W9-BOB-041

Other Avon Books by Donna Boyd

The Passion

The PROMISE

The Promise

D O N N A B O Y D

AVON BOOKS NEW YORK

This is a work of fiction. Names, characters, places, and incidents either are the product of the author's imagination or are used fictitiously. Any resemblance to actual events, locales, organizations, or persons, living or dead, is entirely coincidental and beyond the intent of either the author or the publisher.

AVON BOOKS, INC.
1350 Avenue of the Americas
New York, New York 10019

Interior design by Kellan Peck
ISBN: 0-380-97450-9

Library of Congress Cataloging in Publication Data:

Boyd, Donna.
The promise / Donna Boyd. —1st ed.
p. cm.
I. Title.
PS3552.087757P38 1999 99-20949
813'.54—dc21 CIP

First Avon Books Printing: October 1999

Printed in the U.S.A.

FIRST EDITION

QPM 10 9 8 7 6 5 4 3 2 1

www.avonbooks.com

Grateful acknowledgment is extended to the following distinguished personages for their invaluable contributions toward the completion of this project:

To the ladies of PAWS: Sandra Chastain, Virginia Ellis, Nancy Knight, and Deborah Smith, without whom, quite literally, none of this would have been possible.

To Shannon Harper, research assistant extraordinaire. Any inaccuracies herein are due to the quality of the author, not the quality of the research.

To Ann McKay Thoroman, a gallant soldier who performed her duties nobly and well under the most trying of circumstances. It did not go unnoticed.

The PROMISE

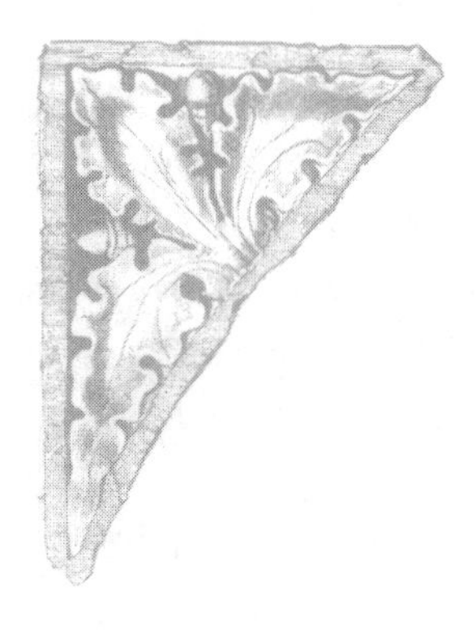
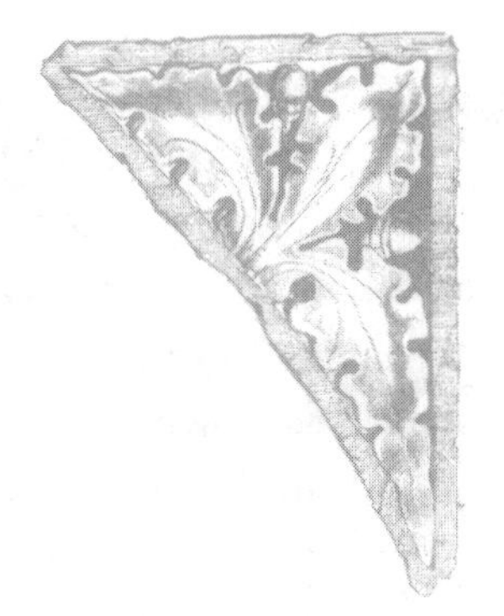

Prologue

AND SO, HUMAN, WE MEET AGAIN. I HAVE BEGUN A TALE THAT LEFT you curious, uneasy in the way of one who has suddenly been given reason to question all he holds true and to recoil a little, in dread and distaste, at the answers. You look over your shoulder more now, don't you? You stare long and hard at patrician faces behind bulletproof glass in dark-colored cars, and when by chance the occupants of those cars turn their gazes to you, you look quickly away, heart pounding, knowing.

You see me now, watching you from the shadows, and it thrills you and terrifies you to know I am there. I have always been there, of course, the gleam of my eyes in the darkness alert and predatory, the set of my mouth amused. And you have always known it, in that deep visceral part of you that once stalked the savannah, hunter and hunted, that burrowed into the bloody skins of its prey for warmth and shook its sticks at the face of evil. But until now the knowledge was an easy thing to ignore. Until now you never saw the eyes.

Who am I, then? What power have I over you? I am the tall fellow with the striking features and the long hair who strides before the cameras to accept the Academy Award. I am the designer with the Italian flair who changes the face of fashion. I am the voice you hear on the radio whose pounding rhythms and twisting melodies have the power to control the beat of the human heart. And those, my dears, are just my hobbies.

I am the face glimpsed behind a tall window backlit with the glow of computer monitors and nothing else. I am the silent bidder in the back of the room, the voice on the phone that closes the stock market for the day. I am the reason your flight was delayed two hours while my private plane was restocked, and it should not surprise you to learn I am also the owner of the airline whose name you cursed while you sat waiting on the runway. My apologies. More pressing matters called at the time.

You have seen my photograph, blurred and hazy, on the front pages of newspapers around the world. I was the one in the background at the summit conference, turning away from the camera at the site of the airport bombing, bent over the computer keyboard when the Mars probe landed. I am your investment banker, your communications expert, your jeweler, your engineer. I am all this, and more. You know this, and instinctively you shrink from the knowing even as your curiosity—ah, that lovely curiosity which is the curse and the boon we both share!—draws you forward. Poor human. The worst is yet to come.

We've kept our distance, you and I, all these years, and, through a mutual history that's emblazoned with blood and glory, we've come to an uneasy peace. In your memory, we are only shadows in the dark. But in ours, you are much, much more. I have come now to restore the balance.

So come with me now, human, to a place before time, where a creature moves low and silent along the edge of the forest. His eyes are narrow, slits of yellow light and his breath trails fresh steam on the cold damp night. For days he has stalked his prey, drawn by a scent, a heartbeat, a sound upon the night that struck his curiosity and raised his head from the hunt. When he began the journey his belly was full and he walked upright, climbing high trees to snatch birds from the nest and drain fresh eggs, using hands and long fingers to build shelter for himself and his mate. But then he caught the scent, and the heartbeat, and it resonated something familiar inside him, and he followed his curiosity.

Now he travels on all fours with a tail for balance, and his body is covered with thick coarse fur that protects him from the cold, and he can no longer remember the reason he began the journey in that other form. He has crossed mountains and swum rivers. He has fought off predators and outrun those he could not. Now his belly is empty and tight, his muscles scream for nourishment, and every heartbeat pounds out *hunger, hunger, hunger* . . . Hunger. It is an instinct stronger even than curiosity.

The smell of smoke has led him to its source, and now he sees them, the sparsely furred creatures with no tails, squatting on their haunches around the fire. He crouches low, blending into the forest, watching, his jowls dripping. The other predators have been driven back, deep into the shadows, by the smell of smoke and the fear of the fire. But he is not afraid. He has made fire himself, in that other form, that other life. He knows its warmth and its comfort. He is puzzled, in a part of his brain that is distant and separate from the hunger, that these creatures should know it too.

He is puzzled by something else. The shape of their forelimbs, the four long digits on each and the shorter, manipulable fifth. Their longer, heavily muscled hind limbs and they way they sit upright, grunting into the fire. The noises they make, the features on their faces, the way they move . . . how like him they are. And yet how completely different. Their smell is rancid and sharp, which must explain why they have not yet caught his scent. Their eyes are small and round and must be half blind, because they have not yet found him in the bushes. Their ears, though much like his own in his other form, are apparently defective, for not one of them turns to follow the sound of his heartbeat, or the breath of the stranger who has come so close to their fire.

The predator decides that the creatures, though they have assumed a form similar to his, are an inferior species and cannot pose a threat. They are prey. And yet they have fire, and he is curious. He leaves the cover of the shadows and creeps toward them.

And just as individual destinies are so often decided in a fraction of a second, by the spin of a wheel upon random chance, so too is the history of the world, or the fates of species. The creature who crept from the shadows had the body of a wolf, but the reasoning to question why. He had the hunger of a beast and a soul that reached higher. The hominids who huddled around the fire might have looked at him and seen themselves. Instead, they looked up and saw monster.

The creatures around the fire see him when it is almost too late. They begin to screech in terror, trampling one another in their haste to flee. A female snatches up an infant and runs. A youth pauses to show his teeth and fling a handful of stones, then begins to scream again and run. The scent of their terror is intoxicating; the excitement of the hunt, the allure of the challenge, the rich life-charged odor of prey in its last, most intense moments. He is the hunter, and instinct commands he give chase.

He allows the young and the agile to escape, but springs upon a lame one who has fallen behind, and brings him down in a single leap. Ah, the rush of hot blood into his mouth. Ah, the crunch of bone and sinew beneath his teeth. Ah, the raging beast of hunger within him that bursts free and tears at flesh, gulps soft tissues, buries itself muzzle-deep in the steaming corpse and gorges until it can hold no more. He is the predator, and his nature has been fulfilled.

But later, sated and drowsy, he curls himself into a ball before the dying embers of the fire, and he dreams the dreams no other beast of the forest dreams. He remembers a shape, a form, a face, a hand with five digits, a covering of smooth skin, the absence of a tail. He remembers himself. And he remembers the creatures, so familiar and so strange, whose scents had lured him here. He looks into their fire, and he is sorry they are gone.

That, then, so the legend goes, is how it began between us all those centuries ago. Predator and prey, a choice and a decision. And that is the way it might have stayed between us, except that something happened over the centuries, to both of us. And that's the story you have come to hear, isn't it? Because today we face another choice, another decision. And the action we take today, just as it did on that long-ago night before the fire, will determine the course of all the rest of the world.

Come with me, then, to a city called New York, in a place called America, where a young werewolf mourns the end of an era. In his hands he holds the key to a dynasty, and in his head a secret that could change your destiny forever, and mine. Hear his howl of sorrow reverberate around the earth, feel his loss chill your blood. Watch now as he rises, and moves to the window, and stares out unseeing at a cold gray morn. He thinks the worst is over.

He is wrong.

The drama that began all those hundreds of thousands of years ago is approaching the final act, and the curtain rises here, in this room, on this night. When it drops closed again, neither you nor I, nor any other of our kind, will ever be the same. So draw closer to the fire, human, and make yourself comfortable.

I have a story to tell you.

PART ONE

Born to run and born to prey
we live and die in Nature's way:
Killers all until we say,
"I shall not kill today, my friend . . .
I shall not kill today."

—FROM A CHILD'S JUMPING-SONG
TRADITIONAL WEREWOLF

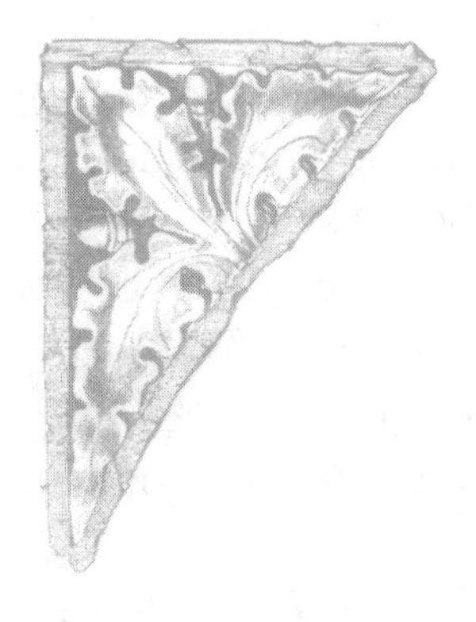

One

13:43
Greenwich Mean Time
November 23, 1998

In London, the Westminster chimes began to toll out of synch and out of tune for the first time in the one-hundred-forty-year history of the most famous clock in the world. A computer failure was blamed for the unexpected shutdown of the underground, and the BBC was off the air for an entire four minutes. No explanation for the missing time was ever offered.

In Beirut, electrical power flickered and went out, and in Iran, thirty-six oil pumps suddenly ceased production. In Moscow, three windows in St. Basil's Cathedral exploded outward, and a crack appeared in a three-hundred-year-old mirror. In Paris, in Rome, in Tokyo and in Hong Kong, traffic jams of monumental proportions resulted when traffic lights ceased to function. In Geneva and Lucerne, millions of dollars in transfers were lost when banking computers shut down. St. Mark's Square was deserted in the middle of the day. Ships at sea cut their engines. Planes in flight bowed their wings.

Around the world, humans turned away from meals uneaten,

fighting a sudden wave of nausea; they awoke from their beds, shuddering in a cold sweat; they broke off in the midst of a sentence and stared, helplessly, into a pit of despair they could not understand. They would later recall a cold chill, a stabbing pain behind their eyes, an electrical prickling at the base of their necks as around the world the howl went up, too loud and too high for their ears to hear yet releasing with it all the depths of agony a soul can know: *He is dead, he is dead . . .*

In the Park Avenue apartment, Nicholas Devoncroix turned from the window and back into the room where the bodies of his parents lay lifeless on the bed. After the accident their remains had been brought here, away from the prying eyes and probing questions of human officials, so that their children might have a few moments to say their goodbyes before the preparations for cremation began. Nicholas had not been in time to say goodbye, of course. Alexander Devoncroix had died instantly beneath the wheels of a fast-moving vehicle in the dark depths of Central Park, as had the bodyguard who had flung himself before the automobile in an attempt to save his leader. Elise Devoncroix, Alexander's mate for over one hundred years, had died of separation shock and grief only moments after her spouse.

The driver of the vehicle, presumably human, had not been found.

Nicholas went over to the two wolf-formed bodies on the bed. His hand shook as he touched the silver-gray fur of his father's neck, cold now, lifeless and dull. He was a magnificent figure even now, devoid of breath, robbed of power. His body was over six feet long, his head massive, his muscles lean, and for the viewing he had been arranged so that his injuries were not visible, and his demeanor retained its dignity. But Nicholas knew that if he lifted his father into an embrace, the corpse would sag limply in his arms, loose bones and organs sloshing beneath their fragile capsule of skin; fur would deteriorate beneath his touch, and his hand would slide into a cold open wound on the back side of his father's neck. Their bodies deteriorated very quickly after death. In only another hour or two they would begin to rot.

Anguish clenched Nicholas's throat and burned his eyes. "Father, why?" he whispered hoarsely. "Who has done this to you?"

And he could almost hear the walls of the room echoing back, *You have, my son . . . You have.*

Alexander and Elise had been on their way to see Nicholas when the death vehicle burst out of the night, and the reason they had crossed Central Park so urgently in the middle of the night in wolf form was to try to stop their son and heir from making a mistake . . . what they believed was a mistake, and what he insisted was their only salvation. The last twenty-four hours between Nicholas and his parents had been filled with threats and recriminations, challenges and anger.

And he had been too late to say goodbye.

He looked at his mother, near the same height as his father but lighter, her pale fur longer and silkier, a portrait of delicate strength and regal bearing even in death. He wanted to kiss her. He wanted to fling himself upon her and bury his face in her fur and inhale the sweet soft fragrances of pine resin and mother's milk, of silk and pearls and hearth fire and power . . . but those scents were gone now and the fur was cold.

Alexander and Elise Devoncroix, leaders of the pack for over a century, were no more.

It was a blow. But the pack would survive. He, Nicholas Antonov Devoncroix, would make certain that it did.

Slowly Nicholas straightened up, letting his hand linger for just another moment in the air above his mother's head, and then he dropped it to his side. "I am sorry," he said softly, thickly, "for all I have done. For all I must do."

Nicholas Devoncroix was thirty-eight years old; young for a species whose elderly were still sound at one hundred fifty years. He was the youngest son of the family that had ruled the pack undisputed for almost a thousand years, and as such he had been groomed from the moment of his birth for the position he held today. Born into a world of virtually unlimited privilege and wealth, he had nonetheless spent the first year after his weaning fighting his eleven brothers and sisters for his meals, defending his sleeping space and his running space and his playthings and even the attention of his teachers and parents with his wits, his teeth and his claws. If he was not fast enough or strong enough, he went hungry and he slept on the floor; if he was not clever enough or aggressive enough or inventive enough, he was humiliated, scorned by his peers, and that was a punishment far worse than hunger, or even banishment from the fire.

Most cubs learn to control their ability to change forms by age three; Nicholas had mastered it by his second birthday. He brought home his first killed deer at age five and he received the accolades of the pack. But he earned the thunderous approval of the pack and was named Champion of the Hunt when, on that same occasion, he added the trophies of his six older brothers, which they were not clever enough or fast enough to protect, to his own bounty. By the time he was ten, it was generally agreed that the future of the pack was safe in the hands of Nicholas Devoncroix.

He held degrees from the world's major universities in the arts, sciences and humanities. By age twenty he had climbed Everest in human form, had won the Grand Prix and had composed and conducted a symphony. It was he who had designed the satellite communications system upon which pack security around the world was based, and had, as an incidental benefit, earned several hundred million dollars by selling various harmless bits of that technology to humans. He was a skilled negotiator, a shrewd financier, a brilliant engineer.

He was frequently photographed with the world's most enticing females, both human and werewolf. He dined with human kings, presidents and diplomats. He had a villa on the Riviera, an apartment on Ile St. Louis and a ranch in the Hawaiian islands at which ministers of finance and chairmen of various international boards were frequent guests.

When human factions went to war—whether they were nations

or corporations—at the inconvenience of the pack, he made peace. When greed or shortsightedness caused a division within the corporate pack, he made corrections. When crises arose, he made decisions. He made improvements, he made suggestions, he made deals. Most important of all, he made himself indispensable. Over the past ten years he had gradually insinuated himself into every area of administration of the pack and its hundred-plus corporate divisions. His personal number was on the Rolodex of every important CEO, investment officer, prime minister, king and president in the world, right next to that of Alexander Devoncroix—sometimes above it. A pack in crisis did not function well, and nothing would plunge it into confusion faster than sudden change. Every precaution had therefore been taken that the transition between a pack leader and his successor should be seamless.

But there were some eventualities against which no precautions were effective. No werewolf could be prepared for the legacy left to Nicholas by his father. And nothing could prepare the pack for what Nicholas must do now.

Nicholas made his eyes focus one more time on the inert forms upon the bed. "*Au revoir, mon père, ma mère,*" he said. "*Je vous adore.*" And in English he added, "You have ruled well. I will protect what you have built in the best way I know. I swear it."

He turned and left the room.

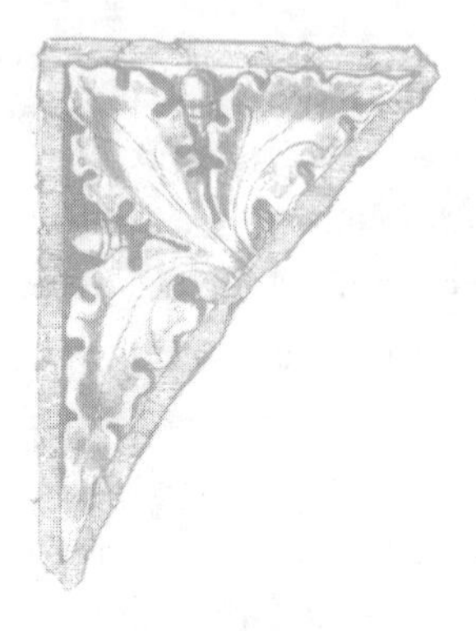
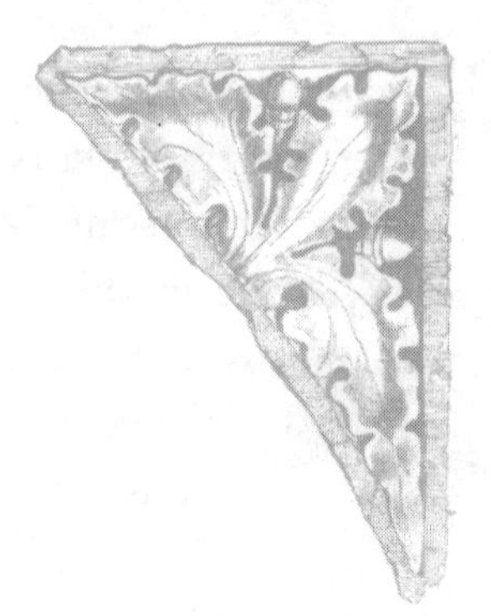

Two

NICHOLAS CAME OUT OF THE BEDROOM INTO A SEA OF SILENCE. THE most important werewolves in New York were gathered there, having rushed to the Park Avenue apartment of their pack leader the moment their senses felt the blow of his passing. Others were coming—from Washington, Montreal, California, Britain, Sri Lanka, Baghdad; from all over the world they would follow their instincts home.

They were confused, disoriented, shaken and uncertain, rudderless in a vast and empty sea. A hundred years had passed since the death of the last pack leader, a hundred years of peace and prosperity and burgeoning power. Now suddenly, without warning, violence had struck down their leader and shattered the pack. They waited for assurance that they were not alone.

Nicholas looked out over the cathedral of a room filled with faces, all turned his way. A rich sensual chamber of scents and textures, of fear and sorrow, greed and ambition, anxiety and need . . . most of all need. So much need. They turned to him, those sleek, well-groomed bodies in their Chanel suits and kid gloves, with their expensively coiffed hair and dramatically made-up faces, their eyes wide and their mouths pinched and their nostrils flared, drinking in the scent of him as he did of them . . . looking for weakness, looking for fear.

He thought distantly, *They are mine now. Mine to shepherd, mine to guide, mine to protect.*

In rather recent history, a tradition was established by a human monarch to assure his subjects of the continuity of the throne. To celebrate the longevity of this monarchy, a ritual announcement has evolved which is repeated upon the demise of each ruler and the ascension of the new one. But it has never had quite the power of the pack ritual from which it was derived so many centuries ago.

They were a people of ritual. The words must be said.

Nicholas stood tall and spoke loudly. "The leader of the pack is dead," he said.

Not even a heartbeat passed. From the assemblage a single voice was raised, loud and clear: "All hail the leader of the pack," it cried. "May he live forever."

The bitter dead smell of grief that issued from a hundred close-packed bodies transformed immediately into relief and triumph, power mounting and cascading like clear water through a sluice.

"May he live forever," echoed the audience, and the words reverberated around the room with enthusiasm and fervor, *May he live forever*, for his life was their life, and without him they were nothing, a pack without a leader did not exist. All hail the leader of the pack. May he, and they, live forever.

The first thing that happened was that Nicholas was surrounded by guards. Silent and unobtrusive and for the most part ceremonial, they had served his father and now they would serve him. In many ways they were as symbolic as groomsmen at a wedding, but their purpose was a deadly serious one. Never was a new ruler more vulnerable to attack and overthrow than in the first few days after the death of the old ruler, particularly if he was unmated. Though it was far more likely these days that the challenge would occur on the battleground of Wall Street than in a Park Avenue apartment, and that the weapons used would be margins and commodities rather than teeth and claws, the ritual persisted. They thrived upon ritual.

Nicholas scanned the crowd until he caught the gaze of the one he sought: the owner of the voice which had first hailed him leader. With neither a nod nor a blink, with the simple communication of his eyes, Nicholas signalled his request. The other werewolf lowered his own gaze in acknowledgement.

Nicholas made his way through the crowd, which parted for him respectfully, eyes following, hands moving toward him instinctively, just to touch him, to steal a whisper of his scent and take it home to those who did not rank a place in this room, to say when they were old that fortune had favored them and they had been here on this day, at this moment, when the old had passed to the new.

He left the guards stationed outside the door and entered the study. He closed the door and leaned against it, for he could go no further.

His parents had been fond of the opulence of their Victorian youth, and all of their residences reflected the same. High molded ceilings, touches of baroque gold trim, mural walls, heavy draperies, enormous chandeliers, intricately carved woodwork, Carrara marble. This room was no different, for all that its function was far more utilitarian than any other room in the house. A massive mahogany rolltop desk, decorated with baroque scrollwork and supported on legs carved to look like wolves' feet, occupied one corner. Built into it was a secure satellite telephone and a computer system from which Alexander Devoncroix could access any file in the world. Two gilded, five-foot mirrors on either side of the room concealed sophisticated video cameras and recording devices, and a bank of security monitors was hidden within a sliding panel to the left of the emerald marble fireplace.

The twelve- by thirty-six-foot mural that covered two walls had been painted by Fragonard on special commission, and it depicted a palace in Lyons, France, its grand entrance guarded by two enormous stone wolves, its sweeping grounds and elaborate gardens peopled by beautiful men and women in artfully draped garments of gossamer and gauze, picnicking and bathing and playing musical instruments and gathering flowers; an idyll of peace and innocence. One had to look hard to see the wolves peeking out from beneath the shrubbery, sunbathing on craggy rocks, painted into the shadows on the lawn. The mural concealed nothing at all. Alexander Devoncroix had merely liked it.

The brocade settees and overstuffed chairs had held heads of state and international financiers. Kings and king-makers had sipped tea from the gold-rimmed Limoges cups displayed in the mirrored cabinet, and toasts had been drunk from the Baccarat crystal that sealed the fates of nations. The room was filled with the scent of Alexander Devoncroix, the empire he had built, the history he had made, and for a moment Nicholas's knees went weak from it.

It was no street accident that had killed Alexander Devoncroix. He had been murdered. And only Nicholas knew why.

He pushed away from the door and crossed the room in three swift strides, tearing at the catch to the window, flinging open the casement. He leaned out into the cold, breathing deeply.

In a time before technology, werewolves had struggled to keep their secrets from others of their kind, whose hearing was on average five hundred times more acute than that of a human. But with the advent of radio a simple device had been fashioned which, by emitting an oscillating high-frequency wave, could soundproof any room from werewolf ears. This room was so equipped, and when Nicholas threw open the window, the contrasting roar of noise was as tangible and as forceful as a breaking wave; he actually gulped for breath with its impact.

Like bits of flotsam riding on that wave, voices gradually separated themselves from the thunder of traffic, the blare of horns, the buzz and burr of telephones, the crank of machinery, the chatter of humans.

"It was a human, you know, a human who killed him—"

"Dreadful irony, after he worked all his life to further the state of humanity."

"I never thought it was right and I don't care who knows it. Always knew it would come to a bad end, this human-loving—"

"It was an accident. Accidents happen every day, to humans as well as to us."

"He was Alexander Devoncroix! Such accidents should not be allowed to happen to such a creature!"

"At least he didn't suffer. Unlike Analise, who lingered six hours when she was struck by that truck."

"Perhaps it's best to go quickly. But at the hands of a human . . ."

Cell phones chirruping all over New York, messages flying, speculation and rumor, information and misinformation. It would be the same in Rome and Paris and London, in Johannesburg and Frankfurt and Sydney and Seoul. Less than an hour had passed, and already the details of the demise of the leader of the pack and his spouse had made their way around the world.

"Will you go to Alaska? But we must go, we're Devoncroix!"

"I heard only six to a family—"

"I had a meeting scheduled—"

"No, hold your shares, you fool! Haven't you ever *met* the young Devoncroix?"

". . . air traffic will, of course, be rerouted for the next couple of days—"

"We should have instructions by noon—"

". . . as strong a werewolf as ever I did business with—"

"No, cancel it, cancel them all, let the humans take care of it for a day—"

Nicholas drew in the sounds and let them soothe him, for even in chaos they were good sounds, familiar sounds. His people. His pack.

He stood there, leaning out into the rain, watching them scuttle by two stories below. His pulse steadied and slowed, his breathing grew more regular, and gradually his head began to clear. Umbrellas clashing, shoulders hunched, werewolves and humans surged together, eyes straight ahead, expressions intent, each a world unto himself. Cold rain splashed upon Nicholas's hands as they gripped the sill, and soaked his silk cuffs. The window was only twenty-five feet from the pavement, not so far a leap for a werewolf as young and as strong as he was. For a moment he considered it: stripping off his clothes, springing through the window and, with a mighty cry, changing in midair as his father once had boasted of doing, landing in full wolf form in the middle of Park Avenue and running, just running until he found some place open and green and running still with the wind in his face and the turf flying beneath his paws, running until his legs collapsed and his lungs burst, just running.

He heard the door open and close behind him, and he spoke without turning. "I think it can be safely said that there are more of our kind in New York at any one time than in any other city on earth. Except perhaps London."

He could hear the faint smile in the other man's voice. "Or Venice at Carnival."

Nicholas closed the window and turned reluctantly away from it. The absence of sound from the street was acute and isolating, and it hurt his ears. "There was a time when one would have to look long and far to find those who were not our kind. A time when ours were the only voices on the planet and the sound of our song drowned out all other noises."

Michel inclined his head in agreement. "The modern age has brought many changes. Not all of them for the better."

Nicholas agreed softly. "Yes."

There was a silence, respectful yet awkward, the first uncertain moment between two colleagues who realized their status, and therefore their relationship, had changed forever. Michel had been Nicholas's personal assistant since Nicholas had taken his last degree and entered the world of business, and the relationship had long since grown beyond that of manager and secretary. Every detail of Nicholas's day was managed by Michel, every secret of his affairs known to him. Michel was advisor, confidant, friend. And Nicholas was about to test his loyalty in a way neither of them had ever imagined before.

Nicholas smiled faintly, sensing the other man's awkwardness. "And so. I am a creature of import now, and we can no longer be at ease with one another."

Michel relaxed slightly. "You were always a creature of import, sir. Nonetheless, I don't envy you your position now."

Nicholas's effort to smile faded. "No ambition to be king, eh, Michel?"

"I have never had one," confessed Michel. And his eyes crinkled slightly at the corners with his own attempt at humor. "I far prefer to be king-maker."

"It is good to know, then, that I can mark one possible challenger off the list, and rest easy knowing I have only several thousand more to guard against."

But the joke was feeble and fell flat, and another awkward silence followed, heavy with grief and weariness, and the burden of things too powerful to be said in words.

It was Michel who recovered himself first, rallying as he always did. He drew up his shoulders, dropped his head and said formally, "My fealty is yours to command, sir. May I approach?"

Nicholas nodded. Michel came forward and kissed his lips.

Nicholas placed his hands upon either side of the other man's face and said, "Michel, son of Gault, you have served me well, as your father served my father for all of his life. Is it your wish to continue to do so?"

And Michel replied without hesitation, "Until death."

Then he stepped back and, with his eyes still respectfully lowered, said quietly, "You will want to know, sir, that the incident at the laboratory has been taken care of as you requested. The debris has been removed, and the environment sanitized. Garret is on his way and will no doubt make a full report."

Nicholas regarded him without expression. The debris to which Michel referred consisted of four bodies, three victims and one assassin. The "incident" was murder. And Garret Landseer, Nicholas's closest friend and chief of security, was the only person in the world Nicholas could trust to dispose of the evidence.

He murmured, "Five murders in less than two days. And this from a species which has less than one such crime in a decade. We are proud of saying we do not kill our own kind. Yet somehow . . . we have managed it."

Michel looked startled. "Five murders?"

"If one doesn't count the death of the assassin who attacked the laboratory and died of the wounds inflicted upon him by those who were fighting for their lives."

Michel blanched. "But . . . your parents. It was a street accident, a reckless human. Surely you're not implying . . . ?"

Instead of answering, Nicholas moved behind his father's desk, lifted the rolltop that revealed the computer monitor and keyboard and tapped in his own security code. "Call the car around. I want to leave for the airport in a quarter of an hour. My sister Sabine will attend to the cremation and bring the ashes home tomorrow. The ceremony will begin on Saturday and is to last for three days. No more than one quarter of any division is to be absent at any one time, is that understood? Assemble the staff, send out the announcements. I will address the pack at zero hundred hours GMT via satellite. But first . . ."

Michel had already started for the door and he turned back.

"You will stand witness to this document, which will be presented to the Council the moment I arrive in Alaska."

Nicholas moved to call up the document, but just then the door opened and Garret strode in, his black hair tangled with wind and jeweled with rain, smelling of cold and anger and grief and determination. He embraced Nicholas fiercely, and he whispered, "My heart breaks with yours."

The genuine emotion of the only person who might truthfully understand his own sorrow caused Nicholas's throat to clench. He returned the embrace, inhaling strength and familiarity, the clean warm scents of the childhood they had shared, memories and comfort.

Garret moved a little away, and kissed Nicholas hard on the mouth. "Until death," he said, before the question could be asked, "and beyond."

The two embraced again, more formally this time, and Garret stepped away. "We found the car," he said without preamble. He stripped off his damp coat and tossed it aside, running his fingers through his hair. "It had been abandoned in an alley, soaked with gasoline and burned."

Nicholas nodded, unsurprised. "Could you determine anything from the remains?"

Garret met his gaze. "Werewolf."

Among werewolves, even when in human form, far more was said in silence than was ever voiced aloud. Nicholas read the questions, the speculations and the truths behind Garret's words that had little to do with the words themselves. He was very careful that his friend should see nothing of the same in him.

Then Nicholas said softly, "So. They have penetrated the pack at an even higher level than we thought."

Michel, who had removed Garret's coat from the leather chair where it had landed, paused in the act of hanging the garment upon the coat rack by the door. His face was hollow with disbelief. "One of our own was driving the vehicle that struck down the leader of the pack?"

"Not exactly," replied Garret, still looking at Nicholas, "one of our own."

It took only a moment for Michel to understand, a fraction of that time for him to conceal his impatient incredulity. "With all due respect, I can't think it would serve the pack in this time of sorrow to dredge up those old rumors about the Brothers of the Dark Moon. Everything that has gone wrong for a millennium has been blamed on them, when it is well known that they no longer exist. Alexander Devoncroix himself dispersed them over a hundred years ago."

Nicholas said, "Recent events suggest the rumors of their demise may have been premature."

And Garret added sharply, "You understand that none of this is to leave this room."

Michel returned a disdainful look. His discretion was absolute. Had it not been, he would not have retained his position for this long.

Garret turned back to Nicholas. "Nicholas, the security people tell me that your parents were on their way here, to see you. Do you know why?"

For a moment Nicholas said nothing. Then slowly he nodded. He sat at the desk and tapped a few computer keys, bringing up a document. "This is why," he said without expression, and turned the screen toward the room. "Michel, you will be good enough to come forward and read it as well."

Michel stood beside Garret and the two of them scanned the screen. Ten full seconds of silence followed.

Garret spoke first. His expression was careful, his tone guarded. "I don't understand. This looks as though you propose to reinstate the Edict of Separation."

Nicholas replied, "My parents objected. They threatened to veto me with the Council. They were on their way to argue their case again when . . ." Only the slightest hesitation there, and very little change of expression at all. "They were killed."

"By those whose ends would be served by the reinstatement of the edict," Garret said flatly. His gaze returned, unblinking, to the screen.

"That seems unlikely." Michel spoke up, his voice high and tight with disbelief. "Even with the pack leader and his spouse gone, even with you, sir, in charge . . ." He inclined his head deferentially to Nicholas. ". . . if the Council chooses to oppose you, which it surely will, it could be months, years, before the entire pack accepts your decree. And in the meantime . . . forgive me, sir, but in the meantime you could be overthrown."

"And the pack would be torn apart no matter what happened

in the end," Garret said. "We might never recover from the turmoil." He turned to Nicholas, confusion overriding the impatience in his eyes. "How did such a thing come to be? I know that events of the past few hours have been—" Again he choose his words carefully. "Unsettling, but surely you cannot have thought such a drastic measure would prove the solution."

Nicholas felt a flare of anger he couldn't entirely control. He and Garret had been raised together from pups; they had run together, hunted together, schooled together, fought together. They had discovered the pleasures of females together, and the various delights, both illicit and celebrated, that could be enjoyed in human form. From the time of first adolescence Nicholas had known that there was only one werewolf who could be trusted to stand at his side, come what may, and Garret had known that his place was then and forevermore at Nicholas's side. There had never been secrets between them, not one. Now Nicholas was forced to keep from Garret the most important secret of his life, and it angered him.

He pushed away from the desk and got to his feet, pacing the room in terse, even strides. "We have forgotten our place in the world this last century. We have been misled by the human qualities of greed and lust, we have wallowed in the pleasures of human flesh. We have lowered ourselves to live like humans among humans, to dine with them and cater to them and take them to our beds. We are hunters grown fat and lazy. We are masters who have forgotten how to rule. The leadership of Alexander Devoncroix has brought us a century of self-indulgence and dissipation which has made us the servants of humans, rather than their masters. But no more." He stopped and turned to face them. "Every ruler is challenged by the necessity of taking the appropriate action at the right time. This is the only appropriate response for the situation that faces us now." And his voice hoarsened a bit, his expression tightened with urgency as he added to Garret, "You may not understand. But I beg you to trust me."

Garret's scent was harsh with incredulity, and he made another swipe at his hair with impatient fingers. "It is your suspicion, then, that someone—some member of the Dark Brotherhood—became privy to your intentions to bring this resolution before the Council, and aware of your father's determination to stop it. And for this reason our pack leader was killed."

Nicholas didn't flinch. From now until the time of public mourning, his pain would be contained unto himself; the pack expected nothing less, and he would not disappoint them with a display of weakness.

Garret continued, watching his friend closely. "And it would not be irrational to assume some connection between this murder and the assassination of three of our most prominent scientists in a secured laboratory."

Nicholas said, "It is your job to find such a connection, if it exists." He held his friend's gaze. "I rely upon you to do so."

The two werewolves were evenly matched, tall and strong of muscle and mind, equally stubborn, equally determined. But leadership is as much a function of resolve as of qualification, of innate power as much as skill. Only a second or two passed before Garret, pained by the effort of meeting the superior werewolf's gaze, shifted his own away.

"I will see to it immediately," he said.

"One moment." Nicholas moved back to the desk. "Such a decree as I have written requires two witnesses that I have made it of my own will and sound mind. Your signature, please. And yours, Michel."

For a moment neither of the two werewolves moved. The startled pace of their pulses echoed in Nicholas's ears, the smell of their shock was static and sharp.

Garret said flatly, "You cannot be serious."

"I assure you, I am."

"Your father was killed because of this!"

"He was killed because he tried to stop it," replied Nicholas without emotion.

Garret stared at him. "Yet you would proceed, you would push this—this obscenity into law, knowing that he gave his life to try to prevent it?"

Michel broke in sharply. "You forget yourself, monsieur! The pack leader answers to none but his conscience."

Garret barely spared him a glance. "We have been at peace with humans for a thousand years—"

"Not so long as that," replied Nicholas carelessly. He unlocked one of the desk drawers and removed his briefcase.

Garret's voice was rising. "Do you have any idea what you will be unleashing with this edict? You would turn us all into savages again, destroy all it's taken centuries to build. And if that doesn't concern you, think of your own fortune! Alexander Devoncroix built an empire based on harmony with humans, but what will become of it now? Is this the way the new pack leader intends to usher his people into the twenty-first century?"

Nicholas's eyes blazed. "Leave it, Garret!" His voice was a decibel below a shout, and the smell of flaring temper was like heat lightning. He caught himself with a breath, then added tensely, "You tread on dangerous ground."

Garret lowered his eyes and took a step backward. "I speak my mind to you as I have always done," he replied. "I wouldn't be of much help to you if I didn't, and what I've said to you today will be echoed ten times in the Council chamber. I meant no disrespect. However, I understand if you think discipline is necessary."

Nicholas gazed at him for a moment, and his expression softened into vague wryness. "I think," he said, "that you play a very poor Marc Antony to my Caesar. There are things you don't know, Garret. I do not make this decision lightly. But please continue to express your opinion openly and at every possible opportunity. I should not recognize you if you did not."

Garret looked at him again. "Then I must tell you this. The pack will never accept this. To do such a thing in the midst of transition is reckless in the extreme."

Michel had watched the interchange with cautious interest, and now he spoke up thoughtfully. "Perhaps not so much as you might think. The pack blames a human for the death of their leader already, and it's no secret that sentiment toward humans has grown less and less tolerant over the past few years. Perhaps now is precisely the time to make such a move."

At Garret's outraged stare, Michel drew himself up. "*My* concern is for the safety of our pack leader, who stands before me, and for the security of his position. What is yours?"

Garret jerked his angry gaze from Michel to Nicholas. "You do this thing," he said lowly, "and a hundred thousand years of civilization has been for nought. We may as well go wild again, sleeping in the forest and killing whatever moves. Do you really want that to be your legacy?

"And I," returned Nicholas in a cold hard voice, "need no lectures on civilization from you. Do you stand beside me or no?"

For a moment the two werewolves locked gazes and the room grew acrid with the energy expended; challenge and question, resolve and uncertainty, outrage and determination.

The faint film of perspiration that misted Garret's face was a testimony to the courage it took to hold Nicholas's gaze, and the strength of will that fought back pain. The battle for truth between them was silent, but it was strong, and in the end, it was won.

Garret lowered his eyes. "You are my leader. I do as you command." He took up the stylus on the desk and impressed his signature into the electronic pad. "My life for you," he said, and, with his eyes still lowered, stepped away.

Nicholas looked at Michel. Michel stepped forward and placed his signature below Garret's.

And it was done.

Nicholas said, "I will read this to the Council as soon as we're assembled. I expect resistance." His eyes met Garret's. "If I had discovered a disease that could wipe out the pack, a disease that was transmitted only by humans, what kind of a ruler would I be if I did not try to protect the pack from it?"

Garret's eyes were quick with question and, almost immediately, the answer. "But there is no such disease."

Nicholas replied simply, "There is. Its symptoms are apathy, indolence and tolerance for the intolerable, among others. It is caused by intimacy with humans and it runs rampant through the pack. How many more must die because of it?"

Garret was silent for a moment. "The irony cannot have escaped you. The Brothers of the Dark Moon have spent centuries trying to find a way to wipe the human curse from the planet and establish themselves in dominance once again. Some might say that with this edict you've taken the first step toward accomplishing their goal, and for it they would hail you as prophet and savior."

Nicholas showed not a flicker of expression as he replied, "That is indeed ironic." He pushed the button that would print the document.

Michel stepped forward, staying his hand. "Sir, if you'll permit me—it would be more efficient to send the document electronically, so that the Council will have had a chance to study it by the time you meet with them. Also, it might be best to have no hard copies just yet, if you know what I mean."

Nicholas hesitated, then aborted the print. "Perhaps you're right."

Michel said, "I'll see to your car." He turned for the door, then back. "And, sir, it occurs to me that it might be more efficient if I stayed here for a few hours to supervise the final arrangements rather than accompany you home just now. I'll be with you in plenty of time to help you arrange your presentation to the Council, however."

Nicholas waved him away impatiently. "Whatever you think best."

When he was gone Garret stood alone before the desk, his hands clasped loosely behind his back, and he regarded his friend studiously. "Can you tell me now?" he demanded.

Nicholas looked up, and in his eyes was a brief flash of gratitude for the understanding the question implied. "No. Not yet."

Garret nodded. "I have known you for thirty-five years," he

said. "I owe you my life a half-dozen times over. It should be enough. I'm sorry if I suggested otherwise."

Nicholas said roughly, "You did more than suggest." And then his scowl eased, he gave a toss of his blond head in the symbolic gesture of shaking off unpleasantness, and he managed to relax his features into something very closely resembling a smile. He said, "It never happened."

Garret hesitated. "Do you want me to make any announcement to the pack about what we know about your parents' deaths?"

"No. To do so will only give the killers warning. I want you to continue as you have done, and bring what you find to me alone."

"Of course."

Garret hesitated for another moment, then stepped around the desk and embraced his friend again. "Good journey, Nicholas. I will keep you in my heart."

Garret had been gone only a moment when the intercom on the desk chimed. It was Michel, informing him that the car was waiting. Nicholas reached for his coat and briefcase, then put both down again. He opened his briefcase. There, lying on top, was a small book bound in red leather. He took out the book, and looked at it solemnly for a moment. He could hear his father's voice so clearly he almost glanced around for its source. *Have you read the book? You promised you would read it! How can you know the truth until you have done so?*

I will read it, but nothing in it can change my mind. I know enough already to understand what must be done.

Do nothing. Stay where you are. Your mother and I are coming to talk to you.

Those were the last words Nicholas had ever heard his father say. He had been killed before he had reached Nicholas's door.

Nicholas opened the book and scanned the first few pages. The very sight of it was painful, and the smell . . . He brought it swiftly to his face and inhaled old ink and crisp paper, binding glue, leather . . . and Alexander Devoncroix, rich, alive, strong, the essence of him lingering like fine oil, glossing and enriching everything he had touched. Nicholas's throat clenched, and he closed the book, locking it in his briefcase. He had promised his father he would read it, and he would. But he could not bear it now.

He moved away from the desk, put on his coat, picked up his briefcase. He looked back at the computer monitor, the screen having blanked to the Devoncroix logo, silver on black. Almost hesitantly, Nicholas touched the keyboard, and the document reappeared. He let his hand fall away.

He thought of the remains of his parents lying in the back room. He heard their voices in his head. He felt their scent upon his hands, his clothing, his hair. *Do nothing . . .*

But the pack was his now, and he would do what he must to ensure their survival.

"I'm sorry," he whispered to the ghosts of the room.

Then he turned back to the computer, lifted his hand to the keyboard and pushed the button that would change the world.

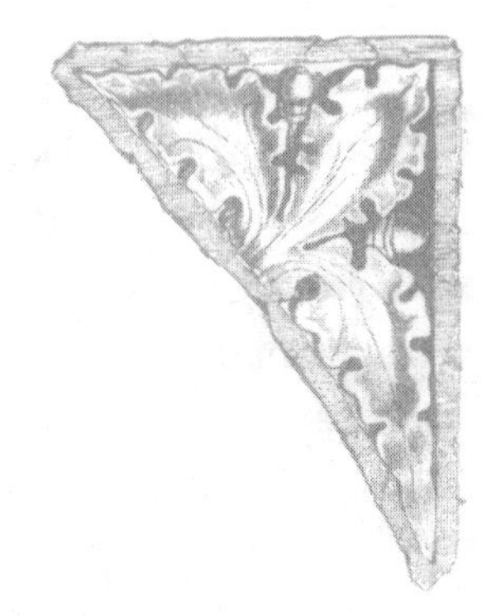

Three

THE WILDERNESS OF NORTHWESTERN ALASKA 05:16 ALASKA STANDARD TIME NOVEMBER 23

ONE BY ONE THEY CAME OVER THE CREST OF THE HILL, MATERIALIZING like ghosts through the fog of a lightly falling snow. First the beta male, a pale gray, shaggy-coated beast with a white blaze across his face, and then his silver-coated mate, the beta female. The remainder of the pack spread out on either side of them, forming a fan at the top of the hill, eight in all, and waited.

He came, the big white male, the alpha, cresting the hill in the exact center of the fan formed by the other wolves, a military formation with the beta male on his right and the beta female on his left. Immediately the pack began to move down the hill, silently and efficiently, each step choreographed with an eerie precision so that they did not appear to break formation once. They surrounded the small group of musk oxen—two adults and a calf—from a distance of about ten feet and held their position, as still as ice carvings, making no sound or movement, nor scent or shadow, to reveal their presence. The beasts did not even look up, but continued to paw the snow and munch at the frozen vegetation underneath.

From the hill, the alpha sat watching, his form majestic and still. The wind that ruffled his snow-encrusted fur was the only movement upon the landscape that surrounded him. And then, without previous sign or warning, the wolves below moved in upon the herd. They wasted no time or energy upon the chase. For less than three minutes the snow was a blur of snarling bodies and flashing teeth, of blood spatters and flailing hoofbeats as four of them attacked the adults, driving them off in a flurry of sound and fury. Three others swiftly brought down the calf. The beta male rent open the viscera, tearing out the entrails. His mate began ripping chunks of flesh from the haunches.

On the hill a quarter mile away, a camera shutter clicked. The white alpha, still in place upon the crest of the hill, pivoted his head toward the sound, and stared for a moment directly into the lens of the camera with pale, eerily thoughtful eyes. Then he turned and made his way down the hill to feast.

Hannah Braselton North felt her heart beat, fast and hard, pounding into the hard-packed snow of the ground upon which she lay, and she had a moment of eerie certainty that the wolf could hear that too. Every hair on her body was standing on end. It was impossible, she knew, that the male could have heard her camera click from that far away. More impossible still that he could have seen her when he looked around. Yet when she had seen those pale penetrating eyes focused upon hers through the long-distance lens of the camera, her breath had stopped in her chest and she had been unable to force herself to draw breath since.

With a curse she realized that the camera had gone limp in her hand, its focus lost, the opportunity to photograph the magnificent beast full-face missed. Quickly she brought the lens into focus again, swinging it down to follow the feast at the bottom of the hill.

Afterward, she would never be able to fully describe what happened next. It began as a prickling sensation at the base of her spine, escalating like a flash of electricity to a stabbing in her temples, a ringing in her ears. The camera slipped from her suddenly numb fingers and her face contorted in a rictus of pain as she drew herself to her hands and knees, twisting her head around and upward toward the blank gray sky as though in search of the source of the sound that was stabbing like ice picks in her ears. She saw nothing.

Below her, the wolves backed away from their feast, dropping bloody chunks of meat and leaving them where they lay. Turning their backs upon their kill, they formed a perfect circle around the white alpha male, and raised up their voices in one long, strong, heart-piercing howl.

Four

The Wilderness
16:10
Alaska Standard Time
November 23

"I SAW THEM TODAY. AFTER ALL THIS TIME, I'D HALF STARTED TO WONder if I'd imagined them, but you were right—this is their winter hunting ground. You should have been there, Tom. You should have seen them. It was the most phenomenal thing, the way they hunted, not like the other packs we've studied—these guys meant business. They attacked, they killed, they ate. Why weren't you there, anyway? It's not as though you had some place better to be."

There was no reply, but Hannah had not expected one. Tom had stopped talking to her months ago. She caught the edge of her right glove with her teeth and tugged it off, working her stiffened fingers for a moment before pulling off the other glove and wrapping both hands around a mug of Sterno-heated tea. She was still breathing hard, with exertion and excitement, and she moved around the small tent as she spoke, working the circulation back into her feet and legs while she waited for the solar heater to raise the temperature above freezing.

There had been a time when she spoke into the tape recorder, for appearance's sake if nothing else. She didn't bother any longer.

"There were only eight of them, though," she went on, holding the mug close to her cold face. "The beautiful silver was gone, and the one I called Midnight, and a couple of yearlings. I like to think the two young ones went off to start their own packs, but I know they're probably dead." She hesitated, for the next was even harder to say than she had imagined. "The Great White's mate wasn't with them, the alpha female. Maybe that doesn't mean anything. There's no law that says she has to be on every hunt. She might have cubs. It doesn't mean . . . I'd hate to think she's dead, Tom. I'd hate to think he's alone."

In the silence that fell, the wind whistled through the spare trees that sheltered her camp, and snapped at the flaps of the tent. In a moment she continued, forcing a lighter tone. "There have been a few births, though, I saw some new faces. The youngsters look healthy—but why shouldn't they, with these hunting grounds?"

Still no answer. Hannah sipped the tea, found it barely potable and sat down on the edge of the cot to remove her outer boots. The temperature inside the tent was approaching minus two degrees Celsius.

The Arctic dome tent was sparsely furnished with a folding cot lined with a sleeping bag, a camp chair that served as a table, desk and countertop when needed, and two metal cases filled with supplies. All would pack neatly and compactly onto the sledge when it came time to move on. The supply cases were a great deal lighter now than they had been when she left base two weeks ago, and she estimated, if she thought about it at all, that she had enough food and water for another ten days. After that she would simply . . . move on.

Hannah Braselton North had come to the wilderness to die. That was not what she had told her family and colleagues, who believed she was spending the winter in a Canadian wildlife park and who were so relieved to see her getting on with her life that they did not question her plans too closely. The human capacity for grief was, after all, limited, and the consensus of opinion was that it was time for mourning to end. So Hannah went to Alaska, and she knew she would not be coming back.

Base camp was a comfortable log-built compound thirty miles to the south where, for six months out of the year, a select team of scientists, photographers and professional observers studied the flora and fauna of this small section of the Arctic world. Their research was funded by the privately, and lavishly, endowed Wilderness Project, whose only goal was wilderness preservation. The estate of Henry Jacob Braselton, media tycoon, was the source of the endowment.

They called the facility Station Alpha, and it had been a dream of Tom's long before he married the daughter of the man who could make it come true. Somehow over the years the dream had also become Hannah's: a completely independent, fully equipped compound situated in the heart of a wilderness that was as untouched as any place on earth could be said to be, a place where the researchers who came to study the environment could actually become a part of what they studied.

Hannah Braselton, wildlife biologist, had met Tom North, zoological veterinarian, when she interned at a wolf habitat maintained by the Wildlife Management Institute. He knew who she was; the name Braselton was a legend in corporate America and her father's death three years earlier—along with his vast endowments to the arts and sciences—had made news for months. There were some problems with that, of course; Tom was not comfortable in the high-society world from which Hannah came, and Hannah had no patience with reverse snobbishness.

But, as one of Hannah's first professors in the biology program had pointed out, "manure is a great equalizer," and by the end of her first week at the habitat most of the staff and interns, including Tom, had decided Hannah Braselton was okay.

On their third date Tom had said, "I will endeavor, Ms. Braselton, not to allow your vast fortune to get in the way of my falling in love with you."

Tom was tall and lanky, with an unruly lock of jet-black hair that persisted in falling over his left eyebrow and an irritating Midwestern drawl that got more pronounced when he was angry. He was also one of the most dedicated veterinarians Hannah had ever worked with. She fell in love with him the first time she saw him beat his fist against a tree in impotent fury over a gunshot animal he had been unable to save.

"So, High Class," he said, holding her in his arms on a blanket under the stars after the first time they made love, "you gonna make an honest man of me or what?"

"I'll do better than that," she told him, pushing back that persistent lock of hair over his eye. "I'm going to make all your dreams come true."

"You already have," he told her.

They were married four days later.

They bought a run-down ranch in upper Montana and turned it into a refuge for sick and injured wolves, most of them victims of the less-than-warm reception given them by ranchers when they happened to wander outside the boundaries of Yellowstone National Park. Before the Norths had even moved in all their equipment, someone burned down their barn. Hannah had been afraid Tom would want to leave, to find a more hospitable location or even a less hazardous line of work. But he had spent a few minutes surveying the damage and kicking around ashes, then said, "Well, what are you waiting for, High Class? We got work to do."

They spent five years developing the ranch, building bridges to the community and rebuilding with every setback. They developed an education program and employed a staff, mostly volunteer, to help with organizational duties and animal care. Summers they spent in the high country, in Canada or Alaska, as members of various research teams tracking and observing wolves in their natural environments. All the while Hannah was working on setting up the foundation, from her father's various endowments, that would one day become The Wilderness Project.

Station Alpha had been completed three years ago, with an eight-year plan that would eventually take them to Phase Four, a fully operational facility which could support as many as fifty personnel year-round and which would include a meteorological center, a state-of-the-art veterinary clinic and a broadcasting capability. The project was still in Phase Two, with the concentration of research on cataloguing and tracking the indigenous wildlife. That was how Hannah and Tom had discovered the Great White's pack two springs earlier.

"I still can't believe they were here," she murmured into her mug. "It was almost as though they were waiting for me, you know? I mean it, Tom, if you could have seen the way the Great White looked at me . . ."

She was silent for a moment, sipping her tea, remembering the click of the shutter and the turn of the majestic head, the look in those fierce Arctic eyes as they met hers through the camera lens. Only a wolf could manage to look proud, contemptuous and disinterested at the same time. And that was only one of the many reasons the species had fascinated scientists, researchers and preservationists for so many years.

"It was like he remembered me," she said softly, gazing at the low mist of steam that had congealed in her cup, "or that he knew why I had come . . . or at least that's what I want to think. And who's going to argue with me, hmm, Tom? Certainly not you."

The wind snapped the flaps of the tent a couple of times and then died back to a low, soft hum that scuttled snow across the frozen ground and stirred the branches of evergreens at the far end of the valley. But for that soft constant murmur of wind, there was absolute silence, and sometimes Hannah liked to simply stop and listen to that silence. A part of her was always hoping to hear a familiar voice borne upon the wind, a shout of laughter or discovery: *Hannah, over here!* or *Hannah, due west!* which was Tom's preferred method of communicating across the tundra, despite the ready availability of thousands of dollars' worth of sophisticated communications equipment. Sometimes she listened so hard that she actually thought, far in the distance . . . but then she would rush outside and stand straining to hear, and there would be nothing but the wind.

One day, she knew, she would hear the voice, and she would follow it, and not look back. Until then, she would wait.

She frowned now, recalling the bizarre behavior of the pack right after she had taken the photograph. What was it they had heard? Some kind of seismic disturbance or supersonic wave? The pack howl had lasted almost three minutes, reverberating off the glaciers and echoing over the plains, and when it was finished they had disappeared into the snowy woods as quickly as they had come, abandoning their kill.

"I wish you had seen *that*," she muttered to Tom. She finished off the tea and poured the rest of the hot water over the same bag, swirling it absently by the string. "You always had an explanation for everything."

Tom had discovered the hidden valley the first June they spent here, and had speculated that it was protected enough to actually support a variety of wildlife through the winter months. He had found the droppings of musk oxen, frozen in less than a foot of snow, and had seen signs of winter-hardy vegetation beneath. He had spotted the mud slick in Little Claw Creek, where the wolves went to drink, breaking through the crust of the ice with their massive paws and leaving tracks frozen in the snow. But an entire summer's worth of searching had not produced the pack to which those tracks belonged, nor any sign of their den.

That was when Tom suggested the valley might be the winter home of the pack, and insisted on staying late into the season to prove it. Hannah stayed with him.

It was October when the wolves showed up, and left the first fresh paw prints in mud leading down to the fast-flowing stream. Tom and Hannah followed the tracks for over a mile on foot in dry, blowing snow and wind chills ten below zero. They were clever, stalking silently and downwind, but the wolves were cleverer. The tracks did not lead to their den, but to a blind bluff where, when Hannah looked up, the Great White and his mate were watching them from atop a stone escarpment, perhaps twenty feet over their heads. Hannah gripped Tom's arm in a moment of intense communication and he looked up as well, and for the longest time the four of them simply acknowledged one another in silence: man, woman and wolves.

They never discovered how the wolves got up there, and they never found the trail. Neither did they know where the rest of the pack was. But one thing was clear: the wolves had been watching them, following him, since they left the creek. They had deliberately led their human trackers away from the den and the rest of the pack.

Hannah and Tom stayed for two more weeks, before the weather became so inclement that they knew they would have to either leave or resign themselves to wintering over. During that time they saw the pack twice, but never found the den. And although they never got closer than the distance of their highest-powered binoculars, they always had the feeling that the Great White knew they were there, and that they were allowed to watch only at his sufferance.

Hannah had wanted to stay, but Tom had always been the practical one. Even with Station Alpha fully operational, which it was not at that time, it would have been a suicide pact to mount such an expedition alone. But they began to make plans then to return to the wilderness and winter with this remarkable pack; to learn what it had to teach.

They had talked of little else during that winter and spring, even though they knew the project might be as much as three years in the future. Hannah wanted to include a *National Geographic* film crew, Tom wanted to keep the personnel down to the essentials, and they had argued, as they always did, over the relative merits of public-awareness programs. The discussion was tabled temporarily as they made arrangements to return to Alaska for the summer; Tom hoped to be able to piece together a picture of the pack's winter habits from whatever evidence was left behind.

Hannah was as anxious to get back to the wilderness that summer as Tom was, but part of the stipulations for endowment for The Wilderness Project provided that the project be thirty percent self-sufficient. And that meant that a certain amount of time and effort had to be devoted to fund-raising and public relations.

Tom, who had to be wrestled into a black tie, accused her of enjoying the lecture circuit, of looking forward to the banquets and the ballrooms and shaking the politicians' hands, as though the ability to do so were something to be ashamed of. She would return hotly that if not for the lectures and the politicians and the banquets, neither of them would have a job, but the truth was, she *did* enjoy it. And she *was* ashamed to tell Tom so.

He hadn't wanted to accompany her on that last junket to Chicago, but then, he never did. She insisted it was the Braselton-North *team* that persuaded people to take out their checkbooks, and this was in part true, because Tom was a great deal more persuasive—and charming—than he gave himself credit for. But the real truth was simply that she did not like to go to fund-raisers alone. When she dressed up in her Versace gown and her mother's pearls, she wanted her handsome husband at her side. So he went, although he never wanted to.

They were driving back to the hotel on the night before they were to fly to Fairbanks. They had attended a dinner with board members of the Braselton Foundation, and Hannah had presented a progress report and a slide show of the new facility. It had gone well, no one had asked any hard-to-answer questions, and Tom was in an ebullient mood because it was over, and they were headed home to the wilderness.

They stopped at a red light at an almost deserted intersection, Tom was loosening his tie and talking in an easy relaxed way about something—and it was so odd that, as many times as she had been over the scene in her head, Hannah could not remember what, exactly, he had been talking about. The night was mild and it had rained earlier, leaving the air misty and clean-tasting. Tom had his window open to enjoy the breeze, and Hannah remembered seeing the reflection of the traffic light on the damp pavement as it started to change on the opposite side from green to yellow. Tom eased his foot off the brake.

And then a predator came out of the shadows with a forty-four magnum and a crack of thunder, and then she was on her hands and knees on the pavement while the car screeched away and someone screamed in her ears, crawling toward Tom, who was facedown on the sidewalk, slipping on the oily asphalt; then reaching him, dragging him into her lap and realizing that the screams were her own because the slippery substance was not oil but blood, and the left half of Tom's head had been blown away.

Three weeks later she went back to the ranch, alone, and tried to do the things everyone told her she should do: pack up Tom's clothes and papers, and distribute his personal effects. Instead she sat down in the big rocker in front of the window that overlooked the meadow, and she rocked, and she looked, and she didn't move. Volunteers came by to feed the animals, and they tried to offer their awkward condolences, but she sent them away. Neighbors who had petitioned to have the ranch closed down when she and Tom had first moved there came by with pies and cakes and pointless murmurs of sympathy, and she nodded wordlessly and took their food and sent them away, and she went back to the rocker.

On the fourth day she went into the kitchen and found Tom's coffee cup sitting in the sink, where he had left it before the trip to Chicago, its bottom crusted over with dried coffee too heavily sugared, because he never *would* learn to put his dishes in the dishwasher. She picked up the cup with both hands and simply gazed at it for a long time. Then she drew back with a scream of rage and threw it against the opposite wall. She opened the cupboard and pulled out one glass after another, throwing them, smashing them, and when the glasses were all gone she started on the china and then the serving bowls and then the pots and pans, until she couldn't find anything else to throw and she stood in the middle of the littered kitchen with her face wet and her chest heaving and her hair tangled around her shoulders.

Tom stood watching her from the corner, arms and ankles crossed, mouth turned up with a grin, shock of hair grazing one eyebrow.

"You about finished here, High Class?" he said. "Because we've got work to do."

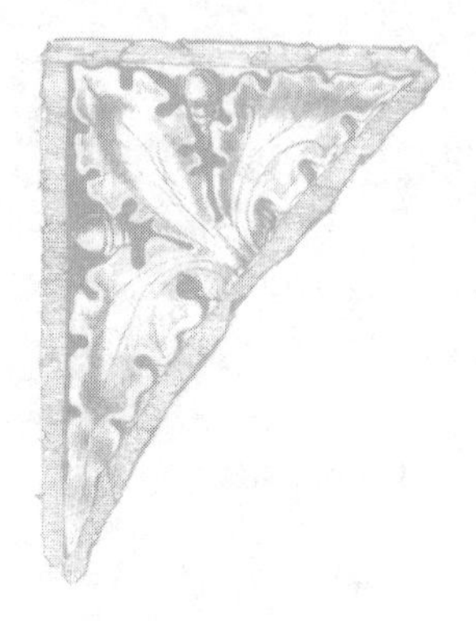

Five

A FAINT SOUND OUTSIDE THE TENT MADE HANNAH FROWN, DISTRACTing her, marring the stillness of the perfect solitude. It took her a moment to identify it. Helicopter blades. She heard them sometimes, and they never failed to annoy her. This one was far away and headed in the opposite direction, so she did not bother getting up to check the sky. But there were simply some sounds that did not belong here, and it irritated her.

The sound of Tom's voice, carried on the wind. *That* belonged here.

"Even in the middle of the goddamn wilderness with glaciers on three sides, huh, babe?" She lifted the tea kettle, but it was empty. "Is any place safe from civilization?"

She wiped her mug and put it away, gazing thoughtfully at the corner of the cot where Tom should have been, hunched over his notebook or fiddling with his camera equipment. He was a much better veterinarian than photographer, but that did not stop him from loading himself down with lenses and film every time they went out.

"You know," she told him, "I've been thinking about what you said, and I don't think this pack has ever been studied before, and I doubt they have ever seen humans. I know you thought that because they didn't act afraid of us, or even curious, it was because they had been acclimated to humans before. But I think they're just not interested. Like today. The White knew I was there; he just made it a point to stay out of my way. The sound of the snowmobile doesn't seem to startle or alarm them, but I think it's because they know it doesn't have anything to do with them—it's no threat. I've been tracking them for weeks, and all they have to do to avoid me is take a path that's too steep or rocky for the snowmobile."

Again she frowned. "Yeah, laugh if you want to, but we've both seen how canny these animals can be. Besides, if you've got a better theory, speak up."

Silence.

Hannah shivered and moved closer to the heater. "I wish you could have seen him, Tom, one last time. I wish you could have said goodbye."

She paused, and the wind whistled outside the tent and the glacier cracked and moaned as she simply sat there, watching the radiant glow of the heater, thinking nothing at all. She had trained herself not to think, just as she had trained herself to tolerate the cold and the isolation and the endless feeble gray sun that never set and never rose, that just hung there on the horizon in a perpetual state of uncertainty that was, in its own way, a metaphor for life—and death.

Sound carried with exceptional clarity in the cold, and she could still hear the helicopter, obscenely intrusive even though its gentle beating was muffled by the increasing force of the wind. She wondered how far the wolves had had to travel to reach their den and if she had made her own camp far enough away. She did not want to scare them off. She didn't want to intrude upon their valley in the same way the sounds of modern mechanization were intruding upon her solitude. She had planned to go out again today, and try to pick up their trail. She doubted she would have much luck, but there was tomorrow, and the next day, and until she found the den. This she would do for Tom. After that . . .

The percussion of the blast caused the water kettle to rattle against the heater and toppled several packages of freeze-dried camp meals Hannah had arranged on the chair. She said, "What the—?" and jumped to her feet, pushing quickly out of the tent and into the frigid day.

She never really had a doubt as to what had caused the sound. It was an explosion, and she was just in time to see the last of the fiery trail twisting and spinning and sinking like a stone into the jagged crevice of the eastern glacier.

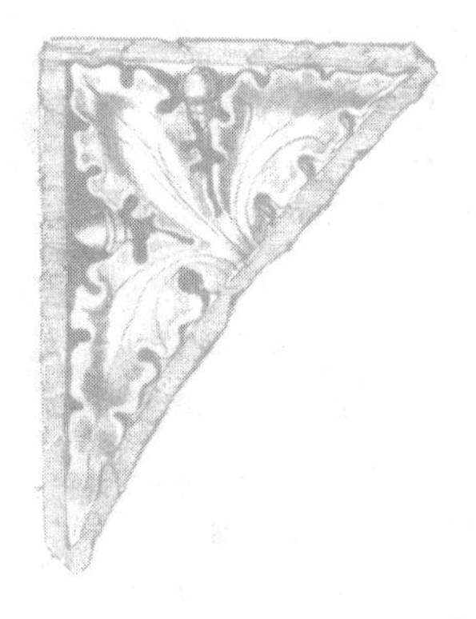

Six

HANNAH ALMOST DIDN'T GO TO INVESTIGATE. IF THE FIREBALL HAD descended on the far side of the glacier instead of on the near, she would have turned away, and forgotten it by the time she went to sleep. She might have convinced herself that it was nothing more than a meteor fragment, or a bit of space trash. Whatever it was, it had nothing to do with her.

But she knew exactly what had caused that blast, and it was not a meteor or a burning stream of debris that had crashed into the frozen hillside. It was the helicopter. Soon the air would be thick with the percussion of others looking for their lost member, and if they found it they would come here by the dozens, swarming over the tundra like black ants on the beach, and there would be no chance of escaping them, not for her, not for her wolves.

She could not stay where she was. Her camp would be a signal that would bring them closer. She estimated that the crash site was five or six hours away by snowmobile, and the closer she could get to it, the better chance she would have of keeping the intruders away from the wolves.

She broke camp and packed the sledge, and within an hour was on her way.

She didn't think about possible survivors. Had there been any when the plane went down, they would not last long in the subzero weather; not long enough for the rescuers to reach them, not even long enough for Hannah to get there. Corpses, and pieces of corpses, were all that awaited her on the side of that mountain, but the prospect brought neither dismay nor revulsion. It was simply a fact.

A light punishing snow began to fall about a hour before she reached the wreckage, and the wind that blew from the northeast carried with it the smell of hot twisted metal and burned flesh. The black plume of smoke that had guided her way across the tundra became harder to see as the terrain grew more hilly, and finally died down altogether. The snowmobile sputtered and spun on steep icy grades, causing the sledge to sway dangerously. Spitting snow froze on her mask and goggles, and she had to stop repeatedly to clear them. She considered veering west, away from the carnage that did not concern her and the intrusion of the outside world she had not invited. But then she saw a movement, on a slope just beyond her, that made her heart stop.

"Tom?"

She cut the engine and listened, peering into the curtain of snow, futilely trying to part it with her gloved hand. There was definitely a shape on the crest, a shadow . . .

"Tom, is that you?" No answer.

She restarted the engine and put it in gear, moving closer. The shape shifted, turning to look her full in the face for a moment before heading off and disappearing into the snow. It was the white wolf.

She did not consider changing direction after that.

She continued travelling toward the east, where she had last glimpsed the column of smoke. Within half an hour she began to see the first signs of debris—a twisted piece of unidentified metal, a walnut door with a brass handle that might have been part of an interior cabinet, a leather-covered headrest—all of them rimmed with snow and obscenely out of place in this silent wilderness. The smell of burned things was as thick as a toxin in the air now, and when she crested the rise she saw the crash site less than a hundred feet below.

There was very little left of the helicopter. A portion of cliff had been sheered away by the impact, and a river of melted snow had refrozen around it, locking the machine in a shroud of broken stones and filthy, smokey ice. One blade of the front rotor was missing, another was buried in the cliff. The body was broken in two, with the rear half dug into a snowbank a hundred yards from the front, and both portions so twisted and buckled as to be barely recognizable as machinery at all. The ground was littered with debris, black and gray-blue and brown flecks of color against the white, for almost a quarter of a mile. It was impossible for Hannah to guess which of those spots of color might represent portions of human bodies.

With the greatest reluctance, Hannah guided the snowmobile down the slope as close to the site as she could get. She cut the engine and, removing her goggles, trudged through the snow and a sea of detritus the rest of the way. Most of the remnants of the crash were unidentifiable: scraps of cloth, slivers of plastic, shards of tinted glass. There was a portion of a burned seat, its leather covering peeled away and its insides fused into a single mass of blackened springs and caramelized synthetic padding. There was a portion of teak panelling, unscarred except for a ragged tear along one side, and a small microwave oven minus a door. She began to suspect this was not an ordinary helicopter.

There were no bodies, and she was not surprised. As she got closer she could see that the fire had been so intense it had melted the paint on the outside of the helicopter, and not even the ID numbers were readable. The stench, intensified by the cold air, was almost unbearable—a combination of burned oil and burning rubber, of the yellowish fumes emitted by mattress fires and the choking toxicity of chemicals. Beneath it all was a sweet-sick cooking odor whose origins she did not like to imagine.

She forced herself to move toward the mangled shape of the forward section of the helicopter, slipping on the slick, fast-frozen ice more than once and falling to her knees. Holding her breath against the odor, which was more intense at this range, she grasped the jagged edge of the fuselage and peered inside. There was nothing but wreckage burned beyond recognition, cables dangling overhead, seats strewn and fused to the floor, rubble piled into unidentifiable heaps. The lumps of material near the cockpit were not recognizable as human and might, in fact, have been nothing more than melted equipment components. Releasing a slow soft breath of relief, Hannah backed away.

Something crunched beneath her foot.

She looked down at what appeared to be a charred stick, broken beneath her boot. Only it wasn't a stick. At one end were four distinct and recognizable digits, grotesquely deformed by heat but unmistakable. Not a hand. A paw.

Hannah gasped and lurched backward, losing her balance and landing hard on her buttocks. It was then that she caught sight of another fur-covered grotesquerie protruding at an angle from the snow to her right; swinging her head around wildly to search with newly intent eyes, she spotted a muzzle, half buried in the snow, one ear burned away and the eye socket empty and staring into the sky. Otherwise it was a perfect wolf head.

"Jesus Christ," she whispered.

She turned her head and vomited into the snow.

Gray day and spinning snow swirled violently around her for an endless time. Her heaving gasps for breath were punctuated with the smell of burning bones and singed fur. Hannah clawed at the ice to put distance between herself and the mangled animal corpses, then rolled over onto her back with her eyes squeezed tightly shut, drawing long wet breaths through flared nostrils.

"Shit," she whispered. "*Shit.*"

The teak panelling, microwave oven and leather seats were instantly understandable now. This was not a military chopper, a supply transport or a survey craft. It was a luxury corporate vehicle, out for a weekend of sport. Its passengers were hunters. Its cargo, the quarry. Wolves.

With a wave of rage so intense it left her shaking, Hannah rolled onto all fours and rose to her feet, facing the wreckage. "Rot in hell, you stupid sons of bitches," she said lowly, balling her fists. "I hope you're still burning."

The moisture of perspiration and tears had stiffened her mask and was beginning to freeze into a film that burned her cheeks. She bent to scoop up a handful of snow and forced it into her mouth, but spat it out immediately. It tasted worse than the residue of sickness and death that clung to her tongue. Hannah started back up the hill toward the snowmobile.

She slipped halfway up and fell to one knee. A glint of metal caught her eye, and somewhat hesitantly she made her way over to it. It was a slim square box, half buried in the snow, and as she dug it out Hannah realized it was a briefcase with most of the leather burned off, leaving only the metal undercasing. The lock was warped and a significant gap was noticeable between the two halves; it looked easy enough to pry it open. Inside there was undoubtedly something to identify the owner—the murderer. Hannah clutched the case to her chest grimly and continued up the hill.

She almost didn't notice the shadow behind the boulder, so much a part of the deep cobalt shadows of a day devoid of sunlight that it seemed just another depression in the landscape. There might have been a sound, but she didn't think so. Afterward she could not say exactly why she looked, and looked again, and realized that what she was seeing, half-hidden behind a boulder twenty feet away, was the fully intact body of a wolf.

She didn't want to go over to it. She tried to turn her feet in the other direction. But a morbid fascination, if nothing else, drew her closer.

As she approached she could make out, barely discernible

through the snow, a blood-splattered trail where the wolf had dragged itself to shelter behind the boulder, indicating that, as incredible as it seemed, the creature had been alive at the time of the crash. And then a new and horrible thought struck her: perhaps all of the wolves had been alive before the crash; not victims of the hunter's bullet after all, but live zoological cargo. That the crash had taken human lives was unfortunate, of course—despite the fact that those humans had most likely been engaged in immoral and illegal activity—but that it should have so horribly mangled and killed those captive animals who had no chance to save themselves was doubly horrifying. Yet it appeared there had been at least one survivor.

The wolf was lying on his side facing her. He was huge, five feet long or more. The wind blew and parted a ruff of pale flax-colored fur around his neck, revealing a dark wound just below the ear that was still seeping blood. The top foreleg was broken at elbow and wrist, causing it to protrude at two different angles. A knob of white bone was visible under the elbow. A pool of blood had darkened the snow beneath him, and Hannah moved reluctantly closer, dreading what she would find. What she found made her draw in her breath and stop short.

"Dear God," she whispered.

The wolf was still alive.

Most of the fur had been burned away from shoulder to hip, and the skin below it was blackened and suppurating. But she could see the rib cage rising with quick shallow breaths, see the faint puffs of steam from the nostrils and, yes, hear the wet gurgling sound as that breath passed through blood in the airway.

"Oh, Christ," she said softly, then moved carefully closer. "Oh, shit. You poor bastard. Fuck. Fuck." Now she was whispering, and her throat was so tight she could barely make the sound.

Fur was missing in half a dozen places that she could see and the skin that was revealed looked like raw hamburger. Bleeding wounds she could not see saturated what remained of his fur with dark patches, and the choking, gurgling efforts he made to breathe were heart-wrenching to hear. Blood stained his lower jaw and the snow beneath, indicating internal injuries about which she could only speculate. After surviving this long, the poor fellow didn't have a chance. It was only a question now of how long it would take him to die.

Hannah climbed the hill back to the sledge, moving faster and with more determination the closer she got. She unlashed her rifle and checked the chamber. Setting her jaw grimly, she returned down the hill.

She came as close as she could get and positioned the barrel directly over the wolf's head, for a bad shot would be no mercy at all. She eased off the safety and curled her finger around the trigger. "I wish there was someone to do this for me, fellow," she said huskily.

Her eyes suddenly went hot with tears and angrily she shrugged her shoulder to wipe them on the sleeve of her coat. When she repositioned her aim, the wolf was looking at her.

His eyes were blue, like the Arctic eyes of Great White, only darker and not as clear. They were cloudy slits, in fact, and no doubt didn't focus on her at all, but it was disconcerting nonetheless, and her hand shook. The eyes closed again, and the long gurgling release of breath sounded like a sigh.

"Fuck," she whispered, and lowered the unfired rifle.

She went back to the sledge, her heart pounding with exertion and anxiety, and unpacked her medical kit. She returned quickly to the scene, sliding the last ten or twenty feet on her backside, and she half expected him to be dead. She opened the insulated med kit and took out a syringe, tearing off the paper with her teeth, and a bottle of Stadol. She could hear the wolf breathing, light and rapid, now slow and labored, now choking, now still. And now quick and rapid again. She started to draw up a measure of the liquid into the syringe, then hesitated, glancing at the animal. Two milligrams would act upon the respiratory system like ten milligrams of morphine. A full syringe would be a quick and painless death. In his condition, anything less would be cruel.

Hannah tightened her lips, drew up 0.1 milligram and injected it into the muscle of his neck. Then she began to look around for something to use as a splint.

The lodge was less than two hours away by snowmobile, but Hannah did not expect the wolf to still be alive when she reached it. In fact, he seemed to be breathing a little easier by the time she pulled up in front of the shuttered, snow-covered building. Before transferring him from the sledge to the smaller sled that was used to transport supplies and firewood from the outbuilding to the main house, she injected a small dose of the tranquilizer benzodiazepine. She waited for his breathing to stop, knowing that if it did she had neither the skill nor the equipment to start it again.

But when she returned from getting the generator started and clearing out a work space in the main room of the lodge, he was still alive. She began the long and arduous process of moving the animal inside.

Hannah had worked at close range with wolves, both tranquilized and alert, before. But she had never had to handle one alone, and had never dealt with one this badly injured. She knew the chances of his surviving the night were slim, and that her clumsy efforts to save him were only prolonging his suffering. But that he was alive at all was a miracle, and every moment he continued to breathe was such a stubborn defiance of all probability that Hannah felt obligated to give him every chance.

She got him inside, out of the blowing cold, and filled both the wood-burning furnace and the room's fireplace. She was a strong woman accustomed to heavy lifting and carrying, yet her arm muscles were shaking and her back ached dully by the time she had both fires going. She unzipped her parka and covered her outer clothing with a sturdy canvas apron, replaced her Arctic gloves with thin latex ones and knelt beside her patient.

"Tom, help me, for Christ's sake. Tell me what to do."

She set up a liter of oxygen, cleaned the open wounds and replaced the field bandages with sterile gauze. She injected massive doses of ampicillin, debrided the burns and set the bones as best she could. Out of the corner of her eye, now and then, she thought she could catch a glimpse of Tom, watching intently from the shadows by the door, nodding with occasional approval. She knew that should make her feel better, but it didn't.

With no small amount of difficulty she established a saline IV, yet there was nothing she could do about the crushed ribs or the undoubtedly punctured lung, nor about the internal, soft-tissue injuries she could not see. After an hour or so the wolf seemed to be responding to the oxygen, and began to stir. She cautiously administered a one-third dose of Stadol, and moved him into a large portable crate they used to transport tranquilized animals to and from the compound. Hannah rolled the crate close to the fire, and went to unload the rest of her supplies from the sledge.

Bad weather was approaching, with a high biting wind and blue-black shadows chasing the snow. Hannah barely noticed. By the time she put away the snowmobile and trudged the ten yards from the storage shed to the lodge, she was staggering with exhaustion. Wind and snow chased her into the building and she struggled to get the door closed behind her. She peeled off her outerwear and let it lie where it fell as she made her way over to the crate and the wounded creature inside who struggled to live. He was still breathing.

Next to the Great White, he was the biggest wolf she had ever seen.

"Are you part of the pack, fellow?" she asked softly. "Are you one of Tom's wolves?"

She stretched out on the floor beside the crate, and fell asleep with Tom watching her approvingly from the shadows of the flickering twilight.

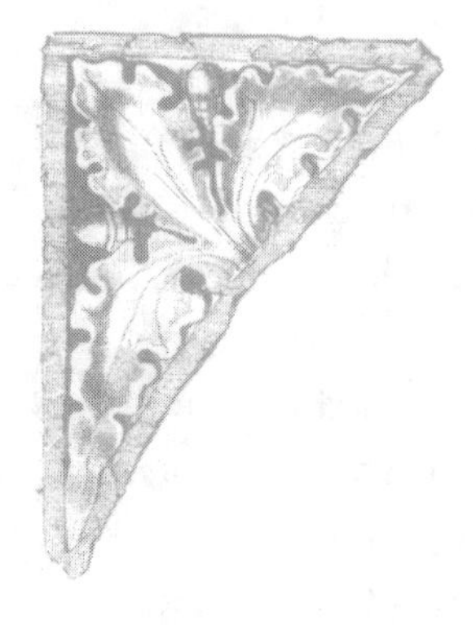

Seven

THE PAIN CAME IN SLOWLY, LIKE A TIDE FILLING AN EMPTY POOL. When the pool was filled, when every part of him was saturated with awareness, the agony was so intense that all of his remaining strength was required not to cry out with it, to scream, to howl until his voice filled the heavens and turned the skies black. The pain was not in his body, which felt oddly light and free. The pain was in his consciousness, in his memory, in his soul, and it was filled with the smell of burning bones and boiling blood.

Dead. They were all dead. Friends, employees, trusted advisors. The stench of death was in his fur, the taste of it on his tongue, the hot white flash of it burned into his retinas. Dead, all of them. His people. And he had not been able to do a thing to save them.

Like the tide, the soul-pain of consciousness receded, slowly, and gave way to another kind of memory, more distant and confused. Another death. Ah, it was too much. So many dead, so many gone, so much darkness sucking out the light.

The pain. The pain.

Sir, the leader of the pack is dead, and with him his queen.

Long live the leader of the pack.

No, don't let it be . . .

The smell. What was the smell? Fire and burning flesh, toxic smoke, thick and purple, fuel . . . yes, fuel. And more. Accelerant. Explosives. A bomb.

The helicopter had not fallen from the sky. It had been sabotaged.

Voices clattered around in his brain like lost children, echoing, bouncing back upon one another, making no sense.

What will you do?

What I must.

What will you—

Must—

Must do . . .

Shouting now. His father's voice raised in anger. *You would do this thing? You would destroy all that we stand for with a few strokes of the pen—*

And then his father was dead, and his mother with him. *Dead.* The pain.

A bomb. A bomb so cleverly disguised that not even werewolf senses could discern its presence until after it had detonated. But who? Who had done such a thing? And how and why? The answers were there, nudging at the back of his brain, and he could hear them if it weren't for the pain . . . the pain, and the voices.

His father's voice: *I cannot let you do this thing!*

You know there is no other choice! It should have been done long ago. What has happened here must never happen again and there is only one way to prevent it, you know that!

He saw his hands, his own human-formed hands, clenched around a book with a battered red cover. It must never happen again. No one must know. What has happened here must never happen again.

The leader of the pack is dead . . .

Half a millennium of peace . . .

Ends here. Ends now.

Long live the leader of the pack.

I, Nicholas Devoncroix, do by my own hand this day set down these words . . .

Words. Voices. Pictures fading in and out in his head. A broken promise, the smell of fuel. A bomb, a saboteur . . . *who? why?* There was so much he couldn't remember, and none of it mattered now. The tide was rising again, the smell of pain, the taste of pain, Mother, Father, flesh and fur burning in the snow.

He was Nicholas Devoncroix, leader of the pack, and death stalked his dreams.

Hannah awoke with a start two hours later and immediately checked on the wolf. He was still alive. In fact, his breathing seemed to be a little steadier, and she could no longer hear the gurgling sound with each exhalation. The burns were still ugly and raw, but the antibiotic ointment she had applied seemed to be doing its job and the wounds were no longer oozing blood. She didn't want to agitate him with a closer examination, so she arranged a blanket over the crate to simulate the feeling of a den, and she left the wolf alone.

Tom was no longer there.

She went around the room turning on lamps and picking up bloody rags and discarded plastic wrappings, moving stiffly and aching in every muscle. She stopped before the silent radio and looked at it thoughtfully for a moment. She could call Denali for a real veterinarian, but by the time they got someone up here—if in fact they could send anyone at all—the wolf would be either dead or past the need for emergency care. Almost as an afterthought, she considered calling in news of the crash, but didn't linger over the idea. There would be teams of search vehicles combing the mountainside as soon as the weather cleared, and she felt no obligation whatsoever to make the search for the dead bounty hunters any easier.

She heated a can of stew in the narrow galley kitchen and ate it standing up, almost gulping it, and felt the strength flow through her calorie-starved body with each bite. She made a mug of steaming tea and carried it back to the main room to check on the wolf again. He was breathing quietly, his splinted legs straight and still. She did not know what else to do for him.

"A word from you, my love," she murmured to Tom, "would be appreciated now."

And that was when she remembered the briefcase she had picked up at the site. The twisted frame came apart with the aid of a crowbar, revealing contents that were relatively undamaged. There were a few folders, damp at the corners where ice had seeped inside and melted, an electronic organizer, a Mont Blanc pen, eight hundred dollars in cash and an untitled book with a battered red cover.

The cash didn't interest her, and she left it in the case. She glanced through the folders first but found little of interest—a velum-bound prospectus on a company called Infotech, a contract regarding a merger of two other companies whose names meant nothing to her, some memos whose recipients and senders used initials, a copy of a ruling by a U.S. Supreme Court judge regarding a environmental issue that concerned yet a completely different company. Several of the memos were on stationery that bore a vaguely familiar logo, but there was nothing of a genuinely identifying nature. She opened the book.

On the first page was written, perfectly centered: "Being the true writings of Matise Devoncroix."

It took Hannah a moment to realize that it was handwriting on the paper and not typesetting, so fine and precise were the letters. The paper itself was soft and expensive, and as she flipped through the pages she saw that the book had been hand-bound with several different kinds of paper in varying shades of ivory and white, as though the writing had taken a long time. She frowned a little, curiously, and tried to reconcile this odd little book and its precise penmanship and old-fashioned phrasing with all those cold corporate documents. For that matter, why would a businessman bring a briefcase full of sensitive documents along on a sporting trip anyway?

"Devoncroix," she murmured out loud. "Where do I know that name from?"

She didn't expect an answer.

She put the book aside and tried to access the electronic organizer. Either the battery was dead, or it had been damaged in the crash. She could not even get the display window to light up.

A sudden downdraft caused the fireplace to sputter and spit sparks, and she went over to add more logs. She refilled the furnace and checked the supply of wood in the adjoining shed, estimating that it would be several days before she would have to brave the elements to resupply from the woodpile behind the building. The wind had died down but it was snowing heavily now, and the temperature gauge mounted just outside the furnace room door read minus twelve degrees Celsius.

She secured the house against the night, checked the fuel in the generator and tightened the insulating shutters. The Foundation had built this compound to be self-sufficient in temperatures down to sixty below, but as far as Hannah knew, no one had ever tested it before. Fuel and food would be restocked in the spring, but there was always enough of both on hand and to last a six-member team two weeks in case of an emergency. They were stationed at the end of the world, and emergencies were, more often than not, a matter of routine.

Hannah wasn't afraid of the dark, and the cold was her friend. But she worried what both would do to the creature inside the compound who had fought so hard to live and was still holding on by a thread.

The metal shutters were operated from the inside with a lever, and sealed off the windows like draperies. Hannah was closing the last one when she caught a glimpse of something in the snow just beyond the compound. A streak of gray, a flash of movement . . . It looked like a wolf, but was gone too quickly for her to be certain.

Her wolf had not moved, but the sound of his quick shallow

panting, distressing as it was in itself, assured her he lived. Hannah spent some time searching through the various books the team had left over the years for a veterinary text, but found nothing helpful.

Her eyes fell on the red book, and she picked it up again, flipping forward a few pages. She scanned a page, then stopped and read it more slowly. "Tom, for heaven's sake, will you listen to this?"

She read out loud: " 'We first met Man in the time of the great plains and forests, when we all ran as wolves and rarely desired to be anything else. That initial encounter, so the legend goes, did not go well for Man, but it inspired us to a greater awareness of ourselves, and of our potential. Man had hands to make fire, so did we. Man had legs to climb trees, so did we. And we, of course, had something Man would never have: a quick and superior intellect, and our two forms' . . ."

"Two forms?" she repeated, frowning. "What in the world?"

A sound from the cage made her stop and look up. The eyes of the wolf were open and, though unfocused, seemed to be searching for the source of the voice.

"Do you like to hear me talk, fellow?" Hannah asked softly, moving closer to the cage. "It interests you, doesn't it? Makes you think it might be worth staying alive, huh, if for nothing else than to protect yourself from me?"

The wolf made the sound again, low in his throat, something between a growl and a whine, and his eyes drooped closed. His breathing was rapid and shallow, punctuated erratically by faint, sharp sounds of pain or need. Hannah doubted whether the sound of her voice meant anything to the wild creature at all, or whether he had truly even noticed it, but she liked to think otherwise. And the sound of her own voice might at least block the howl of the wind, and the wolf's soft, unconscious moans of pain.

"Besides, like they say, what can it hurt?"

She took the book over to the fireplace and sat down. She glanced over at the wolf, then turned to the beginning of the book and began to read out loud.

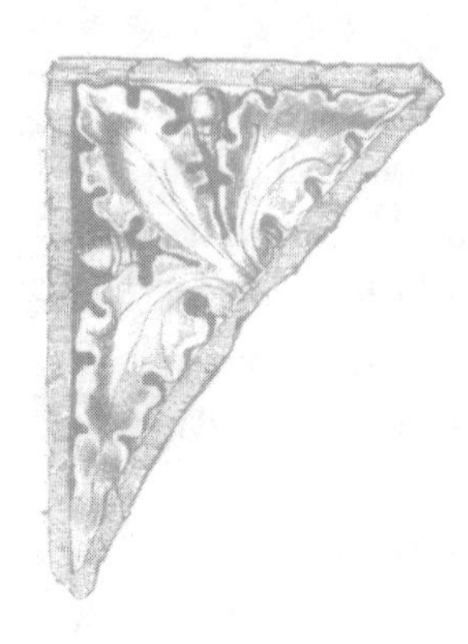

From the Writings of Matise Devoncroix

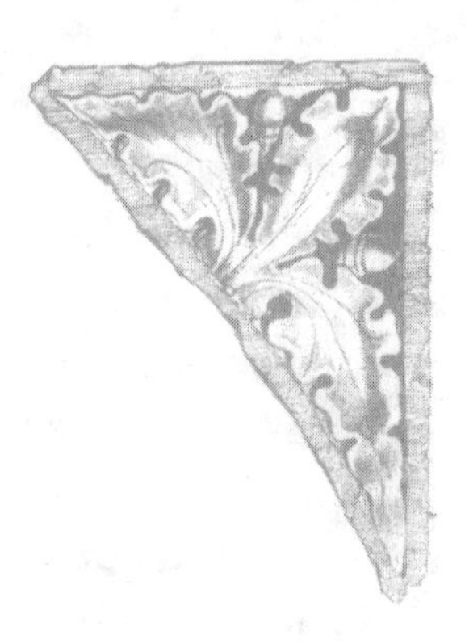

I

I've spent a lifetime entertaining others with my little tales, my philosophies, speculations and imaginings. How strange it seems to me now, as I put to paper the most important words I've ever written, to know that they must never be seen by any eyes but your own.

I hope that you will not be too quick to condemn me for the secrets I've kept, for already I've tormented myself far more than any righteous accusations could ever do. I saw the only woman I have ever loved almost destroyed by such secrets, but it was the telling of them, in the end, that brought her to ruin. I've done my best to protect you from the same fate. Perhaps I was wrong to try.

I will not defend my choices to you, for by the time you finish this chronicle either you will understand them or it will no longer matter. I don't know how much longer we will have together. I have done my best for you. I've tried to teach you well. But how could I prepare you for your role in the world I could not even imagine? How could I help you choose when I don't even know what the choices are?

All I can do for you now is to tell you the truth, and try to explain how it came about. But with the knowledge comes a great responsibility, for the burden of responsibility, like the burden of power, is your birthright. It did not begin with you and me, you see, although I would like to say that it did, nor even with Brianna, whose story this really is. To understand how we came to be at the point we are today, we must look farther back than that, to the time that even history has forgotten. Understand these things, and you will understand Brianna, and me—and yourself.

I've taught you so many things in our time together; I've told you so many stories. Did I teach you enough? Did I tell you this one?

Read my last tale with care, then, and commit it to your heart. The blood of a thousand generations has been spilled for your sake; the blood of a thousand more mingles in your veins. This is their story.

And ours.

II

WE FIRST MET MAN IN THE TIME OF THE GREAT PLAINS AND FORESTS, when we all ran as wolves and rarely desired to be anything else. That initial encounter, so the legend goes, did not go well for Man, but it inspired us to a greater awareness of ourselves, and of our potential. Man had hands to make fire, so did we. Man had legs to climb trees, so did we. And we, of course, had something Man would never have: a quick and superior intellect, and our two forms.

We soon learned the advantages of building shelters near the good hunting grounds, rather than denning in faraway caves that might flood or be breached by predators. We sharpened tools of stone for digging out earthen caves and found them to be even more efficient than our claws. Soon we fashioned axes for felling trees to warm our shelters, and scrapers for curing the hides of beasts, for by now we were discovering more and more advantages to the two-legged form, and needed to clothe ourselves against the elements while in it.

We did not hunt Man then. That came later.

We had little need to associate with humankind during those days, for the world was big and their numbers small. But there is evidence in prehistory that our paths crossed—drawings in ancient human caves of upright creatures with the heads of wolves, for example—and it seems reasonable to assume that a species so ill-suited to survival on this planet could hardly have gained a reputation as one of the fiercest predators in the jungle without some assistance from the masters of the art. This is the legend that tells how it happened:

A young wolfling strayed too far from the den one day and fell into the river, whose rising tide swiftly swept him away. When he stumbled to shore again, half drowned, he could smell nothing that was familiar to him, not his mother, nor his littermates, nor his hunting grounds, nor his pack. He wandered for days and nearly starved before he caught the scent of roasting meat. He had no fear of approaching a stranger's fire, for the smell of cooking meant home to him, and the human who saw the small bedraggled pup creep into his camp with tail and belly lowered to beg for nourishment had no cause to fear, either. He was, in fact, surprised and curious to see a wolf behave in such a manner, and because he had meat to spare, he gave him some. Man and wolfling feasted together, and fell asleep beside the fire.

The next day the man found a young boy at his fire in place of the wolf, and he was greatly amazed. The wolfling stayed some days, and together he and the man hunted, the wolfling in four-legged form to chase and kill, and changing to boy form when the meat was cooked. He showed the man how to make a shelter of leaves and branches to keep out the rain, as he had seen his elders do, and how to clothe himself in the hides of beasts to keep off the cold. Then one day while they hunted together, the wolfling caught scent of his own pack, and he knew he could not stay with the man. But he worried how the man would hunt without him, for he was too slow and too frail to bring down any but the sickest and the oldest and the skinniest of the beasts. He would soon starve.

And then the wolfling had an idea. He attached a long stick to a sharpened stone digger, and showed the man how to throw it through the air as fast as a wolf could leap, so that it would fell the beast before it could run away. The man was happy with his gift and learned to use it well, and the wolfling left his friend to return to his own kind, pleased that the man would not starve.

Some years later, when the wolfling was full-sized and had struck out on his own to find a mate and form his own pack, he caught scent once more of his old friend the man. Joyously he ran to greet the man, eager to show off his mature wolf form and to hunt again as they had done before. But as he approached the camp, the man rose up from his sleep and gave a great cry—and killed the wolf with his spear.

This was not perhaps the first betrayal, but it is the one we remember. It was from that moment, you see, that one of our strictest taboos was born: an aversion to weapons of any sort among our kind. You will hear it said that weapons are the last resort of a weakling human, and that is an onus no one of us would have brought upon himself.

That's true enough, I suppose. But the comparison to helpless humans is not the real reason our collective unconscious recoils so instinctively from the concept of weaponry. It is, rather, that the idea of using an artificial tool to harm another stirs that memory in us, a memory so deeply buried even now we do not recognize it for what it is, of a gift offered and a trust betrayed. And the hurt of remembering is more than we can bear.

III

GIVEN OUR ALMOST ENDLESS FASCINATION WITH HUMANS, IT SEEMS odd now to realize that until we were ten years old, neither Brianna nor I had ever actually seen one. But it's true. We, eldest children of the rulers of the pack, spent our formative years sublimely convinced that we and our kind were the only creatures on earth with sentience. Of course, even after we understood about humans, it was a long time before I changed my mind on that score, and sometimes, to be honest, I still am not completely convinced I was wrong.

To understand how we could have gone so long in the modern world without once meeting a member of a species so prevalent that not even the remotest wilderness is untouched by them today, you have to understand how it was with us at the turn of the century. Mostly, you have to understand about Brianna.

She was born in the spring of 1900 on a mountaintop in Alaska, the first in a thousand, thousand years to be born in the Ancient Place, the secret cave-castle that once had sheltered a huge, vastly advanced pack whose fate is unknown to us and whose legacy has somehow been lost in time. Alexander and Elise Devoncroix went to Alaska, discovered this wondrous fortress of a long-forgotten people, and Brianna was born. There was magic attached to her name even then. Word travelled back to the pack of these two miracles, and soon they started to come, werewolves from all walks of life and of every description, crossing the tundra and swimming the rivers and climbing the mountains, to see for themselves. Just by being born, she became a legend.

That, it goes without saying, is something of a challenge for one small child to live up to.

Brianna was born in the spring, and had already assumed her human form by the time she was presented to the pack, for she was precocious from birth. The Devoncroix stayed through the summer, parents and infant, while the pack continued to come, bearing gifts for the firstborn and undisguised curiosity for the rumors they had heard about the Ancient Place. Paths were cleared, herd beasts were driven in and held in the high meadows to fatten for their sport and their nourishment, streams were cleared and made to flow again, and, bit by bit, the forgotten castle was brought back to life.

Perhaps you have never seen this place. Perhaps you walk its halls every day and know its secret passages and hidden rooms, its dark, damp stones and sudden gardens far better than I ever shall. But let me try to describe it to you as I recall it from my youth, for it was vastly different then, so much more filled with mystery and wonder, with shadows and whispered breaths of things long dead; it was a sanctuary frozen in time, a tomb opened and empty, it was the smell of the earth and the sound of heartbeats long stilled.

The edifice that you see now was only half cleared away then, so that as one approached on foot from the mountain pass, all that was visible, and then only if you looked hard, was the chimneys. The big wooden doors seemed to grow right from the hillside, and the carved-stone wolf heads that decorate them were not there then; I remember when Papa commissioned them and brought in the artist to do the work. At any rate, few used the doors then. The entrances that the werewolves preferred were narrow tunnels carved into the hillside—I think they have all been sealed up now, for security reasons—and those tunnels led to more tunnels, which, for the most part, could be negotiated by scent alone. Can you imagine what fun I had as a child losing myself in those tunnels, relying only on my senses to lead me to new discoveries? And what discoveries I made.

The tunnels eventually gave way to anterooms, which were the oldest part of the structure and which we think were enlarged from natural underground caves. When I was playing there, it was still possible to find bits of cookware and stone pottery that have been dated to 500,000 B.C. and which we suspect are even older—long before we previously believed werewolves had use for such tools of civilization. Of course, all those artifacts are on display now in the museum hall. But I considered them my playthings.

The great indoor gardens were overgrown with ropey vines as thick as tree trunks; the pools—except the hot springs, of course—

were stagnant and cold. But what an adventure it was to go creeping through those forbidden places, treading the marble floors that had been worn by a hundred thousand long-stilled feet, pretending to track the great mastodon or long-toothed tiger. At any moment it was possible to stumble upon a chamber heretofore unknown, to gaze up, openmouthed, at a ceiling painted in azure and gold, to touch a swath of gossamer drapery that swept the breadth of a room and have the whole thing crumble into dust in your hand; to sweep your fingers across a tabletop blackened with time and discover an inlay of precious stones beneath. The great rooms have all been restored now and the pack members stroll the halls and gasp at their opulence; they admire the gardens and the pools and the thermoelectric heating system and the channelled light from windows they cannot see, and they wonder over the cleverness of their ancestors and think they know something of their heritage. But I tell you that seeing that place as it once was, when the dusty forgotten rooms still smelled of the dreams and ambitions of a race of werewolves long lost to us, when every step was an adventure waiting to unfold and around any corner might lie the clue that would tell us all the story we had been longing to hear—*that* is to know your heritage. That is to know who you truly are, and that is the greatest gift any child can possess.

I had such a gift, when I was young. Would that I could now impart it to you.

They came from France, from Britain, from Germany and from America that summer after Brianna was born, and they stayed to tear down rotting draperies, to shore up sagging timbers, to lovingly brush new life into faded tapestries. And although Papa always claimed it was his idea to move the pack headquarters from Palais Devoncroix in Lyons to this hidden fortress in Alaska, I think the decision was made that summer, by the pack. They knew they had come home.

It was no coincidence that gold strikes were being realized up and down the great Alaskan rivers that year and in those following, for many of our kind, making the journey out of curiosity or to impress the pack leader, were stopped by the scent of precious ore beneath the ground, and found a reason to linger. So you could even say Brianna was the reason for the sudden increase of pack wealth upon which our twentieth-century fortune was built . . . but that might be stretching it a bit.

By the end of autumn my mother had gone into her confinement, and in December I was born. I know the story as Brianna tells it, and the images are so locked in my mind it is almost as though I can see it with my memory: a newborn cub, watching his own Presentation Day.

They all assembled in the small meeting hall, the forty or fifty pack members who had taken up residence for the winter, and Brianna was brought from the nursery by Aunt Euphonia to wait at the front of the throng and be the first to meet her new brother. She tells of how the air smelled of flowers in the middle of winter with a blizzard howling outside, and how toasty-warm it was in the hall and how beautiful, softly lit by the glow of hundreds of ceremonial candles that flickered gently in the breeze that was created by moving bodies and whispered voices and the gentle waft of the newly discovered forced-air furnace.

There was tension in the room, though, too, restless whispers and uneasy murmurings as everyone awaited news from the birthing chamber. Two years earlier the pack leaders had lost a son only hours after birth, and though Brianna's birth had done a great deal to dispel concern about the ability of the pack leaders to produce a living offspring, the pack awaited with some anxiety the birth of a male. Would he be healthy or no? Was the Scourge that had killed the first infant a curse of the Devoncroix males?

The sudden suspended stillness was like a collective held breath as the sound of footsteps rang in the corridor, and the scent of the pack leader electrified the air. All heads twisted to look as Alexander Devoncroix strode into the hall from a side room, in waistcoat and shirtsleeves, with his hair loose and tangled around his shoulders, smelling of sweat and birth blood and the labor of his mate.

There was not a rustle or a sigh or the blinking of an eye as he mounted the short steps to a stone platform at the front of the room and stood before them.

Alexander Devoncroix parted the folds of the blanket he carried and lifted from its depths a small, sleeping cub. His face transformed from exhaustion to purest joy, his scent became infused with triumph, and he held the tiny creature up, with its damp curled fur and its blind eyes and its now mewling mouth, for all the pack to see.

"A son has been born to the queen!" he cried, and a great cheer went up throughout the hall. "A strong and healthy son!"

The roar of the crowd was so great that Brianna, barely more than an infant herself, covered her ears and began to shriek with protest. Laughing with joy and the irrepressible nature that was, in his youth, his trademark, Alexander scooped Brianna from her aunt and into his embrace. "Behold your brother, little one," he declared. "His name is Matise."

Brianna stopped crying and sniffed the stranger experimentally. The scrape of his soft, pearly claws on her naked skin made her giggle, and she touched his fur, which was already beginning to dry into wispy brown curls, and counted his paws, and touched his small cold nose. For a moment she didn't seem to know what to make of any of it.

It was then, I am told, I began to lick her face, and she laughed out loud with delight. Hers was the first laughter I ever heard, hers was the first touch I knew after my parents', and hers was the scent I took back with me to my nursing bed. We were destined to be, from the moment of my birth, the very best of friends.

A portrait was painted of that occasion, so rich in symbolism and historical significance, when Alexander Devoncroix stood before the pack in the ancient ceremonial hall, holding his firstborn children close to his heart, the one in wolf form and the other in human. It was, I'm sure, a fine work of art. But it was destroyed long ago.

IV

IT'S QUITE UNUSUAL AMONG OUR KIND FOR CHILDREN TO BE BORN SO close together. Brianna and I were practically twins, and for another four years we were our parents' only offspring, the darlings of the pack. I was a strong cub and thrived in the harsh Alaskan winter. By spring I was weaned, and had assumed my human form, which is the way it is with our young.

We were beautiful children, Brianna with her unruly mop of red curls and porcelain-white skin, and I with my golden complexion and wavy chestnut hair streaked with blond, both of us with big blue Devoncroix eyes. We had the looks and we had the charm and we would have been stupid children indeed not to take advantage of both. We worked at it from morning to night and still could not get into all the mischief we devised for ourselves, although I must say we gave it a fair go. One might say we terrorized the household, except that a healthy cub is expected to do precisely that, and although we met our share of cuffings and scoldings, I think we were greatly indulged—and not because we were the youngest children present or because we were the offspring of the pack leaders (which should, in fact, have caused us to be held to a higher standard than most), but because we were adorable. I say that without conceit. We were.

As the winter winds gave way to sunny days and warmer temperatures, we toughened our human skin by digging caves in the remaining banks of snow and splashing through barely thawed streams. We honed our reflexes by chasing—but never catching—spring hares. We ran naked over stubbly winter fields and used our newly developed toes and fingers to climb trees like little monkeys. We tested our new teeth on each other and rolled and tumbled together down ice-slick hillsides. We explored the narrow tunnels and hidden passages of the castle side by side, and together we grew in wonder.

Together we learned to dine at the table with implements instead of our fingers, to dress ourselves in clothes with many fastenings and to wear shoes with leather soles, all of which was very trying to impatient children who were accustomed to playing naked in the snow, sleeping where we fell and eating our fill of whatever we pleased whenever we could find it. But such, we were told over and over again, were the necessities of a civilized people, and it seemed to be very, very important to be civilized.

"Why must we be civilized?" I would demand when I was feeling particularly fractious, and in the care of an elder I knew could be counted on for a certain amount of indulgence.

"To give the humans something to aspire to," was the reply from a patient nanny.

"What are humans?" Brianna asked before I could.

The nanny returned in exasperation, "They are perfectly worthless creatures whose only great talent is to eat noisy children who bedevil their elders!"

We could tell by the twinkle in her eyes that humans did not really eat children—at least we didn't think they did—but now we were curious. We asked perhaps a dozen people that day, and got a dozen different replies.

"What nonsense. Haven't you anything better to do than concern yourself with humans? Why aren't you at your music lesson?"

"Humans . . . ah, yes, I remember them. I had one for dinner once. He was tough."

We didn't understand the uproarious laughter that went around the group.

"Humans," said another, "are nature's way of making us grateful we are what we are."

And the most outrageous answer of all came from our mother, who looked at us for a long and solemn time before drawing us both onto her lap. "Humans," she said, "are really very much like us. They look like we do, they speak like we do, they move like we do and in some ways—not very many, I'm afraid—they even think like we do. But they haven't our minds, my dears, or our skills. They can barely hear a whisper across the room, and they have no sense of smell at all. Saddest of all, they can never change shape.

They have to keep this body—the one you have now but will soon outgrow—forever."

Brianna said, with big eyes, "They don't have tails?" We had both spent an hour that afternoon chasing our cousin's tail, admiring its fullness and its flexibility and its taste, and discussing how soon it might be before we could have something so fine.

Maman smiled tenderly at her and smoothed her hair. "I'm afraid not. They can't run the wilderness or chase down the deer or climb a mountain face in the snow. They would freeze without their clothes."

This made a very big impression on us, because we despised wearing clothes.

"They are really quite pathetic creatures," our mother said, "which is why we must help them when we can, and never, ever harm them. Do you understand?"

We both nodded, and she kissed us with sweet milk-smelling kisses and sent us off to bed. That night as we lay upon our pallets in the nursery, watching the shadows that played off the grate of the dancing fire, Brianna whispered to me, "I don't think there *are* such things as humans after all, do you?"

I was silent for a time, thinking it over. I always tried to think things over, even at that age. "I don't know," I replied at last. "But if there are, I surely wouldn't want to be one."

She nodded vigorously. As with most things, we were in perfect agreement on that.

V

LIKE MOST CHILDREN, I WAS UNCONCERNED WITH THE WORLD AND everything in it except as it applied to me, so I admit I may have a somewhat skewed remembrance of how it was with us in those first idyllic days of Alaska. Still, I think it's important to try to share with you what I do recall, because there will never be a time like that again. That much I do know.

In those days the pack, such as it was, was scattered all over Europe and the Americas. Our little group in Alaska was comprised mostly of close relatives and retainers, those adventurous and enterprising souls who followed the gold trail, and the security guards and household staff who came over from the Palais in Lyons.

For some six hundred years the pack headquarters had been my mother's ancestral home in Lyons, an elegant, sprawling château on the Rhone surrounded by several thousand acres of park and wooded running grounds, heated pools, sunning rocks and elaborate gardens. The Palais held all our treasures, our art galleries, our relics, the symbols of our antiquity, and it was a marvelous place for gatherings, celebrations and court occasions. But nothing really *happened* there. This was because, until Alexander Devoncroix married Elise Devoncroix, pack leadership was largely a symbolic role. In truth, there wasn't much of a pack to lead.

Before the turn of the century the pack was divided into small family, clan or community groups, each with its own agenda, its own interests, its own business or trade. It was my parents' dream to unite the pack into a single, powerful unit that spanned the globe, that in fact *controlled* the globe, using what they very wisely foresaw would be the weapon of choice for the twentieth century: money. It was really absurdly simple. Humans are so greedy, so shortsighted. And when one has the advantage of ears that can hear secrets whispered across a city block, a nose that can smell fear, lies and desire with far less energy than it takes a human to conceal the same, not to mention the effortless skill that is necessary to master technology and the sciences—well, you can see how easy it was for us to dominate the world of international business, industry and finance. Oh, it didn't happen overnight. But it was destined to happen.

I say all this to set the stage for how it was for Brianna and me as we grew. Our parents were not only the strongest, wealthiest, most powerful werewolves in the pack, they were well on their way to becoming the most influential creatures on the planet. They amassed fortunes between lunch and dinner. They manipulated destinies in their spare time. They created nations out of pocket change and in between appointments they somehow found time to raise a family. And they did these things with flair and style, an effortless panache that even now, after all that has happened and all that I know, makes me look back upon those days and everything they accomplished with absolute awe.

By our fourth winter in Alaska there were perhaps twenty children living there. The responsibility for raising children belongs to the entire pack, and this is true whether you are the child of a Devoncroix or of a cook's assistant; we are very democratic that way. During the day we had our lessons together, which consisted in great part of hours of instruction in all things civilized—how to read words written on a page and speak with the proper vowels in various languages; how to style our hair and plan a proper dinner; and how to address, with honor and respect, those both above and beneath us in status. We learned how to do amazing things with numbers and abstract concepts, and how to gauge the weight of a jewel by the feel and its quality by the sparkle; we learned the language of music and the form and substance of art. Yet, as always, the most interesting lessons were not in the classroom, but on the playground.

It has forever struck me as worth noting that children must be taught to be civilized, but to be savage they need only to follow their instincts.

Between our classroom lessons we had supervised play—which, of course, was not really play at all but merely another way of learning. There were games like Steal the Dog, a very odd-sounding sport in which the object was to snatch a knotted rag from the opposing team without being caught. There were games of coordination and balance, like skipping stones, of speed and strength, like baton racing; and of skill and stealth, like Master of the Hunt. And, of course, Seek and Find, which developed our sense of smell; and Kill the Whisperer, which honed our ears. A favorite was Night Hunter, which was played under the light of the moon and tested the development of all our senses.

Brianna and I did well in most games and exceptionally in some.

The only critical report either of us ever received from a supervisor was that Brianna refused to participate unless she was on my team, and on the one occasion when we were forced to play on opposite teams, she shouted the warning that helped my team win the game. She earned the wrath of her teammates and a broken tooth for that trick, despite my best efforts to defend her, and—as was usually the case—we ended up fighting on the same side that day after all.

I remember that Papa just shook his head indulgently when he got the report, and he sat Brianna on his knee and talked to her at length about the importance of teamwork.

She returned indignantly, "But he is my brother!"

Papa kissed the top of her head and I could tell he was trying not to laugh. Later, I heard him telling the story to my mother and they both laughed, in the pleased proud way of parents, and Brianna and I got extra pudding that night for supper. The broken tooth was soon replaced by a whole healthy one, and I don't think either of us learned very much about teamwork that day after all.

As we grew older we discovered another game that caused both of us a great deal more trouble than we could ever have imagined. But it's selfish of me to say "both of us." The trouble was all Brianna's; all I did was pick up the pieces.

We are, of course, all born in wolf form, but gradually begin to assume the hominid form over the next few fragile months. By the time we are weaned, the human form is more or less stabilized, and that is the form in which we remain for the first two to five years of our lives—an interesting choice Nature has made, I've always thought. Sometime around the age of three, a growth hormone is released that enables the children to resume their natural, or wolf, form, and the next few months are spent in exuberant practice of the newfound ability to change forms and in diligent instruction on how, and when, to control it.

In a group of children of mixed ages there are always a few who are recklessly experimenting with their new maturity, a few who look down their noses at their younger companions' shameless exuberance, having mastered their own Changes weeks or even months ago, and a few who are jealously waiting for their own fur and tails.

Meanwhile, the games go on—games in which those children confined to hominid form are the prey, while their faster, more powerful wolf-form brethren—the "pack"—chase them and tumble them and bite them with their teeth. This may sound cruel and even dangerous, but it is a marvelous lesson in life and the balance of nature: with four legs you can run very fast, but with two hands you can climb trees. Besides, we all knew—all of us huddled up there in the trees, tossing stones down on those who howled and scrabbled below—that sooner or later *we* would be skimming across the ground with the wind in our fur while someone else scrambled up the trees.

Brianna was not very good at this game. She wasn't very fast or very nimble, and not much stronger than a cub half her age. She was therefore a natural target. We each took our share of blows, nips and tumbles but had the usual tough skin that did not bleed easily, and any wounds entailed were to the ego. I did my best to protect her, pushing myself in front of her whenever I could, taking the body slam that was meant for her, giving her a chance to escape while I dangled from the lower branches, my toes and ankles easy prey for snapping teeth. *That* was what I thought of as teamwork, and with a little practice, running away was something we became very good at.

It happened on this day that four of us, the "prey," were being chased by a pack of six or eight. It was summertime and we were in the high meadow, with our supervisor watching sleepy-eyed from a sun-warmed rock on the hillside. Brianna made it to the branches of a low tree and I earned points for cleverness by burrowing into a thicket and hiding there, for these young werewolves were too stupid with their own enjoyment of themselves to remember they could scent prey as well as chase it. Two younger children, who hadn't had our experience in hiding and climbing, were perfect distractions as they squealed and ran hither and yon, and Brianna and I settled in for an enjoyable view of the spectacle.

All would have been well except that, just as the pack was racing past her tree, the branch upon which Brianna was stretched out broke and she fell hard into their midst. I could hear the breath leave her lungs in an explosive whoosh and she lay as helpless as a turtle on its back, gasping for breath that would not come, while a fury of scrambling paws and flying tails descended upon her.

I could smell the sudden hot terror that flooded her skin and I plunged from my hiding place with my heart pumping adrenaline and every fine hair on my body standing on end in fear and fury. "Bri!"

I raced to her as the pack leapt upon her, tearing at her clothes, nipping her skin, flinging her this way and that. She cried out then, "Matise, don't—" but the words were cut off on a choking sound as someone slammed a heavy paw against her throat.

This is what I remember about what happened next. I was rushing for her with every cell in my body ready to fight, pulse roaring, teeth bared, fists balled; furious and anxious and hollow with fear. I could hear Brianna's choked cries and see her ineffectual flailing against the wolf bodies that pummelled her, I could smell the sharp excitement of the hunt and the greedy hunger of triumph and I was hot with anger and determination—no, I was *on fire* with it, I was roaring with it, I was fierce with it. I gave a mighty cry and I leapt toward the fray and I came down in the midst of it, tearing out mouthfuls of fur with my teeth, slashing with my claws, barely aware that I had Changed.

I grabbed by the scruff of the neck the wolf who had pinned Brianna down and I flung him aside, then whirled with teeth bared and every hair bristled to take on all comers. I did not see Brianna stumble to her feet and run to safety, for I was a beast of the jungle now, savage and fierce and enjoying every moment of it.

My first fight was a good one, for I made up in sheer passion what I lacked in experience. I took down a male a year older and twenty pounds heavier than I was, and drove off a female with a nasty bite, and I hardly even noticed when someone tore a chunk out of my ear. Oh, it was glorious, rolling and snapping and dashing and retreating, the sting of pain, the smell of exertion, the roar of victory in my blood. And when at last even the older males backed off and looked at me with narrow-eyed respect, I was a little sorry the battle was over.

With a great display of indifference, the attackers wandered off, and I shook myself in self-congratulatory delight and embraced my human form once again. I looked around for Brianna, bleeding and grinning and ready to relive the tale of my grand triumph with the person who had made it all possible.

But she wasn't there.

Brianna locked herself in the nursery all day, refusing meals, refusing comfort, refusing to participate in the celebration of my maturity and great heroism. I missed her, of course. But such a day happens only once in a wolfling's life, and I was very much involved in enjoying it to its very last nuance. I strutted around the castle with my chest puffed out to twice its normal size, suffering my hair to be tousled and my ribs to be elbowed and soaking up the praise and the teasing alike.

"What a fighter you are! Just like your papa at this age!"

"Wait until Alexander gets back from Paris to hear of this! Will he burst his buttons with pride!"

"How many of them were there again, young sir? Twelve, fifteen?"

"And it'll be three dozen of the rascals he banished by the time his papa gets back to hear the tale."

"It was a fine, fine lesson you taught the others today, Matise. Anyone can take advantage of the weak, but it takes genuine superiority to defend those who cannot do so for themselves."

It was after supper before the excitement began to die down, and I had a thought to spare for my missing sister. It was not very sporting of her, I decided, not to share in my celebration when she knew nothing was much fun without her. Although, I had to secretly admit, being petted and praised and made the center of attention was a sensation that very little could spoil.

I went to the nursery door, but she had bolted it closed. "Bri? Why are you hiding up here? Why is the door locked?"

"Go away!"

"*Maman* set the table for us in her chamber," I told her eagerly. "It was great fun. Why didn't you come? Everyone asked about you. Cousin Mathilde said it was because you couldn't eat with your broken lip. Does it hurt? Can I see?"

Brianna flung open the door, eyes blazing. "Go away! I hate you!"

I took a step backward, startled by the fire in her eyes and hurt by her words. Why was she angry? Didn't she know I had done it all for her?

I was about to tell her so when her eyes went to my mangled ear and she gasped. "What happened to your ear?"

I grinned. She had only a swollen lip as a souvenir of that day's battle, but my ear looked like a piece of raw meat—a matter of some pride with me. "Leon took a bite out of it. There's a hole right here, do you want to see?"

I made to show her, but she flung herself at me, hugging me so tightly she threatened to choke off my breath. "Oh, you horrible, horrible creature, why didn't you wait for me? Why did you get yourself half eaten?"

I replied, struggling to unwind her arms from around my neck, "I didn't get half eaten, only a little bite. And how could I wait for you when you were running away?"

That seemed to make her angry and she pushed me away. "The Change!" she cried. "How *could* you do it without me? Why didn't you wait for me?"

That surprised me, and I had to think about it. "Well, it's not something one plans, is it? It just . . ." My heart started to swell up with the memory, and then to race with the struggle to put it into words. "It just sort of—*happens*—and, oh, Bri, you can't imagine, you can't *begin* to imagine what it's like when it does!"

Her eyes flashed with tears, and only then did I understand how much I had hurt her. "We always do things together!" she cried. "Now you've ruined it forever!"

"Oh, Bri." My joy turned to chagrin and I grabbed both of her hands in mine. "I didn't mean to, honest. And I'll teach you how to Change. It's easy, the easiest thing in the world. Then we can do everything together from now on, okay?"

I saw hope start to stir in her wet, angry eyes, and she looked at me cautiously. "Promise?"

"Promise," I returned. "We'll be together forever and ever, you and me, and I'll always take care of you. Always."

"I'll always take care of you too," she promised solemnly.

I grinned with the confidence of youth and the joy of a problem easily solved. "But I was a fine wolf, wasn't I?"

"Very fine," she told me, grinning back. "But I'm going to be finer."

VI

AND NOW I MUST TRY TO PUT IT INTO WORDS, THIS THING WE CALL the Passion, this Change, this transmutation from one state of being to another. I, who have spent a lifetime transmuting ideas into marks upon a paper, find myself at an utter loss as I attempt to describe what it is like to be of not one but two natures, neither beast nor man but a blending of both, and as if that were not marvel enough, to be able to call upon the coiled power deep within oneself to Change that form at will. Has ever so remarkable a species ever walked the earth? Has ever so nearly perfect a creation been designed by Nature?

Obviously not.

And yet I say "nearly perfect" because, as with all things in a mostly random universe, there is a certain percentage of expected failure. This is a truth I came to know intimately, as you shall shortly see.

In English we call it the Passion; in French *le Metamorphose;* in German, *Veranderung;* in Russian, *Metamorfoza;* in other languages, other things, and in our own language, the language of the wolf form, we have no designation for it at all, it is so much an essential natural part of our being. *We are; therefore we are* is the closest possible translation. I think, however, that word—*passion*—implying as it does the passage from one thing to another as well as intense emotion and, yes, even the suffering without which no great thing is achieved, is the most nearly descriptive word of what the transformation is to us. It is as natural as a snake shedding its skin, as spectacular as a lightning strike blazing to fire, as powerful as an orbiting moon that changes the pull of the tide. It is what we *are,* and what we are is magnificent.

From my earliest memories I knew of the Change and recognized it with the same easy familiarity that I welcomed the sound of my parents' voices or the warmth of their naked skin or their smell, cold and musky and rich with fur and blood, straight from the hunt. As an infant, I crawled over my wolf-formed relatives and tugged on their fur and felt the warning cuffs of their paws when I tugged too hard; I saw them change in a dazzle of light and the smell of exotic residue, each scent unique to the individual and each equally as enticing. Even as an infant I was delighted by it, it made me laugh out loud with pleasure and eagerness; as I grew older I could feel the pull of it, taste the need for it, and I would stand enchanted in the wake of it, poised to be carried on to my destiny. And it *was* my destiny, as it is the destiny of everyone of our kind, the promise of mastery and maturity that is our birthright.

In the weeks that followed my first Change, I was as absorbed with wonder and as self-indulgent in that wonder as any wolfling has ever been. I practiced my Change in public, to show off to my peers and demonstrate my style and my scent and my growing elan to my elders, who watched with indulgent pride and more than a few tactful suggestions. And I practiced in private, exploring every level of pleasure and power, revelling in it, drinking it in like a forbidden sweet, intoxicating myself with the utter fascination of what I was becoming. And all the while I was cloaked in guilt, because my pleasure and my pride, my wonder and my delight, were necessary secrets that separated me from Brianna.

I recall when Papa returned to hear the story of my maturity, and how pleased he was, and how I was fairly bursting with pride to see the dance of approval in his eyes. Then Brianna told him how she had cut her lip in the fight and almost broken a tooth. Papa took Brianna's face in both his hands and examined it closely, then pronounced with pleasure, "There, now, not a trace of a scar. You're a strong healer, Brianna, and it's a good thing, because we can't have anything spoiling that pretty face of yours."

Not to be outdone, I fingered my ear, which had healed crookedly from the bite, and boasted, "Teacher says scars of battle are nothing to be ashamed of. He says I should be proud to have one already at my age."

Maman returned scornfully, "Scars are a sign of poor nutrition and bad judgement, nothing more. I shall be pleased to tell your teacher so at the first possible opportunity."

"Quite right," agreed Papa seriously, although we both knew he had several scars of his own. "You must always remember two things. First, there is only one battlefield worth risking your hide on—or any other part of your anatomy, for that matter—and that is the field of honor. Second . . ." He grinned suddenly and darted out a hand to tug playfully at my ear. "Mind your ears when you're fighting, son, they're your most vulnerable part. I once tore an ear right from a fellow's head in the heat of battle, and spat it out on the ground. They don't grow back, you know."

This alarmed me quite a bit, and gave me pause for years afterward whenever I had the impulse to start a fight I might not win. I brought a worried hand to my ear, and both my parents laughed.

Brianna, always a master at directing wandering attention back to herself, piped up eagerly. "Matise is going to teach me how to Change."

Another look passed between our parents, and then Papa smiled. "I'm not sure it's something that can be taught, dear heart.

But you mustn't be jealous of your brother. Everyone develops at a different rate. Your time will come."

"Then I will be sure to mind my ears," she assured him somberly, and he laughed again, and kissed us both, and sent us off to bed.

They went walking in the woods that night, as they often did. Sometimes they went to run as wolves, to chase the moon and hunt the wild and bloody things, and they would come back smelling of musk and sweat and fur and cold and wild unvarnished power, a thrilling mixture that wafted through corridors and seeped into walls and made everyone within feel strong and alive. Sometimes, though, they went just to be alone, away from the children and the aunts and the uncles and the retainers, to talk between themselves of things they wanted to remain between themselves.

At any rate I did not hear how the conversation began, but Brianna's insistent shaking of my arm aroused me from a contented half slumber, and when I scowled at her and slapped her hand away, she raised a finger to her lips and mouthed in the dark, "Listen."

Brianna's ears have always been better than mine, and I was fuzzy with sleep, so it was a moment before I could focus through the layers of household noise to discern the voices.

I heard my Papa say in an odd, strained tone, "Then we must be very careful that her blood is never spilled again."

I frowned in confusion and rubbed my eyes. Brianna whispered in my ear, "They're talking about me."

Mother said, "She is so very precious to me, Alexander. I couldn't bear it if—"

But the wind turned the other way, and we heard no more. Brianna went back to her bed, and we thought in silence about what we'd heard. None of it made much sense to us, and the only conclusion we drew was that Brianna was, for whatever reason, different from the others.

By then, I think everyone already knew that.

VII

I DID MY BEST TO KEEP MY PROMISE TO HER. AT THE VERY FIRST MOMENT we had free to be together we were clattering hand in hand down the stairs, through the dusty corridors, wriggling through the crack in a huge stone door and crawling through a forgotten tunnel to one of our "secret" places in the bowels of the castle. I cannot tell you what the room is used for now, although I do know that it is no longer a secret; that entire section of the building was opened up to renovation sometime in the thirties. Whatever its function today, though, however grand its restructuring or important its use, it cannot serve any more noble purpose than it did in my youth, when it was the refuge of two children in search of magic.

We came into the chamber through a corridor too narrow and too low-ceilinged to allow any but a wolf form or a child to enter, which makes me think now that the place might have had some ceremonial significance in days of old. There was no door as such, but a rounded opening of about three feet in diameter where the tunnel opened into the chamber.

Inside, however, the ceiling was high and domed, as most of the ceilings are, and the sloping walls were lined with benches of the sort that could comfortably accommodate wolf or human form, halfway up. The remaining walls were decorated with the most magnificent marble friezes ever created, and even as a child, I knew enough to be in awe of them. Giant wolves, their eyes and teeth blackened with age, seemed to grow right from the walls, with every detail of fur and form so magnificently sculpted that if one glanced quickly away, the illusion of movement caught by the peripheral vision was real enough to draw a gasp. Wolves in polished marble leapt and twisted in the air in a joyful dance, they devoured monstrous beasts in the forest, they strode in giant leaps over odd, fantasy-looking cities, they played and frolicked in the ruins of fallen columns and twisted rubble.

There must have been hundreds of scenes, for the room was enormous, each of them telling a different story in marble, and between the scenes were stylized depictions of wolf heads, some roaring in fury, some narrow-eyed and watchful, some smirking and amused; and some, the most impressive, were simply bold, proud portrait studies. Have you seen the monuments of Rome? Do you think the sculpture of Greece or the friezes commissioned by the French kings are magnificent? They are but pale imitations of an art form mastered by our race in times we had forgotten long before those transient human civilizations rose and fell.

The place smelled of rich entombment and moldy earth, of forgotten secrets and age beyond imagining. Marble dust. Tiny burrowing creatures. Air gone so stale that it has preserved memory, or a form of it, in every molecule, and the memory is of creatures with fur and power whose blood was once hot and whose teeth were once sharp, and whose breath filled this room and made it alive. This was the smell of the place; it wrapped itself around us and drew us in. We revelled in it even as we were in awe of it.

The floor was of heavily veined rose marble, its color barely distinguishable now except where our feet had scuffed away centuries of dust and neglect. In the center of the floor was an enormous circle formed of earth; perhaps it had once been a planted garden or ceremonial display, or perhaps it had been a playing field of some sort, for we have always been particularly fond of organized games. Maybe it had been a battlefield or a killing ground, or maybe it had been used then for exactly what Brianna and I were using it for now.

The lighting had originally been supplied via a series of mirrors that reflected and multiplied light from a small opening to the outside and directed it here; we could see the glass panels in the ceiling which were meant to refract that light throughout the enclosure. But time had dulled mirrors, earthquakes had damaged the delicate engineering, and now only a few of those panels received light. They reflected it back into the vast chamber in a dim and dusty haze that left long-toothed wolves crouched in the shadows on the walls, and slithery things watching with beady eyes from beneath cracked stones. We feared neither the long-dead creatures whose scent still drifted on tendrils of cold damp air, nor the living ones that might dart at us from high rafters or low corners. We were young, we were werewolves, we were invincible.

We crawled through the opening and stood to our full height, dusting the grit from our knees. We were naked now, as we almost always were at that age when unsupervised; savagery, it seems, takes more than a few lessons in manners before it gives way to the almighty force of civilization. Besides, such business as ours was best accomplished without the encumbrance of clothing.

We looked around for a moment, appreciating the almost reverent pleasure we took in being back in this place, and drew deeply of the cold, old-scented air. It tasted of the Passions of a hundred thousand ancestors, their lingering electricity still ghost-dancing upon the ether of memory, and I knew that if ever the miracle of Change were to come to Brianna, it would be here in this magical-smelling place, with my help.

Only I wasn't quite sure how to begin.

Fingers linked, and without pausing to consult on the matter, we crossed the grimy marble floor and walked straight to the center of the dirt circle. I faced Brianna and tried to look authoritative.

"Well," I began, with an air of great importance. "The first thing you have to learn is how to take care of your clothes." We all learned before our first Change that there was nothing cruder or more vulgar than the sight of a wolfling attempting to transform fully clothed. You might be forgiven an accident once, or even twice, but after the third time you hardly dared to show your face in public again.

Brianna made an impatient face and gestured to our obvious lack of need to concern ourselves with that rule.

"Well, then," I went on, still very full of myself and of the knowledge that I enjoyed being in a unique position to impart. "The next thing you have to be careful of is that there's no furniture in the way and no humans about, and that you are not in an enclosed place that will be hard to get out of without hands, and—"

"I *know* all the rules," Brianna exclaimed in proper exasperation. "What I need to know is *how*. What do I do?"

This, of course, was exactly what I did not know how to answer. I studied on it for a moment, then answered, "You don't *do* anything. It just happens."

I saw the familiar flare of temper in her eyes and knew I was very close to being hit. "You said you would teach me!"

"Well, I will!" My own indignation flashed as I defended against the possibility of being caught, however inadvertently, in a display of incompetence. "Just let me think about it, will you? Nobody's ever put it into words, now, have they?"

She had no argument for that, and was temporarily—and reluctantly—mollified. The adults around us spent a great deal of time talking about how *not* to Change, and when it was inappropriate, and when we should be especially wary of giving in to our instincts—during moments of great trauma or anxiety, in rage or in sorrow, and especially during times of sexual arousal whereupon one might unexpectedly find oneself badly mated. And they talked about the times it was permissible, even desirable, to give over to one's nature—in the presence of a werewolf of superior rank who had already Changed, for example; in moments of great exuberance and joy, as part of the courtship ritual toward one you are considering as a mate, during times of serious illness or injury to promote healing . . . oh, there were a hundred, hundred rules governing the when and the why, but not one word had ever been spoken within my hearing as to the how.

Yet even then I was fascinated by words, with the challenge of taking thoughts out of the unknown and making them concrete through the simple expediency of language. I was determined to make the magic real for Brianna, even if the only alchemy available to me was that of words.

"All right," I declared with firm resolve, and snatched up both her hands. "All right, I can tell you. It's like this."

I placed her hands on her bare belly, my own hands covering

them. She kept her eyes on my face, curious and intense. I drew a long sweet breath and let the magic begin.

"Feel that?" I demanded, my voice husky with excitement and anticipation. "That's where it starts, right there, hot in the belly, not fire yet, but warm and good and excited. Do you feel it?"

My face was hot and my eyes as dark as coals; I could see the light of them reflected in Brianna's. Her hands felt cold beneath mine, which were fevered with power, and she seemed small, weak, confused as she tried to pull away.

She whispered, "No." She tugged harder at her hands. "I don't feel anything."

I clamped down on her fingers, my heart racing, leaping and bounding to keep up with the flood of chemicals that were gushing into my bloodstream. The coil of excitement in my belly unfurled and spread its fiery tendrils throughout my body, strengthening, swelling, maddening me with promise. Yet I held on to Brianna, reckless in my excitement, determined she should not miss this.

"Then it's a fire," I went on, but I wasn't really speaking to her now, or even looking at her, as my vision began to blur and her figure receded to little more than a hazy shape somewhere in the distance. It was coming upon me quickly now, and all I remembered was that I had to keep talking, I had a promise to keep, I could not leave her behind. "It's a fire that gets bigger and bigger until it fills your chest and dries up your throat, and your skin feels like it's frying, it tingles and stretches—can you feel that?"

Distantly I heard her heartbeat, a faint pattering against the thunder of mine, and her quick uneven breath. "No!" she cried, and I could smell her fear. She tried again to pull away from me, but I held her hands tight with all my strength, drunk with the coming Change and the insanity of power it induced, certain that I could make the magic for her because I could do anything; I would not leave her behind.

"No, Bri, feel that!" I cried hoarsely. My voice was already starting to slip away from me, and I jerked her forward with the enormous strength that, in the throes of the Passion, any werewolf might forget to restrain. I pressed her hands to my own belly, hard with tension and transforming muscles, and this time she did not try to pull free.

This is how Brianna told it to me later. I do my best to reproduce her recollection here, for guilt and terror have colored my own memory of the event far beyond any reliability.

My skin was hot, it was on fire, and my fever enveloped her, making her sweat. My scent was hot and sweet and sharp and tangy, mesmerizing her into stillness and wonder. She sank closer, wanting to drink in that scent with her mouth like water and breathe it into her pores like perfume. Electricity coursed from my fingers to hers, stinging like the bite of insects, then catching along her spinal column and making her numb. She went limp. She was in the thrall of my Passion and helpless to fight it, and not even wanting to.

She could feel my heartbeat, not just hear it but *feel* it inside her body, pounding, thundering, smothering the painful lurching stammer of her own heart and leaving her weightless with total surrender, powerless now to control even the coming and going of her own life force. The air was like honey, hard to breathe but wonderful to drown in, melting on the back of the tongue and clogging up the throat. Breathing seemed very unimportant then. The flow of blood through one's veins was a matter of smallest consequence. Life itself became a small and incidental thing in the wake of the pleasure that swelled and swirled around her, the magnificence of what ensnared us both.

Our eyes were locked together, though mine were long past seeing aught but the colors, textures, flavors and shapes that danced and swirled and caught me in their midst. Brianna, helplessly captured by what I could not control, watched with perfect clarity as the familiar face of the brother with whom she had always shared everything grew hard and sharp, eyes like flame, lips white and cheeks purple with fever. Strands of hair seemed to take on a life of their own, now lifting, now swirling, now writhing like snakes, and she watched, helpless and horrified and enchanted and yearning, as I began to dissolve before her eyes.

It was as quick as that. A sound like a shout, an explosion of triumph, a burst of light and color that for one brief blinding moment swept her along with me to the brink of paradise, a taste of pleasure so intense that afterward its absence was like pain, and then—then it was as though the hand that held hers was suddenly and forcefully jerked away, the bond that buoyed her was suddenly severed and she was plummeting, falling fast into terror, and it felt like dying.

That was what she told me later. Had I known . . . had I been less selfish, less reckless, less *young*, and had I known what my own grand rapture was doing to my sister, could I have stopped? Would I have wanted to? The question tormented me for a long time, and when I finally found the answer it was not one I wanted to admit.

I saw Brianna collapse on the ground in her human form, but was far too lost in the exuberance that follows the Change to concern myself with her, or to even feel disappointment that she had not Changed with me after all. I scampered around the dirt circle in a grand chase, kicking up dust, leaping and spinning, and only when the first burst of my abundant energy was expended did I return to Brianna, bowing and grinning and inviting her to play.

It was then that I smelled the wrongness on her.

Her skin was slick with a cold-smelling sweat, bathed in the sour odor of dead, cast-off cells and misfired neurons. She was hunched over on the ground, trying to vomit, gagging and choking, but bringing forth nothing but a thin stream of yellow bile. Her lungs quivered, yet I could hear no breath passing through, and her heartbeat was like the erratic tapping of a small bird's beak. She coughed and gagged and bloody foam dribbled from her lips.

I came close to her, whining and pacing with concern. I nuzzled close, trying to warm her shivers with my body heat, gently licking the taste of sickness and sweat from her cold face. The wrong smell was thick and terrifying and there was a part of me that wanted to back away from it, to *run* from it, even as another part of me wanted to fight it off with bared teeth and lunging, neck-snapping blows before it hurt my sister.

Brianna reached for me feebly, eyes big with fear and pain, but her fingers barely brushed my fur before the convulsions began. I stood paralyzed by terror for an endless moment, watching as the muscular spasms tore her poor body this way and that, arching her back, twisting her neck, causing horrible choking, bubbling sounds to issue from her throat. Then I turned and I ran.

I remember little of that frantic flight back through the tunnels, of finding my parents where they were inspecting a newly renovated theater room off the great hall. It was my first attempt at communicating while in wolf form, and I remember little of that either, except that I must have been successful, because I recall the alarm that transformed my mother's eyes and the acid scent of my father's swift Change, and then we were racing back through the tunnels in a blur of urgency and fear.

At some point, with my directions clear in their heads, my parents outraced me. I entered the room limping and shaking with fear and fatigue, panting hard, terrified to go further and terrified to go back. I was so drained and confused that I Changed back into human form without waiting for permission, but it was all right: my parents had Changed before me.

They made a poignant tableau in the center of the vast room, their human forms strong and naked and still bright with the residue of their transformation. Motes of dust swirled around them and were captured in a shaft of light as it streamed down from its high source, spilling a dim illumination over my mother, her silky light hair cascading about her hips as she sank onto one knee, and over my father, who lifted my sister's limp form into his arms.

I huddled in the shadows while my tears fell fast and hard, shimmering the scene and dulling my hearing with the slow thick rush of my own breath. Dimly I heard my father calling Brianna's name, and then he said, "It's all right, Elise, she's alive, she's all right."

Relief dried my tears and stopped the frantic snuffling of my breath as I heard my mother's little cry of joy and watched her encircle both of them in a grateful embrace. Cautiously I crept closer, until I could hear Brianna's low breathing and the steady beat of her heart, and feel her small body begin to warm with the heat from our parents.

I let the strong scents of a world gradually righting itself seep into me: Brianna's sweet petal scent obliviating the smell of sickness and vomit; the bitterroot scent of Papa's worry, the salt of his skin, the remnants of wolf form and the musty tunnels through which he had followed me to reach this place; the charcoal fragments of his hasty Change to human form mingled with that of my mother, like burned violets. I smelled my mother's anxiety and sweet reassurance, the warm comfort that flowed from her fingertips like milk from a breast as she stroked Brianna's tangled hair.

Brianna looked around until her eyes found me. I tried to smile for her but couldn't quite manage it.

"Did I Change?" she murmured groggily. "Was that it?"

Something sharp and bitter pierced the air between my parents, and both sets of eyes went to me in demand and accusation. I swallowed hard and answered, "No, Bri . . . not exactly."

My mother drew back her arm and slapped me so hard that I lost my balance and tumbled across the floor. But the throbbing of my jaw was nothing compared to the pain of disappointment I saw in Brianna's eyes, and smelled on her skin.

Still, Brianna's thoughts were for me even then and she struggled to free herself from Papa's arms, crying, "*Maman*, don't! It wasn't Matise's fault, it wasn't—"

Mother swung me to my feet by my arm, her eyes blazing and her hair swirling about her, a glory of magnificent rage. "*Never* try to take another into your Change!" she told me furiously, giving my arm a shake. "Do you have any idea how dangerous that was? Only a mated couple is properly attuned to share the Passion. You might have damaged your sister permanently, or even killed her."

"I would never hurt Bri!" I cried, outraged enough to raise my eyes to hers. That was a mistake, and I quickly lowered them again.

"Matise didn't hurt me!" Brianna insisted loyally and, wiggling free of Papa's arms, ran over to me. I noticed she stumbled a little as she ran, and my stomach cramped to see it. "Don't be angry with him, *Maman*, please—it wasn't his fault!"

Papa smiled a little, watching as Brianna insinuated herself between her angry parent and me. "Of that I have little doubt."

Mother gave her a look that was eloquent in its mixture of reprimand and pity, relief and anger. She turned back to me, but her voice was gentler when she spoke next. "I know you wouldn't hurt your sister, *chéri*, not intentionally, but look at Brianna now. Ask her whether she thinks your little experiment was worth it."

Hesitantly I glanced at Brianna, and the blaze of triumph I saw in her eyes startled me. As clearly as if she had spoken it out loud, I saw her answer: *Yes!* Yes, it was worth it! For a glimpse of what I had become, a moment of the rapture she had shared with me, she would endure any hardship, suffer any pain. With that one radiant, secret look she forgave me, blessed me and terrified me.

Mother gave an exasperated shake of her head as she knelt before us, and her long blond hair rippled like a silk veil stirred by a breeze before it settled again over her bare shoulders and breasts. I loved the smell of her and the look of her, the beauty of her movement and the fierce adoration that blazed from her eyes as she opened her arms and took us both into her embrace. She held us tight for one long moment, her hair making soft little crackling noises against my ear and the sound of her pulses flooding my brain, easing my fear, soothing my soul. "I'm sorry, *Maman*," I whispered fervently. "I will never do it again."

I felt Brianna's startled objection, but ignored it. Mother said, kissing my head, "I know you won't, dear." She kissed Brianna, too, and held her close for another moment.

Papa extended his hand to us, and we cautiously left the safety of my mother's arms to approach him. He tried to sound stern, but we could smell the return of the good humor that was almost always present when he dealt with us. "You must use your minds, both of you," he said, "and think before you act, for that is the one thing that separates us from the humans."

"I thought it was the ability to Change that separated us from the humans," Brianna returned, bravely raising her chin to him. "And I guess that means I'll never be better than a human, never."

There was a brief poignant silence, and I knew another one of those looks passed between my parents. My mother took a short sharp breath and her muscles tightened briefly before she forcefully, visibly, relaxed them. She came over to us and, gently but firmly, set her hands upon Brianna's shoulders.

"Brianna, listen to me," she said quietly. "There is something you must hear, and try to understand. You are old enough now—"

"No." My father's voice cut sharply across my mother's, and in a single motion he swung Brianna onto his hip and away from my mother's gaze. It was the first—and only—time I had ever heard him interrupt my mother or contradict her, and I shall forever remember the surprise in her eyes that mirrored my own.

"No," he repeated, firmly but less loudly. He held Brianna's face in his hands and made her look at him. "We will not have you speak of yourself in such a way. You're a strong young werewolf, Brianna, with the eyes and ears to best anyone in the pack, and I've seen you out-track your own brother in the hunt. I'll not tolerate this foolish self-pity, not from anyone in *my* family, do you understand me?"

Brianna nodded uncertainly, but I could see that her attention, like mine, was mostly held by my mother, who stood stiff and silent beside us, her nostrils flared and her lips pressed tightly together. I knew the smell of her anger, and of her disappointment, but what I smelled from her now was neither—and it was both.

Papa turned to me then with a stern look. "Matise, you were fortunate. You came into your maturity early. It is therefore up to you to protect your sister, not to endanger her, is that clear?"

I ducked my head and murmured some sort of apology, but I

could hardly concentrate at all for the tension that emanated from our mother, and could hardly take my eyes off her. Brianna and I were young enough then to still expect our eyes to tell us truths they could not possibly know.

Papa turned again to Brianna, gripping her by the waist and holding her away from his body, dangling her in the air so that her face was even with his. His expression was very stern, and his eyes dark, and he smelled of firm resolve and unquestioned power and, oddly, sorrow. He swallowed before he spoke as though his throat hurt him, and then his voice was a little husky. "You remember this, Brianna Devoncroix, for all the rest of your life. You are a miracle. You are the daughter of one of the most powerful werewolves who ever lived, and you bow your head to no living creature."

I could hear her heart beating, fast and hard, and it barely matched the pace of my own. We both knew something momentous was passing in that instant, and neither of us knew what. It elated us, confused us, frightened us. The air practically crackled with things unspoken, and the weight of an unknown future made my small shoulders ache.

Brianna glanced at me for reassurance, and then said obediently, hoping to please, "Except to you, Papa."

He clasped her to his breast and I heard his swift inhalation of breath. "Except to me," he agreed. His voice was thick with emotion.

Brianna patted his shoulder in a very grown-up way and spoke soothingly. "Now, there, Papa, all is well. You mustn't be worried for me; it's all over now and no harm done. Don't be sad anymore."

Her conciliatory manner, so obviously adopted from our mother, made Papa chuckle, and even drew an indulgent, reluctant smile from *Maman*. Papa set Brianna on her feet with an affectionate pat on the bottom, and for a moment I allowed myself a breath of relief. Perhaps everything was going to be all right after all.

But then I caught a glimpse of the fierce and faraway look in my sister's eyes, and I knew my own troubles had only begun.

VIII

IT WAS LATE THAT NIGHT, WHEN MOST OF THE ADULTS HAD GONE running and those left behind to mind the children were fast asleep, before Brianna and I had a chance to talk privately. A mirror of polished stone set high in the ceiling somehow managed to catch the moonlight from outside and reflect it over our stone sanctuary like milk mist, etching the room in ghostly whites and preternaturally deep shadows.

I pretended to be asleep, but Brianna was not fooled; she pounced upon my bed and said with decision, "We'll try again tomorrow."

My eyes flew open wide; I had not expected her to be this direct or this rash. Anyone might have heard. I sat up straight and as far away from her as possible, and I whispered furiously, "Are you mad? Go back to your bed!"

"When is your free hour? I can meet you at—"

"Brianna, quiet!"

I slapped a hand over her mouth, but she twisted away, eyes snapping. "Don't order me about, you foolish boy!" The scowl of temper left her and was replaced by the curve of an arch smile and a toss of her copper curls. "Didn't you hear Papa? I bow my head to no one."

"Keep your head where it is, but you'll bow your will to me or I'll plant my foot on your backside!"

Bickering was a form of play with us, and I won that round only because she had more important things on her mind. She leaned close to me, serious again, and said urgently, "It almost worked, Matise! Today, I could feel it . . ." She grabbed my hand and pressed it against her belly. "Here! And here." She pressed my hand to her chest, hard against her bony sternum and between two small budding breasts. Her eyes were aglow. "Another moment—I know it would have happened for me, I know it! I didn't try hard enough, that's all—"

I jerked my hand away, chilled with horror and hot with anger. "You could have died! You heard what *Maman* said!"

"I don't care!"

In the eerie white light she looked like something from the netherworld, her eyes burning like coals in a pearlescent face, her hair an aureole of fire; an alabaster sylph of a child with the will of a goddess. Her fingers dug into my arm. "Don't you see, Matise, I felt it! Even if I didn't Change—it was worth it just for the feeling!"

Irritably, I tried to pry her fingers away, but she dug into my flesh more insistently. "Would it stop you?" she demanded. "If *Maman* said you could never Change again, would you obey her?"

I wrenched her fingers from my arm and the muscles throbbed with the pressure she had exerted. I looked at her long and hard. "Brianna," I said at last. "You have to Change on your own. I won't help you again."

"I can't!" she cried, and she burst into sobs. "Don't you see I can't Change on my own? I can't! You have to help me—you promised!"

That was the first promise to her that I broke.

Helplessly I patted her shoulder, I wiped her tears, I mumbled, "Bri, don't be stupid, you'll Change, you heard Papa, it just takes time, that's all. You don't need me, you can do it yourself."

"No," she said. Suddenly quiet, her shoulders slumped with defeat, she moved away from me. Her head was bowed, her face wet, and she did not meet my eyes. "I'm different. There's something—wrong with me. I think I've always known that."

I didn't know what to say. I don't think I really understood the consequences of what she was saying, only that it hurt her to say it, and that she was at that moment the saddest person I had ever known.

"C'mon, Bri." Awkwardly, I put an arm around her shoulders. "Don't talk like that. It's going to be all right, I promise. I said I'd take care of you, didn't I?"

In a moment she nodded, and snuggled into my shoulder, and we lay down together and, in the way of children who so easily cast off burdens, we slept.

But as it turned out, that was the second promise I broke.

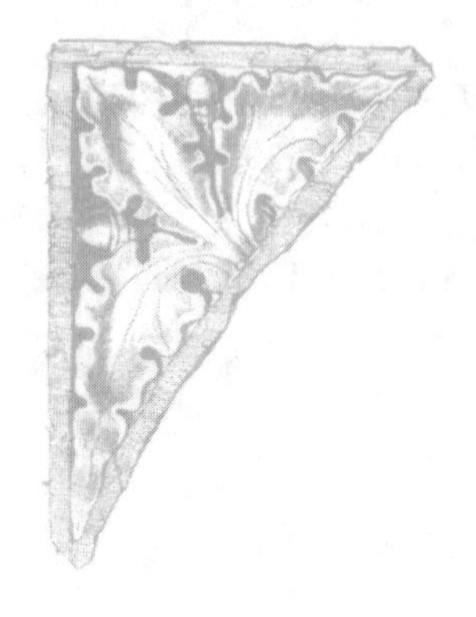

Eight

THE WILDERNESS
07:36
ALASKA STANDARD TIME
NOVEMBER 24

HANNAH STOPPED TO REST HER VOICE, WHICH AT SOME POINTS IN THE narrative had dropped to barely a whisper, so fascinated was she by the content. She stared at the little book. *Being the true writings of Matise Devoncroix . . .* A fiction, of course. Charming and compelling, but a fiction.

"Don't you think so, Tom?" she murmured, hardly aware of having spoken out loud. Then she frowned and shook her head a little, standing. "Like I should take the word of a ghost on the subject of werewolves."

She put the book aside and went into the kitchen, warming herself over the small stove while she heated water for tea. It was odd, though. Those names. Alexander Devoncroix. Elise. Somewhere in the back of her mind a picture was floating, of a tall, regal woman in a Dior gown—yes, definitely Dior—with a coronet of blond braids atop her head and a pearl-and-diamond choker around her neck. Where had she seen her? Television? Newspaper or magazine?

She had to give herself another shake. There was no such person. She was sure of it.

And yet she was equally sure that the name Elise Devoncroix belonged in the caption of a newspaper photo taken at a New York fund-raiser sometime within the past five years.

"Well, hell, why not?" she said aloud. "The woman can turn herself into a wolf and she can't go to a party in a Dior gown?"

But the words didn't sound as funny as she meant them to be, and the chill she felt was not entirely from the temperature of the room.

She cupped her hands around the steaming mug of tea and went over to the wolf, looking down at him with new eyes, and with a trepidation she had not felt before. He was unconscious, partly due to the sedation she had given him and partly due to the deep healing state to which all seriously injured animals instinctively revert. His sides rose and fell rapidly with shallow breaths; his eyes were slightly slitted but still.

He was so big, bigger than any wolf she had ever seen, so big he crowded the cage which had been meant to allow a convalescing animal pacing room. She had studied wolves for fifteen years and this one did not conform in size, appearance or coloring to any breed she had ever seen or heard about. Look how long and finely formed his front paws were. Almost like . . . hands. And the shape of his face . . . was the muzzle shorter than common, the eyes farther apart? The fur, what remained of it, was silky and long, more like that of a pampered, carefully bred domestic dog than a wolf. And she remembered that his eyes were Arctic blue. Weren't the Devoncroix eyes blue?

"Jesus, Hannah, you'll just believe anything, won't you?" She tried to make her voice sound derisive, even amused, but could not quite manage it.

Carefully, very carefully, she knelt beside the cage and opened the door a crack. Her heart was pounding as she reached her hand inside and lifted the wolf's jowl a fraction, checking the gum color for signs of worsening shock. Ah, those teeth. They definitely belonged to a wolf. And she had no doubt that they could tear her hand from her arm should the paralyzing effect of the medication suddenly wear off. His nose leather was hot and dry, as were the tissues of his mouth, but that was to be expected.

She closed the door of the cage and sat back on her heels, cupping the mug again, regarding him thoughtfully for a long time. "Who are you?" she whispered at last. "*What* are you?"

Nicholas was swimming in a sea of nauseating scent: sickness, death, human, burned fur, charred flesh, human, antiseptic, blood, chemicals, human, terror, pain and human, human, human, underscoring all the sensory tracers, stirred into the soup of muddy impressions like spoiled cream: human.

He was deep inside himself, existing barely on instinct, knowing but not caring, aware but not present. He felt neither shock nor confusion, curiosity nor fear, pain nor anxiety. His body was raging with fever as white corpuscles mounted a furious attack against invading infection, adrenal glands flooded his bloodstream with healing hormones, liver and kidneys neutralized toxins with super-enhanced efficiency. His body did not know it had been assaulted to the point of death; it knew only that healing was required of it. The astonishingly efficient physiology that was werewolf did not retreat in the face of crisis, it merely performed more efficiently. Bones knitted because they were broken, cells speeded up reproduction because they were needed, scar tissue formed because the integrity of the skin was damaged and fur began to grow because it was needed to protect the skin. Damaged lung tissue repaired itself because oxygen was needed to fuel the bloodstream, and the heart pumped more strongly because the healing hormones carried in the blood were needed in great quantities very quickly, and enormous amounts of energy were expended; so much, in fact, that soon, if calories were not replaced to fuel the stores, his body would actually begin to consume itself in order to continue to meet the crisis of demands that were made upon it. But not yet. Now it simply healed, and Nicholas, from within his deep and faraway place, allowed it to do so.

Aware but uncaring, he allowed his senses to form a memory map of past and present. Charred fur, pierced flesh, exploding fuel, torn metal, death. The helicopter crash. Antiseptic, chemicals. He had been transported to a clinic of some kind. Human. Human. *Human*.

The sound of a human voice, yes. A human voice reading words she had no right to see, learning secrets she should not know. The secrets of Matise, his brother. And Brianna. *Brianna . . .*

A bloody massacre, and four werewolves dead, all because of Brianna. His parents dead, because of Brianna. No. Not because of her. Because of him. Because he had done . . . something. Something horrible. Something that would change the world.

Something necessary.

His mother's voice, pale face, large eyes: "What will happen if you do this thing?"

And his reply, quiet and still: "What will happen if I do not?"

He allowed his eyes to focus. It took a very long time, but time meant nothing to him. For several hundred heartbeats he could see nothing but large vertical no-colored stripes in front of his eyes, a blur of nothing surrounding. Bars. Gradually he understood they were the bars of a cage.

He tried to move his arm, and then his head. He had no sensation in any part of his body, no movement at all. This did not concern him. He could smell the chemical in his bloodstream, he knew it was responsible for his paralysis. *Human*. A human voice, spinning a narrative that belonged to him. How had she come by these words? How could she know his secrets?

The book. *You promised you would read the book . . .*

Hours passed. Or minutes. Slowly, and in small increments, he focused his senses. His ears. His sense of smell. His eyes.

He saw her, a tall woman sitting in a leather chair across the room. Unruly black hair was tangled around her shoulders. She sat wrapped in a quilt of contrasting colors with one foot tucked beneath her. The other foot was clad in an acrylic pile-lined boot. There was a mug of tea on a table beside her, and beside that was his attaché case, open. He made his eyes sharpen, and a stab of pain went through his head with the effort. He saw it.

She had the red book in her hand, and she was reading it. Her voice wandered in and out of his consciousness, weaving a tale, compelling him to listen. Many pages had already been turned. Too many.

And even from inside that safe, deep place, Nicholas recognized that something fundamental and terrible had occurred.

The human was reading the book. And she would have to die.

From the Writings of Matise Devoncroix

IX

It happened long ago in the land of bright sun, when werewolves lived openly and humans hid their faces from us, that a prosperous builder of roads and towers sought to impress a female he wished to mate. He showed her his house with its many rooms, but she had seen houses as grand. He showed her his baths with tumbling waters, but she came from a land with many hot springs. He showed her his great walled gardens, but she was annoyed by the bees. There remained nothing with which to impress her except for his large pot of gold, which he kept buried in a secret place and would show no werewolf, not even the one with whom he wished to mate.

The female was bored, and the builder was at a loss as to how to please her.

"I know," he declared suddenly. "You will enjoy my dancing human!"

The female was intrigued, for she had never seen a dancing human.

Unfortunately, neither had the builder.

But he went quickly and found one of his humans, who was cleaning out the cooking pit and stealing away bits of charcoaled meat he found there, and the builder said, "Human, quick, come with me. Do this dance as I tell you, and I will give you this basket of eggs, fresh from the nest."

The human preferred fresh eggs to charcoal scraps, so he went with his master and he studied the movements of the simple dance the master performed and then he repeated them, albeit clumsily, for the female.

The builder gave him the eggs as he had promised, and the human ate them all then and there.

The female was delighted. "But oh, how grand it would be," she said later, "to hear a human sing!"

So the builder went and found his human, fast asleep in his nest of straw, and he said, "Human, quick, come with me. Make these sounds as I tell you and I will give you a leg of mutton, fresh from the kill!"

The human liked fresh mutton even more than he liked fresh eggs, and so he followed his master and made the warbling sounds as he was told while the builder played the flute. The female clapped her hands and laughed aloud with pleasure, and the human gorged himself on mutton leg.

"What a clever, clever human you have!" exclaimed the female to the builder when they were alone. "But wouldn't it be amusing if you could teach your human to speak?"

Now this was more of a challenge, and the builder knew it would take many days to train the human to form vowels and consonants, and put the sounds together into coherent words. "But," he cajoled the human, "if you will work hard and learn this task, I will dress you in fine silks from the East and bathe you with perfumes, and sit you down at my own table and serve you meat and wine."

This appealed to the human very much and he worked diligently night and day with scholars and teachers who came from throughout the land, and he learned to form vowels and consonants and put them into words, and words into sentences, and sentences into thought. Finally the night came when he was bathed with perfumes and dressed in silks and brought to his master's table, and the female found him very comely indeed.

"Tell me, human," she said, greatly amused, "what is it that you know?"

The human replied, "I know that my master has buried a large pot of gold underneath the fifth paving stone in the sunrise garden."

Whereupon the female rose up and overpowered her host, and stole the pot of gold from the place where it was buried, and she and the human ran off together and lived forevermore.

And this, so they say, is how humans learned to talk.

Which werewolf in long-ago Sumeria actually decided that these creatures, heretofore regarded only as beasts of burden, might be educable, is anyone's guess. However, it is worth noting that our legends from this time deal mostly with the iniquities of humans, not the accomplishments, and that we like to portray ourselves during this era as the vigilant defenders of civilization against human barbarism. It is therefore possible that the story of the education of humans has been lost through simple embarrassment.

At any rate, humans did take to the complexities of mathematics and written language, albeit slowly, and gained from us over the next few centuries a certain grudging respect. We could communicate with them. We could teach them. We could share our grandeur with them. We could, in some small measure, ease our loneliness. And what unimaginable pleasure we must have taken from bringing these poor savage creatures out of the filth and hopelessness of their own ignorance into the glory of our creation.

We tried living apart from humans in those early days of our history, for our memories are long and our natures unforgiving. Was it curiosity that at last brought us creeping back into human camps?

Or was it compassion, loneliness or perhaps simple arrogance? We could not live alone; that much I know. We have never been able to do so.

Less than ten thousand years ago we were building walled cities to keep the humans out, yet even our own history barely makes note of the fact that the great gardens of Babylon, the temples of Assyria, and even the magnificent city of Ur were all built upon the blood and sweat of humans. How ironic it is to think that some of the finest accomplishments of the ancient age might not have existed without the labor of the human slaves we held in such contempt. And it is more ironic still to note that the humans themselves, in recording their own history, scarcely recall their enslavement while taking such very great pride in their achievements. Well, allow them their deceptions and their conceits. It is little enough in repayment, I suppose, for the captivity of a race.

Imagine how it must have been, then, when we came upon the struggling encampment on the banks of the Nile River—a band of half-wild humans living in mud huts and worshipping the rise and fall of the river tide, haphazardly feeding their families on the grain of their patchwork fields. What an opportunity this was to indulge our scientific bent, to satisfy our curiosity, to expound our theories. We took it upon ourselves, for our own amusement, to change the world. And we did.

We took this tattered beginning of what might one day have been a moderately respectable human settlement and transformed it almost overnight into one of the greatest civilizations the world has ever known. The great pyramids are but the merest sample of our architectural expertise. The paintings, the sculptures, the exquisite craftsmanship in ivory and gold—all are evidence of an era of accomplishment theretofore unparalleled in our history.

We laugh at human scholars who to this day puzzle over the sudden, inexplicable flowering of civilization in so unlikely a way, who search for mystical explanations for the appearance of the pyramids, which seemed to spring full-grown from the mind of the builder with no historical precedent, and who to this day cannot duplicate the methods we used to hollow out rock crystal into the delicate jars and vases that have survived five centuries. Mysterious Egypt? It is a joke among us, for all the questing human has to do to solve the mystery is to look to the jackal-headed god carved upon the columns, the temple walls, the stone tablets that remain from that ancient place . . . but humans couldn't even get that right, could they? Wolves are not indigenous to Egypt, so modern scholars, unearthing the ruins, assumed the creature with the body of a human and the head of a canid to be a jackal-god. It is clear to anyone with an eye for the truth, however, that these carvings are merely stylistic representations of the builders: the creatures of two forms, the gods that were later known as werewolves.

Egypt was our first and grandest experiment, and it succeeded gloriously.

But here is a nuance of the truth so often overlooked by our own scholars that I think we are not much better than humans when it comes to the selective retelling of history. *Egypt succeeded only because humans made it possible.* We built a civilization because, for the first time, we were able to capture and keep vast numbers of human laborers to support it. We came into the fertile valley of the Nile, but we didn't know what to do with it. We were hunters, masters, creators and inventors; we had no interest in nor talent for agriculture. Yet these pathetic ragged humans lived their lives around the flooding and receding waters, the planting and harvesting of fields. *They* had the knowledge, the skill and the experience to feed the millions of humans we would eventually bring into that valley: the quarrymen, the builders, the toolsmiths, the personal servants and yes, even more farmers. We were the builders of Egypt, but humans were the reason.

Most of our scholars view Egypt as the first example of werewolf intellect conquering human bestiality to form an enduring civilization. I think it might be more accurately said that Egypt was the first example of human and werewolf working together to rise above the expectations of either. It has always been a truism that humans need us to advance. But in Egypt, we perhaps discovered for the first time that we need them as well.

Even then, we needed them.

X

BRIANNA AND I WERE TEN WHEN WE LEFT ALASKA FOR SWITZERLAND, and we saw our first humans. The reason for this long delay in the expansion of our education was simple: for most of our childhood, the only safe way to make the passage to and from our wilderness compound was in wolf form. There simply were no roads. I could have gone, of course, on one of the numerous forays the youth of our compound made to inspect human settlements, or I could have accompanied my parents on one of the trips they were always taking to Europe or the lower United States. I could have gone, but I couldn't have borne to leave Brianna behind—or rather, I could not face the look in her eyes when I returned. I had betrayed her once already.

Eventually, of course, passes were built to accommodate the great wagonloads of furnishings and equipment that were imported from Europe while we were in the process of modernizing the castle, not to mention the personnel who were required to do that modernizing and who, perforce, wanted to bring their tools and personal belongings with them. At any rate, by the time Brianna and I were ready to complete our schooling, there were roads—more or less—that allowed us to cross the wilderness in style.

After that disastrous day when I tried to take Brianna into my Passion, everything began to change for us, although I didn't really understand how much until far later. We continued to have our indoor lessons with the others, but when it came time for athletics or play, the supervisors always found something more pressing for Brianna to do, or she was required to stay inside to perfect her penmanship, or Cook had arranged special lessons for her, or she was awarded the soprano part in a difficult operetta which required long hours of concentrated rehearsal. As a consequence she was separated from her peers, both physically and by preferential treatment, and as anyone who has ever been a child knows, once you stand outside the pack, the ranks tend to close very quickly. It's difficult, if not impossible, to find your way back in.

Brianna's ebullient spirits were not outwardly affected by this. She was developing an extraordinary voice and a magnetic stage presence, two qualities which are highly admired by even the crudest of our kind, and she flaunted both to the maximum degree. Further, she was exceptionally bright, and the extra attention given her by her teachers made her a natural target of resentment by her classmates. She loved to show off her expertise at games of skill involving auditory and scent discrimination, and her eyesight was the best in the pack. Even Papa would sometimes take her with him to survey outlying lands or track the movement of a herd, for she could see details in a valley from the top of a mountain, and tracks in the snow even in bright daylight. But another summer passed, and another, and Brianna did not Change.

She never gave a hint that she minded, of course, nor that she considered herself to be anything less than perfect. Mother assured Brianna that there was nothing unusual at all in First Change being delayed for so long, and told her stories of legendary werewolves who hadn't Changed until they were twelve or thirteen. I think Brianna knew she was making up those stories, because when the aunts got together to whisper about it, they talked about rare medical conditions and genetic flaws. Brianna pretended not to hear, and tossed her head at the cruel taunts thrown at her by the other children, and never lost an opportunity to push herself to the front of the pack, almost as if in defiance of what she knew she could not do.

Between the ages of four and ten, Brianna grew into a beautiful, accomplished, determined and generally obnoxious young werewolf, and I gained a reputation as one of the best fighters in the pack. I had plenty of practice.

XI

BY AGE TEN, WE WERE ALL EVALUATED ACCORDING TO OUR VARIOUS talents and degrees of educability and sent off to one of several dedicated schools in Switzerland—and by "dedicated," I mean that humans are never allowed within. It has become quite fashionable of late to take advanced degrees from human universities—which is only sensible if one is going to function in the human world—and many of our finest educators amuse themselves by accepting professorships at such institutions. But by the time we have completed the six or eight years of formal instruction at our own schools, we are far better equipped to pursue our chosen vocations than any human university could make us, and degrees from human institutions are mostly redundant.

Papa escorted us personally, as he had business in Europe, and Mother, who was by then expecting our fourth sibling, elected not to travel. Brianna and I were resplendent in our travelling clothes, Brianna in blue velvet with her bright curls caught back at the nape in a stiff satin bow, and I in high leather boots and a natty checked cap. We travelled by closed coach, a magnificent affair with high yellow wheels and the family crest emblazoned in azure and gold upon the door. Needless to say, we made quite a spectacle as we came into Nome, and at any other time we would have basked in the attention. On this most singular of occasions, however, I was trying far too hard to pretend a savoir faire I did not feel—and to disguise my absolute dismay over this, my first glimpse into the grand and glorious world of humans.

There is simply no describing the smell of a human if one has never experienced it for oneself. Stale, overripe, darkly necrotic, faintly putrid, cloyingly sweet—this is but a rough approximation that barely approaches the reality of it. We had caught traces of the human scent on others before, of course, so that it was not entirely a shock, but never in such strong quantity. Never so close.

And the city. To this point we had known no life but the high clear air of the mountains, the towering evergreens, the rushing rivers, the deep virgin snow. We knew the smell of fur and woodsmoke, the taste of wind when it rushes across a glacier, the sounds of a hawk calling to its mate and of our own sweet voices raised in song. But in this place of humans there was the smell of churned mud and horse offal, of engine exhaust and rotten vegetables; there were the sounds of strident voices, angry shouts, sharp commands, turning wheels, squeaking boards, screeching saw blades, rumbling mechanics; the low moans of ships' horns from the harbor, the creak of cranes, the clatter of movement from a thousand directions at once—it was all too much, in fact, for a young werewolf's ears to absorb at once.

They urinated in the streets here. They washed themselves once or twice a week and drew their water from the same stream in which they soaped their filthy clothes. It was the most disgusting place I had ever seen, and despite the scented handkerchief I kept pressed to my nostrils, I could hardly stop from being sick.

"Bri, the smell!" I moaned, gesturing for her to close the window.

She glanced at me disinterestedly and immediately returned to her bright-eyed survey of all the passing sights and sounds—and smells—of this exciting new world. "It's not so bad, once you get used to it. Papa, is that our ship? The big white one?"

"It is indeed, *chérie*. She's carrying a cargo of precious metals and rare woods to sell to greedy humans in Europe . . . as well as two very precious children, of course."

Brianna giggled and bounced in her seat, her color high and her eyes alight with anticipation. "Will we meet many humans, Papa? Will they be on our ship?"

"No humans sail on this ship, *chérie*, although there are several in our fleet that are run entirely by humans. They make passable sailors, all in all."

"How much like us they look!" Brianna exclaimed, flitting like a small, grandly plummaged bird from one window to another. "Look at that pretty creature there, in the red coat! And what a handsome man standing in the doorway! That hotel, Papa, is that like the one where we'll stay in London? Will there be many motorcars there?"

Papa laughed out loud at her ebullience, and I sat up straight with the protest "They are nothing like us, Bri! They're filthy and awkward and—short!"

She shrugged away my dismay. "I like them. They're interesting." She turned to Papa with bright dancing eyes. "Might we meet one, Papa? Do you see any you know?"

He tweaked her chin, still chuckling. "I think that might be arranged, precious girl, if you will mind your manners and remember what your mother has taught you."

I said, still smothering my face with my handkerchief, "I think I will forgo the pleasure, if you don't mind, Papa."

Papa looked at me with no trace of humor on his suddenly stern, aristocratic features. "I do very much mind," he said. He leaned across the seat and deliberately removed my hand from my face and placed it in my lap. "You are a Devoncroix, and you will conduct yourself as one, beginning this moment, in this place. There is no excuse for uncivil behavior, Matise, not even to a human."

"Most particularly not to a human," piped up Brianna, blithely quoting one of our teachers' favorite axioms, "because they are our inferiors, and we must set an example for them."

I risked shooting her a fierce scowl, but already her attention was distracted toward the window again as the coach rolled to a stop.

We stepped down onto the soiled and reeking boardwalk in front of a false-fronted hotel that exuded the odors of overcooked meat and raw humans. Brianna and I looked around wide-eyed while Papa made arrangements for our luggage to be transferred to the ship. Well, perhaps Brianna was a bit more wide-eyed than I. I was trying very hard to breathe shallowly and keep my lips from wrinkling into a sneer—an expression of which I was certain Papa would not approve.

A human man opened the door of the hotel to a flood of chattering, scuttling human sounds, and called out cheerfully, "*Alors,*

Monsieur Devoncroix, welcome! I had not expected you again quite so soon. And who are your handsome companions?"

The creature beamed at us, and Papa greeted him with a smile. "Henri, my friend, it is good to see you. May I present my children, Brianna . . ."

Brianna made a curtsy as pretty as a hundred nights of practicing before the mirror could make it, and the human cooed with pleasure.

"And Matise."

The human leaned forward and offered me his pudgy oily hand. Manfully I drew a breath, inhaling the sour-milk odor of human skin, damp wool and dirty hair, a wave of hot breath stained with garlic and rotting teeth—and I vomited all over my new boots.

Brianna snatched back her skirts and Papa gave me a look of mild reproval, but the human only clucked sympathetically. "*Pauvre enfant* hasn't got his travelling stomach yet, has he? Well, we'll put a remedy to that. Come along, *petit monsieur*. Madame will take care of you, eh?"

It could have been much worse, of course. But I couldn't help wondering how jovial the human would have been if it had been *his* new boots I'd ruined.

After that inauspicious beginning, the remainder of the day was little more than a blur to me. I was attended by a plump woman with a fat towel who did a rather poor job of polishing my boots but was just as annoyingly cheerful as her spouse had been. Then I was taken up to join the others in a red velvet salon that smelled, rather more palatably, of wine from my father's private stock and sweet cakes warm from the oven and human females wearing Devoncroix perfume. This was where the humans had gathered to await the departure of their ship, which sailed a few hours after ours did, and although I didn't realize it at the time, only the first-class passengers waited here. It was difficult for me, at that time, to tell the difference between an aristocratic human and a derelict one. Except for the perfume, they all smelled alike to me.

There were perhaps a dozen humans in the room, and as I entered they were all gathered in speechless admiration around the piano, where Brianna was rendering a Brahms concerto with her usual aplomb. Papa stood some distance away with a glass of sherry in his hand and an indulgent smile on his face, watching her. I recall thinking how out of place he looked, the tall, elegant werewolf with his flowing mane of honey-brown hair distinctively arrowed with white on one side, his piercing blue eyes, his impeccably tailored clothing, his long tapered fingers, curled so delicately around the cheap stemmed glass, concealing a strength that could have effortlessly snapped the neck of any human in the room.

I went over to him, and he dropped an affectionate hand upon my shoulder.

"Papa," I said, keeping my voice low so as not to disturb the beauty of Brianna's music. "How terrible it must be for you to have to work with them and eat with them and travel with them and talk to them every time you try to do business. I never realized before."

He gave me an odd look—amusement mixed with disappointment. "It's not so bad as you might imagine, once you get used to it," he answered, mimicking Brianna's words from earlier. He sipped his sherry and nodded encouragement to Brianna, who was approaching a rather intricate arpeggio. He returned his attention to me, and he said seriously, "Matise, you were born into a world that was vastly different from the one I knew, and by the time you are ready to take your place in it, the world will be more different still. There is no room for petty prejudices and blanket judgements in a century that is destined to move as quickly as this one does, and we can no longer keep ourselves separate from humans if we are to thrive in the future that awaits us. Your mother saw this years ago, and that is why she is the greatest queen who ever lived."

He paused, acknowledging my somber nod of agreement, and took another sip of his sherry. He said, "You have a long ocean voyage ahead of you. It may well be the last one you make. We are working on a device now by which we can fly across the ocean, and

I shouldn't be at all surprised if you return from your schooling by wing rather than by sail."

My eyes went round and he smiled. "You heard correctly. We've had the design for twenty years at least, but until now the pack was so scattered, our efforts so divided, that we had no hope of developing it. It was your mother's vision that brought the pack together, and your mother's vision that made the development of our technology feasible. Can you guess who will be paying for our flying machine, Matise? Can you tell me what the market will be?"

I shook my head mutely, my mind racing excitedly from one possibility to the next over what adventures I would have in such a device.

"Humans," Papa told me. "Humans will pay for it, humans will build it, humans will fly in it. Do you understand what I'm telling you, son?"

I nodded vigorously, though of course at that time I did not. "Papa," I said a little breathlessly, "I would like very much to fly in this machine when it's finished."

Papa smiled and ruffled my hair. "I will see to it that one is delivered to your door."

At that moment Brianna finished her concerto and there was a spontaneous burst of applause, accompanied with exclamations like "Magnificent!" and "Prodigy!" and "What a future the child has!"

I clapped politely, even though I knew it wasn't Brianna's best effort, and Papa raised his glass to her, smiling fondly. "Look at your sister," he said. "Isn't she lovely?"

"She's a little showoff," I muttered, because it was exactly this kind of behavior that so irritated our peers that I generally ended up in a fight afterward. It took me a moment to realize I would not be fighting tonight. The humans adored her.

Brianna ran over to us, her eyes alight and her cheeks flushed, and hugged Papa tight around the waist. "Oh, Papa, I adore this place!" she cried. "Can we stay?"

He laughed and tweaked her curls. "You are vain, *petite*, and I would be a foolish father indeed to indulge you in it. You missed the E flat in the second movement."

She pouted. "No one noticed."

"Except your papa."

Then, to raise her falling spirits, he kissed her soundly and said, "Get yourself a cake, *chérie*, but mind you don't make yourself sick like your brother. I'll return for you upon the hour."

When he was gone, Brianna and I both helped ourselves liberally to cakes, and to Madeira in teacups—for humans have the most astonishing notions about the age at which one should drink wine—and settled together cozily upon a settee in a corner.

"I think they're rather dull," I said, diminishing with my words what I *really* thought of our first encounter with humans.

Brianna responded dreamily. "I think they're magnificent."

I couldn't disguise my first incredulous look, but remembered Papa's speech and tried to be more tolerant. "Well," I conceded, "they do try to be civilized. And they affect a passable imitation. But, Bri—that woman over there, in the yellow satin. All that finery on the outside, but her petticoats are stained with muck from the street and her hair hasn't been washed in a week and her undergarments are stiff with the excretions of her monthly flow and she thinks no one will notice."

"No one will," replied Brianna reasonably. "At least no human will."

"It's disgusting."

"I think it's quite marvelous."

I had to swallow a mouthful of wonderfully sticky goo before I could respond. "Why? How can you think such a thing?"

"Oh, Matise, don't you see?" She turned to me with eyes shining with intensity. "They don't *know*. They think I'm wonderful and they don't *know*."

"Know what?" I asked impatiently, for I really was beginning to tire of hearing about how wonderful Brianna was.

"That I'm different," she responded earnestly. "That I'm not like you or any of the others . . . that I can't Change."

She shifted her gaze from mine briefly, because this was the first time that she had brought the subject up since that night so long ago when I told her I could not keep my promise to her. We were both uncomfortable for a moment.

Then she looked at me with a quick, bright twinkle of the eye. "They think I'm a prodigy! They adore me. They don't care if I can't Change!"

I wanted to tell her how ridiculous it was to be flattered by the adulation of humans, who were so lacking in accomplishment that they would have been impressed by any werewolf, and to scold her for setting her standards so low. If Papa had been there I'm sure he would have done so. But all I could think when I looked into her happy, dancing eyes, was how sad it all was. How terribly, terribly sad.

It would be five long years, you see, before Brianna saw another human. And I didn't want to break her heart by telling her so.

Nine

THE WILDERNESS
09:00
ALASKA STANDARD TIME
NOVEMBER 24

THE SOUND OF THE WIND FLINGING SOMETHING AGAINST THE SIDE OF the building made Hannah start and get to her feet, her heart pounding. The book and the quilt slid to the floor and she stepped quickly over them, going to check the doors and windows for damage. The metal shutters which she had closed on the windward side of the house were secure, and so were the doors. But when she went to close the shutters on the front window she found the mechanism frozen, the shutters inoperative. Outside was a whiteout; visibility zero.

Devoncroix. She knew where she had heard the name before. She turned from the window, experiencing a strange reluctance to prove what she knew was true. Then she went over to the work area, took out the portable computer from its locked drawer and plugged in the power pack. The hard drive whirred; the opening screen came up. Hannah logged on to the database and typed a simple search command. Seconds later she had the answer she sought. Two years ago the Wilderness Project had received a donation of twenty thousand dollars from Atlas Energy and Oil, a division of the Devoncroix Corporation.

Hardly daring to breathe, Hannah typed in another search and waited for the answer. When it came she stared at it for another long unblinking moment: Alexander Devoncroix, President and CEO, the Devoncroix Corporation.

Hannah sat back and released a slow breath. For several minutes she did not move. Then she turned off the computer, replaced it in its drawer and got up.

That information proved nothing, of course. And everything.

The wolf was awake in the cage, lying with its forelimbs stretched out before it and its head held straight, looking at her with eyes as blue as an Alaskan night sky.

The sight made Hannah's throat grow dry.

She approached the cage cautiously. The wolf was panting hard, its shrunken abdomen puffing and collapsing with each rapid breath. Its tongue was pale and dry, its nose leather dull, its fur gummy and lifeless. But those were peripheral things, barely noticed. What Hannah's eyes were fixed upon was the long patch upon his torso from shoulder to flank where once there had been nothing but raw, oozing skin; now the area was covered with downy fur through which the new growth of skin shone pink and healthy. The splints which had bound his forelegs had been removed and placed neatly in a corner of the cage; the broken bones were straight and only a glossy pink indentation of flesh remained at the former puncture wound.

"Christ," she whispered.

No creature could have healed that quickly. None, at least, that was recognized by human science.

She dropped down to her haunches in front of the cage, staring, half expecting a trick of light. But it was no trick. The burns, at least half of which had been third-degree, were completely healed. The bones were straight, even though all logic suggested that in the process of removing the splints and shifting around in the cage, he should have done considerable damage. And how had he been so quiet, after all?

Hannah had been around wolves coming out of anesthesia before, and they had never reacted timidly. Disoriented, sick, caged, they had exercised their instinct to lash out violently the moment they were strong enough to do so, desperately seeking freedom. This one had quietly removed his splints . . . and waited.

The only explanation, of course, was that the creature before her now was not a wolf.

Hannah tried to swallow, but found she lacked the wherewithal to do so. "You're scaring the hell out of me, fellow," she whispered shakily. And then, on a breath so soft that it barely made a sound, "Who are you?"

Blue eyes stared back at her, keenly intelligent, imperially demanding, piercing and hypnotic. Hannah couldn't pull herself away from those eyes, as though if she looked long enough she might find her answers there. And that possibility terrified her.

Nicholas was starving. Fever had burned away every calorie; healing had consumed all stored reserves of fat and protein. Waste had been converted into survival fuel, but even that was now gone. The adrenals could produce no more hormones, the pancreas and liver were shutting down, and if his body did not receive food quickly and in great quantities, it would simply break down its various parts into their simplest components, and he would cease to be.

The brain, that most unique and vital werewolf organ, would be the last to lose function. Even now, though his body was almost too weak for him to continue breathing, his mind had demanded that he rouse himself, that he shake off the effects of the drug, that he remain alert. His brain had known that removing the splints would get the attention of the human, for the human who was responsible for his captivity was also his only chance for survival.

Food. Rich dark broth, bloody meat, glistening fat, protein, food, masses of it, gallons of it, swimming in red pungent juices, food. The thought of it, the need for it, the desperation for it filled every synapse and sinew, ached in each cell and oozed from his skin. *Food, human, bring me food. I must have it now or I will die . . .*

Hannah lurched to her feet with such an effort that she staggered backward, freeing herself from those eyes. She looked around the room sharply, quickly, peering into every corner, behind every shadow, but she was no longer certain what she was looking for. Tom? Oddly, her mind could barely bring forth a picture of him. That should have disturbed her, but it didn't.

And then her eyes fell upon the red book, open on the floor. She started to pick it up, and then she glanced back at the wolf. Still staring. Blue eyes.

Hannah went quickly into the galley, flinging open cupboards one after another. Cans of stew, desiccated vegetables and freeze-dried dinners, powdered eggs, pasta, coffee, sugar, flour, legumes. Then she remembered the still room.

She flung on her parka without zipping it and went through a short breezeway to a freestanding pantry off the galley. The last of the previous season's meat supply was hanging from the rafters: a slab of salted bacon, two smoked turkeys, a haunch of venison. All had been maintained at a constant twenty degrees Fahrenheit since September.

She stood on tiptoe to tug the venison down, pulling at the knot with clumsy, frozen fingers. When the rope gave way the falling meat almost knocked her to the ground. Frozen, it weighed almost thirty pounds. She snatched a slab of bacon in the same manner and carried one under each arm back to the kitchen.

She returned to the galley, jerked open the microwave door and dumped the roast inside. She set the temperature to maximum and pressed the power button. The lights dimmed as the oven hummed into operation and she knew she was straining the generator to its fullest using fuel she could ill afford. Nonetheless, she put the largest pot she could find on the stove and began to fill it with cans of beef and chicken broth, tossing in the bacon to boil.

She thawed the roast just until it was soft enough to carve, then dropped the pieces of diced raw meat into the stewpot with the broth and bacon. The soup mixture had by now cooled to room temperature, and she stirred it all together, and dished it into a bowl.

In front of the cage, she hesitated. The wolf had lowered his head, chin resting between his paws, and looked less alert than before. He was no longer panting, but his breathing was labored, and he was weakening visibly. Still, she would be foolish indeed to open the door of the cage not knowing what state of sedation the animal was in, or how much of his strength he had regained.

But a tranquilized wolf could not eat. And if this one didn't eat soon, he would surely die.

Hannah knelt, slipped the pins out of the cage door and opened it. The wolf did not lift his head, did not move. Hesitantly she reached in and set the bowl on the floor beside the wolf, then quickly closed the door. Only then did the animal turn his head and, in a moment, lap experimentally at the broth.

Hannah barely released a breath until the bowl was empty; then she once again opened the door and reached inside the cage. The wolf simply watched her. She removed the bowl went quickly back to the galley, refilled the bowl and returned.

She repeated this process until most of the contents of the stewpot were depleted and until the wolf, sated, placed his head upon his paws and closed his eyes. Hannah shut the door of the cage one last time and then stood over it, looking down at the wolf thoughtfully for a long time.

"Do you think I don't know?" she said softly at last. "I'm a woman who talks to dead men. Do you think I don't know the truth about you?"

You know nothing, human, Nicholas thought. He was drowsy with gorging, physically content, but his strength was returning. He was alert. *You know nothing of what you keep here in your cage, nor of what your clumsiness might cost us all . . .*

Yet she had tended his wounds. She had fed him. Somehow she

had known what to do and when to do it and that made him uneasy. Was it possible for a human to be that perceptive?

His father had thought so. And so had Brianna, it would seem . . .

You are a foolish, foolish human, Nicholas thought sadly as he watched her go back to her chair. *Soon I will be strong and it will be because of you. You may yet wish you had let me die . . .*

Hannah sat down, tucking her feet beneath her, picked up her quilt and the book, then suddenly turned to look at him, a small puzzled frown on her face. But in another moment she seemed to dismiss whatever had troubled her, and she found her place in the book and began anew to read aloud.

Outside, the howling of the wind sounded like the voices of wolves.

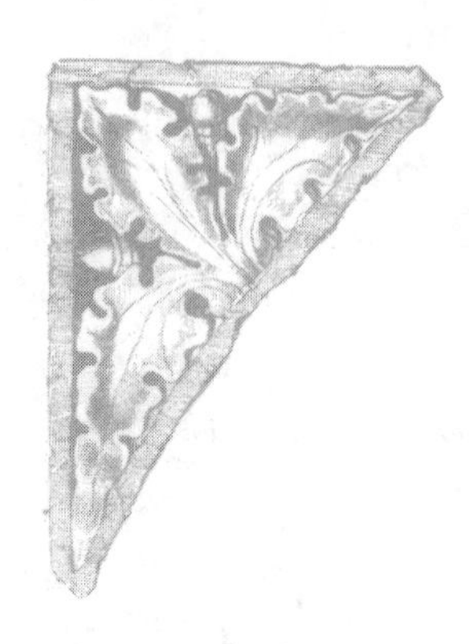

From the Writings of Matise Devoncroix

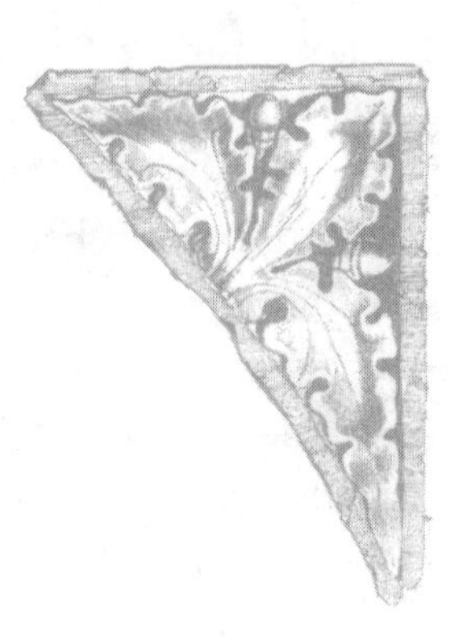

XII

HERE IS THE STORY OF A WEREWOLF WHO WOULD RULE THE WORLD, and the legacy of intolerance and mistrust he never meant to leave, but which refuses to die to this day.

There are those who say that Greece might have developed without us, and for proof point to the Bronze Age cultures of Mycenae and Crete. Are they trying to affect modesty with this claim, I wonder, or assuage their consciences? In any event I make no argument against the finely developed civilization of those early Greeks, which was indeed quite admirable for the human race, nor will I speculate upon how much of it they brought from Egypt, or gained in trade with us. Perhaps Greece would indeed have existed as a mercantile and cultural center without us; but it would never have flowered into a great civilization.

For this I offer the most obvious evidence of all: history itself. Look at what happened to those bright, upwardly striving Mycenaeans after the Trojan War. Look at what happened after the Dorian invasions. For centuries that jewel of the Mediterranean was lost in a Dark Age; humans who once worked bronze and gold and played musical instruments and built frescoed palaces and mighty fortresses now retreated to rude villages and primitive farms, whatever potential they once possessed completely forgotten.

Then, with a suddenness that is inexplicable even to human historians, Greece began to rise again. In the mere blink of a historical eye they went from half-naked sheepherders living like savages to a people who could discourse intelligently on geometry, music, philosophy and atomic theory. It is, of course, a matter of absurdity to think they did it alone.

It began, as far as we can determine, with a werewolf called Usolodes, the Great Manipulator, who brought the concept of coinage to the people of Lydia, and in the process accumulated an obscene amount of wealth—all courtesy of the humans he pretended to help (his legend is often confused with that of Croesus, especially by humans). We were masters of commerce even then, and if anyone is foolish enough to think the idea of making money by trading with humans is a new one, I invite him to read his history.

There were others, of course, whose contribution was invaluable: shipbuilders, traders, winemakers, masters of the deal, as we would call them today, whose names have been lost in antiquity but who, over the course of a century or less, were responsible for establishing Greece as the commercial center of the known world. We did it for ourselves, but in the process humans benefited. They became wealthy enough to own the slaves we discarded, to build the cities we designed, to spend their leisure at our feet, learning from us.

Who were we? The great philosophers, artists, mathematicians whose names you know already. We were the architects, the designers, the musicians and the playwrights. Those are our likenesses you see preserved forever in marble, those are our techniques. You may recall the human myths about Olympus, and the gods who brought them light, fire, dance and poetry, music and art. For once, the humans were right.

We called ourselves Zeus, Athena, Apollo, Aphrodite, Dionysus, Ares and Artemis. We were playful lovers of humans, stern rulers, indulgent dictators. We were the bringers of civilization.

Look closely into human myths from the ancient times. You will find much of our history there.

We set the stage, we created the ambition, we had the vision. And there was none among us more ambitious or more visionary than young Alexander.

Truth be told, I think the old gods had grown tired of Greece by then. So many of them had moved on to the next great adventure: Rome, our first modern nation. Times change, we all grow, much is left behind. Greece, the birthplace of civilization, was the perfect spot from which to launch the grandest, maddest scheme ever yet conceived by man or werewolf.

He was born of a Macedonian leader and the half-wild, half-mad Olympias, young Alexander with his scheme to conquer the world. What grand plans must his mother have put into his head even as an infant, what reckless ambition, what deranged dreams? Or was his development inevitable, a natural consequence of the world we had created, just as smoke is a result of fire? Yet, taken in its whole, his plan was not so flawed, nor his ambition so wrong. Some have said—even humans—that his only mistake was in dying too soon.

Look at the world as he must have seen it, this young genius, this obsessed visionary; try to imagine his point of view. Here was the grandeur of the Greek civilization, designed by werewolves and inherited by humans; humans who had sat at the feet of Pythagoras and Aristotle and Socrates, learning our secrets, mastering our ways, and even—yes, it was true—beginning to compete with us. Perhaps they used the principles of design we taught them only to build temples to honor us, but they *did* use them. Perhaps the methods of trade and commerce we taught them increased our coffers far more than they did theirs, but humans profited. Humans built ships, discovered trade routes, flourished under our benevolent guidance. And did we care? Ah, no. We were gods. We were adored. We were little concerned with the tiny lives of those who served us.

But Alexander saw, and he was concerned.

He saw a human population which could replenish itself far faster than we could, a fierce fighting machinery that had no scruples, an unlimited greed which was boundless in its potential for exploitation. He saw quick retentive minds that were easily trainable and perhaps a little too quick to adapt. He saw great potential in the fast-breeding, hardy-fighting, infinitely educable human species. And he saw great danger.

His design was to conquer the world, to secure the trading posts, to dominate the cities, to control commerce, to enslave humans. And he did it so beautifully, so effortlessly, that the world never knew it had been conquered, the humans never guessed they had been enslaved. He reclaimed civilization for his own kind, he took control of what was ours, and in the end he changed the course of history forever.

Humans continued to grow and to learn, but they grew only as far as he allowed, they learned only what he taught. Commerce thrived, and the lion's share went into his pocket. He established the role of the sacred monarch, and all humans bowed down to him. He was responsible for the dissemination of Hellenism, a civilization with a common language, literature, art and political organization. All the world was one, and all the world turned its face toward him.

He founded seventy cities and completely saturated the barbarian world with all that was best of Greece. He ruled the world, a single world, united for the only time in history. The humans never knew the full extent of his ambition. To this day they call him Alexander the Great.

All in all, it was not a bad scheme. He was the first leader of the Brotherhood of the Dark Moon.

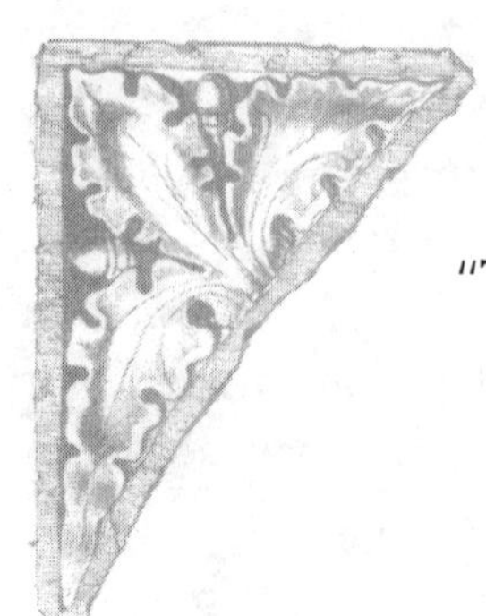

Brianna—
Pages from
a Journal Labeled
"The Switzerland Years"

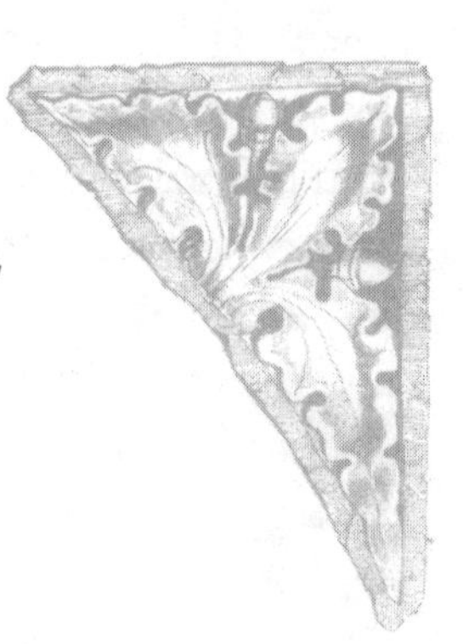

XIII

AH, MATISE, IF YOU KNEW HOW I HATED YOU FOR WHAT YOU'D DONE to me! Hated you with a child's single-minded intensity for what you could not help but should have known; hated you for your beauty, your freedom, your magnificence in the Passion; hated you for the joy that was yours to claim anytime you wanted and the rapture that I had been allowed to taste so briefly . . . and I loved you for all of that and more.

Up until you claimed your First Change I can't remember *not* loving you, and I suppose it is the same for you. We were lucky children, indeed, to be so close in age, and that was a great part of our attachment to one another, I'm sure. But it was more than that. My earliest memory is of you, and the smell of beeswax and birth blood in the great chamber where we all gathered to welcome the firstborn son. How peculiar you seemed to me then in your mewling wolf form, and how delightful. Tiny pearl claws, damp silky fur, barely formed blind eyes . . . I am not sure whether I adored you because of our differences or in spite of them. I knew only that you were mine, and I treasured you.

I had never known betrayal, or imagined what it might feel like, until you entered your First Change without me. That you did so to protect me from pack bullies completely escaped my selfish reasoning, of course, and only later did I understand the pattern that was established that day. But then I made you promise, and I know you felt guilty for a long time because you couldn't keep your promise. But don't you see? I didn't blame you because you couldn't teach me to Change. That wasn't your fault. No, the worst thing you did to me was to let me taste it, to bring me that close that one time to the only thing in the world I wanted and the one thing I knew even then I could never, ever have.

I knew you couldn't teach me to Change. But it would have been better to die never knowing what I had missed than to spend the rest of my life aching for my lost birthright.

By the time we went to L'École, I had built up quite an armor against pain, disappointment and humiliation. There was a part of me that was still convinced my own First Change might descend upon me with the morning sun, and, oh, I cannot count the hours I spent secreted in profound meditation, in earnest, sweat-filled effort, trying to call down a magic I had not the faintest idea how to generate. But I could remember it, yes, and I could smell it on others, and I could want it so badly my teeth ached. I simply could not make it happen.

So I tried to make it not matter. I learned early on that it was far more desirable to be the center of attention than to spend one's life skulking in the shadows—and also that there was less chance of being bitten that way. So I excelled in everything I undertook—which, when one is easily the brightest child in a school of twenty, is not difficult. At L'École des Arts et Sciences, enrollment two hundred sixty, not including the most brilliant and demanding professors on the face of the earth, it became something more of a challenge.

But there was an advantage in that too. While the other students used their free time for pack hunts or recreational runs, I always managed to be otherwise occupied in private lessons, recitals or conferences with my professors. I was Brianna Devoncroix, after all, and I had a reputation for excellence to maintain.

The school of the arts and sciences was one of the most popular divisions, second only to the school of mathematics, and rating far ahead of the schools of engineering, business and finance—the latter being considered such natural skills they hardly needed refining, and often were the last resort of those whose talents were so ill-defined they couldn't qualify anywhere else. All the schools were located in the high Swiss Alps, each a hundred miles or more from the nearest human settlement. But the school of the arts had the most desirable location, six thousand feet above sea level in the high lake district, with a vista of sky and clouds, snowcapped crags and verdant slopes from every window. Herds of elk were kept for hunting, and beef cows and sheep dotted the mountainsides. Waterfalls cut sluices out of the grass in the summer and in the winter formed magnificent ice sculptures that were arrested in time on their way to the sea. In the valleys below, lakes glittered like jeweled islands. Some of the most magnificent paintings the world has ever known have come from artists who spent their formative years being inspired by the view from L'École des Arts et Sciences.

Testing is rigorous and competition is fierce for the few places that open up each year in the school of the arts. Desire does not enter into the picture, and children of the pack leader would not be given preferential treatment even if we had thought to ask for it. I had no doubt I would be assigned to L'École des Arts, but I was surprised—and enormously relieved—when my brother was as well. Still, any delusion I had that we would be together in the same way as in Alaska was dashed during the first week.

The first thing some well-intentioned supervisor did was assign us to different dormitories. Second, Matise was put into the Creative

Arts program—which included everything from invention to composition—while I was assigned to Performance. None of our classes or instructors were the same, and even our mealtimes were different. The only chance we had to see each other was during our free hours. And the only thing that worried me more than not having my brother around to defend me in those early years was the free hour.

It was during the free hour that all the students came together, young and old, forming games and athletic competitions and impromptu hunts, swimming the rivers and plunging through the snow, running as wolves and Changing at will. In the classroom hours we were expected to master the discipline required to maintain human form for extensive periods of time, but in the free hour we were expected to Change.

It took all my skill to avoid detection. As much as I could, I spent my free hours in study, but when the supervisors drove me out into the sunshine, I quickly sought out Matise. If anyone teased me or challenged my human form, he was there to drive the devil off.

As time passed I managed to deceive myself into thinking no one knew the truth, and those who engaged in unflattering speculation about me, or even outright confrontation, were quickly cut from my circle. It's amazing what a little bit of confidence and a great deal of arrogance can do, and if, by my second year, my circle of friends was growing quite small, I easily managed to convince myself I didn't care. I was a prodigy, and soon all the world would know it.

At least that was what I believed until I happened to repeat the sentiment to my music mistress.

She was a demanding teacher with a strident personality and very little tolerance for imperfection. She instructed me in piano and voice, and was a juror in all second-level competitions and auditions. When I failed to gain the lead role in an operatic production of *Antigone*—the first time I had ever lost any role I wanted—I went to her and demanded to know why.

She sat alone in the music conservatory with its polished pale floors and light flooding through the enormous Palladian windows, making musical notations at a spinet prettily painted with edelweiss. She wore a loose dark gown and no shoes, and her long black-and-white-streaked hair flowed over her back and hips and brushed the piano bench on which she sat. When I entered she glanced at me over half-rimmed spectacles, but did not stop the fingering notations she was making on the score. I tried not to be intimidated.

I approached within six feet of the piano.

"Speak!" she demanded.

I blurted, "Why did you pick Michelina over me?"

"Because she is better than you," replied Madame brusquely. "You will kindly transpose Chopin's Polonaise in E flat to C sharp and have it on my desk by eight A.M. as a reminder of the folly of questioning your elders."

I plunged recklessly on. "Better than me? But she can't even hit a G-octave without going flat!"

"But her whole notes are rounder than yours and her soprano is deeper. Also, she takes direction a great deal better than you do. In addition to the Polonaise, you will also write a counterpoint duet to Beethoven's Sonata in E, using only the isotonic scale, please."

I stared at her, openmouthed. "But—Madame—if you would allow me to sing the part for you again, I'm sure I could get my notes rounder!"

"Brianna, unless you would enjoy spending the remainder of your evening writing a symphony, you would be well advised to leave me now."

"But," I cried, "you don't understand! I am a prodigy!"

She looked at me now with both eyebrows raised very high over her spectacles, and she inquired, "My dear child, who in the world told you that?"

I could feel myself wading deeper and deeper into the mire, but had gone too far to back down now. "Why—well, everyone knows it. In Alaska, in the city where the hotel was, all the humans cried out and rose to their feet when they heard me play Brahms!"

She removed her spectacles, staring at me with eyes that grew bright as they filled with amusement. "Did you say—humans?"

I knew for certain then that I'd made a blunder but saw no graceful way to remedy it. I nodded bravely.

She looked for a moment as though she could not decide whether to laugh or scold, and then gave an angry, impatient shake of her head that smelled of distaste and exasperation.

"Well, now, if this is not a perfect example of what comes from a policy of tolerance! A bright young werewolf like you, thinking the best she can aspire to is to be applauded by humans. I would like to see the look on Alexander Devoncroix's face if he could hear his own daughter now!"

She finished with an angry sniff that flared her nostrils and tightened her lips as though she was savoring the imagining. And while I enjoyed being called a "bright young werewolf," I suspected uneasily that she had just insulted my beloved papa, and I wasn't quite sure how to defend him.

Her expression softened into mere impatience as she returned her gaze to me. "Listen to your mistress, young one, and let's have no more foolishness. To be called a prodigy by a human is no better than being called clean by a pig; all is relative. You have some talent and you will spend the rest of your time at L'École developing it, but it is not developed yet and you are not, I assure you, a prodigy."

I did not know whether to be dejected, humiliated or angry, but I did know that I had been unmistakably dismissed. And that I was not getting the lead in *Antigone*. I dropped my gaze and turned to go.

"Brianna."

Quick with hope, I looked back.

Her expression was guarded, oddly enigmatic. "Brianna, you are a child of the leaders of the pack, a unique and rather... weighty position for anyone your age. Your parents are great idealists and will no doubt be remembered accordingly by history, but reformists are rarely regarded with universal acclaim during their own time. Do you understand what I mean?"

I nodded sagely, though of course I hadn't a notion.

A small frown creased the smooth flesh between her brows. "There are many within the pack who disagree with the Devoncroix policy of dealing with humans—of letting them into our homes and businesses, of educating them and employing them. I heard only last week that the queen has actually begun to place humans in management positions in one of her factories overseas."

She looked as though she would say more, then changed her mind. Instead she fixed me with a steady gaze. "You have enough problems, Brianna. I think the less you talk about humans while you're here, the better."

Since I had nothing more to say about humans, I did not find that a difficult suggestion to accept. But later we talked about it, Matise and I, in our free hour, while the others were basking naked in the sun or chasing the herds on the lower slopes or tumbling each other playfully in the tall grass. We chose our own rock to sun upon, and we mused over what Madame had meant about humans in factories, and why she should care at all.

"Papa says he is building a flying machine," Matise remarked lazily, eyes slitted at the sun. "He says humans will pay for it and humans will build it and humans will fly in it. I never fancied them smart enough."

"Well, I'm sure he didn't mean they would do it *alone*. We would have to help them."

"Then what's the point at all?"

"*Maman* says one day humans will feed the pack," I said, remembering an overheard scrap of conversation.

"Liver pudding, I hope."

I punched him in the ribs and he grinned and punched me back. We wrestled playfully for a moment; then he rolled over onto his stomach with his chin propped up on his doubled fists, gazing in the direction of the hills below, where a couple of undisciplined youths in wolf form chased the fat off our dinner mutton. They thought they were too far away to be seen, and they were—by anyone but me. I debated the advantages of reporting the incident to a supervisor.

Matise said, "I wish I could be in your dorm."

"Don't you like yours?"

He shrugged. "You're not there."

I stretched an arm over his bare buttocks, which were pebbly and cold from their contact with the rock. "At least you're in my section. What if they had sent us to different schools?"

"My counselor thinks I have a talent for composition."

"Music?" I had heard Matise sing and thought this unlikely in the extreme.

"Words."

"Plays?"

"And poetry."

"You must write a play for me in which no one else can play the lead. You must put that in the stage directions."

"I don't want to write plays. I'd rather build flying machines."

But I could feel his attention begin to stray as a change of wind brought the hot-fur scent of playful excitement and the sound of running paws on soft grass. His head turned in that direction and a few moments later a group of young werewolves crested the hill not a hundred meters away, two females and a male, panting with happy exertion and tossing their heads to the wind. Matise's skin tightened beneath my fingers and his scent grew faintly sharper, and I knew he wanted to join them.

I said irritably, "It's stupid to build things that humans can do. If you don't want to write plays, why are you in the art school?"

He seemed surprised. "Why, to take care of you, of course."

"They don't just put you in a school to take care of your sister!"

"They do if the pack leader says so."

I was hurt, astonished, angry, embarrassed and incredulous all at once, and I did not entirely understand any of the emotions. I knew that I was not angry *at* Matise but *for* him, that he should have been sent to a school where he didn't really want to be, that his whole future should have been directed to take care of me, that he couldn't even run with the others when he wanted to because of me . . . that, because of me, he was even ashamed to Change.

I got to my feet, pushing back my sun-dampened hair, glaring down at him. "Well, I don't need you to take care of me, what do you think of that? I do very well without you!"

He was watching the werewolves across the hill, so still and so intent that his hair did not ripple in the breeze. I could smell his need and it ached in my belly. "Oh, go on!" I cried, kicking at him with my bare foot. "Go run with them, you know that's what you want."

"Ow!" He scowled and rubbed the place where my foot had contacted his arm. "What did you do that for?"

"You're boring and I have better things to do," I retorted. "Go play with the others."

But the catch in my voice must have betrayed me, because his scowl faded and he caught my hand. "I don't want to play with the others. I came out to take the sun with you."

I wouldn't let him pull me down again, so he stood up and tried to coax my good humor back. He kissed my mouth and licked away the sun-sweat from my face, hoping to make me smile. "Come on, Bri. You know you're the only one here who's smart enough for me to talk to. What would I do with my free hour if you weren't here?"

I looked up at him—for by then he was already several inches taller than I—and I said, "You would run with the others. You would build flying machines. You would be what you're *supposed* to be, Matise!"

He looked confused. "But I don't want to—"

I knew if I stayed I would only embarrass myself further, so I jerked my hand away and turned to go. "I have a transposition to do."

"Two," he reminded me.

I didn't look back.

But when I knew he could no longer see me, I circled around

and hid in a tree, and I watched him Change. It was so beautiful it made me cry.

XIV

THE ONLY TIMES I DREADED WORSE THAN FREE HOURS WERE FESTIVAL days. When lessons were suspended and even the supervisors and professors gave way to the reckless bacchanal spirit of the celebration, there was no place for me to hide. Studiousness and sobriety were frowned upon, if not actually forbidden, and the doors of the dormitories were closed for the duration. The lessons that were taught on feast days were the lessons of life, and they could not be learned in the classroom.

Oh, but I was clever, and contrived many inventive ways to avoid the humiliation of being called to run with the pack—and of being unable to comply. During my first winter festival I came down with a nasty cough, and created the most bad-tempered and ultimately convincing fuss when I was made to stay indoors, away from the festivities. With the midsummer festival my parents visited, and everyone accepted the fact that Matise and I would celebrate with them. Matise, in fact, did. My mother looked at me with sympathy and stroked and nuzzled me a lot; my papa pretended nothing was wrong.

And so, between various excellently acted illnesses and indispositions, it was the summer of my thirteenth year before I experienced my first real festival. Looking back, I'm not certain whether I really ran out of excuses or whether curiosity and desire simply got the best of me. I guarded my secret and was terrified of having it uncovered, but I was so very tired of being left out. In the end, I think, fear of isolation won out over fear of discovery—and there was also the ever-persistent hope that this time would be *my* time. This time the Passion would be mine.

We awoke that morning before dawn to the crackling air of excitement and the enticing aroma of food in great quantities and of every description wafting across the hills and seeping into the valleys: sweet breads and starchy grains, mutton sizzling in fat and ladled with gravy, roasted beef and stuffed sausages and puff pastries dripping with sugar sauce. We streamed out of our beds and into the dining halls in exuberant spirits, the clothes of civilization abandoned for loose Changing robes or nothing at all. We flung ourselves upon the laden tables with unpretentious gusto, grabbing with our fingers and tearing with our teeth, laughing out loud with the sheer pleasure of it, for in many ways this opportunity to cast aside civilized manners and indulge ourselves in our hedonistic sides was the best part of the day.

Even now I can transport myself in an instant to the thrill of that cool summer morning, the taste of fresh cheese and sugared cream and rich dark blood sauce, the smell of healthy young werewolves and blossoming sexuality; and everywhere, in every breath and throbbing pulse and tingling nerve, was the promise of discovery. The high rafters rang with the sounds of our voices, our playful squabbles, our challenges and occasional impulsive, exuberant howls. No one corrected us, no one restrained us. Today we lived by different rules.

We stuffed ourselves shamelessly, faces shiny with grease, arms reaching and hands snatching at whatever treat caught our fancy. We would need every calorie we could hoard for the athletics, the hunts, and the Changes that were ahead of us, and there would be no more prepared food this day. When next we ate, it would be what we caught. I loved thinking about this, imagining that I might, indeed, become a huntress before this day was done; and I loved indulging my appetites with the rest of them, licking my platter and tossing it on the floor, snatching a leg of fowl from the mouth of another with my teeth, scooping up soft cheese with my fingers and licking it away.

It has always seemed so odd to me that, as adults, we choose to begin the feast days with the penultimate in civilized behavior—lavish banquets of many separate courses served in the finest silver and crystal dishes, symphonic and operatic performances which we attend after hours of painstaking grooming and elaborate costuming. Only as the day deteriorates do we allow ourselves to discard the layers of our civilized behavior and indulge our true natures. It seems to me that the way children observe the festivals—by simply letting go and letting be—is far more healthy and honest.

On the other hand, I suppose, when adults finally do allow themselves to celebrate the glory and the intensity of their true natures, they do so with a passion their children could not even imagine. There is balance in all things.

As the first golden rays of the sun topped the high peaks, turning the grasses spring-colored and softening the lingering puddles of snow, we all tumbled outside, drunk on sugar and our own irrepressible selves. I shall never forget the glory of that morning: the taste of the air, redolent with alpine flowers and high cold rivers and the sweet-spicy-musky-hot, crackling, dancing, achingly tantalizing odors of a hundred young werewolves on the verge of Passion. Should anyone imagine that just because I could not Change I lacked any of the other facilities of a normal healthy werewolf, let me dispel that notion immediately. I was as drugged and as stimulated by the sights and sounds and smells as anyone present, perhaps more so. I could taste the Passion in the air and I wanted to bury myself in it, to lift up my arms and let it fall over me like rain, to draw it into my pores and have it fill me and become my own. My skin ached and tingled, my heartbeat raced, every sense was intensified, recklessness and desire coursed through my veins. The grass was sharply cold and wet on my feet and I could feel every blade. The melody of cowbells on a hillside three miles away was a symphony to me. The air felt like honey on my tongue and the sun on my face was as warm as a kiss. I dropped my robe to the ground and laughed out loud, turning round and round in an impromptu dance of delight.

I fell into the embrace of a fellow student by the name of Aramis, and we tumbled to the ground in a shower of laughing licks and teasing caresses. I was filled with joy and I could not imagine why I had avoided this marvelous display of public celebration for so long. Of course I revelled in the pleasure of Aramis's playful nips upon my shoulders and thighs, the lovely suckling of my breasts; I loved the taste of his skin and the sparkle of his eyes and the feel of his lithe young body beneath my hands. But most of all I adored being part of the whole; of being, for that one brief moment, one of the many who laughed and danced in the sunshine and made love in the grass. I loved being wanted, I loved being right, and I loved, for that too-short time in Aramis's arms, being me.

He caught my hands and knelt astride me and pulled me to a sitting position between his knees so that our noses were touching and our scents were blending and my vision was filled with the wicked, wonderfully provocative twinkle in his eyes.

"Come run with me," he invited, and my heart leapt to my throat.

This was, of course, an invitation no sensible werewolf would refuse. To play the sex games as we had done was fine enough in a casual way, but nothing one might not do with a brother or sister. But to run with one of the opposite sex . . . well, that's quite a different thing altogether, isn't it? This was a pairing, a courtship ritual, and though we were far too young to mate, it was the manner in which we learned the ways of mating and of choosing one's mate that would serve us well in later years. Until a male and a female have run together in their natural forms, they cannot say they have known each other intimately; until they have known the scent of the other on the wind, tasted the fur at the nape of the neck, matched paces through a wood or across an open field and known the silent language that is wolf—until a male and a female have *been* together, they are but the merest acquaintances. And to be asked to run with an attractive member of the opposite sex is the highest compliment that can be paid.

As a young female whose human form had barely reached its final maturity, I could expect to run with many males before I chose a final mate. But this was my first invitation, and I wanted beyond all that was reasonable to say yes.

He must have smelled the desire on me, because he sprang away from me with the grace of a gazelle and, moving a few paces away to show his splendid human form to its best advantage, he leapt into a pirouette and Changed.

Oh, my, what style he had. I had never seen it done like that before, almost in midair, and it quite took my breath away. I clapped my hands together and gave a cry of delight and he came down on all fours, slightly askew but in very good profile, a gorgeous particolored wolf with green eyes. I opened my mouth and threw back my head to inhale his fragrance, hot vanilla and burned citrus; intoxicating.

His fur was still shimmering and crackling with static electricity, so eager was he, when he turned and bowed to me, inviting me to join him. Oh, yes, I wanted him. My blood raced and my belly ached and my skin burned with wanting him. He knew it, he smelled it. To refuse him now would be the worst kind of insult. Blood feuds had begun on less. Yet what was I to do? Leap up and try to call down the Passion, as I had done so many times before—and fail? And if I failed now, before him, before everyone, what would become of me?

He began to smell my hesitation, and a warning growl, almost too low to be heard and completely unconscious, I'm sure, issued from deep in his throat. I got uncertainly to my feet, my heart pounding hard—but not from excitement now.

Head low, chest rumbling, he took a step toward me, the challenge implicit. I didn't know what to do except to retreat. I took a stumbling step backward.

I don't know what might have happened next. In the reckless atmosphere of the festival, filled with adolescent bravado and frustrated sexuality, he might have charged me, and in my human form I would have had little defense. Perhaps I would have been badly hurt. It is not unknown, though it is unspeakably shameful, for such "accidents" to result in death.

Then suddenly he was there, with a scrabble of claws upon stone and flying clods of turf, silver-tipped fur bristling and blue eyes glinting, my brother Matise. He issued a savage bark-growled challenge and Aramis forgot me, turning to the thrill of battle. The two males met in a clash of teeth and claws and brutal invective, snapping and tumbling, rolling and leaping.

It lasted less than a minute, but long enough to draw a crowd, and it was magnificent. How I longed to be among them, thinking fast, reacting faster, my face in hot fur, my teeth clamping down on vital tendon, ducking, rolling, coming up with a mighty roar to leap again . . . And yes, I circled with the others, who even in the heat of battle managed to retain their human form, cheering the combatants on for nothing more than the smell of battle and the love of a good fight. It was over too soon. I smelled hot blood and heard Aramis's yelp. Matise backed away, and Aramis, with his tail tucked low, fled.

There was no shame in it. He had fought well. But Matise was better.

A few other squabbles had broken out in the interim as immature werewolves succumbed to the primal spell, and those who retained control of their senses simply lost interest and moved away. Matise stood before me, a magnificent wolf of muscle and sinew, all powerful form and glinting eyes. His fur was damp with the saliva of combat, and he quivered still with excess adrenaline; his excitement tasted like cinnamon wine to me.

I ran to embrace him and he sprang to meet me, but my fingers had barely brushed his fur before a group of the others bounded up, encircling Matise with their playful challenges and congratulations. He laughingly cuffed a few and tumbled another, and then a pretty auburn-haired female invited him to chase, and they all were off on a run, leaving me, forgotten, behind.

It was a scenario we had played out many times before. Whenever it looked as though I was about to be put into an embarrassing position or called upon to Change, Matise would appear and distract the others until they forgot about me and I could walk away with my pride and my secret intact. It was something we did so naturally that we had never even discussed it, and I had certainly never thought to resent it.

But today I found I did not want to be left behind. I did not want to be forgotten. I wanted to be the sleek young female who was running flirtatious figure eights around a handsome male. I wanted to splash through the streams and roll in the grass and leap fallen logs in a single mighty spring that made me airborne for an endless, sun-brightened moment. I wanted to *run.*

And run I did, alone and on my two human-formed legs, as fast and as long as my human-formed lungs would take me, away from the others, downwind of the pack, just running. Brambles snagged my hair and branches slapped at my fragile human-formed skin, but I barely felt the pain for the anger, the frustration, the *need* that consumed me. I could smell them, those others with their four strong legs and thick shiny fur; I could hear them quick-scuffling-darting-dashing along wooded paths, across open meadows, leaping and tumbling and nipping and snuffling. They did not have to hide, they did not have to pretend. The scent of their Passion was like acid in my throat; their yelps and howls and cries of pleasure hurt my ears.

And then, through the sound of my own harsh breathing and roaring pulses came a savage cry of triumph and a screech of terror; the smell of hot blood gushing and the thrashing sounds of an animal dying, then the clashing of teeth and scrabbling paws and bickering over the kill. Warm, fresh flesh, but none of it mine.

I ran faster, away from the feast, away from the pack.

There is a kind of euphoria that overtakes a werewolf who is running, a self-hypnosis, if you will, which wipes the mind clean and leaves only the body: legs stretching, heart pumping, lungs breathing in and out. Rhythm. Awareness. Running. Running. Running until—it has happened—the need to run is all that is left, and you run until you collapse.

In human form, of course, the lungs are smaller, the legs are shorter, the heart weaker. I ran for miles, but my strength was gone long before my will to run was. I collapsed near a stream with my chest on fire and air raking through my throat like the sound of sobs. I buried my face in the cold water and let the rush of it flow into my mouth; I swallowed as much of it as I could and vomited it back up immediately. I was able to drag myself far away from the stream so that I wouldn't drown before I fell facedown on the ground and into the deep and dreamless sleep of utter exhaustion.

XV

I AWOKE TO THE SMELL OF FRESH KILL, AND SO HUNGRY I WAS SHAKING. I crept to the stream and drank some more, but the water only sloshed around in a painfully empty stomach. *Blood. Warm flesh.* The soft, baby-sweet smell of downy fur. Rabbit. Someone had killed a rabbit, and not very far from me. I followed the scent stealthily, and as helplessly as if I were drawn to it on a string.

I found the rabbit with its neck broken and its gut torn open in a thicket two turns in the stream to the north of me. It had barely been eaten at all: just the heart and a portion of the stomach, as though the killer, having caught it, had lost interest.

I was so hungry I plunged right in and snatched it up without giving a thought to whose dinner I might be stealing, or what would become of me when the predator came back to claim his prey. I could smell the scent of werewolf all over the rabbit and throughout the thicket, so strong that if I had thought about it at all, I would have thought to look over my shoulder.

But I wasn't thinking, couldn't think; I was consumed by hunger and primal need. I could barely tear open the chest cavity, my hands were so weak and shaking so badly. I buried my face in the rich wet innards and tore with my teeth, swallowing whole without tasting—soft tissue, muscle, small spongy bones. The carcass was still warm, the blood barely congealed. I snapped a thigh and sucked out the marrow. I scraped the flesh off a strip of hide and discarded the fur. I licked the empty body cavity and snuffled for overlooked scraps like a dog. I made an utter spectacle of myself.

And it was then that I felt the eyes upon me. It was then that I caught her scent.

All I had to do was turn my head thirty degrees to the right and there she was, a slim black wolf with chocolate eyes, so still and so dark that she was almost a part of the brambles in which she had chosen to hide—except for the eyes, which were watching me.

My heart went still and the half-chewed flesh in my mouth was suddenly dry and tasteless. I looked down at the remnants of the carcass in my hands. Some fur, the large bones, an empty skull. I struggled to swallow the tasteless lump in my mouth and hesitantly, apologetically, held out the remains of her kill to her.

She came out of the brambles slowly, body low, eyes watchful. I saw she was close to my age, and not much larger. In wolf form, we would have been evenly matched. But as it was, I hadn't much of a chance.

Still, I held her gaze, because I was Brianna Devoncroix, and I bowed my head to no one. I did wish at that moment, however, that there was some way to hold my head high and protect my throat at the same time.

She came close, and sniffed the desecrated remains of her dinner. Then she took a polite step back, and sat down. The effect was as if to say, "Thank you, I don't care for any."

The effect on me was enormous relief.

I placed the remains carefully on the ground and backed away. When she made no move to rush me, I relaxed enough to turn my back on her, and went to the stream to wash up.

I busied myself with splashing the blood from my face and cleaning the strings of meat from my teeth, but that doesn't mean I wasn't aware of the smokey herbed scent of her Change, a whiff of burned fur and a faint crackle in the air, evidence of a hasty, careless transformation of more function than form. I pretended disinterest and preoccupation with my grooming, but in fact I was waiting for the water to clear so that I might see her reflection without turning.

But as it happened, the water ran too fast and in order to satisfy my curiosity I had to turn around and face the female, who, having failed to humiliate me with her teeth and claws, no doubt now intended to do so with her scorn.

She was round-breasted and lean-hipped, with wavy black hair that fell midway down the length of her back. She had big dark eyes and a rather sharp nose, but was not otherwise unattractive. She regarded me with a frank curiosity that almost matched my own.

After several moments of looking at each other without a word springing to mind, she said, "I wanted to see if I could do it. Catch it, I mean. But then I found I wasn't hungry."

I gave an awkward little shrug. "I was."

She grinned suddenly. "I suppose you were, running all that way on only two legs."

My eyes narrowed and I went stiff with suspicion, ready to defend myself against the challenge I knew was coming. "You were following me?"

She lifted her shoulders in a disinterested way. "Not intentionally. Now and again I caught a whiff of you. You're Brianna Devoncroix."

I nodded cautiously.

"Your brother is in my dormitory."

"He never mentioned you."

"He never noticed me," she replied matter-of-factly. "No one does."

"So who are you," I demanded, "that no one ever notices you?"

"My name is Freda Fasburg." She started walking upstream, then tossed her next words casually over her shoulder. "I'm a princess."

"A what?" I hurried to keep up.

"A princess. My father is the Prince of Auchenstein, and that makes me a princess."

I was very confused and perfectly intrigued—as she had no doubt intended me to be. "A prince?" I scrambled over a fallen log. "Do you mean—like a human?"

She laughed. "Something like that. The other humans think we are, anyway—human, that is. We've had the principality for, oh, I don't know, centuries, and that's why the pack cast us out."

"Cast you out?"

She gave me a sharp, half-amused, half-uncertain look over her shoulder. "You're certain no one has told you this?"

I shook my head, fascinated.

Freda shrugged. "Well, you should smell it on me, anyway. I'm an outcast, just like you. Except that now your father has decided to bring us back into the pack. I'm not sure we want to come, though. My sister says your father only wants us for our money. We're extremely wealthy." She flashed me a grin suddenly, and her dark eyes sparkled. "That's what happens when you're royalty—humans want to give you all their money."

This was all a great deal to absorb at once, and I hardly knew which point to question first. Then she surprised me again by saying, not unkindly, "You're an anthropomorph, aren't you?"

That stopped me in my tracks. I had never heard the word before. "What's that?"

We had reached a place where the land sloped away from the stream and the grass was tall and thick. Freda sank down on the ground in a slanting patch of sunlight with the soles of her feet planted together and her hair streaming over her breasts, and she looked up at me earnestly. "I've heard the teachers talking. It happens sometimes, they say, even in the best of families, and no one knows why. They call it anthropomorphism. When a werewolf can't Change."

I stared at her, aghast. They were talking about me. She knew. The teachers knew. Everyone knew. I had no choice but to attack her.

I flung myself upon her, ready to bite and kick and scratch and pummel with my fists if I could, but she was far too nimble for me and rolled aside and to her feet in a single fluid motion. I found myself clutching handfuls of grass, but only for a moment. I swung around, ready to lunge, and she exclaimed, "What are you, some kind of savage? Even humans have better manners than that!"

That stopped me cold. I, Brianna Devoncroix, had been accused of many things, but never of a lack of manners. We had been so well drilled since birth that I wasn't entirely sure what, precisely, even constituted bad manners. I knew only that bad manners were one thing you never, ever wanted to have.

Angrily, Freda brushed grass off her thighs and out of her hair. "The humans have a word for creatures like you," she continued spitefully. "Lycanthrope! It means a werewolf who acts like a wolf while in human form. And when they catch one, they put it in a cage with iron bars and take it around from city to city so all the other humans can stare and laugh and throw things at it!"

All the breath left my lungs and the heat left my face and I sat down hard, staring at her. Lycanthrope. I *had* heard that word before, but I had never known what it meant. Suddenly I understood why my parents and teachers had worked so hard to instill in me the manners of civilization, why they had insisted so strictly upon an unbreachable code of behavior. Because if I were captured by humans . . . because if I could never assume wolf form . . . Lycanthrope. They put them in cages.

"Cages," I whispered out loud, and through lips that were so numb they could barely form the word.

Remorse filled the other girl's eyes and she took an uncertain step toward me, then another, bolder one. She sat down beside me. "I didn't mean to say you are one," she said in a tone that was something between apologetic and defensive. "Only that you *acted* like one. Besides, I don't think humans really put them in cages, at least not anymore. They probably put them in hospitals."

At my questioning look she explained, "Buildings for diseased people."

I considered this alternative for a moment, and did not like it better than the first. I said, as steadily as I could, "I'm not a lycanthrope. Or an anthropomorph. I'm just—late, that's all."

She thought about that for a moment. "I'm not sure there has ever been anyone as late as thirteen without Changing. I could look it up for you, though," she volunteered. "I'm in the science department."

I drew up my knees and encircled them with my arms, pretending a great disinterest. "You can if you want. But I'm not an anthropomorph."

"It wouldn't be the worst thing in the world if you were."

I returned a contemptuous laugh. "Very easy for you to say!"

Now it was her turn to affect a casualness she very clearly did not feel. "A great lot of good it does me to be able to run as a wolf when there is no one to run *with*."

Curiosity drew my attention away from my own troubles—albeit reluctantly—to her. "Why won't the others run with you? Because you lived with humans?"

Freda nodded. "Because we *ruled* humans. And because we interfered with their government—that's what royalty does, you know—and because we let them think we *were* human. It's complicated. But now your papa says all is forgiven and we should return to the pack, and so I have to go to L'École even though no one wants me here, and *my* papa has to live in Venice and renounce his throne."

I was by now utterly and completely fascinated, the words "lycanthrope" and "anthropomorph" all but forgotten. "You lived among humans? You went to their houses and had them as guests at your table and played games with them and ate their food? What was it like?"

She slanted me a glittering glance. "Well, if you really want to know . . ."

"I do." There was perhaps a shade too much eagerness in my voice, so I mitigated it with a deliberately casual "I'm sure my papa would want me to learn all I can, after all, about how such a peculiar thing came to be as werewolves who took the names of human royalty."

Freda flopped over onto her back and gazed up at the clouds through the canopy of trees, and she said, "Well, it was hundreds and hundreds of years ago, before the time of Queen Eudora even. That nasty plague had wiped out most of the human population, and bodies were piled up in the streets, and they were eating their own children, so the story goes . . ."

I gave an elaborate and appropriate shudder but, wide-eyed, bade her continue. Her lips upturned with satisfaction at her captive audience, and she went on.

"It was a matter of sanitation, I should imagine. All those unburied bodies, the smell, no one to take the humans in hand and teach them how to care for themselves again . . . My great-great-great-great-grandmother Isolde decided to take matters into her own hands, and brought her pack out of the Black Forest, where they dwelled, to clean up the village and drive off the wild animals that were preying on the sick and the weak, and to re-civilize the humans. She brought the medicines of the forest, and set the strong to caring for the weak. She drove the vicious animals away from the village, and cleaned up the streets, and taught the humans hygiene and nutrition. She organized building crews to restore the crumbling structures of the village, and the first thing the humans built was a palace for Isolde, and they named her their queen . . ."

The day slipped by as Freda told me the stories of her family, and my eager ears absorbed every word. The others chased down the deer and had sex on the hillside and proved their prowess in games of strength and skill. I would not have chosen to be anywhere else.

By the time the long shadows of an endless midsummer day turned from cobalt to midnight and a brilliant yellow moon appeared over the top of the highest hill, we were the fastest friends. We lay on our stomachs, human skins prickling a little in the rising cold, and looked down over the moonswept trails and valleys.

"I would run with you if I could," I said, breaking one of the comfortable silences that had fallen between us.

Freda folded her hands beneath her chin and replied matter-of-factly, "You will, someday."

I smiled at her and believed, for the first time, I think, that I really would.

We both heard the voice, a mile or two away, carried on the wind. My brother Matise, looking for me. I called back.

"He's very handsome, your brother," Freda commented.

I glanced at her. "Are you in love with him?"

She thought about it for a moment. "No. But if I were to be in love with anyone, it might be him. He smiled at me once."

"He's very charming," I agreed.

"Everyone says so."

I squinted down the hillside as Matise came into view, a smooth swift shadow with an easy bounding stride, closing the distance between us effortlessly. "He's brought us pheasant," I announced happily. "Two of them."

"I smell them," Freda said. "How do you know there are two?"

"I can see them."

She cast me an admiring glance. "Your eyes are better than the average werewolf's—or even human's."

Since the only slight advantage human physiology has over ours is in the strength of their eyesight, I knew to take that as a compliment.

Matise approached cautiously, sensing the stranger, and I awaited his reaction to my new friend with equal parts eagerness and anxiety. I wanted him to approve of her very much, but if he had not done so I would have turned my back on her without question. That was simply the way it was with us.

He drew within a few dozen meters of us and stopped to analyze her scent. Then he dropped the pheasants and politely Changed into human form for us. We watched with admiration and appreciation as he scooped up the birds and came near.

"Matise," I said, "this is Freda Fasburg. She's in your dormitory."

He looked her over. "Hello."

"Her family was exiled, did you know that?"

"Not exiled," corrected Freda. "Just shunned. Anyway, we're not anymore."

Matise sat down before us, holding up the pheasants. They were fine and fat and freshly killed. "I thought you might be hungry."

I glanced at Freda, and burst into uncontrollable giggles. "No, thank you. I've eaten."

Freda started to giggle too, but she was polite enough to take the birds from Matise. "Maybe we'll roast them," she suggested, and began to pluck the feathers. "Who can make fire without a match?"

"I can," Matise said, "but I'd rather not."

I said, "Freda is in love with you."

Matise grinned and stretched out on the ground, loosening his muscles. "I shouldn't doubt it. So many females are."

Freda murmured, "And I can smell most of them now."

We both laughed then, and in a moment so did Matise, and I was content. Later, Freda ran back to the dormitory for matches, and we roasted the fowl and feasted under the full moon and we listened to the howls of the others echoing across the mountainside, but I had no desire to join them. I felt no loneliness. I had my brother and my only friend, and they had me, and we all had one another. I could ask for nothing more.

Looking back, I suppose that was the most significant feast day of my life.

Well, perhaps the second most significant.

XVI

THE FIRST TIME I SAW THE PALAIS AT LYONS IT TOOK MY BREATH AWAY, just as it was designed to do. The approach was through the verdant French countryside and rambling vineyards—Devoncroix, of course—which were so different from the Alaska of my childhood and the Alps of my youth that my eyes hurt from trying to take it all in, my head swam with the effort of sorting all the scents and sounds. We went through a set of tall iron gates emblazoned with the Devoncroix crest in gold and worked with griffins sporting wolf heads at the top, and then down a long quiet road paved with crushed shells and striped with the shadows of well-spaced chestnut trees.

The year was 1915, and we arrived in a long sleek Daimler automobile, Matise and Freda and I, so excited we could hardly keep still. We had come to celebrate our Ascension from L'École, and a special feast day had been called for it. Members of the pack from all over the world had gathered at the Devoncroix ancestral home in Lyons to celebrate the Ascension of the two eldest children of the leaders of the pack—along with all the rest of our class, of course—into adulthood.

By this time Palais Devoncroix had been virtually deserted for almost fifteen years, although a staff had been left behind to maintain it. This was the model after which the grand human palaces of Versailles and Tuileries were designed, and though it might no longer be the showcase for pack treasures, not even a decade of relative disuse could detract from its grandeur. As we came up the long drive we held our collective breath for the first glimpse of this marvel, so fabled in legend and in song.

It did not disappoint. We rounded a curve and there it was, arranged like a giant wedding cake atop a gentle green hill, reflecting its own glory in a wide, still lake at its base. It was fashioned of the finest pink marble in the Italianate style, with many curved balconies and fluted turrets, stained-glass windows and hanging gardens. The facade seemed to pour gracefully down over the hillside with three separate sets of wide, curving steps, each leading to a pair of beautifully carved and decorated doors that were two stories high and etched with gold. The part we could see was enormous, but the part we could not see—the myriad of rooms and galleries and indoor gardens—took up almost ten hectares of land.

I could not suppress a gasp, straining to get the best view of the approach through the Daimler's windscreens. "Why—it's almost as grand as Castle Devoncroix!"

"Not nearly," corrected Matise. "But," he had to admit, "it's quite impressive. As it should be, since it was home to our mother's ancestry and retainers, literally, and the world pack, figuratively—not to mention its function as a cultural center and social seat for all the pack—for centuries."

"You do take such a great lot of words to say the simplest

things," remarked Freda without bothering to glance at him. Her gaze, like mine, was fixed on the spectacle ahead. Then she added, almost absently, "I should like to see Castle Devoncroix someday."

"I can't think why you shouldn't," Matise answered, for he was never offended by Freda's criticisms. "We're going home this summer. You should come with us."

"Not me," I replied gaily, climbing onto my knees for a better view. "I have the whole world to see first!"

"And I'm going to see it with her!" Freda said, and then gasped, "Oh, my!" and craned her neck backward as we passed through another set of tall iron gates filigreed with gold which opened magically at our approach.

The driver slowed the vehicle as we crossed the arched stone bridge that spanned the lake, and we were all three appropriately silent, appreciating the spectacular view.

Then Matise said, "Papa says this will be the last pack gathering here. In the future, the official pack headquarters will be in Alaska."

"I can't think how that will be convenient," observed Freda, "since all of the pack is in Europe."

"Well, it's the humans, you know," Matise told her, sounding very sage, "and their silly wars. Papa feels it would be safer if we watched from afar. We do stand to make a great deal of money, though."

"From Alaska?"

"No, from the war. Neutralities always flourish when nations battle, and we are ultimately neutral. In addition, we own all the steel and chemical factories, and those are the commodities humans require to make munitions, not to mention the shipyards and—"

"Oh, bother the humans and their silly wars!" I exclaimed impatiently. My eyes were fairly bursting with the effort to see everything at once, and when the Daimler rolled to a stop in front of the center set of steps, I tumbled out almost before the wheels had stopped turning. I stood there silently for a moment, my breath completely stolen away, filled with the awe of my ancestral home.

"Matise," I whispered as he and Freda alighted from the car and stood beside me, "can you believe we're here?"

For there we were at the bottom of the curve of the great steps so often depicted in painting and tale, within the shadow of the great statues of Armaden the Great Mother and Silos, who had claimed pack dominance for the Devoncroix a dozen centuries ago. Lining the steps in a double column was the honor guard, each wolf chosen as much for his or her magnificent good looks as for skill in battle—a perfectly matched set of black-furred, broad-chested, chocolate-eyed wolves standing at fierce attention to announce the presence within of the leaders of the pack.

All around us were the sights and sounds and smells of celebration—elegant werewolves in gala attire with their parasols and walking sticks and lovely big hats trimmed with yards and yards of chiffon; and werewolves in their unfettered natural form, chasing one another in the sun, dozing on the rocks, splashing in the streams. The air was scented with wonder and anticipation, and it tingled in my bones.

Despite our parents' efforts to protect us from the unsightliness of the humans' war, we had passed through shocking evidence of violence and folly on our way here: gutted cities, burned fields, marching soldiers and crying, orphaned children. But in this haven of our people, in this deep protected valley, it was as though the war that raged in the north of France did not exist. Suffering and death could not touch us here. Human foolishness was banished from our doors. An invisible shield marked our territory and within it were only elegance, surety and magnificence.

"There's magic in this place," I said softly, and hugged the possibilities to me like a delightful secret. "Can't you feel it?"

Matise put his arm around my shoulders and Freda squeezed my gloved hand with her own and the moment was so poignant, so filled with promise and expectation, that I can see it to this day with my mind's eye, as sharp as a photograph. What a beautiful trio we made, standing together ready to conquer the world: Matise, so exquisitely handsome in his gray-striped trousers and stylishly cocked straw boater, with all that gorgeous striped hair caught behind his collar with a black ribbon; and Freda, in the emerald green that was her best color, with her hair swept up in a chignon to the side of a wide-brimmed hat of pale green trimmed with ostrich feathers and mauve ribbons; and I, stunning in a white linen hobble skirt and mid-length coat sashed with wide scarlet satin and a marvelous, enormous black hat tied with white chiffon streamers. Oh, we were beautiful. We were strong, we were bright, we were confident. We were ready to conquer the world.

And on that bright summer morning in that most reverent of all places, I honestly believed we could.

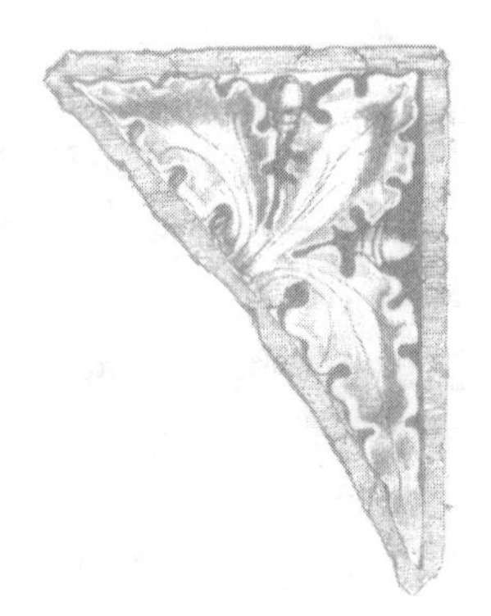

Ten

The Wilderness
12:08
Alaska Standard Time
November 24

THE VOICE OF THE HUMAN, MILDLY HOARSE WITH SO MANY HOURS OF sustained vocalization, cracked and faded on the last sentence. She made an airy coughing sound, then closed the book and left the room. In a moment Nicholas heard water being poured into a kettle, and smelled an electric burner.

Nicholas thought about Brianna and Matise and Freda Fasburg, and wondered what their story could possibly have to do with him; with scientists massacred in a laboratory, with the assassination of one pack leader and the attempted murder of another. It all tied in to Brianna, Nicholas knew that. His father had known it too. He had been so insistent that Nicholas read the book . . .

Restlessly, Nicholas tried to put together the pieces of the past few hours—or was it days? Desperation flooded his veins as he wondered how long he had been ill. How long had the pack been unprotected, without leadership? Were they searching for him even now? Or did they think he was dead?

A speeding automobile in the night. A bomb hidden on a helicopter. Werewolves turning upon one another, murdering each other like humans . . . such were the times in which they lived. Such were the dangers to the pack. And he was here, helpless and confined, powerless to prevent whatever catastrophe the Dark Brotherhood had in store.

Their plan was obvious, their genius absolute. For almost a hundred years this subversive group of human-haters had gone underground, had managed, even, to convince the pack that they no longer existed, biding their time until they could resurface and take control in a single dramatic coup. They had quietly infiltrated the pack over the past decade, doing their jobs so effectively that to this day not one of their members had been positively identified. They had learned the secrets of the Devoncroix administration, its weaknesses and its strengths, and they had formulated their plan.

The plan was brilliant: to assert themselves when father and son were divided, to assassinate the old leader and take over the pack before the heir could assume power . . . and to use Nicholas's own edict to do it. Garret had been right. He had played right into their hands.

But it made no sense. Alexander had been killed because he opposed the edict, but Nicholas had championed it. Had he been left unmolested, he would have inadvertently proved a friend to the Dark Brotherhood, not a threat. Then why had they tried to kill him as well as his father? Unless . . . Something tickled the back of Nicholas's memory. What was it Michel had said? *If the Council chooses to oppose you . . . it could be months, years, before the entire pack accepts your decree . . .*

And the Dark Brothers had not the luxury of time. They must move swiftly while the pack was weak, while it was without a leader, while the most powerful decree ever written was waiting to become law.

But how had they known? How could they have known what Nicholas was planning? His security system was impenetrable. No one except his parents had known about his intention to issue the edict, and every conversation they had had about it had been on a secure line.

And then, without warning, something else Michel had said came back to him. *It might be best to have no hard copies just yet, if you know what I mean . . .*

Michel had insisted that he send the edict electronically. Because hard copies would have been destroyed when the helicopter went down?

It might be more efficient if I stayed here for a few hours . . . rather than accompany you home . . .

Nicholas felt a chill with the remembrance, and his heart began to pound. He had to get out of here. He had to warn Garret. He had to protect his pack.

The human woman returned, a mug of tea sweetened with honey in one hand and a dish of fresh water in the other. He watched her carefully, eyes narrowed. If she opened the door of the cage, he could bolt. He could overpower her effortlessly. But he had not the strength to Change, not yet. And without Changing he could not use his telephone or high-frequency radio, or even work the locks on the doors.

But she did not open the cage door. There was a slot at the bottom of the cage, too narrow for the bowl in which she had brought him food earlier, but just the right size for the flatter dish that held the water. She slipped it through, up against his paws.

"Drink, fellow," she encouraged softly. "Your body needs to stay hydrated in order to get well."

What do you know of what my body needs? he thought contemptuously. *What I need is to get out of this place, to hunt, to feed, to return to my people . . .*

She knelt beside him, studying his nearly healed wounds through the bars of the cage with a mixture of horror and amazement. "How do you do that?" she whispered, raising her eyes to his. "What kind of creature are you?"

He thought desperately, *Worthless human! Call someone! Tell them about the crash, about what you've found. My people will be monitoring every broadcast, every report. But how can they begin to search for me when they don't know where to look?*

Hannah sipped her tea and said absently, "I suppose I should try to get a message through about the crash. But with this storm building, no one could get out here. And it's not as though there were any survivors . . . except you," she added softly.

His heart gave a single powerful thud before resuming its more-or-less usual rhythm again. Impossible. Not even the most accomplished werewolf could communicate with a human while in wolf form. Human brains were far too small to allow them to understand the unspoken thought, everyone knew that. And yet . . . how many werewolves, he wondered, had ever *tried* to communicate with a human while in wolf form?

He caught her gaze. He formed a picture in his mind of his SCU—Satellite Communications Unit. It was a device that, though not yet on the market for humans, allowed him to receive radio and television broadcasts, to send faxes and electronic mail, and to make secure telephone calls from anywhere in the world using the Devoncroix communications satellite. He knew she would not be able to master the complexities of making a satellite telephone call with the device, but if the transmitter switch were simply turned on, it would send a locator signal that would instantly alert Garret.

Go to the briefcase, he commanded her. *Find the small black box there. Bring it to me.*

She sipped her tea, observing him intently. "Who are you?" she whispered. "Are you—Matise?"

Stupid human, listen to me. Go! Go now to the briefcase!

She frowned and rubbed a spot just above the bridge of her nose, as though it hurt her. She said, "I know you're no ordinary wolf, but is it possible . . . is it possible this book isn't just a piece of fiction?" Then she made an impatient sound low in her throat and shook her head. "Of course it's possible. Why shouldn't it be possible?"

Look at me, human. Let me see your eyes. Do what I tell you. Bring me the box.

She looked at him then, and frowned again. Nicholas watched her, hardly daring to breathe, as she stood up, glanced around uncertainly and walked away.

Idly Hannah flipped open the top of the briefcase and surveyed the contents there, wondering if she had overlooked something that might identify him . . . *might identify the owner of the briefcase,* she corrected herself mentally. She opened the folder of papers and thumbed through them again. There were signatures at the bottom of one of the contracts, and an international telephone number—Paris, she thought—on the face sheet. But she didn't have a telephone, so that was of no help.

The box, human. Bring me the box!

She picked up the electronic organizer again, pushed what appeared to be the "on" button, turned it over, tried the button again.

Yes, that's it. Bring it to me.

Hannah discovered a slider switch recessed into the side of the organizer, and when she pushed it up the device jerked open like a pocket phone. She lifted an eyebrow in surprise. Inside there were several buttons and toggles, but no keypad. She had never seen anything like it before.

She tried the "on" button again and this time the small screen glowed green. So the battery was operative, but apparently the database had been damaged. She tried a few of the buttons in rapid succession, but got nothing more than muted bleeps.

It's voice-activated, Nicholas thought urgently. *You can't access the functions without a verbal command. Bring it to me. I can press the switch that will send the locator signal.*

Nicholas watched in despair as she turned the device off and put it aside with a shrug. She picked up her quilt and the red book, then settled close to him on the sofa. She glanced in his direction and smiled. "Shall we finish this chapter?"

Once again, she began to read aloud.

From the Writings of Matise Devoncroix

XVII

BRIANNA

THE ASCENSION CEREMONY WAS PRECEDED BY TWO DAYS OF FEASTING and celebration, of pack runs and athletic competitions and theater performances and symphony concerts. We, the one hundred three young werewolves about to enter adulthood, were the honored guests, the featured artists, the focus of all indulgent attention. Matise competed in two races; he won the first and came in third in the second, yet such a fuss was made over him as though he had won both races.

I sang a Verdi aria on the outdoor stage upon which so many of my illustrious ancestors had performed, and when I happened to glance toward my parents' elevated seats I saw my papa's eyes glisten with tears as he brought my mother's hand to his lips, and my mother's face was misty with pride. Lost in the thunder of applause and the wash of stage lights and the sweet, sweet smell of the adoration of hundreds and hundreds of werewolves, I was so transported I trembled with the glory of it. With only the smallest of efforts I could have raised my arms and leapt into the Passion at that moment, I was sure of it. But I did not.

I had other plans.

There is always at least one mating ceremony at feast celebrations, for what would any celebration be without an acknowledgement of that most essential part of what we are, and thus why we are able to celebrate anything at all? These ceremonies are both joyous and solemn, ribald and passionate and profoundly sentimental. Everyone who is able attends, from the just-weaned cub to the gray-muzzled grandfather: friends, relatives, distant acquaintances, enemies, business rivals, all come together to participate with delight and awe in this, the beginning of new life, and the continuation of what we are.

While the bride and groom were being feted by their closest family and friends with exotic wines and gourmet delicacies, while they were being massaged with scented oils and serenaded and petted and pampered and otherwise prepared for the solemn moment of their union, hedonistic bliss ruled the pack. Great tables were set up in the halls of the Palais and in the parks, each laden with sides of mutton and beef, wheels of cheese, steaming breads, thick blood puddings and sweets of every imaginable variety. Huge barrels of Devoncroix wine were tapped and the glasses passed freely beneath the flow. Because of the nature of the occasion, we all wore loose changing gowns or nothing at all, and, out of respect to the prospective mates, we all maintained our human forms. There would be plenty of time for Changing—for running and flirting and conceiving young, if one were already mated—after the bride and groom had had their hour of glory.

Despite the restriction to human form—or perhaps because of it—gluttony ruled the day. We had already feasted until we were bored with eating, yet we somehow found a way to force down one more dollop of head cheese, one more bite of pastry dripping in caramel sauce. And there was sex, the indulgence of the day, the ultimate gluttony, and the air was thick with the smell of it.

How we loved each other, in the heady, drunken eros of that midsummer day, beautiful bodies hot with the sun and slick with passion, lips and tongues caressing, fingertips stroking, arms and legs locked as we tumbled, kissing, suckling, adoring, on the soft meadow grass and fell into the perfumed fields of flowers. Ah, it was ecstasy . . . at least for those who were asked.

Freda and I enjoyed it all from the gently swirling waters of a hot pool in the high meadow, overfilled glasses of wine in our hands, a platter of sweets on a floating table between us. Warm fingers of water caressed our toes and our nipples and stroked between our thighs. The fragrance of blended lavender and patchouli was almost as drugging as the wine, the kiss of the sun rich and soporific. Lost in a sensual haze of sweet butter creams and dark, strong wine, of swirling heat and gentle sexual pleasure, I envied no werewolf in the world.

Freda sighed deeply and settled her shoulders beneath the water, letting bubbles tickle her chin. The steam rose and slickened her face, pasting to her skin the tendrils of dark hair that escaped from her topknot. "Ah, those Romans," she murmured. "What clever werewolves they were to invent the baths."

"The Romans did not invent them," I corrected drowsily. "They simply perfected the design."

"Nonetheless, I shall be sure to send them a thank-you note." She lifted her glass above her head and, extending her tongue, spilled a stream of wine onto it. Of course she could not catch it all and we both burst into giggles as red wine dribbled down her chin and into the water, and she pretended to lap up droplets from the bubbles. I splashed water into her face and she snatched up a candy and tossed it at me and I caught it with my teeth, which sent her into another gale of giggles. And then at the same time we became aware of the lovely familiar scent of hot male skin and werewolf musk and we turned in the pool to watch.

It was Matise, and a light-haired female from one of the other schools, and an auburn-haired vixen named Aenid from the Science department at L'École. They played a laughing game of chase across the meadow, lithe young creatures with long slim muscles and glowing faces and wind-combed hair, and my brother was the most comely of the threesome.

In the school of the arts we had access to representative pieces from all the Great Masters, and one entire hall was filled with nothing but exquisite werewolf bodies worked in marble. Not one of them could have compared to Matise, with his powerful shoulders and lean waist and long thighs and firm buttocks. His hair, colored like caramel marbled with butterscotch, fell to his shoulder blades in thick waves that smelled like forest and sunshine and cool spongy moss; you wanted to gather it up by the handfuls and bury your face in it whenever he was near. He had a good face with a mouth that was always ready to laugh or to kiss, and eyes like Papa's, full of devilment. He was a joy simply to watch.

Speaking my thoughts out loud, Freda said, "My, he is beautiful."

I turned onto my stomach and let the buoyancy of the mineral water lift my legs as I folded my arms upon the tiled wall of the pool and rested my chin upon them. Matise chose that moment to allow Aenid to capture him by tagging his ankle, and the two of them went down in a laughing dance of tangled hair and entwining limbs and greedy tasting mouths. When the blond, only a step or two behind, caught up with them, Matise grabbed her wrist without ever removing his mouth from Aenid's breast, and pulled her into the fray.

"Do you know," Freda remarked, "humans have their sex in secret, even on their mating day."

"How odd." I grew bored as Matise focused his attention on pleasuring the blonde and Aenid began to caress his genitals with her tongue. I turned over and took up my wineglass again, sipping thoughtfully. "Have you ever thought about it—what it must be like to be mated? To have another person's heart beat in time with yours, to carry in your head all the secrets of their life and to know they carry yours? To know their *thoughts?* Not even Matise and I know each other's thoughts. It's really quite terrifying, isn't it? To be bonded like that to someone for all your life."

Freda nodded solemnly. "I think humans are more sensible about it, actually. They simply have sex and have babies."

I agreed.

I thought about mating a great deal; of course I did. I thought about it in the same way I thought about the Passion, with hope and determination and no small amount of desperation. Since one can mate only in wolf form, the two were integrally connected, of course. But we were fifteen, Freda and I, and no one would expect us to mate until we were thirty at the earliest. There was time. And on that fine summer day, when the air was charged with hope and promise I believed it more than I ever had before. It would happen for me. I knew it.

I asked, sipping my wine, "Who will you mate with, Freda?"

She shrugged, trying to look unconcerned. "We always mate with our cousins. Although now the queen—your mother—says we mustn't anymore because the pack needs more variety in its gene pool."

I tried to think why this should make her unhappy enough to pretend it didn't matter at all, which was what she was doing. Her tone was easy and her posture relaxed, but her scent was distinctly troubled and I could hear a heaviness in her pulse that hadn't been there before. "But that's good, isn't it?" I prompted. "Isn't it better to have the whole pack to choose from than just a few cousins?"

"I suppose." Her smile was a little wan. "Provided, of course, someone in the pack chooses me as well."

And that, of course, was why we were alone in the pool, instead of enjoying the company of strong young males. Freda was beautiful in human and wolf form; she was bright, she was fast, she was cunning. It infuriated me that she should be shunned simply because she had had the misfortune to be born into a family whose ancestors, several hundred years ago, had exercised bad judgement.

If Freda's enrollment at L'École had been my parents' experiment in returning the Fasburgs to the pack, it had, in my opinion, failed miserably.

"*Maman* will *find* someone to mate with you," I declared loyally, squeezing her fingers under the water. "I'll tell her so."

"Never mind, Freda," offered Matise gaily, coming upon us from behind. "If things grow lean enough you can always mate with me!"

He sprang into the pool with a tidal wave of exuberance that splashed our eyes and soaked our hair and spilled our wine. We squealed and slapped at him with appropriate outrage, and Freda replied darkly, swiping at her stinging eyes, "I shall never be desperate enough to choose you for a mate, Matise Devoncroix!"

"Ah, but you mustn't be premature. You have no idea what an excellent lover I am."

"Everyone in the pack knows what an excellent lover you are," I returned, scowling as I picked up and discarded a soggy pastry.

He clasped Freda suddenly by the shoulders and covered her mouth with his, kissing her deep and hard with tongue and teeth, making her pulse race and her skin flush. I watched with amusement at first, and then with a growing uneasiness. I think that was the first time it occurred to me that one day Matise would mate.

He would mate, and we would be separated.

I tugged his hair sharply and he released Freda with a yelp of pain. He turned on me with his hand raised and I bared my teeth to him. We would never have dared display such savage behavior, even in play, before anyone but Freda, and she laughed—albeit a little breathlessly.

"Very well," she admitted, eyes sparkling, "perhaps your reputation as a lover is deserved. But you really must work on your finish."

Matise grinned and ducked under the water, staying long enough to wash away the scents of all the females he had been with that afternoon. He came up gasping and streaming, parting the wet hair away from his eyes and raking handfuls of water off his face.

Again Freda and I squealed and shielded our wine as he shook a great spray of water over us.

"Go away, you horrible beast," I commanded, pushing at him with my feet. "We were having a lovely time without you. Go back to practicing being a great lover."

He slipped his arm around me and kissed me tenderly, tugging at my lower lip gently with his teeth, breathing his sweet-scented breath into my throat. He snuggled his face into my neck, inhaling the essence of my scent, and I did the same with him, stroking his wet hair with my fingers. "That was nice," I admitted, smiling at him. "Now go away."

"No time," he said. Settling back against the wall, he stretched out his arms, encircling my shoulders with one and Freda's with the other. "The bride and groom have left the house, and we must discuss what we're going to do tomorrow. Do it quick, or we'll miss the mating ceremony."

I could see Freda's hand stroking Matise's thigh beneath the water. "Tomorrow," she announced, waving her glass high in the air, "we shall be free! We'll run, we'll dance, we'll commit all kinds of excesses, and when we are done . . ." She glanced at me across the top of her glass, eyes twinkling. "Brianna and I are going to get on a train and go to the land of the humans, where we will do all those lovely things all over again!"

"Just make certain you do them outside of Europe," Matise counseled sternly. "Papa says no Devoncroix is to be in the path of human weapons and that means you, Bri. Now, as for the problem at hand, I thought we could do it like this." He looked at me. "They will call the names alphabetically, so Freda is already behind you in line. All I have to do is make sure I am too, so that when they call your name, each of us will still be in human form—"

I understood. The Ascension Ceremony, like most of our rituals, was simple and straightforward: one by one we would be called forward in human form, our accomplishments recited, our intentions declared, our maturity claimed—and we would Change. A dozen times before, Freda and Matise had covered for me in similar situations; we had our routine down so patly we hardly needed to discuss it. But Matise wanted to make certain I was protected from humiliation on this, the most important day of my life. I loved him for it, and for a moment was fairly bursting with the need to tell him my secret, to tell them both they needn't worry about me any longer.

I lay my fingers across his mouth, stopping his words. "I have taken care of it," I assured him.

He could hear my heart speeding—they both could—and smell my excitement, and puzzlement registered in his eyes, and in Freda's. Matise said, "Bri, don't do anything stupid. You can't miss your own Ascension Ceremony—you'll never forgive yourself."

"If you're afraid we might not be able to cover for you," Freda put in, "let's talk to your papa. He's the leader of the whole pack, he could—"

"No, there's no need," Matise said impatiently. "We'll create a distraction, you and I—"

"No need." I caught Matise's hand, and Freda's, and held them each tight, my certainty so strong it practically glowed through my skin. "Matise, no need. I don't have to hide any longer. I can Change!"

Confusion shadowed Freda's eyes and wonder slowly lit Matise's. "Bri—do you mean it? When? How—"

But I held up a hand to silence him, cocking my head to listen. "Wait—they're here. We're going to miss the mating!"

We scrambled out of the pool and hurried toward the meadow. Once Freda caught my arm and whispered, "Bri, what do you mean, you can Change?"

But I shushed her and wove my way through the crowd toward a place in the front.

By the time we gained a good vantage point, the ritual had almost reached its pinnacle. The bride and groom stood naked in the center of a wide circle formed by the pack, hands upraised, fingertips almost touching. The thrill of excitement that resonated through the pack was like an electric buzz, amplified by voices joined in song, a slow, wild, sweet melody in a minor key that started out as soft as whispering leaves but grew louder and stronger until it reflected the beat of a thousand hearts before it, in and of its own power, created a wave of sound so sure, so thrilling, that it buoyed the couple toward their Passion and shook the depths of desire within each and every werewolf present.

I could feel it in my bones, swelling in my chest, hot and wondrous: love, need, pleasure, flowing through and around me as it did through every werewolf present; all of us one, all of us powerful. I grasped Freda's hand and Matise's, and felt their return grips hard enough to crush the bones. Ah, the smell of them. The warm thrill of their blood pulsing my ears, the tingle of their electric power in my skin, their nearness, their warmth.

The chorus of sound reached a crescendo and hung suspended in the air, swirling and resounding and gathering power for an endless moment, and then the bride tossed back her head and stretched forth on her toes and leapt into her Passion in a burst of color and light and tangy hot perfume. In less than a heartbeat, before the crackle of her transformation had faded from the air, her intended joined her and the flare of light was so bright it hurt the eyes.

We held our collective breath while the heat rose among us, desire trembled within us and the rich drugging scent of Passion seeped into our pores. The female sprang a few steps away from her husband with an inviting, flirtatious look over her shoulder and the male captured her almost instantly, sinking his teeth into her neck, holding her with his forelegs. She gave a great howl of triumph that reverberated through our souls as he mounted her, penis engorged and unsheathed, and penetrated her with a single thrust. A great cry of joy and celebration went through the crowd as we smelled the gush of hot semen, and all around me werewolves began to Change, surrendering to the magic of the moment, the glory of life, the demand of passion.

I could feel Matise's fingers tightly wound around mine and his thigh pressed against my hip, and smell his heat, hear his excitement. Freda was on my other side, her hand clasped around mine, her breast soft against my arm, her heart pounding in my ears. The breeze, sweeping across my skin, dried the water that lingered there and felt like a thousand biting ants. Every part of me ached: joints, tendons, cartilage, fibers, neurons, cells. I trembled. I tasted my own sweat. The air was singed with Passion, my ears throbbed with a thousand heartbeats, my eyes burned and blurred. My belly cramped with desire. I could taste it on my tongue. I was weak with it, dizzy, as my senses were infused with the coming Passion of my companions.

Matise's hand slipped out of my grip as he spun away from me, caught up in rapture, and then even Freda was gone. I was drunk with the residue of all those Changing around me, vaguely aware of the familiar scents of the transformations of those I loved best. Dizzily I watched as they met each other in wolf form, did a playful little dance of recognition, then ran off together, laughing, celebrating with the others.

My ears were full of thunder and the landscape was littered with color and movement as I staggered toward the shelter of a broad tree and sank to the ground behind it, weak, shaking, wet-faced. I tasted tears now, but they were tears of wonder and joy. I had felt the beginning of the Passion. I *had.*

My time was coming. And it would be soon.

XVIII

THE ASCENSION CEREMONY WAS HELD THE NEXT DAY, AND TRADItionally began at sunset. By the time all the speeches were made and all the welcomes given, dusk would have fallen, and the glow of a hundred Passions, one after another, would make a spectacular display upon the twilight landscape. There then would follow a pack run through the moonlight, and for the first time we would run as full-fledged members of the pack, adults alongside adults, claiming our place.

Excitement crackled through the corridors of Palais Devoncroix like ground lightning, for nothing is more contagious than the exuberance of youth. The day was spent going from feast to feast with our families, being teased and toasted and required to suffer all manner of well-meant advice. I had by this time two more brothers and three sisters, and as part of the ritual, Matise and I were each required to pledge our loyalty to them with a kiss. Late in the afternoon we were sent back to our rooms to bathe and brush our hair until it gleamed and perfume our bodies and prepare our minds for the solemnity of the occasion to come.

Maman came to me in private not long after I had stepped from my bath. Freda, with whom I had chosen to share the room, was polishing her hair with silk scarves in the sunny western window embrasure, and I could hear the tiny crinkling sounds her hair made as it was charged with static electricity from the silk and the sun. Freda got to her feet immediately when *Maman* entered, but *Maman* waved her down again.

"A word alone with my daughter, if you don't mind, my dear," she said.

Had she said "private," that would have been Freda's command to leave the room and put as much distance as she could between us so that none of our words could be overheard. As it was, however, the polite thing for Freda to do was to turn her back and pretend not to hear. It's such a silly thing, really, for werewolves to try to keep secrets.

Maman took my hands and stepped back an arm's length from me, smiling as she looked over my form. "What a beautiful young female you've grown to be, Brianna. All that red hair, such a lovely figure. You bring joy to your father's heart and mine every time we look at you."

I grinned back at her. "I agree. I am quite striking to look at. But I owe you and Papa the thanks for that."

She laughed and tugged at my hands, bringing me to sit with her on the brocade divan adjacent to where she stood. She gazed gently into my eyes and filled me with contentment, my mother, symbol of all that was good and strong and correct, this perfect female, this quintessential werewolf. She had skin of porcelain and eyes of crystal and a pale rich abundance of hair that tumbled over her shoulders and caressed her hips. She smelled of sunshine and flowers and things that were good to eat; sometimes just inhaling her scent could make me weak with adoration.

She said, "We are so very proud of you, Brianna. Your voice, your spirit, your accomplishments at your studies . . . you have a magnificent career ahead of you, and what you may yet mean to the pack only history can tell."

I wanted to acknowledge her faith in me, but she held up a finger for silence. Now a rather odd intensity came into her eyes, as though she were looking inside me for something she could not quite find. "You came into my life at a time when I had all but lost hope," she said, "and you brought healing to the heart of your papa, which I had thought was broken forever. You gave us back our lives, Brianna, my darling girl, and for that you will always have the most special place here." She pressed the area just below her left breast, smiling at me. "And because of that, because you asked it, we have granted your request and altered the ceremony slightly, so that all the names will be called before yours, and everyone will have had a chance to Change. When your name is called, stand forward proudly and recite your designation, then simply walk back and stand with your family, who will protect you. No one will think the less of you, and the ceremony will not be disrupted."

I lowered my eyes. "They will think the less of me," I said softly.

She was silent for a moment. I could feel her pain, and thought for the first time how humiliating it must be for her and for Papa, leaders of the pack, to be parents of a child afflicted with my condition. Stunted, incomplete.

She said, "Brianna, you are a clever girl to have avoided this moment for so long, but you cannot deceive the pack—or yourself—forever. You are not the first to suffer this affliction and you won't be the last. Very often what is lacking in one area will be compensated for in another—your extraordinary eyesight, for example, is no doubt related to your inability to Change. You must never think of yourself as less of a werewolf because of it. In many ways you are more."

I wanted to jerk my hands back and stalk away from her platitudes; I wanted to cry out that she knew nothing about it, *nothing*. But I held my tongue. Today I was an adult. Today I would begin to act like one.

"I don't want to shame you, *Maman*. Or Papa."

She cupped my face tenderly with her hand and stroked my cheek with her thumb. "You could never do that." She let her hand fall away from my face, and lowered her eyes briefly. "Long ago I wanted to tell you . . . well, it doesn't matter now. Your papa was right, and you have grown up to be everything we hoped for and more."

Then she kissed me, and gave me a smile that adored and strengthened. "Destiny is in your eyes, my darling. You will change the world."

And I believed her. I honestly did.

Freda waited until my mother's footsteps had faded through the corridors, until we both had to strain to pick up the sound of her voice engaged in another conversation up a set of stairs and a half-dozen rooms away. Then she flew from her sunny window seat and abandoned all pretense of propriety as she descended on me.

"What are you plotting?" she demanded in a whisper. "First you told your brother that you can Change, that you're *going* to Change, and now your mother—"

I pressed my fingers to her lips until I was sure she would be silent, then cautiously left her to scramble beneath my mattress for the book, which I presented to her triumphantly.

She glanced at the cover. "You stole this from the science library!"

"I did not! I borrowed it." I sat down beside her, one foot tucked under me, and quickly began to flip the pages. "It's that text on anthropomorphism you told me about. This physiologist Zelder did a whole research project on it, and look—this is what he says." I found the place with my finger. "' . . . the ages between thirteen and fifteen appearing to be the time in which the young werewolf is particularly susceptible to the pheromones given off by another's Change . . . evidence that repeated exposure to those pheromones can cause a buildup in the bloodstream and initiate a Change where none was possible before . . .' He even talks about the power of places," I told her excitedly, closing the book, "places where thousands of Changes have occurred over a long period of time—places like this! Like the mating grounds, and the ceremonial pavilion where we'll be tonight!"

Freda looked troubled. "I've read this book, Brianna, and it's not considered—"

I shook my head impatiently. "You don't understand! It's working—I felt it the moment I set foot here, and every moment since. And I was remembering, the first time I almost Changed, it was in that ancient circle, where we could still smell the Passion of the Old Ones—and then yesterday, at the mating ceremony, didn't you notice? I was almost there, I *could* have Changed, but I held back, because tonight, after everyone has Changed before me, after the buildup of all the pheromones since I've been here—*then* it will happen for me! It will be . . ." I could hardly find the word in my excitement and my certainty. "Effortless!"

Freda still looked unhappy. "Brianna, your mother was right. There's no shame in it if you just walk away. But if you step forward into the circle of the others—"

"That's exactly what I'm going to do!" I assured her.

"But you *haven't* ever Changed," she insisted. "What if—"

I just laughed at her. "Freda, you didn't really think I was going to live my life like this forever, did you? I've been brave and I've been clever and I've been quiet. But it's my time now!"

"You can't just *command* something like that!"

I tossed her a look over my shoulder as I went to get dressed. "Watch me!"

XIX

I WILL NEVER FORGET THE MAGIC OF THAT MISTY EVENING AS TWILIGHT faded from pink and gold to dusky blue. There were storm clouds in the distance, swollen gray and thunder blue, but that only added to the power of the night and the color of the sunset. The grass was spongy with dew beneath our feet and a soft breeze rose up from the river. I could taste the faint ozone on the air, but whether it was from the approaching storm or my own excitement I could not be sure.

All the pack were gathered beneath the arch-roofed pavilion, in human form and in their most formal Changing robes, solemnly occupying the tiered benches that encircled the pavilion according to status, with the highest ranked at the top. We, the students, filed out in a single row to a stately canon performed by strings and a chorus. We wore white gowns of gauzy muslin with deep cowl collars and long full sleeves that hid our hands, feet bare and hair loose and unadorned, the shape of our strong young bodies beautifully outlined beneath the veil of gauze. The arena was lit only by footlights which grew subtly stronger as the dusk deepened, but which never grew so harsh as to dispel the mystical aura of soft fogs and yellow glows.

The students were seated in a semicircle at the eastern curve of the pavilion as the chorus came to an end, and during the break in formality caused by the rustling of skirts and the finding of seats, Matise, who was beside me in line, grabbed my arm. "Have you lost your senses?" he hissed in my ear. "Freda told me you've never Changed at all and you're planning to try it tonight!"

I pinched his leg hard enough to leave a bruise but did not alter the serenity of my expression by a fraction.

His fingers tightened on my arm, and that *did* hurt. "Don't do it, Bri," he warned, his voice low.

I suddenly realized my folly in not having taken Matise into my confidence sooner, as a dozen possible ways he could spoil my plan flashed through my head all at once. I turned to him, my expression quick with panic, and begged, "Matise, don't stop me, please! Don't you see—if not tonight, when? When in my whole life?"

I saw the struggle in his eyes: his own stubborn reason warring with sympathy for me, understanding of me, absolute commitment to me . . . and the desperation he could smell from me. He let go of my arm and muttered, "I couldn't if I wanted to."

All the pack rose to their feet in a howl of approval as my mother walked to the center dais to open the ceremonies.

She looked exquisite in her favorite blue, and she gave a beautiful speech about the beginning of life and the rallying of the pack toward a new tomorrow. The smell of the crowd grew sweet with adoration of her. When she was finished and the roar of the assembly died down, my papa strode onto the dais, all power and majesty, and kissed *Maman*'s hand and escorted her to the marble throne chair on the east side of the dais. Then he addressed the pack.

He was a commanding speaker and could hold a crowd. His eyes flashed like blue lightning at times and the thunder that rolled in the distance was to great effect. I recall that when he spoke of sending his children "into a world we have made and we will control through peace and cooperation," all eyes turned to Matise and me, and I was as proud as if I myself had created that world. He talked about the conflicts raging in Europe, and about the necessity of werewolves "disassociating themselves from the petty politics of humans"—at which point I glanced at Freda, wondering if she would be insulted, but she was looking at me and hardly seemed interested in Papa's speech at all. Then he went on to relate how this would be our last pack gathering in Lyons, and that the new pack headquarters in Alaska would be officially dedicated in the spring. He spoke of the technology that would enable us to rule the world from a place even so far away as Alaska, of the miracles that awaited us all if we joined together and how very, very rich the humans were going to make us. By the time he had finished, the audience was on its feet, cheering and shouting.

When the speeches were over, there was the Naming. As the name of each and every living family member of each and every student was recited and recognized, my tension mounted, as palpable as the humidity that thickened the air. The list was endless. Then came other speeches, from our teachers and counselors and supervisors. Endless.

Matise and Freda kept glancing at me with poorly disguised curiosity. I ignored them.

Finally, it was our time. The sky was dark blue by now and rimmed with purple in the rolling clouds. Occasionally a flash of silent lightning etched a thunderhead in fluorescent lavender, and when my papa stepped up to the podium again, a warm gust of wind billowed his hair and molded his robe close to his body for a moment. He lifted his arms to the sky and announced exuberantly, "A good night for a pack run, my children!" A rumble of thunder seemed to echo his words and everyone laughed and cheered. Oh, it was magical. Even the atmosphere of the earth was charged with expectation on my behalf.

Then Papa turned to the students and, stretching out his hands to us in a silent command to rise, said, "As it was in the time that ended darkness, so it is today. You enter into your full maturity responsible for yourselves, your family and your pack. Yet since the time of the good Queen Eudora we have embraced another responsibility, with the full and clear understanding that the world is our pack, and we upon it merely caretakers. You are the children of tomorrow. Do you make this vow of your own free will?"

As one, we lifted our voices to reply, "I take this vow of my own free will."

Papa commanded, "Speak it, then."

And so, with our faces turned east and the warm, sharp-tasting winds of the coming storm brushing them, we took Eudora's Vow, and we became full-fledged members of the pack.

Then there remained only the individual introductions to the pack, and with the same great ponderousness with which time had seemed to move before this point, it now speeded up crazily; too soon, too soon, and the excitement was making me nauseated.

One by one they went before me: "I am Cassandra D'Eauville

and I am a master of the visual arts." She stepped free of her gauzy robe and executed a stylish Change. "I am Marius Arquette, and I am a master of engineering." He swept off his robe and Changed with a flourish, and the next in line hurried forth to face the pack. "I am Lindser Meechaum and I am a master of gastronomic science."

"I am Adelaine Rosche and I am a master of theoretical mathematics . . ."

". . . master of management and craft . . ."

". . . master of dance . . ."

". . . of drama . . ."

". . . of chemistry . . ."

". . . of physics . . ."

". . . of practical art . . ."

Finally it was: "I am Freda Fasburg, and I am a master of physiology."

And at last Matise, who by this time was as feverish as I was from the scent of the hundred Changes and the crescendo of murmuring heartbeats from the crowd and the taste of electricity—meteorological and physical—in the air. Nonetheless, he remembered to squeeze my fingers, quick and hard, before he too stepped forth to face the pack and declared in a clear strong voice, "I am Matise Devoncroix, and I am a master of language."

He stripped out of his robe and tossed it into the air—it really was magnificent—and before it settled to the ground again he had Changed and come down on all fours. And I was alone.

This is how it was, how it is burned upon my brain in scent and sound and magnificent color: the milling crowd of just-changed wolves, nipping and snapping at one another in excitement, restless and eager, waiting for the leader of the pack to give the signal that would free them to the night; the tiered benches filled with others waiting to Change, anxious to Change, their heartbeats a cacophonous symphony of anticipation and their scent like hot wine, weighing down the air; my parents upon the dais with their hands linked and their eyes glowing blue fire and their chests swelling with pride and pleasure as they looked out upon their bounty. In the distance thunder rolled and a magnificent fork of lightning touched the far horizon and cast a cerulean glow across the sky. I heard one fat raindrop strike the clay-tiled roof, and then another. Zephyrs of warm wind chased my skirt and tickled my ankles and brought the taste of wet earth and electric charges to my tongue . . . and werewolf, everywhere, in shades of rose and wine, cinnamon and oak, orange and moss and vanilla and sandalwood and sea spray and hot musk, werewolf power, werewolf glory. I could feel it. I could taste it.

I stepped forward and I said loudly, "I am Brianna Devoncroix, a master of music."

In a single motion I loosed the ties of my robe, twirled it aside and spun around on my toes, arms stretched high, head thrown back, reaching for the Passion, inhaling it into my lungs, tasting it rich and solid on the back of my tongue. Trembling with it. *Feeling* it.

Thunder crashed, loud and hard. Electricity snapped in the air around me. Muscles ached, dizziness swirled, I cried out with ecstasy, for I was on the verge, the Passion was mine to claim . . . but just as it had done so many times before, it eluded me.

I am not quite sure when I became aware of this. Something changed around me. The sound of the crowd, the smell of the air. I heard a shout, and felt a sharp pain in my leg. I looked down and saw a welt rising on my thigh. Someone from the crowd had thrown a stone at me.

I heard the growling behind me and turned quickly. My classmates were staring at me, heads low, teeth bared, gazes filled with contempt. I took a stumbling step backward, suddenly cold, suddenly weak, suddenly vulnerable. But when I turned around, the spectators, many still in human form, were pouring out of the tiered benches, fists raised at me, voices angry and jeering. I had failed. And in so doing I had mocked them, I had humiliated them, I had insulted what we were. I had separated myself from them. I stood alone, brazen and different, and I must be cast out.

I heard my mother call my name and somewhere in the crowd, almost drowned out by the snarls and growls of the others, I heard Matise's wolf-voice. Frantically I looked for a break in the throng, a way to reach my parents or my aunts. I started to run.

All still might have been well had I escaped, had I hidden myself until they forgot me or had I reached the shelter of a family member who was still willing to protect me. But my scent was sheer terror, my mind was still cloudy and my muscles were weak from my attempt at the Passion, and as I made it to the edge of the covered pavilion my foot slipped on the wet grass and I fell.

The pack's instinct toward a fallen, frightened adversary is to attack. And that was what I was to them then: an adversary. Something to be disposed of, conquered, triumphed over. They rushed me all at once.

I can write no more of the details of that night. I took a chance and I lost, and I now must pay the price.

I knew my life with the pack was over when I looked up and saw my parents watching it all with a cool dispassion, holding the arms of my brother who fought to rescue me.

XX

MATISE

I CANNOT LET THE TELLING END THERE. PERHAPS FOR BRIANNA IT WAS indeed over, but for me the tragedy was just beginning. The rest of that night is my story, my horror, my shame.

My memories of the first few moments of chaos are not very clear. Snapping teeth and glinting eyes, sharp claws, fur-sheathed muscles wrestling and writhing in their eagerness to get to her. The taste of dirt in my mouth as I stumbled in my urgency to reach her. The smell of blood, the smell of war.

I could see Brianna on the ground, her arm caught between a pair of powerful jaws which shook her like a rag doll. When he let her go for a better grip, she managed to crawl a few feet away but was slammed to the ground again, facedown in the mud. She tried to cry out but choked; she managed only to cover her head and face with her arms before the next assault.

And then I did a shameful thing. In my confusion, in my anxiety, tossed this way and that by my own body's immature reaction to the pheromones of a hundred different Changes, I myself Changed into human form.

I tried to reach her, but was quickly driven back. I called out for her and heard her sob my name. I saw Freda, still in wolf form, trying to break through the crowd. I shouted to her. She looked around for me and was challenged by a young female who took exception to her intention. A brief, vicious skirmish ensued, with Freda the victor. She bared her teeth to another challenger and fought her way forward.

I struck out against muscled fur and sharp teeth with my bare hands, trying to get to Brianna. Suddenly my arms were caught from behind and held strongly. My father said firmly, "Leave it be, Matise. This is not your fight."

I gave him one incredulous look and began to struggle furiously. "Let me go! Look at what they're doing to her!"

My mother said very calmly, standing beside me, "They won't kill her."

I stared at her in disbelief, but her features were cool and composed. Desperately I sought out Brianna, and what I saw sickened me. They had her on the ground, snapping and snarling, darting at her occasionally with nipping teeth that tore her skin or a disciplinary shake that bruised her bones. Her hair was matted with mud; rain and tears streaked her face. And as I watched, one arrogant young wolf pushed his way forward and urinated on her face.

I cried, "How can you let them do that?" I tried to pull my arms away. "Why don't you stop them?"

My father said, "Brianna is an adult today. She must be responsible for the course she chooses."

And my mother said sternly, "You do her no favors by fighting this battle for her, Matise. Leave it be."

Another wolf sidled up and marked her with the sign of his contempt, and they all were laughing, mocking her, tossing her about in sport. Skirmishes broke out among the pack as the level of excitement grew.

My mother passed a concerned look to my father. At some point, I realized, he had released my arms. Now the expression on his face as he observed the travesty being executed before him was simple disappointment.

"It is enough," he said.

He left me, and went to the Calling Rock. He cast aside his robe and lifted his arms to the sky and in a flash of thunder and purple lightning he called down the Passion; in almost a twin motion, my mother followed. Their scent was a powerful drug that perfumed the night, that was carried on the thunder and sizzled in the rain. I felt it in my blood and crawling on my skin, urgency and need.

The pack was restless, anxious. Brianna was all but forgotten as they paced and milled and surged close to their leader. I managed, with an effort, to tear my attention from the power of my father and searched for Brianna. I was able to find her only because Freda, in defiance of everything that was proper, had changed to human form. Freda was bleeding from injuries she had sustained in battle, but the pack was little interested in her. She knelt down to lift Brianna out of the mud just as my father put out the call to run.

Oh, it is a magnificent thing, that call. It is a single note that stretches into the sky, gathers the force of the night and returns to earth bursting into a thousand fragments of light. It pierces the soul, it boils the blood, it draws the nature of every werewolf within hearing distance as inexorably as the moon draws the tide.

All around me, voices were raised in answer. My hair stood on end, my skin ached, my soul was on fire. The pack called. I needed to answer it.

Frantically I cast my eyes back to Brianna. Freda was holding her, and Brianna's arms circled her friend's neck weakly. The rain was washing away the mud and urine that stained her skin. She did not look at me. I could not go to her.

The call of the pack was maddening, intoxicating. It lifted me, it buoyed me, it sucked me in. I looked at Brianna . . . and I turned away.

Feverishly, wildly, helplessly, I spun into the Passion. I left my sister behind, and answered the call of the pack.

XXI

BRIANNA

I SUSTAINED A BROKEN WRIST, A DISLOCATED SHOULDER, TWO cracked ribs and numerous contusions both inside and out, but for all the pain, not a single drop of my blood had been spilled. Had I put up a fight it might have been worse, but they were growing bored with me by the time Papa had transformed and called the pack to run.

My injuries healed within a week—at least those you could see. The real damage was not to my body, and the wounds deep inside would never heal.

When my parents entered my room I closed my eyes. Matise came again and again, and I pretended to be asleep. He knew I was not.

I could hear the voices throughout the Palais as, one by one, the members of the pack took their leave. "What a disappointment for you. But she does have a lovely voice . . ."

"What a great pity. Such a beautiful human form, those fine Devoncroix genes wasted . . ."

"Well, of course this proves it. If she didn't Change during the worst of it, there really is no hope for her . . ."

"You mustn't despair. So many of them live long and perfectly happy lives . . ."

And some of them ended up in cages, mad things captured by humans and put on display. No one said that. No one dared utter that truth.

Freda, who had sustained a nasty bite on her arm trying to

defend me, was the only one I could bear to face. She moved into the sickroom with me, and took my meals left at the door and brought them to me, and washed me and brushed my hair and changed my linens. But even she said, "Brianna, try not to hate your parents. Don't you see if they had intervened to save you, they would have lost the respect of the entire pack! You issued a challenge by—by doing what you did, and it was no one's fault but your own. They couldn't help you!"

I replied, without very much emotion at all, "I don't hate them. But I don't think I can ever forgive them either."

She said, a little uncertainly, "There was another reason that they didn't stop it. As you know, we all instinctively revert to wolf form when we're in pain. I think they were hoping that the shock, or perhaps the injury, might trigger . . . that you might . . ."

I understood then the murmured words *If she didn't Change during the worst of it, there really is no hope for her*. I almost smiled, although even irony required somewhat more effort for recognition than it was worth. "That I might Change before I was killed?"

She dropped her eyes, a sigh barely repressed, and said nothing.

I glanced around the room, all gold ormolu and frescoed ceilings, silk brocade and intricately carved marble. I gazed beyond, through the tall, open windows, toward the park and the fountains, the bathing pools and the formal gardens; werewolves at play, bounding across the lawn and splashing in the fountains, strolling the gardens in wolf and in human form, nuzzling one another, lying beside one another in peaceful contentment. And I said slowly, only now beginning to understand it was true, "I don't belong here."

I looked back at Freda, my brows knit slightly in puzzlement—not at the truth, but that it had taken me so long to realize it. "I don't think I ever did."

I left Palais Devoncroix that night with nothing except the clothing I wore. I simply walked out of my room, across the garden, out of the gate. I didn't look back. The night was bright with the light of a hundred million stars and a crescent moon shone yellow just above the tree line. I could hear the movement of the river and the chirrup of frogs and the scuttle and rustle of the insects that made their home behind the bark of a tree. I could hear the murmur of voices at Palais Devoncroix, the sighs of lovers as they turned one another in bed . . . and Matise.

He stood downwind of me, so that I actually heard the beat of his heart, the rustle of his clothing, before I caught his scent. I turned, scanning the shadows and silhouettes around me, and discovered him leaning against a plane tree some two dozen meters to the west, arms and ankles crossed, waiting for me.

His shirt was unbuttoned and looked as though it had been pulled on as an afterthought; his feet were bare, his hair was loose. He was scowling.

I walked up to him. I didn't want to, but I knew if I turned away he would only follow. "Did Freda tell you?"

"She didn't have to. What kind of new foolishness is this? What do you think you're doing?"

"I'm leaving," I told him.

"Without me?"

My throat constricted unexpectedly. "Because of you," I said hoarsely. I looked him full in the eye and drew a breath. "Matise," I said, "I'm leaving the pack."

I saw his thoughts as clearly as if they had been my own. He wanted to pretend not to believe me, but he knew that would only be a waste of time. He wanted it not to be true, but he knew it was. He wanted to reason with me, cajole me, threaten me, ridicule me; he wanted me to take the words back. But he couldn't. And he was horrified.

On a quick rush of breath he said, "Bri, don't do this."

I was already shaking my head. "It's done."

Silence. Pounding hearts. A frantic flickering of desperate thoughts, and his eyes reflecting that desperation. He knew me too well. There was nothing he could do.

"Bri, think about this. Will you just take a minute and *think* about this? You're the firstborn daughter of the leaders of the pack—you can't just *leave*!"

"They have already left me, haven't they?" I couldn't have made the words sound bitter even if I had wanted to. I hadn't the energy. "All of them. This is what we do, Matise—we cast out the misfits, the malcontents, the deformed. It's a matter of survival of the pack, and it's as old as time."

"But—" Frantically he cast about to find something to dissuade me. "If you leave the pack, your name will be stricken from the records, never spoken again. No werewolf will ever acknowledge you; you'll have no one to turn to. What will you do? How will you live?"

"Freda's family owns a theater in London," I replied. "I will perform there for the humans."

He stared at me. He smelled my resolve, heard the steadiness of my heartbeat. There was no changing anything. He knew it.

He turned in profile to me, looking back the way I had come, toward the Palais. His shoulders were stiff and his blood was heavy in his veins and the sad, bitter scents of grief and distress bathed his skin and leached into the air. His voice was hoarse and ragged when at last he spoke.

"I tried, Bri. I tried to get to you. When I saw you couldn't—I Changed back so that I could get you out of the crowd, but that was a *mistake*. I should have stayed as I was, I could have fought better. I should never have left you alone. If I had it all to do over again, if I could trade the rest of my life to have that moment back . . . but I can't. I promised to take care of you and in the end I failed you, and I have no excuse for that. None."

I could not bear to see my brother in such pain. I took a quick step forward and touched his arm. "Matise, don't. It's not your fault."

"You don't understand!" He turned on me then, his face torn with anguish and his eyes wild and angry, but I could see the anger was not directed at me, but at himself. "That's not the worst of it, you don't understand!" He took a quick sharp breath, his hands balled into fists at his sides. "When Papa called the pack to run—I answered the call. I left you for Freda and the old aunts to tend to and I went with the pack. I didn't want to—I tried not to—but in the end I went with them, not you! I would give my life to take it back, but now you are leaving and whose fault is it if not mine?"

"Oh, Matise." I looked at him with my heart breaking, filled to overflowing with his pain, and with mine. "How can you blame yourself for being what you are? How can you expect me to blame you?"

I held open my arms to him and he swept me into a crushing embrace, our faces buried in each other's necks, our senses bursting with the presence of each other: heartbeats, pulses, textures, tastes, scents, ah, the scents. I wanted to let him melt into me, to take him into my pores, to capture the scent of him inside me somewhere safe so that I might remove it in all those bleak lonely days ahead to savor, to treasure, to weep over, to adore. *Matise. Matise.*

"I'll go with you," he said hoarsely, and my heart skipped a beat.

But I knew he couldn't do that, and I held him harder, and shook my head against his shoulder, breathless, desperate, dying inside with the thought of leaving him. "You don't belong among humans any more than I belong here. It would destroy you and watching it would destroy me."

"Then we won't go to the humans. We'll go someplace else, you and I, we'll go to the wilderness, to Australia or Malaysia or the South Pacific. I can take care of you anywhere in the world, we don't need anyone else, not the pack, not humans, not anyone. It's always been the two of us and it always will be, we promised, remember? Just tell me where you want to go, and I'll take you there!"

I thrust my fingers through his hair, holding his face close to mine, holding his gaze even though it meant drinking in his pain with my eyes. My own face was wet with tears. "You can't leave the pack," I repeated as steadily as I could. "You can't come with me, we can't go to the wilderness. You have to stay here, and find a mate, and have a life, Matise!"

I saw the dread and the torment fill his eyes and knew then that I had given voice to the one thing neither of us had ever been able to speak before, and that in saying it, I had changed everything. I saw it in his eyes as he saw it in mine, and he covered my mouth with his and I kissed him back, hard; I wound my arms around his neck and I strained on my toes, pushing myself into him, tasting him, devouring him, inhaling him, becoming him, consuming him.

I dragged my mouth down to his neck and his chest, flat-tongued, biting, tasting. He pushed aside my coat and my blouse, buttons popping effortlessly beneath his rough fingers; he tore at my chemise and pulled my clothing off my shoulders and down to my waist. He clasped his hands over my breasts, suckling them, arousing me.

Ah, shall I claim madness? Shall I claim innocence? Simple sex games gone awry, playful intent between brother and sister which opened the gate to a place no siblings should go? But there was no madness. There was no innocence. We knew exactly what we were doing. Our footsteps had turned down our path long ago; our only regret was that it had taken this long to arrive at our destination.

I heard it in his breath, ragged with desire, I felt it flame in his skin and in mine, I felt it in the starburst of pleasure as he thrust his fingers between my thighs and I heard it in my small, helpless, wondrous cries as I pressed myself into him, greedy, desperate, adoring. The wetness of his mouth, the mating of our tongues; the wetness of his hair, the smell of it and the taste; the wetness between my thighs, the smell of musk, the night scented with it, his and mine. Oh, I could feel his heat, an inferno, searing, maddening, I wanted to scream with it. I could hear the rush of his blood, hear the high-pitched strain of his muscles, lengthening, stretching. His penis, fully engorged, pressed against my pubis. The quivering of tension within him was like a hum of electricity along a tightwire. Even his hair was drying from its drenching burst of perspiration, growing static, giving off the sweet intoxicating aroma of fresh pine. It hurt to be near him. My blood sang with being near him.

"Yes," I whispered, gasping, "yes, take me with you, Matise, take me into your Passion!"

"Yes," he muttered. His tongue was hot in my mouth, on my face, on my neck. "Yes!"

I could feel the charge running down my spine, like hot fingers plucking at strings. It hummed in my head, it throbbed in my pulse, it blistered my skin. I cried out, openmouthed, against his face. His fingers crushed my ribs, my fingers raked his back. The coming Passion crackled in the air around us. My hair stood on end, my mouth went dry, my blood boiled, my soul cried out for him, *Yes, Matise, Yes!*

"No!" he shouted, and thrust me from him. His eyes were wild, his hair swirling on end, alive with the static charge; his body crackled with a faint blue light and he shouted again, hoarsely, barely articulate: *"No!"*

I staggered back, nauseated, dizzy. I fell to my knees. Every pore in my body wept for him, ached for him. I lifted my arm, but couldn't reach him. I cried out for him, but couldn't make a sound.

In his eyes I saw the horror of what he had almost done, what we had almost done. In his inarticulate cry I heard the anguish. He took a staggering step backward, and another. His hands tore at his clothing. He turned and he ran.

Sometime later Freda found me, shivering, gasping, weeping. She covered my nakedness with her own cloak and helped me to my feet, down the hill, toward the road. We walked most of the night to the train station in Lyons, and the only thing I remember of the journey is the eyes of a wolf watching me from the shadows.

The loneliness in those eyes would pierce my heart forever.

PART TWO

Caesar, beware your ambition. It has the soul
of the wolf from whence it came,
and is a hungry thing.

—AUGUSTUS SABATINI,
WEREWOLF, A.D. 360

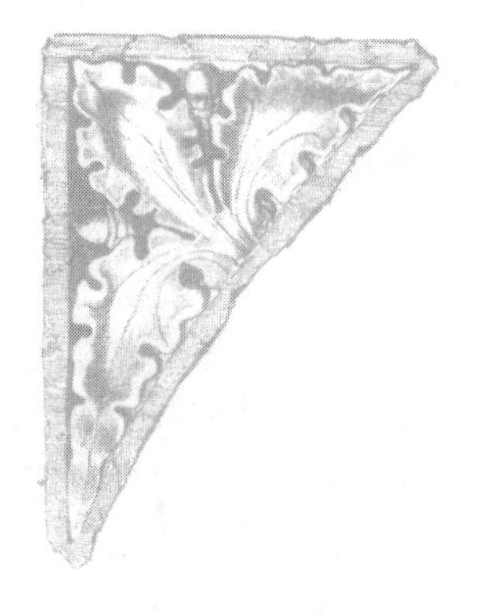

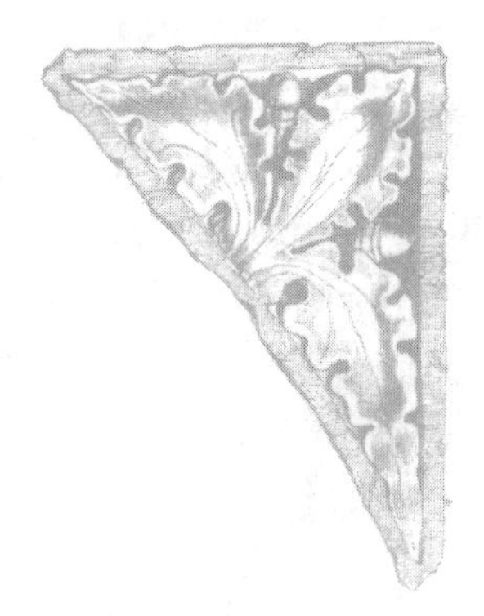

Eleven

THE WILDERNESS
10:34
ALASKA STANDARD TIME
NOVEMBER 25

BENEATH HIS CLOSED LIDS NICHOLAS'S EYES WERE MOVING RAPIDLY back and forth, indicative of deep REM sleep. But Nicholas was not sleeping. He was remembering.

Blood on the oak panelling of the foyer and on the pale blue Aubusson. Blood smears on white silk wallpaper. Sprays of blood on the ceiling. Bloody fingerprints on the glossy ivory woodwork around the doorway. The smell from the death chamber was dark and compelling, and the smell of the human was sick-sweet and nauseating. It was everywhere.

The three corpses, having reverted to their natural state in death, were crumpled on the floor in various stages of mutilation. Moria's neck had been snapped, her throat torn open, both forelegs broken and matted with blood. She had not gone easily. Beneath the north-facing window was Tobias, a magnificent black wolf who in life had been one of the most brilliant biochemists of his time. His spine was twisted into an unnatural position against the wall, his entrails, pink and glistening, spilling out of a wound that split his rib cage. Rene, who was old and sometimes had trouble seeing, was nonetheless a gifted researcher who had been in charge of three of the most important development projects in the corporation. He had been the first to die, his skull shattered by a single blow.

The smell of the human was on their fur, in the carpet, lingering like a miasma in the air. Spatters of human blood were mixed with theirs.

Nicholas dipped his fingers in the blood on Moria's muzzle and brought them to his nostrils, forcing himself to inhale, extracting every nuance of the hated scent from the serum. His head swam with images; revulsion shuddered through him. And he said hoarsely, "Human. How could a human have done this?"

He got to his feet and swung his eyes around the room, scanning for details he might have missed before. There was wildness in his gaze, fever in his eyes. The blood inside his veins was as cold as hate, but pulsed hot enough to burn his skin. He shouted, "No human could have done this!"

He was shaking, quivering with rage and pain. The others in the room could feel his heat and smell the acrid haze of his anguish; a responsive quiver of savagery leapt within them which they controlled only with great effort. His eyes moved from one to the other of them, the guards, the trackers, finally Alexander himself, seeking an answer or a challenge; but all remained silent, as was their place. Only in Alexander's eyes did he see compassion, but it was too little, far too late.

He strode past them, his face marble-white and his breath roaring, and in the wake of him the air was electric. He pushed out of the room toward the back of the house, to the French door that opened onto the cold dark garden, strode through it with a powerful kick that snapped the lock and ruptured the hinges and sent glass spraying like a fine misty rain over carpet and patio; he burst onto the stone courtyard and into the night where he lifted his arms and threw back his head and released a cry, a scream, a howl of torment so intense that it seemed to chill the very marrow of the earth. The night shuddered and writhed with the depth of his pain and when the sound died away the emptiness reverberated.

He dropped his arms and his head, and, alone in the shadows of the winter garden, he stood until the quaking subsided.

After a long time he lifted his head to acknowledge the presence behind him.

"We have his blood scent. My trackers will find him by dawn," Nicholas said. "But the pleasure of killing him will be mine."

Alexander commented neutrally, "It has been centuries since one of us killed a human in anything other than self-defense."

"You don't call this self-defense?" Nicholas gestured brutally toward the slaughterhouse they had left behind. "They were scientists, researchers, *humanitarians*, for the love of all that's holy! He murdered them without warning, without reason. And not just murdered but—" His voice hoarsened and one fist clenched as he ground out the word. "Savaged. Eviscerated. You would have me ignore this?"

Asked Alexander reasonably, "And how will you explain the execution of this human to the authorities who come searching for his killer?"

"What's one dead human more or less to them?" Nicholas's voice reflected impatience and contempt. "Let them dare try to bring us to account. Are you suggesting the weakest of us couldn't handle a dozen or more blundering human policemen?"

Alexander nodded slowly. "So you would kill the policemen. Then you would kill those who came looking for the policemen. Then you would kill to protect those who killed before, and then because some human annoyed you and finally for the sake of killing itself. Where will it stop?"

Nicholas scowled fiercely. "Haven't we been hiding our dead and keeping our secrets long enough? Haven't we turned a blind eye to human atrocities once too often? Maybe the Dark Brothers are right. Maybe it's time to put the balance of power where it belongs."

"And all for the sins of one human."

Nicholas's eyes glittered. "One human who, one time, went one step too far. That's all it takes."

The elder's face remained shadowed, and his silence, this time, went on too long. His voice was carefully devoid of accusation or judgement when he spoke, but nonetheless seemed weighted down with both. "A moral code, once broken, can't be repaired. Think carefully before you plunge us all into war."

"*He* has started the war!" roared Nicholas. "It is done, can't you see that?"

"I think," said Alexander quietly, "you let your passions overcome your judgement."

Nicholas drew in a sharp breath and released it slowly. It was a moment before he spoke, although the beat of his heart was loud in the ears of the other werewolf. "You were a wise and compassionate ruler," he said stiffly. "I, perhaps, am neither. But I will do, as you have done, what the times demand."

He moved back into the room, footsteps crunching loudly on broken glass, and toward the door in long, controlled strides. As he passed him, Alexander said quietly, "It wasn't a human."

Nicholas spun on him, his shoulders square and his nostrils flared. The fire in his eyes leapt brightly for a moment with shock and disbelief, then was ice again. "You are insane, old man." His voice was barely above a growl. "His blood scent was everywhere, even you cannot have failed to read it. You're trying to distract me from what you know I must do—"

Alexander said harshly, "Try again."

Nicholas stared at him.

"Your fingers," Alexander commanded. "Smell them."

Nicholas's eyes narrowed as he looked at the older man. Slowly he lifted his fingers, still stained with the killer's blood, to his nostrils. He stiffened. His features went sharp. He brought his fingers closer.

He raised his eyes to Alexander. "Werewolf," he whispered.

In the pulse of silence he could hear the soft thrum of blood through his elder's veins, the expansion and contraction of lungs with steady, even breaths. He could hear the quiet rustling movements of the werewolves in the other room as they went about the business of attending to the dead; he could hear the painful, sickening sound of blood drying on wounds, muscle and sinew contracting as rigor mortis set in.

Nicholas demanded hoarsely, "How was it done? How could he produce such blood? Which is he, human or werewolf?"

Alexander replied quietly, "Both."

And then his father had taken him to a solitary place and told him an incredible tale of crime and passion, and when it was done the foundation of everything Nicholas had ever believed about himself and his world was changed forever.

Ah, but you let me think it was over, Papa. You lied to me . . .

"Promise me you will read this," Alexander had said when he pressed the red bound book into Nicholas's hands. "All your answers are here."

Nicholas had promised, and he had intended to keep his promise, but more murder and mayhem had intervened. Now, thanks to the human, he was hearing the words his father had been so determined he should know, but what difference could it make now? Nicholas had done what he must for the pack. His choices had been taken from him, and nothing between the covers of that book could restore them.

A moral code, once broken, cannot be repaired.

Ah, but, Father, you did not want to be the one to break it, did you? You knew what had to be done and you would not have history remember you so unkindly. You left it to me . . .

His mother's face, via the video conference call she had placed from Europe, blue eyes flashing, tension palpable even over the inadequate conduit of the monitor. "Five hundred years ago we made a vow," she said, her voice throbbing with passion. "Do you think it was to protect the humans? No, you foolish boy, it was to protect ourselves from the chaos our own savagery can unleash. How can you fail to understand that?"

"There has never in the history of the world been chaos like the chaos that will attack the pack should the truth be known. How can *you* fail to understand that?" Nicholas shouted.

The power of the implication was like ice in his blood and tightened Nicholas's throat. He added hoarsely, "I have only restored the natural order of things."

"Perhaps the natural order of things is not yours to decide."

"You know what has to be done, you've both known for decades! Your great experiment has failed, and our association with humans has led to nothing but disaster. Now that we know what is possible, we must make certain it never happens again. We must do *everything in our power* to make certain of it!"

"Your decision must be read before the Council before it becomes law. Your father and I will oppose you there, and the Council will follow our lead . . ."

But Alexander and Elise Devoncroix had been killed in a senseless street accident only hours before the Council convened. Alexander Devoncroix's reign of human tolerance was no more, and his legacy . . . chaos.

Dead. He is dead.

Ah, the pain.

Four dead in a research facility in New York. The leader of the pack and his queen, gone too. Six dead in a helicopter crash in the wilderness of Alaska.

And it had all begun with one human.

From the Writings of Matise Devoncroix

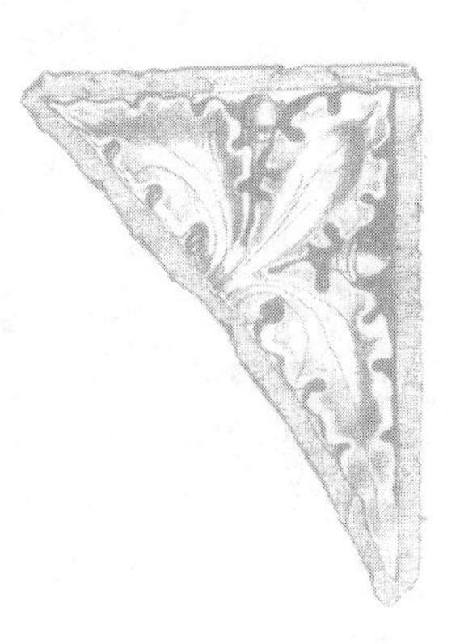

XXII

IT CAME TO PASS THAT THE FEMALE CLIOMEDES, A TRADER IN SILKS OF some modest success, heard of great bargains to be had in a land to the east and insisted on making the journey, even though she was in her fifth month increasing. "Don't be concerned," she told her mate, "for there are two of us, aren't there? If we should travel slowly and the time comes for me to take my wolf form to give birth before we reach the silk merchants, you can negotiate for me."

This seemed a very sensible solution to her mate, and the bargains were exceptionally good, so they set off.

The bargains were even greater than they had expected, and they loaded down their beasts to such an extent that they quickly saw they would never be able to arrive home in time for the birth. Aware of their dilemma, the merchant with whom they had bargained told them of a shorter route he had heard of, though never travelled, that might shorten their time by several weeks.

But the route they were given required crossing mountains and barren fields under the hot sun, and the journey was exceedingly difficult on the gravid female. Soon her time was upon her, and she resigned herself to giving birth in this strange empty land with none of her family around her and nothing but the cries of wild humans at night for company. She comforted herself with the thought that when she returned to civilization she would be very, very rich.

She was to be even richer than she imagined. She and her mate took shelter in a cave that was worn into the highest of seven hills, and she gave birth to not one but two sons. She called them Romulus and Remus, and became the mother of an empire.

By now I'm sure you've realized that most human myths and legends have their bases in reality, although they barely realize it themselves. And you may be sure that whenever there is mention of wolves interacting with the human race, we were, in some form or another, involved. Take, for example, the legends of great men suckled by wolves: Tu Kueh, Zoroaster, Siegfried the hero, Romulus and Remus, among others. For what manner of creatures might suckle at the breast of a wolf mother but rise to walk as humans, except our kind? It is all there for humans to read in their history books, if they but had eyes to see.

It is to the story of Romulus and Remus that I address myself now, and how the great city of Rome grew up around these legendary twins. Twins are such a rarity among us that of course their birth is cause for celebration, and naturally the story of this phenomenon attracted werewolves from far and wide. The human settlers who had spread their encampments over the seven sunny hills must have been quite taken aback by the splendid creatures who descended upon them with their silk tents and gold-spoked chariots and caravans of elaborate furnishings—all to honor the twins who were suckled by a wolf in a cool dry cave in central Italy.

They brought with them the best of a newly civilized world: elaborate plumbing, irrigation and waste-disposal systems, innovative architecture, a taste for luxury and a knack for commerce. As they had done in Greece, the simple shepherds and farmers insisted upon making gods of these brilliant creatures, and few werewolves objected. They took the names Artemis and Juno and Bacchus, and they lived among the people of Rome with all the tenderness and tyranny with which they are depicted in myth.

They were enthusiastic builders, these Etruscan werewolves, and sublime egoists. They designed the most elaborate system of roads and bridges in existence, all leading to their central capital, for where else might anyone wish to go? And what did they care if the humans used that road system to ride out and conquer other humans, for in the end it was only more lucre to fill their coffers, only more humans to adore them. And when the great civilization of Alexander the Great began to crumble and fall, they were poised to step in to pick up the pieces, these new gods with their cynical wit and endless greed. They intended to live forever, but they lived as though there was no tomorrow.

Shall I tell you, then, what happened to that beautiful city of the seven hills? Volumes have been written about its demise, the hows and the whys of it, the mistakes that were made, the bad fortune that couldn't have been avoided. Did they become indolent, these great gods of Rome? Did they become lazy, drunken, careless and disinterested? Perhaps, as they progressed so swiftly into the age of enlightenment, it became too easy for them to laugh at themselves, and therefore for the humans to do the same. Perhaps the answer is as simple this: they gave too much to the humans, educated them too highly, indulged them too well, supervised them too little. They forgot they were supposed to be gods.

Yes, they were hedonists. Yes, they were drunkards and fornicators with humans and wallowers in their own exquisite sensuality. But has there ever been a time when we all were not, to some extent at least, all of those things? They did not desert their holdings, abandon their universities, grow bored with commerce. Yet they watched helplessly as everything they had built was destroyed by the very humans for whom they had built it, and eventually they themselves were cast out of their own paradise. The last great civilization fell to ruin not because its keepers hunted humans, hated humans, or ignored them, but because they loved humans, far too well.

Many say there is a lesson in that for us all today.

But I think the lesson of Romulus and Remus is a much simpler and more immediate one. It always reminds me of Brianna, for she discovered the same truth at a very young age: humans need someone to worship. And a werewolf is nothing without humans to worship him.

XXIII

LONDON, 1928

MATISE

THERE WAS NOT A DAY THAT PASSED OVER THE NEXT TEN YEARS THAT I did not recall, in one manner or another, the night of my Betrayal, or the night of my Horror. Sometimes it was a shadowy shame that lurked in the back of my mind as I prepared for a pack run, a shrinking away from the memory of the time I had answered the call of my nature instead of the call of my sister, and had left her broken and bleeding on the ground. Sometimes it was an awakening in the night with a cry of anguish caught in my chest and a shroud of icy sweat swathing my body and the feel of her, the smell of her and the taste of her in every pore, a fever in my blood and my empty hands stretched out to embrace air. On such occasions I would stumble from my bed and Change in the night and run and run, through cold and wind and snow and rain, in dark, open country or through city streets, a shadow among shadows, running until my mind retreated and the memory faded, and then I would kill, and with the blood of some small creature spurting into my mouth and its death throes weakening between my jaws, the fever would fade, at least for a time. It would fade, but not disappear.

There was no one to whom I could talk about this, no confessor to ease my black and troubled soul, no friend to whom I could entrust the secret of my shame. Sex for us is such a beautifully simple, yet unfathomably complex, thing. When we function true to our nature and all is well, our sexuality is the most perfect part of being werewolf. But when something goes wrong, it goes wrong disastrously. There is no remedy for it. There is no hope.

We learn to arouse and pleasure each other at a very young age. It is a gesture of friendship, of comfort, even of respect. The delight we experience in these human-form pleasures is genuine but shallow, and they are often shared male to male, female to female, brother to sister and by mated couples with those not their mates. The significance of such experiences is little more than a shared meal or a thoughtful gift offered and received; it has nothing at all to do with mating, nor even with love.

In wolf form we share a deeper intimacy that rarely has anything to do with physical pleasure yet is far more meaningful—and in many ways more dangerous—than sex games. In wolf form we are naked to our souls, the only language we speak is the language of truth, and we are as vulnerable—and as powerful—as we will ever be. But because we mate only in wolf form, we must always take care to guard our instincts. One must be far more discriminating about whom one runs with than about whom one has sex with.

We mate once, we mate for grand and passionate love, and we mate for life. We mate with our cousins, our nieces and nephews, our aunts and uncles. The only taboos that exist against mating are between parent and child and between brother and sister. So unthinkable are such pairings that Nature itself has provided a fail-safe remedy against them, for the hormone that is necessary for arousal is simply not released when two such close relatives are involved.

Or at least that is the physiology of it. That's the normal, healthy, *right* way of it. But that was not the way it was with Brianna and me.

I could relive that night a hundred thousand times, each time trying to give it a different ending in my mind, trying to make myself believe I didn't feel what I felt and didn't want what I wanted and, most of all, that I didn't do what I did—but to no avail.

Not even in my imagination—in my haunted, tormented, shamed and desperate imagination—could I betray the truth of it. For I *did* want her, you see. I wanted her with every fiber of my being and every cell in my body, hungrily, desperately, madly. I came to understand, in that moment of blind unreasoning passion, that I had always wanted her just so, the other part of me, the completion of the bond that had begun only hours after my birth when her face, her touch, her scent, the sound of her laughter were imprinted on my senses for all time. Yes, I wanted her. I wanted her emotionally, intellectually, sexually. I wanted her in my blood, in my head, wrapped up inside my soul so deeply she could never escape; I wanted her for my mate and I wanted it so badly I would have killed her for it.

And that, you see, is the shame of it, and the horror. I would have taken her inside my Passion, my poor fragile beloved; I would have let my greed and my lust consume her and she would have paid the price for my love willingly, eagerly. She was my sister, yet she aroused me to the edge of Passion. It never should have happened, but it did. And my punishment for this forbidden lust was in being condemned forever to love the only woman in the world I could never have.

XXIV

We went our separate ways over the next decade, Brianna to London and I to Alaska . . . and Australia and Africa and Egypt and Brazil and Asia Minor and India, anywhere that she was not. And still I saw her face in every crowd, caught the hint of her scent, always just disappearing, at every street corner upon which I paused, and heard her footsteps in every corridor I passed, always just fading away, causing me to turn and search the emptiness with heart pounding and breath stilled. I pray you never know such madness. Yet I could wish no greater gift than that you should know such a love.

I wrote texts and scholarly manuals for the pack; I crossed the ocean in a flying machine not once but many times. I even designed one or two, and watched my designs take shape from imagination to reality much in the way well-crafted words give substance to thoughts. Should I have left the pack when Brianna did? Should I have turned my back on my family, my education, my comfortable and well-fitting position in the carefully ordered social structure to which I belonged? Of course I should have. Do you think I was not tormented every moment of every day by my own cowardice? Yet I returned to the pack when Brianna did not for the same reason I answered the call to run when Brianna could not. Because it was my nature.

My love for Brianna was a fire in my brain, consuming every thought and ambition, devouring reason and philosophy, making me half mad with wanting. But my shame was a force even more powerful, one that a passion as grand as what I felt for Brianna could not subdue. I returned to the pack in a desperate attempt to cure the disease that was my unnatural desire for my sister. But I think I must have known from the beginning that there was no real escape from what I carried within myself.

Eventually I wandered back to Europe, drawn by a dark compulsion I could no easier resist than understand. Brianna was there. The rest of the world held no more charm for me.

I admit a certain fascination for the brazen gaiety with which humans first set about destroying everything they loved and then brashly, determinedly and with more enthusiasm than ever before began to build it all up again. Papa, needless to say, had been right about the war and our position to profit from it. I spent those years of flying machines and exploding weapons exploring the jungles of the Himalayas, so that I barely knew about it except for what I heard in passing; and I remember sending urgent messages to Papa inquiring about Brianna's and Freda's welfare, until I finally received a note saying that a relative of Freda's had taken both girls to his villa in Greece, where they were enduring the "human disturbances" in far greater comfort than was I.

As the second decade of the twentieth century blossomed, the pack was growing in strength and wealth day by day and so, by no small coincidence, were humans.

The nineteen-twenties were grand and glorious times for both our peoples. To the humans we brought stylish motorcars and outrageous fashions, luxury liners and flying ships, moving pictures, rocket science, jazz and a taste for all things decadent and utterly self-indulgent. To us, humans brought banks and railroads, roads and towers, factories and mines and an endless supply of labor with which to run them; in short, wealth. We supplied and they consumed. It was a very satisfactory arrangement all the way around, and already the pack was beginning to call my father Alexander the Great. The sobriquet was meant with affection.

In London, I fell in with a group of human writers—George Wells and Arthur Doyle and Noël Coward, among others—and found them amusing. Over the next few months I turned my hand to writing the kind of thing that entertained humans—under another name, of course—and met with some success. Some of those early tales of fantastical futures and deeply Gothic pasts survive to this day, I believe, and are still delighting humans.

I say it with such dispassion now, but don't you see? I began to love humans because I loved Brianna. Because she had not been away from my thoughts for a single moment in all those years, and because being in the world of humans meant being in her world. I could resist no longer.

And so for some years I lived on the periphery of Brianna's world, moving with ease between the life of the pack and life outside it. I began to travel in the circles of human intellectuals, and I didn't find the company in the least objectionable. I wrote my little books, I roamed around the Continent, I cut a dashing figure among the societies of both humans and werewolves.

It was a grand high time, those middle years of the nineteen twenties, a time of wide flannel trousers and silver flasks, of sporting cars decorated like sailing boats, of lawn tennis and croquet and passionate secret rendezvous in exclusive country houses. Venice became a favorite spot of mine, and the werewolves there most entertaining. I loved Paris, the bustle and the charm, and my parents had so many friends among the human aristocrats there that I was welcome wherever I went. But it was to Britain that I always returned, to the theaters of London and the elegant suite of rooms overlooking Hyde Park. If I could have been said to have a home during these restless years, that was it.

And did I see Brianna in all this time? you will wonder. Ah, yes, I saw her.

I saw her in *Saint Joan* and she brought tears to my eyes. I saw her in *Pygmalion* and she was magnificent. I saw her in *Carmen* and in *La Bohème* and I saw her in a concert entitled "An Evening with Brianna Cross"—she had changed her name, you see, to a nice, human-sounding one—at the Royal Albert Hall. I stood at the back of a standing-room-only audience, so awash in her, so transported by her, that I was oblivious to the roar of applause that went on for curtain call after curtain call, unaware even when the humans began to file out, jostling and pushing me; I simply stood there, still and silent, breathing in her scent and hearing the echo of her voice, until I was the only one remaining inside the theater. And then I left.

That night I found a human woman with red hair and snapping blue eyes, and we danced until we were drunk with dancing, and then I took her to her room and my hands shook as they explored the dark secrets beneath her satin skirts, and my mouth drank of the dewy skin that tasted of Brianna, that smelled of Brianna, that was not and could never be Brianna. Her sweet supple fingers wanted to caress me but I held them tight; her pretty mouth cried out in ecstasy as I pleasured her with my own, suckling her, stroking her, first tenderly, adoringly, then with increasing madness and demand until she writhed beneath my ministrations and gasped for breath. Her skin was drenched and flaming, yet mine was cool and dry. She kissed my lips and begged me to lie with her, but I did not even take off my coat. I held her face hard between my hands and covered her mouth with my own and thrust my tongue deep inside, drinking of her, demanding of her, searching within her for what simply was not there. She melted beneath me, she shuddered in my hands, but what I needed from her she could not give, for she was not, after all, Brianna.

I do not remember the human's name, yet at the end of that night I staggered out into the alley and fell to my knees, retching. I felt an emptiness to the core of my soul.

The next day I sent my card to Freda Fasburg.

XXV

DO YOU REALLY IMAGINE THAT BRIANNA HAD BEEN UNAWARE OF MY presence at all those performances? We travelled in the same circles, we knew the same humans; Noël Coward had on three occasions invited me to parties given specifically to honor Brianna, and I had on all three occasions refused. More than once my eyes had met Freda's, as she watched me from her private box or entered through the stage door, and there had been the warmth of greeting there, but always she had turned reluctantly away. I knew that she lived in Mayfair not far from Brianna, and that they had remained the closest of friends. If Brianna had wanted to see me, Freda could have made it possible. Yet the truth was that I was almost as afraid to face Freda as I was Brianna.

I was therefore surprised when Freda not only acknowledged my card, but agreed to meet me for lunch at Claridges the next day.

"You are the most peculiar fellow," she remarked, after we had kissed, after we had settled down at our corner table with two glasses of cabernet on the white cloth between us. "Everywhere one goes one hears the name Matise Devoncroix, at all the best parties and in all the most fashionable homes, but always I say to myself, No, it certainly cannot be my old school friend Matise, for he would never be so discourteous as to refuse to send me a note, or even to call me on the telephone. And now, after all this time, I find it was indeed you! I can only imagine your busy social schedule has left you no time these past years for old acquaintances."

I smiled at her. "Thank you for coming, Freda."

She reached across the table and clasped my hand, her expression tender. "Did you really think for one moment I would not?"

She was as beautiful as ever, dressed in emerald wool trimmed with ermine and a flirtatious little cloche hat over a tightly pinned and slicked hairstyle that imitated the fashionable bob most flatteringly. She smelled of hyacinths in the dead of winter, and of Brianna. The warmth in her eyes was like the glow of a candle, slowly dispelling the chill in my soul.

I squeezed her fingers, and let the touch say what words could not. In a moment we both picked up our wineglasses.

I said, "How has it been with you, Freda?"

"Few complaints." She sipped her wine. "I have an M.D. degree now, which humans find astonishing—not that a werewolf should practice medicine on humans, but that a female should!"

We both chuckled.

She added, "The work I do on humans is quite interesting, actually. I'm trying to amass data on chromosomal structure as related to abnormalities in humans, or even disease. I hope someday to transfer the findings to werewolf physiology."

I said, with only the smallest note of condescension, "I'm not sure I understand how anything you learn from humans could apply to us."

"Certain rules of physiology apply to all mammals," she replied. "It's possible that the research I'm doing now will one day lead to the cause of anthropomorphism."

I said quietly, "You are a loyal friend."

She lifted her glass to me. "And a brilliant scientist."

"And a brilliant scientist," I agreed, and touched my glass to hers.

I allowed a few moments of companionable silence, of the discreet clatter and stir of the city's finest restaurant, of the taste of one of the better cabernets. Then I said, "You stayed with her the night of our Ascension. But I answered the call of the pack."

It had to be spoken. It was the acknowledgement of a debt, and of a shame.

Her gaze was steady and clear, her tone casual. "The call of the pack has always been easy for me to ignore. It does not make me less of a werewolf."

I inclined my head, lowered my eyes briefly. She sipped her wine. So did I.

I said, "She's done wonderfully, hasn't she?"

"Of course." She smiled. "So have you."

I shrugged.

"Your papa came to the opening of *Carmen*. He sent back his card. She turned him away."

I flinched at this.

"Your mother sends pink roses to the theater with every performance, without fail."

I gazed into my glass. "We never speak of it. But they adore her. They always have." I looked at Freda urgently. "They would welcome her back into the pack in an instant, if only she would—"

But even before Freda lifted her hand to interrupt, I regretted having spoken. "That," she said firmly, "is something *we* never speak of."

The waiter set before us platters of wonderfully rare roast beef and little potatoes basted in oil. The fresh red meat was so tender it practically melted on the tongue.

At length Freda said, "Why did you never send your card backstage?"

I put down my knife and fork, arranging them carefully. I touched my napkin to my lips, and picked up my glass. "Would she have received it?"

Freda's smile was gentle, speculative. "She never had you escorted out of the theater, did she? She has done so with other werewolves before."

I laughed. It was the first spontaneous gaiety I had felt in years. "That is just like her!" I allowed. "Imperious to the last."

Now Freda's smile turned faintly sad. "Little enough compensation, I should think."

She finished her meat, and I finished my wine. I said, "You are beautiful enough to break my heart, Freda."

"We have missed you desperately, Matise," she told me.

I paid, and we walked to the door. We stood on the street with the sounds of traffic and newsboys barking and streetcars rumbling, and I said, "If I sent roses, would she toss them out?"

"Ask her yourself." She pulled a card from her pocket and offered it to me by the corner, her eyes faintly coquettish, mildly challenging. "I'm giving a small dinner tonight. Come at eight."

I looked at the card for a solemn moment, then took it. "I wish you had sent this years ago."

"My darling," she replied with eyes soft, "I did not know your address." She kissed my cheek, lingering briefly to take my scent, and caressed my neck before stepping away. I watched until she was lost in traffic, and then I turned and made my own way back home.

From the Letters of Brianna Devoncroix

XXVI

My dear Matise,

How many letters I have written you over the years, none of them mailed, all of them filled with longing and anger and terrible, terrible loneliness. Childish passions, desperate accusations, selfish needs. I have ached for you. I have wept for you. How could you let me leave you? Why didn't you come with me?

I open my mouth and I can taste you. I close my eyes and I can feel you, I can smell you on my skin and in my hair and in every pore of my body. You are in every note I sing. You think that what happened that night happened only to you, but I share your guilt, your terror . . . your shame.

Those are the letters I have written. And then there are those I have not written. About how I have never, for more than a week or two at a time, not known where you were and what you were doing throughout all these years. You went to the ends of the earth to try to forget about me, didn't you? I had only to go to the world of humans. And those are the letters I didn't write you, because they made me sad and ashamed and I know you wouldn't understand. For in the world of humans, you see, I almost did forget you. I almost did escape what I was.

I wanted to tell you. I wanted to tell you about the first time I walked into a room filled with humans and knew I could enchant them. I could make the hearts of the males beat faster and the females sigh with envy and they whispered, when they thought I couldn't hear, how magnificent I was and how talented and how disturbing. I could make them weep. I could make them tremble. I could make them laugh, and I could make them melt beneath my charm. Ah, Matise, who could resist such marvelous power?

And when I am on the stage . . . when I can hear the roar of their applause, the thrumming of a thousand hearts, quick with wonder and delight and excitement; when the heat of their blood rises from the stands and the thick rich perfume of their adoration flows over me . . . This for me is Passion. This fills my soul and takes me beyond myself and for that brief time, however long it lasts, I *am* the most magnificent creature on earth. Never mind if it is only humans who made me so.

And the first time I made love to a human . . . ah, how to make you understand this? I do adore them, you see. How can I not when they so desperately adore me? Their scent, their manners, their foolishness, their clumsiness, their arrogance—all are endearing to me. And, oh, yes, there is pleasure in being caressed by a male, in being kissed by him and holding my secret tight, and perhaps the pleasure is in the secret, in the wrongness of it. But there is a certain delight, too, in the fullness of their penises and the taste of their sweat, and in the simple, unqualified mundanity of it. And yet the first time I made love to a human I wept for the shallowness of it, for the pity of a race of people condemned to know forever nothing more than this great emptiness that pretends to be a mating . . . and for myself.

He was a darling young man, my first human lover, a Spaniard with thick dark curls and snapping black eyes who claimed to have fought with bulls, though I never smelled any bulls on him. He smelled mostly of sunshine and rich dark wine and lust for me, and those were scents I adored. We danced on a piazza in Italy, I in white silk and he in a deep blue uniform of some sort, and I loved how handsome we were together and how we made all the heads turn and how the humans whispered about the glamorous young actress and the dashing bullfighter. The night smelled, as Italian nights do, of veils of jasmine and riotous roses, and I was quite enchanted.

I took him back to the villa Freda and I had leased for the summer, and, oh, how his heart pounded when I stepped out of the pretty little silk gown, how the fever leapt to his skin and burned in his eyes for him to see me without my clothes. It was a heady feeling, to have such power over him. It was also a little amusing.

We came together with energy and eagerness, though I think I might have startled him a little, my lusty bullfighter, with my enthusiasm for the game. But human males are very easily aroused and quite intent on their own satisfaction, and nothing would stay him from his pursuit of pleasure. All in all, it was a most interesting sensation, and I shall not pretend there was no enjoyment in it for me. There was, in fact, a great deal of enjoyment, but at no point did any of it approach the level of sensation one werewolf can generate within another by so much as a simple meeting of the eyes. And when it was over, I laughed—with surprise, with amazement, with simple bewilderment for the impoverished state of human senses, that *this* should be the pinnacle of their sensual experience.

Laughter, of course, was not an appropriate response at such a moment, and my lover was at first hurt and then enraged. I had no patience for him, for by then I had realized something else: that this sexual act, this shallow imitation of making love, was all that I would ever know of mating. Just like a human, I was condemned to yearn forever to meld my soul with another and to know only this two-dimensional reflection of what I was meant to be. I was filled with such a sorrow that I tell you I was weak with it. I stood by the open window, gripping the sill for support, and I shook with the weight of that great sadness.

The human man—even now his name escapes me—was angry and hurt and his smell was beginning to annoy me. Out of patience with him, I threw a vase at him. It was filled with roses—roses that he had given me, now that I think of it—and that threw my aim off. Roses flew and water splashed and all he got was a little wet as the vase exploded against the wall, but he shouted as though he had been gelded.

The sound of it hurt my ears, and that really was too much. I commanded him to leave and he called me a number of unflattering names and then made the very great mistake of putting his hands upon me. I threw him quite literally across the room, where the weight of his body splintered a very fine Louis Quatorze occasional table before crashing against the wall. It's a wonder I didn't fracture his skull, for I really was beside myself with frustration and impatience.

The commotion roused Freda, who appeared in her nightgown and, after casting me a look of reprimand, went to help the poor dazed and bleeding human to his feet. Somehow she got him into his trousers and helped him gather up the remaining pieces of his pretty blue uniform and saw him out the door. I remember the frightened looks he cast me, and I'm sorry to say I never heard from him again. Sorrier still to report that in Spain, my reputation precedes me, and it is not a very flattering one.

Ah, yes, it's amusing now to look back upon the foibles of both human and werewolf . . . amusing, yes, but bitter also.

I confess that when Freda came back I was laughing, but it was a raw, hysterical kind of laughter that quickly deteriorated into an uncontrolled weeping. She held me for a time, until the worst of it was over, and there was an indescribable comfort in knowing that she understood without my saying a word, she understood precisely why I wept.

I think, sometimes, how it might have been had I not one werewolf in my life to remind me who and what I was. And I think in that case I would not have lived very long.

At length Freda took my face in her hands and said, practically, "You stink of human. You won't get him out of your mind until you get him off your skin."

And so she led me to the bath, which was deep and warm and scented with jasmine, and I sank into it with my face hot and swollen from weeping, too exhausted with emotion to even lift my arms to wash my hair. So she stripped and got in beside me, and scrubbed the smell of human out of my hair, and sponged it off my limbs and from between my legs. And when I began to weep again, she drew me against her breast and held me there, stroking my wet tangled hair, until I was calm once more.

I said at length, in a voice thick with spent tears and flat with weariness, "Why did you come with me? You had a chance with the pack. You should have stayed."

"Silly girl. What use have I for the pack? They should come begging to me."

That almost made me smile, but brought a new flood of tears to my eyes instead. I blinked and swallowed and curled my fist against her slim strong neck. I said, "You might have had a mate. If you had stayed. . . ."

She replied, with only the slightest tinge of impatience, "I will have a mate if I choose. We Fasburgs have mated very well among ourselves without the help of the pack for centuries now."

"What about Matise?"

It really was the most extraordinary thing. I don't believe we had spoken your name except in passing since we left you that night in that woods outside the Palais. Certainly I had not planned to speak of you then, and never in that context. Yet it was said, and I really don't know why.

Freda regarded me steadily, in the way that she does when she is determined to show no surprise. "What about him?"

I think it was a means of punishing myself, you see. Or perhaps it was simply another attempt—like having sex with a human—to exorcise you from my brain. I didn't mean to hurt Freda, I know that. I meant to hurt myself.

I pushed gently away from her, the water rippling between us as I moved. I said, quite as matter-of-factly as I could, "Well, you're in love with him, everyone knows that. You should mate with him, and be daughter to the leader of the pack."

Every word was a dagger in my heart. To think of giving you up, even to one I loved as dearly as Freda, especially to one I loved as dearly, was exquisitely painful to me. And yet—and this is odd—it was also hopeful in some way. For to have you near me again, even if it was only as the mate to someone I loved, was almost worth the sacrifice.

But then I saw the hurt and the embarrassment in Freda's eyes, and an awful moment of clarity came, and nothing was worth the pain I had caused my only friend—but it was too late to take it back. She *was* in love with you, you see. I had never been sure of it until then, but it was so clear upon her face: she loved you quite desperately. Oh, my darling, even if I never have the courage to mail this, I hope you will come to understand that truth someday. She deserves that much. But I beg you, do not love her back. I couldn't bear it if you loved her back.

Freda said, a little coolly, "Being daughter to the leader of the pack has not benefited you much, has it?"

That stung, almost as much, perhaps, as had my observation about her secret adoration for you. She saw it in my eyes, and the quick apologetic softening of her features made me ashamed, because she has always been so much nobler than I.

She said, "I am not in love with Matise. But even if I were, it wouldn't matter. Because . . ." And she held my gaze, daring me to deny her next words. "He is quite desperately in love with you, isn't he?"

And so there it was, our fierce secret a secret no longer, and I was filled with horror and rage that she had discovered it, but also with a slow, long wave of relief, because it was a dreadful thing to keep such a secret all by oneself. I wanted to deny it, for the sake of form if nothing else, to be angry and indignant or laughing and dismissive, but I looked into her eyes and knew how foolish that would be.

So I swallowed back all my hurt and my pride and my confusion and my longing, and, helpless and afraid beneath the enormous truth of it, I simply nodded.

I waited to see repulsion fill her eyes, for to suspect a thing and to see it confessed are two quite different matters, aren't they? Yet I should have remembered that this was the woman who had covered my shame for over ten years, who had fought for me when even my own family had deserted me, who had held me tight in the bosom of her protection when all others had turned their backs on me.

All I saw in her eyes was sorrow, and she opened her arms to me as she had done so many times before, and drew me close.

I tell you, without her I should have died of loneliness a thousand times during those years. I should have simply died.

And I have told you all this, my dear, so that I might now find a way to tell you about my Walter . . .

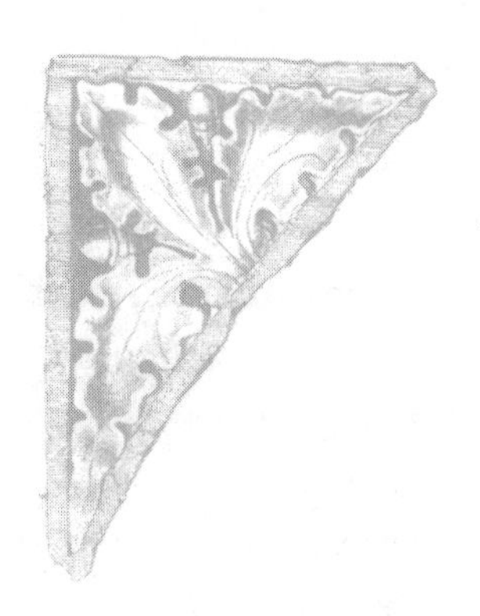

From the Writings of Matise Devoncroix

XXVII

THIS IS HOW IT WAS THAT WINTER NIGHT AT THE MAYFAIR TOWN house of Freda Fasburg: a dozen Rolls and Bentleys parked along the street that was banked with snow, streetlights making wet yellow pools upon the pavement and a curving walkway lined with colorful Japanese lanterns, the sound of music and voices from inside and shapes moving against the tall front windows, raising glasses, bowing heads. The door was opened by a liveried butler and warmth and sound spilled out, scented with the perfumes of Chanel and Devoncroix, roasting meats, candle wax, scotch and gin and rich red wines, cigarette smoke, leather, wool carpets, fine woods, books, fireplaces burning hickory wood, fresh flowers and Brianna, yes, Brianna.

My eyes scanned for her as I was helped out of my coat, as I gave over my gloves and my hat, but little was visible of the room beyond. Then Freda came out with both hands extended, stunning in a black Worth gown trimmed in silver, and she kissed me and welcomed me and took me into the room filled with humans and clatter and music from the phonograph. "Darling, do you know everyone?" and I made my bows to the Prince of Wales and Princess Marina of Greece, and to my young friend Noël and the Duke of Kent, and to George Wells and Lady Colefax and a dozen or so others; and my eyes were searching, my heart was pounding, until I saw her there, halfway down the curve of the staircase, so that she was framed by the arch of the doorway in a perfect pose, my Brianna.

She wore a beaded red gown cut just below the knee and with barely any straps at all on her shoulders, and sheer silk stockings that glistened where the light caught them, and red velvet shoes trimmed with glittering sequins on the crossed straps. She had a paisley silk scarf, embroidered with metallic threads and trimmed with glass beads, knotted on the side of her head, and beneath it a froth of red curls brushed her shoulders, creamy white, strong and perfect. We looked at each other, and I heard her heartbeat but saw nothing in her face, smelled nothing on her skin of either joy or dread, welcome or despite. She was an actress.

She came down the stairs, pretty knees flashing, glass beads jangling, and Freda dropped my arm and took a small step away from me, and others saw her and began murmuring welcomes like "There she is!" and "The lady of the hour!" and "My dear, that gown!" Brianna grinned and added a little bounce to her step, making the glass beads swing, and declared, "I wanted to make an entrance. Did I succeed?"

There was laughter and a smattering of applause as every human in the room fell beneath her spell, as did one werewolf, who in truth had never been completely free of it.

Brianna curtsied to the Prince and he kissed her hand, and she greeted others in turn with hands clasped warmly, cheeks offered to be kissed, flirtatious gestures and pretty moues and tinkling laughter and dancing eyes. And then at last she turned to me.

Caruso was on the phonograph, though I cannot for the life of me remember what he sang. Every other detail of that moment is strikingly clear, however: the pattern of the Aubusson that she crossed to reach me, red and pink roses on a deep blue background; the warmth of the fire upon my left side, and my right side growing suddenly chill with apprehension; the soaring of my heart, the clenching of my muscles; Freda, so still behind me; and the clicking, jingling sound of those little glass beads on Brianna's gown, the whisper of silk on her thighs, her sweet cinnamon-flowers scent, the rush of blood in her veins and finally, finally, the clasp of her hands on mine, the brush of her small, firm breasts against my chest, the press of her lips on my cheek. I was for a moment dizzy with her nearness.

"I thought you would never come," she said softly against my neck.

I looked into her eyes when she stepped back. "I thought you would never ask."

And then someone, it might have been Noël, remarked, "And so you know our lovely Matise already, Bri. I might have known, for you always do have the best of the crop falling at your feet."

Brianna laughed and wound her arm through mine with a possessive familiarity and turned to the room at large. "Everyone, may I present my brother, renowned world traveller and writer of the most deliciously naughty books! Isn't he handsome?"

And someone exclaimed, "Not a bit of it! You don't look a thing alike!"

And someone else: "What secrets have you been keeping, eh? Two mad talents in the same family?"

And there was a great deal of chatter and movement and witty repartee, and I held my own within it, as did Brianna, although at times her laughter sounded so brittle I thought it might shatter like glass upon the air.

I was sorry I had come. And desperately, desperately glad.

We had our dinner at a long polished table set with gold serviettes and cut crystal, a dozen candles banked by fresh flowers; Brianna at one end of the table and I at the other. Freda was an incomparable hostess and Brianna an unflappable wit, and conversation never lagged. There was a human countess on my left, full of bosom and sharp of tongue, and I flirted with her shamelessly. We all drank a good deal of champagne.

Said George jovially, "I refuse to believe you are related to that exquisite creature. Why have you never let it about?"

And the countess said, with her hand upon my thigh, "Your sister is the most charming of young ladies and enormously talented, but you, my dear boy, are quite the most comely member of the family, it's easy to see. Where did you get that gorgeous hair?"

"A little shop in Knightsbridge," I replied lightly. "I shall be happy to take you there when you have a free afternoon."

Her eyes twinkled at me over the rim of her glass, and she squeezed my thigh. I let her.

Afterward we had brandy and the humans smoked cigarettes, and there was one room devoted to cards and politics and another where the furniture was pushed back for dancing, for Freda, the most inimitable of hostesses, entertained in a lavishly casual style. I adored to dance and took Freda as my partner, and we cut quite a figure on the floor, she as light as air and as graceful as a feather floating upon it. Brianna flitted from one room to another and gaiety followed wherever she was, this darling of the humans, this mistress of enchantment. When she danced, all others left the floor to admire her. When she laughed, the whole room joined in. When a debate between Wells, who was a renowned socialist, and the Prince of Wales—who was not—became a little too heated, she sat upon the Prince's knee in a most outrageous fashion and had him chuckling within minutes. She was truly incomparable.

Freda swept another glass of champagne off a silver tray and handed it to me, sipping from one of her own. "It's good to have you back among us, Matise," she said, contentment in her tone. Yet there was a touch of wistfulness there too. "How I wish we could be the happy threesome again."

"You do have a fine life here among the humans," I agreed, lifting my glass. "One could almost be tempted to stay."

She looked at me seriously. "I wanted you to see it. I wanted you to understand."

But now I was curious. I lowered my voice. "With whom do you run, Freda, and where? This is all very grand—" I made a gesture to include the room and all it occupants. "But it cannot satisfy who we are."

She shifted her gaze away, but not before I saw the disappointment there. "I wanted you to understand," she repeated softly. And then her expression brightened, and she raised a hand to someone across the room, and patted my arm and left me.

There was a commotion of gaiety from the other room, and a raucous ragtime tune on the phonograph that I recognized. I put down my glass and went to observe, and what I saw made me smile with all the humans, in sheer delight and admiration of the spirit that was Brianna.

She was engaged in the complex steps of a brash American dance that involved much prancing, posturing and flirtatious glances over one's shoulder, and she had long since left her partner behind. The crowd had gathered in a circle around her, cheering the steps, hooting when she flipped up the hem of her skirt to show her knees, enjoying the performance. I worked my way to the front, and when she spun around and flung out her arm I caught her hand and swung her around and back into the center of the circle as my partner. She laughed and tossed back her head and we finished the dance together in high style, our timing perfect, laughter bubbling like champagne in our eyes and in our throats, delighting in each other and in what we were—children again, for the briefest of times, joyous and alive.

Afterward everyone cheered and applauded, and Brianna and I, flushed with exertion and breathless with pleasure, were jostled apart. Someone slapped me on the back. "I think you must be related after all. Damn fine show, my boy!" I saw Freda, standing near the door, but she wasn't smiling, and when she saw me she turned away.

Towering above the crowd I saw a bobbing purple feather that signalled the approach of the countess. I snatched up two glasses of champagne and departed by the other door.

Brianna was on the terrace, oblivious to the cold in her flimsy, almost strapless little gown, as of course she would be. However she might like to pretend otherwise, she was, in essence, werewolf, and it thrilled me in some obscure way to be reminded of it thus. I handed her a glass of champagne and stood beside her in the dark, sipping my own. Light from the windows pooled and played on the snow-dusted stones around us; the laughter and voices behind us could have belonged to another world. Our breath frosted on the air, and the night was thick-tasting, rich and cold.

I put my hand on her back, warm bare skin welcoming my fingers, and just rested it there. At length I spoke. "So much to say."

She sipped her champagne. "Yes."

I cast about for where to begin. "You have two new sisters and a brother."

"All strong werewolves, I hope, healthy and normal."

"Yes."

"A great comfort to our parents, I'm sure."

"Brianna, they're brokenhearted over losing you. If you would just—"

"My, my, if you've come to start an argument, Mr. Devoncroix, I'm afraid I really must ask you to leave." Her voice was light but had a brittle edge, which she softened with a quick swallow of champagne. She turned to me then, her eyes glittering in the dark. "They all want me now, you know. They buy tickets to my performances, they come to hear me sing—and I always have them removed from the theater. You're the only werewolf I've ever allowed to stay."

I said impatiently, "Brianna, don't be foolish. You can't take revenge on the entire pack for the mistakes of a few. Most of them don't even know why you left the pack."

She thought about this for a moment, then shrugged. "Perhaps you're right. It's pointless to punish them for what they cannot help. What a pity no one ever showed the same consideration to me."

"Are you quite finished? I can't believe Freda puts up with this self-pitying blather day and night, but who else is there?"

She regarded me for a moment, then fought the corner of a rueful grin. "She doesn't," she admitted. "And there is no one else."

She glanced over at the darkened winter garden with its high brick wall and single snow-tipped evergreen tree. I put my arm around her shoulders, and she leaned her head upon mine. We were silent, and warm and comfortable together, and for the first time in ten years, I felt complete.

She said, "You smell like the wild green woods of home."

I kissed her hair, tenderly, as a brother would do. "I have missed you every single day of my life."

"I've hardly thought of you at all."

"Heartless liar."

Suddenly I was eager to be away from this place of humans, away from their smell and their chatter and their ceaseless shallow energy, and to be alone with Brianna, just she and I and the endless night filling up the emptiness of all the lost years. "Brianna, come with me," I said. "Let's go for a drive. I have a Stutz Bearcat—"

She laughed, a lovely musical sound full of delight. "Of course you do!" Then she cut her eyes away, pretending interest in what remained of her champagne. "I can't. I have a late engagement."

I was disappointed to the core of my soul. I dropped my arm from around her shoulders. "So. You haven't forgiven me."

She began in the light false tone of a human. "There was nothing to—"

But before she could finish I seized her shoulders and turned her to me, blood rushing, chest tight. "It was my sickness, not yours, Bri!" I insisted lowly. "You are *not* to blame for what happened that night, and that's what I've wanted to tell you all these years, that's the only thing. Do you think I don't know how you must despise me—do you think I don't despise myself? But it was me and me alone—it had nothing to do with you!"

"It had everything to do with me!" she cried, and now I saw the anguish in her face I had hoped never to see again, now I saw the torment and the desperation and the longing, and that I had brought that look to her face tore at my heart.

"Do you want to know if I have missed you, Matise?" Her color was high and her eyes were bright and I could feel her blood thrumming in her veins beneath my grip. "I have made a *life* of missing you! I awake in the morning missing you and close my eyes at night missing you and with every bite I eat I miss you and with every sip of wine! The sunshine smells like you, did you know that? And so does the rain. I hear your voice on the wind and your heartbeat in the silence. You are *here*," she said, and pressed her fist into her breastbone. Her face was wet with tears now, and her voice failed her. She repeated in a whisper, "You are here."

And then she looked up at me with all the helpless longing of my own wounded soul and I gathered her into my arms and kissed the tears from her cheeks and pressed her into the thunder of my heartbeat and the roar of my breath and I felt weak with the adoration of her. I simply held her like that, enfolded in her and she in me, for the longest time.

"Brianna." I took her face in my hands, trying to press my urgency into her mind. "Papa is in Paris. Come with me, talk to him. The pack scientists are doing amazing research into physiology. If you would let them help you—"

"If I would let them help me, what?" Again her voice took on that high brittle note, and she pulled away from me. "I would no longer be able to arouse my own brother? No, Matise, this sickness goes deep in me and it's not something your scientists can cure."

"Is that it, then? Are you so afraid of me, of what I might do—"

"Yes!" she cried. "Yes, I'm afraid! I'm afraid of what I might do to you, of what being with me will do to you! Matise, you're a strong werewolf with a bright future and a life that doesn't include me—"

"There is no life without you!"

She drew in a sharp breath, and swiped at her eyes with the back of her hand. "Then perhaps you'd better find one. I have."

"Here? Among humans?"

"This is where I belong."

"Brianna." I tried to gentle the frustration in my voice, and I reached for her hand. "Come away with me. I can't hear my own thoughts in this place. We'll drive to the country, where the air is still and the snow is deep, and we'll find a hill to sit upon, and we'll talk the night away like we used to."

She shook her head, and I smelled her regret and her pain. And then her gaze flickered over my shoulder, and she straightened her own shoulders and composed her features. I heard her heartbeat slow. A moment later the door opened and a human came outside, smelling of bay rum and expensive leather and the fur of dead animals.

"My word, Brianna," he exclaimed. "What are you doing out here without your stole?"

She went to him and let him drape the carcass of minks over her shoulders, and she kissed him lightly on the lips and tucked her arm through his. He was blond and tall and well formed in that overbred way of human aristocrats, but he had the smell of too much wealth and too little ambition about him. His lazy eyes passed over me without particular interest, but without challenge either.

"Darling, you're just in time to meet my dear brother Matise Devoncroix," Brianna said. "Matise, this is Walter, Lord Pennington." I remember how very steady her eyes were, how cool the scent from her skin, as she added simply, "My fiancé."

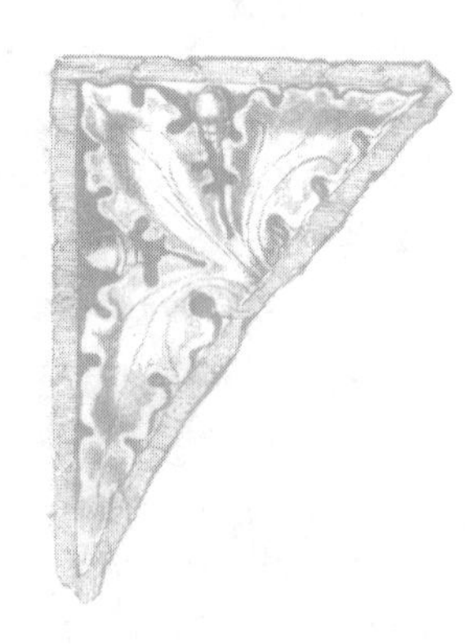

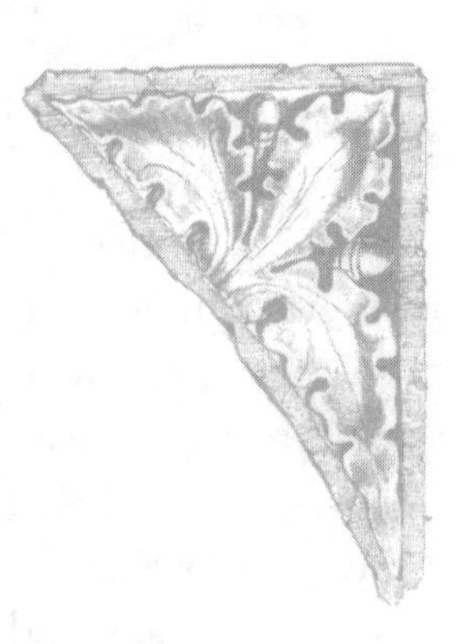

XXVIII

He came to every performance of every show I was in for over a year. He sat always in the same place: third row center, the first to be seated and the last to depart. Many threw roses at my feet when the performance was done; I stood in a veritable shower of roses as I took my bows, but not one came from him. Many tried to gain my favor backstage—among them my own parents, whom I turned away, though you'll never know the pain it cost me—but he never knocked upon my door. My dressing room was awash in flowers, but none were from him. Many stood outside, begging to catch my eye as I left each evening, but though I took up a habit of searching the crowd, he was never among them. Every night he sat there, third row center, impeccably groomed in gloves and tails, smelling faintly of pomade and cabernet and those odd rum-soaked cigars humans like: attentive, intense, *present*, almost as much a part of the show as was the lighting or the orchestra. Ah, yes, he was an impudent creature, this aristocratic human, the Earl of Pennington, yet I confess his plan to intrigue me was quite effective.

It was a year before we met, and by then I had known and discarded a dozen human lovers, but Walter, though he had never so much as kissed my hand, was the most faithful of them all.

There is a wildness in me, my dear, a need to hunt. Never doubt that. As surely as any female among us, I feel the call of the night, the heated stirring of the blood, the lure of prey. My prey upon this occasion was one Walter, Lord Pennington. I only hoped he would not be as unsatisfactory as my previous choices had been.

"You really are quite cruel, Brianna," Freda remarked as we stalked my quarry under pretense of a casual afternoon stroll in Hyde Park. "What will you do with this silly human if you find him?"

I had found him already, for his scent was familiar to me and easy to follow, and I knew that he walked arm in arm with a human female not half a mile beyond. "Why, I'll pluck off his limbs one by one and use his bones to clean my teeth, what do you suppose?"

"It isn't kind to trifle with their emotions."

That made me laugh. "My dear, you must do me a favor and ask any of those with whom I've trifled whether they minded or not. As though you have a right to talk, with your horrid medical experiments."

She scowled. "They are not horrid. They are perfectly acceptable standard medical practices—for humans."

I grimaced. "You cut open their dead bodies."

"Only after you are finished with them," she returned dryly.

I linked my arm through hers and directed her down a curving path that would intersect that of the two humans. For all her high-sounding words, Freda enjoyed our little game as much as I did, and I saw her repress a grin behind her impatient-looking scowl when I spotted my Lord Pennington and placed a warning finger across my lips.

Freda fell a pace behind as I stepped out upon the path directly in front of the gentleman and his lady. I pretended a great astonishment and cool indignation as he stopped and lifted his hat to me.

"My dear sir," I declared, "I do believe you are following me. Must I call the police?"

He showed no surprise, which I liked. In fact, his lips softened at one corner with a smile as he made his bow. "My dear Miss Cross, you flatter me with the suggestion. Please allow me to introduce myself. Walter Edgecourt, Lord Pennington."

I extended my hand with fingers down and wrist up, and he brought his lips within a fraction of an inch of touching my fingertips, so close I could measure the heat of his breath through my gloves and feel the throb of his pulse. All the while his eyes held mine, and I was struck by the quiet, almost cold, intelligence there. They were gray, his eyes.

At length he released my hand and said, still not allowing his gaze to stray from mine, "Miss Brianna Cross, may I present Miss Dorian Winstock. Miss Winstock, Miss Cross."

Oh, the smell of dislike was bitter on her, and the bristling female hormones of defensive jealousy added an amusing spice. She bowed politely to me, but her tone was withering. "Oh," she said. "You are the actress."

I smiled at her, took a step closer and lowered my voice confidentially. "Oh, my dear girl," I assured her, "I am so much more than that."

I saw Walter's lips twitch with amusement, and the girl's eyes grew cloudy with confusion and uncertain insult, but already I had become tired of her. I extended my hand to Freda. "Do you know my friend Freda Fasburg? Freda, Lord Pennington."

He bowed to her. "I am acquainted with your uncle, Miss Fasburg."

She replied, in that way she has when she is growing bored, "How nice for you."

I cast her a quelling look. "I am giving a small supper at my home Friday night after the performance," I told Walter. "I wonder if you would like to come." And I glanced at his companion without interest. "Alone."

The little human female drew herself up like a toad and even her spit curls quivered in outrage, but Walter's eyes took on a spark that was at the same time both hard and amused. "How kind you are to think of me," he replied. And though it was not an acceptance, I knew he would be there.

And I was right.

Freda accuses me of tormenting my human lovers, and it hurts me that she should say so, because I do adore them. Yet I think that as much as I love them, I also hate them and their delightful, decrepit, disorderly world in which I am forced to live, for what they are and what I am not; or perhaps I envy them the innocence of stupidity that refuses to allow them to aspire to anything more. Perhaps the answer is much simpler. I may adore them but I also despise them. Because in the end, you see, they quite simply are not you.

At any rate, I do give lovely parties. And I try always to be on my best behavior for them. On the night that Walter was to come, I was as enchanting as I have ever been: I played the piano and the violin, I served roast oysters and magnums of champagne, I made everyone laugh with outrageous stories of my exploits. I wore a particularly fetching shade of apricot chiffon and a heady Devoncroix perfume. But midnight came and went, as did 1 A.M., and 2. And Walter did not come.

How cool he had been at the performance that evening, occupying his usual seat, applauding in his usual way, even smiling at me as I took my bow. I was insulted, as you can imagine, and quietly furious. Yet the later it grew, the angrier I became, the more delightful I was to my guests. It was only a pity I had not invited anyone I cared to seduce.

By a quarter till three I was saying good night to the last of my guests when I heard the crunch of a footstep upon the walk, caught a whiff of a familiar scent. I turned quite casually back into the house, but did not close the door.

I went down to the kitchen, where the girl was just doing up the last of the glasses. I bade her good night—which only shows that I can, on occasion, be generous with humans—and she scrambled wide-eyed into her coat and hat before I changed my mind. I put away the quail and the biscuits, I drained someone's glass which still had plenty of bubble, I scooped a few salmon eggs onto the tip of my finger and licked them off. At length I said, without turning, "And so, Lord Pennington, you do grace us at last with your presence."

He asked, "How did you know it was I?"

"I could smell you."

"I'm not sure I shouldn't be insulted by that."

I heard his footsteps cross the floor, echoing satisfactorily on the cool stones, but I busied myself by twisting the cork out of another bottle of champagne with my fingers and did not look around.

"What do I smell like?" he inquired.

"Cigars. India silk and wool with snow on it." The cork released with a small pop and I splashed champagne into a glass until it foamed over the top. "Hair cream. Napoleon brandy. Moroccan leather and old books and ink from a well and shoeblack's polish. Oil from a motorcar and slush from the streets, which I suspect you will find splashed upon your trouser cuffs." I turned and thrust the champagne glass at him. "Also, the roast chicken and buttered potatoes you had for supper, along with a not particularly interesting claret. A pity. You would have fared much better here. I served oyster and quail."

He accepted the glass with a raised eyebrow. "Remarkable. But then, I always knew you were an extraordinary woman."

I gave him a cool smile and turned to fill my own glass. "You have no idea."

I leaned against the butcher's table as I sipped my champagne and surveyed him at length. Most humans, I have noticed, are uncomfortable with prolonged silence; few, if any, are able to withstand my gaze for such an uninterrupted length of time. The Earl of Pennington stood bareheaded in a wool greatcoat and slush-splashed trouser cuffs, sipping his champagne, and did not flinch. He rose in my estimation by the moment.

I said at last, "And that's it, then? No apology?"

He replied without hesitation, but with very little sincerity either. "If one is owed, it is yours."

I tried to keep the irritation from my tone. I had, after all, gone to some lengths to obtain oysters on such short notice. "When one shows up for supper five hours late, an apology might be the least that is owed." I felt it unnecessary to point out that there were dozens—no, hundreds—of humans who would have fought for the invitation he had so casually ignored.

A cool smile lit up his eyes. "My dear Miss Cross. Surely you don't think I have spent the last two hundred and eighty-nine nights in the theater, worshipping at your feet, only to share my first personal encounter with you with a dozen others, do you?"

I could smell the sex on him, rich and dark. It made my heart beat faster. "Nicely said," I allowed.

I refilled my glass, but his was barely touched. We stood, separated by eight feet of stone floor, overhead copper pots and drying herbs, and we gazed at each other for a time. My kitchen, I should say, although quite modern with its porcelain electric stove and mahogany icebox, its three big sinks and long, scarred chopping tables, was not necessarily the most inviting of rooms in which to entertain a suitor, and I might have suggested we adjourn to one more conducive to pleasant conversation. But I was still annoyed. The kitchen, with its rough walls and stone floor and shadowy lighting, had the feel of a dungeon about it, which suited my mood very well.

I said curiously, "Why did you attend all of those performances, then? Surely you had other things to do with your evenings."

And he said, gray eyes steady, "I was quite compelled, you see, to discover what kind of creature you were. Surely no human has ever possessed such a voice."

Now *this* was intriguing. "And?" I prompted. "What kind of creature have you determined I am?"

He studied his glass for a moment, golden effervescence rising, dissipating, rising again. "I should say an angel, but I suspect you would laugh if I did."

I obliged him by laughing.

He met my gaze. "I think your power comes from a darker source."

Oh, how he thrilled me, this pale blond human with his narrow nose and sharp cheekbones and gray, gray eyes. The smell of lean, raw strength, determination and greed; good and comforting smells. Avarice, certainty, unvarnished sexuality, these were the things that oozed from his pores, that flowed into me and made me hungry for him.

I crossed to the icebox, intending to take out the platter of quail and make a picnic before the fire in the drawing room. I saw instead a plate of raw beef heart, sliced and ready to be fried for my breakfast, and my mouth filled with saliva. I took out this plate.

"Are you in love with me, Lord Pennington?" I inquired.

He replied without hesitation, "I am."

I smiled, and without removing my gaze from his, I plucked up one of the raw, blood-dark slices of heart from the plate and tore into it with my teeth.

I tell you, his gaze did not waver. Bloody juices dribbled down my chin and I wiped them with my fingers, but he did not flinch. He put aside his champagne glass and crossed the room to me.

His scent overwhelmed me, muting even the lovely sharp taste of the bloody heart, and the sound of his pulses, and his heat; they filled my senses and left me still. He stood very close to me, so that the lapels of his greatcoat brushed the chiffon that covered my breasts, and he looked hard into my eyes, and he reached behind me to the plate on the butcher's table and his long thin fingers closed around a slice of heart, and he brought it to his mouth and, without blinking or shifting his gaze, he bit into it, he tore off the flesh, he filled his mouth with it, he chewed.

The whooshing, pulsing, thundering of blood through veins, valves closing, heart pumping. The click of his teeth, the contractions of his throat, the rush of his breath, the smell of blood. The heat rising as he touched my hair with damp red fingers, then his mouth seized mine and I swept my tongue inside and greedily gathered the bloody juices that lingered there, gathered them, suckled them, swallowed them, and his tongue probed my mouth for the same; ah, a savage mating of raw need it was, a primitive, glorious feast of sensual abandon shared with a worthy mate. He tore the scarves from my hair and the fabric from my shoulders and placed his hot, biting, bloody kisses there. I thrust my hands to his waist, tearing at the buttons of his trousers, and I demanded huskily, breathlessly, "Will you have me now, my Lord Pennington? Will you take me here on the floor like the animal you think I am?"

To my surprise, he caught my hands and held them hard, though I struggled and it must have taken all his strength to do so. His eyes were ablaze above my face, and his breath was hot and tasting of our raw feast and steely need and me. He had my wrists in both his hands, pressed close together, and he brought them between our bodies, next to his chest, and he said, low and harsh, "No."

I could have broken his grip, of course. I could have snapped his bones like kindling wood and tossed him across the room. It was not his physical strength that held me, you see, but his force of will. This brave, reckless, foolish human who dared to tame a werewolf . . . ah, my love, how could I help but adore him? How can you blame me for doing so?

"No," he said, and I drank in the taste of his breath and his perspiration and the heat in his eyes. "When I have you, it will be as the princess you are, and in circumstances befitting your station. When I have you, beloved Brianna, it will be as no man has ever had you before. It will be celestial, it will be wicked, it will be unforgettable. I will have nothing less. You deserve nothing less."

And then, incredibly, he released my wrists and stepped away from me. "Until then, *chérie*, remember." He touched a finger to his lips, and placed it lightly upon mine. *"Vous êtes adorée."*

And then he left my kitchen, and my house.

And unforgettable it was, making love with Walter. Do you notice how I said that? For yes, it is possible to make love with a human—just as it is possible to have dark, wicked, wet and writhing sex with them, oh, yes, and to melt with weakness from the joy of them and cry out with laughter in the midst of it from the pure intensity of pleasure they provide. Walter showed me all of this with his body, his mouth, his clever, knowing hands. He was not afraid of me, you see. He was not shocked by me or discouraged by me or threatened by me. There was a part of him, I think, that was so completely unreachable, nothing could cause him shock or fear, and that in itself was intriguing to me. But despite this—or perhaps because of it—I sometimes looked deep into those cold gray eyes and thought I saw a part of my soul there.

Yet I do precede myself. Walter's courtship of me was long and deliberate and thorough—in a wonderfully perverse, coolly mocking way. He sent me a single blood-red rose with a diamond pin in the shape of a heart attached. It made me laugh because it reminded me of our first outrageous feast together, and you must admit, few humans have so subtle a sense of humor. He took me to dine at his married sister's house, and while the poor woman was desperately trying to make polite conversation with the outspoken actress, his cool, deft fingers were quietly removing my garter under the table.

He was a master of wicked imagination and clever invention, and with him I was above all things never bored. He tantalized me in the most delicious ways with his sensual games, but it was not until the weekend he invited Freda and me—along with several others, of course—to his house in the country that we had sex in the way of humans. That was weeks after we first had met and the anticipation was in itself a sexual experience.

Freda never approved of Walter, but then, she didn't approve of any of my human lovers—which is odd, when you think of it, for it was she who had made me comfortable in human society in the first place, and without her introductions I should have known none of them. But for some reason she took a particular dislike to Walter; I think, perhaps, because she knew he had captured a part of me no human had ever dared touch before.

"He is the most dangerous kind of human, Brianna," she told me. "He is wealthy, he is powerful and he is clever. You would do better to stay with your Italian painters and Irish pony-trainers. Nothing good can come from this liaison."

"Except, perhaps, my happiness."

I remember that night so clearly. Walter's estate was set on several thousand acres of rolling meadowland in Yorkshire, where the nights are cool and the air is bright with stars. His house was one of those architectural nightmares of which humans are so fond—big and old and drafty and rambling, steeped in the smells of a dozen generations of human misdeeds, fading carpets, ancient timbers, birthings and deaths. I rather liked it.

I sat upon the window seat in the tapestry-draped embrasure of my bedchamber, painting the nails of my toes a delicious shade of apple red to match the beaded gown I planned to wear to dinner. Of course we dressed very formally for dinner, but I had a pretty pair of open-toed shoes and I knew such a subtle indiscretion would amuse Walter. The twilight was long, as it is in the north, and a pale moon hung above the tree line. The taste of the breeze through the open window was sharp and clean. Life seemed lovely to me, and simple to understand.

"Your happiness is cheaply purchased," Freda retorted.

She was already dressed for dinner, in a gorgeous jade silk with a chiffon jacket that flowed and billowed marvelously as she paced. She makes a striking figure wherever she goes, of course, and in whatever she wears, and I've often thought what a shame it is that such beauty is wasted upon those who haven't the courage to appreciate it.

I said, stretching out one foot to admire the effect of the paint, "I really think it must be against some kind of protocol to speak so harshly of one's host in his own house. What has he ever done to offend you, anyway?"

"It is not what he has done but what he is."

That made me laugh. "One might say the same thing about either one of us!"

But I couldn't even coax a smile from her. "You are naive about the ways of humans, Brianna. You have no idea what they are capable of. You throw yourself into their graces without the first care as to their nature—"

"Oh, great gods!" I was becoming impatient. "From you of all people!"

"It is precisely *because* my family has lived so closely with them all these generations that I know to be wary. And this Walter of yours is a most peculiar creature, Brianna—"

I started laughing again, because I could imagine, at that moment, Walter's father belowstairs in the great dark musty-smelling library giving him the same lecture about *me*.

"You needn't be jealous, Freda," I teased her. "I can never be a princess like you. The most I can aspire to be is a countess, and then only if I am very, very good to this lovely Earl!"

She scowled at me. "Don't be vulgar." Then she persisted. "It is said he has unusual sexual tastes."

"I am proof enough of that."

"That he is cruel and cold. That he killed a man in Italy, maybe more than one, and still may not return there because of it."

I shrugged. "Humans kill each other all the time."

"Nonetheless, I don't believe it is considered good form to do so in one's own drawing room," she retorted.

I really was growing tired of Freda's complaints. "I think," I said, "you truly are jealous."

She stared at me. "Of that weakling human?"

"Of me. Of the fact that I have a human and you do not."

Her skin flushed and her breath grew quick, though she tried to disguise it. I couldn't help taunting her, for she had irritated me when I only wanted her to be happy for me, and it wasn't fair. "You could have your pick of them, you know, and be as cruel to them as you like. But you had rather be cruel to me! And why? Because you can't make up your mind whether you are of the pack or against it. Because you are too good for humans even though none of your own kind will have you and because you hold out some vain, foolish hope of someday mating with the son of the leader of the pack!"

Ah, that was too unkind of me, wasn't it? I regretted the words the minute they were spoken, for I did not want to argue with Freda, nor did I want to hurt her. But it was too late.

She looked at me with eyes that were shocked and still while the heat drained from her skin. And then she said, "At least I do not attempt to deny my nature."

The words were as sharp as a bite and they cut just as deeply. I got to my feet slowly in what I imagined to be a display of dignity, though I was throbbing with hurt inside. "There you are mistaken," I said. "I have no nature to deny."

She came to me swiftly, remorse flooding her features. "Oh, Bri, don't freeze me out. I know I was hateful and I'm sorry. But listen to me; think of this." She caught my arms earnestly. "If you had your choice, what would you *really* rather be doing tonight? Dining at Lord Pennington's table on cold fish and bits of boiled beef, or running through the meadow with the moon in your eyes and the dew on your tongue, in pursuit of your prey?"

I twisted away from her, scowling, but she could smell the need on my skin.

"Remember the day I first met you?" she insisted. "Remember how you ran and ran on your two human-formed legs?"

"And stole your dinner because I could not catch my own."

"Brianna, *that* is your nature, to be what you *are,* not what I am, not what Pennington wants you to be, not what you think you should be, but *what you are.*"

The beat of her heart was rushing in my ears, the smell of her conviction strong. She backed away from me then, and her eyes were like low-glowing coals. She let the chiffon coat fall from her shoulders and onto the floor, then she reached behind to undo the fastenings of her gown.

"I think," she said, "I will dine out tonight. Will you join me?"

She stepped free of her gown and tossed it casually on the bed, followed by the silk undergarments and satin shoes and embroidered stockings. She freed her hair with her fingers and shook it loose around her breasts. Ah, there was a wild smell about her, a primitive savage gleam in her eyes as she tossed back the veil of her hair, as inviting as laughter, as alluring as a forbidden secret. Could she hear my heart throbbing? I know she could. Could she smell my need? Of course she could. She put out her hand to me and she said again, "Will you?"

I will, I will! I shouted back to her without saying a word. Breath quick and hard, muscles set, quivering, eyes going narrow in their sockets. She smiled to see this, and took some steps farther away from me, and stretched up her hands over her head, fingers locked together, showing off the lovely structure of that thin strong body, hips flexing, calves lengthening, breasts lifting. Head thrown back so that the dark swirl of her hair almost touched the backs of her knees, she drew in a single long breath, gave a half turn and surrendered to the Passion in a soft explosion of pale light and the scent of fleur-de-lis. The heady residue of her Change swirled through the air and made the spacious chamber seem suddenly small; it flooded my senses and left me weak and staggering, so that I fell back, clutching the drapery for support. And when my head cleared she was there before me in strong black wolf form, fur glistening, eyes questioning.

I gathered myself; I pulled open the window more fully for her. She bounded gracefully through. When I looked out she was on the darkened lawn, cast in silhouette by the yellow light of the windows below, waiting for me.

She always waited for me.

I climbed through the window in my white shift and bare feet. It was a drop of some six feet to the next roof, another ten to the ground, but I managed it just as Freda had. Exhilarated, I laughed, and she tossed her head and grinned and beckoned me and together we ran.

Of course she outdistanced me in a flash, but I didn't care. All I cared about was to be running, damp breeze tearing at my hair, bare feet tearing into turf, dodging limbs and branches; lungs straining, muscles stretching, heart pumping, swelling, pumping . . . ah, it was glorious. Even on two legs, it was glorious.

Her scent was always with me, sometimes strong on the grass, sometimes faint on the wind, but always warm, alive, companionable. So, you see, it wasn't like running alone. It was like—it was as close as I can imagine it being like—running with the pack. Our very own small pack, hers and mine.

At length I caught the scent of other living things, their heat and movement and soft grumbling sounds, and I knew immediately where she had led me. I should have turned back. I should have known to say the game had run its course. But something had been released in me that could not so easily be returned to its cage. You know this beast, my dear; you are on the most intimate of terms with it. Do not think that just because I am different from you in that one small way I have never called out its name, have never flung open my arms wide and embraced it to my bosom. Oh, no, the only real difference between us is that I am too often required to keep my beast hidden.

So it was with hot saliva pooling in my mouth that I crept up beside Freda on the hill where she crouched in the shadows, overlooking the lazily scattered flock of sheep below. I dropped down on my stomach on the ground beside her, breathing in her hot excitement and my own rich sweat. She glanced at me. Without questioning how I knew it, I understood. I leapt from my position and with a great ululating screeching cry I plunged down the hill and into the midst of the flock.

It was a child's game, nothing more, and I don't pretend to compare it to the thrill of a real hunt. I scattered the sheep, they cried and milled and bumped into one another in their stupid, clumsy fright and Freda took her time in bounding play, circling, cutting back, separating out the best. But there *was* a thrill to it, I tell you, there was an excitement to be in the midst of a kill with frenzy and glory, the smell of churned earth and fear, the indigo sky, the deep, fast-moving shadows, and now the scream of death, now the spurt of blood. I laughed out loud with the greatness of it.

Freda dragged her kill a little away from the mud and offal the stupid herd had churned up, and by the time I reached her she had already torn open the chest and removed the best organs. I dropped down beside the kill and the wave of hot fresh meat-scent that rose from the open carcass made my stomach cramp. I started to plunge my hand in, grabbing for the stomach, but Freda snapped at me, drawing back her bloody muzzle to show her teeth. I withdrew respectfully, if a little resentfully. True, it was her kill, and true, she needed the nourishment more than I, but there was indeed enough for two.

The wet crunching sounds she made as she tore at the innards filled me with a courage born of hunger, and when she freed a sizeable chunk of flesh and retreated with it, I saw my chance and approached the kill. She watched me but continued to chew, making no move to stop me. I fell greedily to the feast.

I could have used my hands to tear off a delicacy or two; I could have taken the edge off the hunger that was generated by nothing more than the sensual and hormonal flood tide the chase had released within me. But I needed to bathe myself in the experience, to plunge my face deep into the open wound and taste the heat and the blood, to fasten my teeth upon the slippery sinews of flesh that only moments ago had held life, had been life, had surrendered its life to me, to us. I flung my human-formed body upon the animal, I tore at its flesh with my human-formed teeth, I buried my face in damp bloody wool and *I* was alive. For that one endless, glorious moment, I was alive.

Yet even in the midst of the orgy my senses were as sharp as they've ever been—perhaps sharper. I heard the hooves on soft grass, I smelled the horse. I snapped my head up, listening intently for a moment, then whirled around.

Freda was gone.

By this time I knew who approached. And I knew who had told him I would be here.

I had time to clean my face and move away from the kill, but I could do nothing about my stained shift, my wild and tangled hair, the dead sheep on the ground. Nor, if the truth be told, did I care to. So I stood there, and waited.

I think the horse smelled the wildness on me, or perhaps the presence of the werewolf so recently near, for as it came over the hill it shied and reared and gave a scream. Walter handled it with a rude, deft hand, mastering the beast as he mastered his own shock at what he saw outlined in the moonlight before him—the scattered flock, the eviscerated sheep and me.

It had been Freda's plan to make certain Walter saw my true nature, to test his mettle. What she had not counted upon was that I would see Walter's true nature. And what I saw was quite dumbfounding.

He slid off the restless prancing horse and secured its reins to the limb of a tree. He was in full dinner dress, and I can only imagine that the message Freda had arranged to have sent to him had indicated some urgency, to send him out on horseback like this. He strode toward me, and I saw his nostrils flare, heard his heartbeat quicken as he realized that the wet stain that plastered the front of my shift to my breasts and my stomach was blood. I smelled horror on him, and then quick anger, and I understood the anger was because of the first quick flash of fear he had felt before he understood the blood that soaked my garment was not my own.

He stopped a few feet in front of me. He looked at the gutted sheep. He looked at me. I didn't care. I was still half crazed with the wildness of the night and the glory of my run and I didn't care. He came closer, reached out a hand and plucked a dried leaf from my hair. He gazed deeply into my eyes. My eyes blazed back at him.

He seized my shoulders roughly. I lifted my head in grand defiance, chest heaving with full rapid breaths born of exertion and excitement, heart pounding, thundering. I said softly, so close to him that my breath went into his mouth, "Take care not to hold me too closely. I would hate to bloody your pretty white shirtfront."

His gaze flickered to my chest. Now the thunder that filled my ears was his heartbeat, and the fever that flushed my skin was his heat. He released my shoulders, and took hold of my shift on either side of the bodice, and with a single powerful motion he tore the wet fabric from my body. My skin was slippery as his hands glided over it, breasts and torso and abdomen, and then his fingers were wet as they thrust into my hair, and he pressed his hard kiss upon me and we tumbled to the ground, and that is how we first made love, my Walter and I.

You can see why I adored him. You surely must.

The next morning Walter's father remarked about the wild dog that had killed one of his sheep, and Walter's eyes met mine over kippers and sweet tea, but not a word of the incident was ever spoken between us. Nor was there any need to discuss the matter with Freda. She had acted in my best interest, and as any clever werewolf would have done, she had used cunning and deception to achieve her ends. I know she would have liked to see a different result, but in fact it was all for the best.

In the afternoon we strolled among his mother's roses, Walter and I, so very civilized in our whites and our hats, and he said, "You understand, of course, that now you will have to marry me."

I laughed and I laughed.

But the next week was when you returned to London, my dear, and terrified me with my love for you. And the next time Walter asked me to marry him, I didn't laugh at all.

From the Writings of Matise Devoncroix

XXIX

I CAN'T TELL YOU HOW I LEFT FREDA'S HOUSE. HOW ASTONISHMENT gave way to incredulity and disbelief became shock and finally anger. I must have made some manner of terse goodbyes, because I remember Freda clutching my arm in the foyer, her eyes dark and distressed as she begged me not to do anything rash. She needn't have worried. By this time Brianna and her human had gone away in his long black car and I couldn't have followed them had I wished. And I didn't wish to follow them, not then. I was filled with a great roiling emotion that pushed the brink of my control, and I dared not remain near humans.

Freda was right, of course, when she pleaded with me to remain calm. To allow Passion to overcome reason is to negate all we have become, all we have accomplished. But understand my pain, my fury, my longing for all that was impossible, all that I could desire but never command. There was but one remedy, and it was in magic.

I left my Stutz Bearcat parked crookedly on the street before my apartment and I did not even go inside to Change; I stripped naked in the middle of the street, careless of what humans might see, almost defying them to see, although none did. I plunged into the cultivated wilderness and I ran, and I ran, and I ran.

In this madness there is magic, a cure for helplessness and anger and despair; a victory over bondage and restraint and all things human. The bite of the cold, the rush of air into my nostrils, the blurring of lights and the sound of human invention all beneath my power, the crunch of small bones between my teeth, the gush of blood, the triumph, the power. The power.

I tore the flesh from my small catch, I shook it viciously, spraying myself with blood, burying my muzzle in its soft innards sheerly for the pleasure of it. I wasn't hungry. I simply wanted to kill. And it was from the depths of this sensual, self-involved immersion that I caught another heartbeat, tasted another scent. But I was drunk on my own indulgence and did not react quickly enough. She charged me before I turned.

She slammed into me with the full force of her body and knocked me off my feet, and before I could react she dug her teeth into my neck and kicked me hard. This is a perfectly acceptable challenge when one werewolf meets another, yet I sensed a moment of real hostility within it and it caught me off guard, long enough for her to draw blood. I growled and spun around to retaliate but captured nothing but a mouthful of fur; mocking me, she leapt out of reach and then was off in a blur.

I was at least as confused as I was annoyed, and I followed her just as she had intended. She crossed the darkened street and entered my apartment through the open window, and by the time I sprang over the sill, nothing remained of her Change but the scent of it. She made a beautiful nude in the moonlight, tossing back her long tangled hair as she straightened up, regarding me with impatience and disdain.

I myself despise Changing indoors. There is never enough room and necessity quite takes the glory out of it. But I was so put out with Freda at this point that being cornered, as it were, in my own apartment seemed just another inconvenience, so I executed a quick and utilitarian Change, and when I faced her she was stepping into her silver-and-black dress, and twisting her hair into coils.

"By all means, make yourself free in my home," I snapped, irritably rubbing the place on my neck which she had bitten. "Confound it all, Freda, have you gone mad? What's gotten into you?"

"Do pardon me for interrupting your run," she returned sharply, stabbing a coil of hair with a jewel-studded pin. "Running is, after all, what you do best."

Had it been anyone but Freda, I would not have tolerated this for a moment. But she had never challenged me before; this in itself was astonishing enough. That she now could confound her impudence with accusations and sarcasm left me in a state between outrage and bewilderment.

I glared at her. "You knew about this absurdity. You knew about Brianna's fixation with the human and you didn't tell me."

But she was not intimidated. "And did it not occur to you, my fine young friend, that if you hadn't deserted her all those years ago, it might not have come to this?"

Even her attack had not shocked me so, not even her bite. This I had not expected from her. Not from the Freda I knew.

I said on a low and furious breath, "How dare you speak to me thus! You know nothing about it, nothing!"

I approached her in a rage, but she did not flinch. I brushed past her and flung open the door of my wardrobe, pulling a silk robe over my nakedness.

Freda said quietly in the dark, "I know everything."

I spun around, belting the robe closed with a jerk, and the air between us smelled hot and crisp with danger. I felt the crackle of it in my hair, tingling in my fingertips. I repeated softly but very distinctly, *"You know nothing."*

Freda moved away from me, skirting the bed and a big soft chair where I liked to read sometimes, and she turned on a lamp. The glow was gentle, though it hurt my eyes, as it must have done hers. Another moment or two passed before I could focus, and by that time the edge of my rage was gone.

Freda went over to the lowboy, where there was a decanter of brandy and some glasses on a silver tray, and some candies and biscuits that my housekeeper supplied fresh every day. She picked up a biscuit, nibbled it experimentally, put it down again. She said, "You know the story of The Lost Heir."

I said nothing. I tried to make my mind still and my pulses quiet. I watched her.

She said, "In the time before Humans, long, long ago, a powerful queen's last-born, the destined heir, was stolen by an ambitious rival, and replaced with a cub so much alike that even the queen couldn't tell the difference."

She poured a measure of brandy into a balloon glass and offered it to me. I remained stone-faced, motionless. She sipped the brandy herself. "The cub grew as a member of the family, though still loyal to its birth family, who plotted to take over the pack by claiming the cub as their own when the queen died. Do you remember how the plot was foiled, Matise?" She watched me over the rim of the snifter. "You should. You've written the tale with all its proper embellishments for the collected pack texts."

I refused to answer. I could feel a film of sweat beneath my arms and on the back of my neck, and I knew that she could smell it. It was cold and sour, like the feeling in the pit of my stomach.

She continued. "The changeling fell in love with his adopted sister, the queen's true child, and she with him. Their arousal was so intense they couldn't resist the Passion, and they mated. It was in this way that the pack knew the impostor was not the queen's own child, because it is impossible for *a brother and a sister to arouse each other*."

I said hoarsely, "It's just a story, a cradle tale." But I couldn't control my pulse anymore, or the scent of powerful mixed emotions that flooded my skin. I knew what she was going to say. And it was outrageous.

Her eyes flashed with impatience. "Ah, yes, so much easier for you to believe Brianna is at fault! Brianna the defective, Brianna the wicked—"

"I never thought her wicked! It was me—"

"Yes, it was you!" she spat back. "You who were weak, you who were afraid, you who had so little faith in this woman you claim to adore that you would reject the logical for the impossible in order to blame her! You were aroused by her, Matise," she stated plainly, firmly. "The logic of it is that she cannot be your natural sister."

My heartbeat was wild—with hope, with anger, with shame, with expectation and denial. I tried to hide this from her with laughter. "You should be the writer of tales, Freda! What an imagination you have."

"It is perhaps because I have no imagination that the conclusion comes to me so easily," she replied coolly. "I smell the shame on you Matise. I hope it is because you know your error."

"I know nothing," I returned sharply, "except that you are interfering in things that are none of your concern and that your conclusions are spiteful and outrageous. Brianna Devoncroix is the firstborn of the leader of the pack, everyone knows that! To even suggest otherwise is heresy. In the old days you would be tossed into a cage to rot for spreading such gossip."

Now I wanted a brandy. I strode over to her and snatched up the decanter, sloshing a measure into a glass. It annoyed me that my hands were not quite steady, and I knew she could hear the fine trembling of my muscles as the adrenaline surge attacked them. Freda was mad and her suggestions were cruelly incredulous. But what if she was not? *What if she was not?*

I downed the brandy in a single swallow, then looked at her with sudden, sharp suspicion. "You haven't repeated this nonsense to Brianna, have you?"

"There was no point. As long as you were wandering the globe, trying to escape from her, it would have been more cruel than kind to suggest that her heart had been broken for nothing."

"And why come to me with this folderol now? Why wait all these years to decide to torment me?"

She took another sip from her glass, her eyes calm and unblinking. "I met a man a year or two ago. He told me he served as guard to your parents for forty years and came to beg of me admittance to one of Brianna's shows. He said he had a special acquaintance with her—that he had been present at her birth."

I held my breath. I think I had known—surely I must have known from the beginning—that Freda would not have approached me with such an outrageous tale without some form of proof. Yet still I couldn't believe it.

"He lied, of course," she continued casually. "But he had caught my interest—because, you see, I had already wondered about the circumstances of Brianna's birth, just as you should have done. Upon further questioning, this guard admitted he had not been present at any birth at all, but he testifies to the fact that he never left your mother's side during the spring and summer of 1900, and that there was no pregnancy. Your parents went into the mountains and discovered Castle Devoncroix, and when they returned a day or so later, there was the infant Brianna. They declared the child to be their own and it was so. But your mother did not give birth to her. This he swears."

"Then he is a liar." The words came out raspy and dry, without my ever planning to utter them at all. My lips felt numb, my skin suddenly cold. Was it because I wanted so desperately to believe her words, or because I was terrified to do so? Or was it because I knew the truth deep in the pit of my soul, had known it from the moment Freda began speaking, even before?

Freda's voice took on a tight note, underscored by urgency. "Ask your father. Ask your mother. Would they deceive you, knowing what the lie would cost—has already cost? You know it in your heart, Matise. If you loved her half as much as you claim, you would admit it now."

Two children, six months apart. Barely a physical possibility, it had always been a matter of marvel within the pack. Brianna, born unattended in the Alaskan wilderness. And an anthropomorph, the most unlikely result of two of the strongest Devoncroix lines. Sister arousing brother to the point of Passion . . .

The bowl of the empty brandy snifter suddenly exploded beneath the pressure of my fingers. I stared down at the shiny fragments in my hand and on the carpet at my feet without comprehension or care.

Ah, I knew it. How could I not have known? How could I have punished Brianna, and myself, for all these years by refusing to know?

Absently, I brushed the slivers of glass from my hands and from my robe. I looked at Freda. "And you've kept this secret—this secret that might have saved us both—for all this time." My voice was without accusation, and all but with the mildest inflection. I lacked the resources to manage more.

Freda made a gesture of impatient self-defense. "And should I have done otherwise? You left her, Matise; you left both of us. Until you came to me—to her—of your own free will, I had no way of knowing what your real feelings might be, or whether you would only use this information to hurt her further."

She drew in a breath, and for the first time cast her gaze away from mine. "In truth, I might not have told you yet, for in many ways she was better off without you—and without the pack that you were so quick to choose over her. But when I saw you the other day—when I saw her face with you tonight—I realized that you may be the only person in the world who can stop her from pursuing this outrageous marriage. I despise you for what you have done to her, Matise, but I had rather she be with you than destroy her life with this human."

Freda put her snifter down very carefully on the silver tray, and added, clear-eyed, "It's one thing for me to reject the pack. I have my family and we are strong and large, and none of us has ever been alone. But Brianna—if she marries this human, if she makes a public liaison with him through that pagan human ceremony, admitting to having sex with him, to *joining* herself with him—there will be no turning back. No one will be able to help her then, and to the pack she will be dead. Ask your parents, Matise," she said, and now an edge of pleading tightened her tone. "Just please—ask them for the truth."

She turned then and left, closing the door quietly behind her.

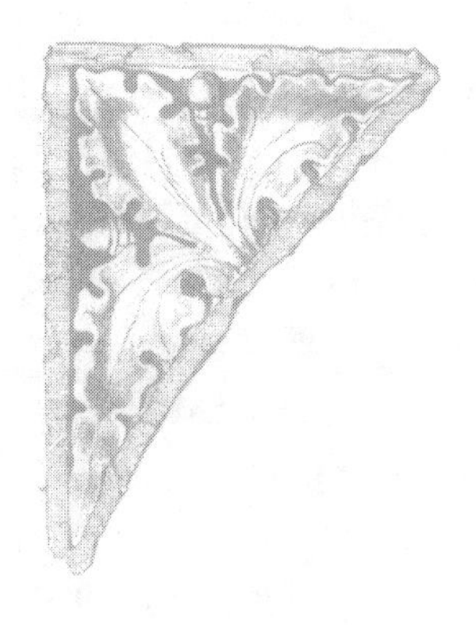

Twelve

THE WILDERNESS
14:58
ALASKA STANDARD TIME
NOVEMBER 25

THE HUMAN SLEPT. DID SHE DREAM OF LONG-AGO TIMES AND WORLDS unknown to her? Were her dreams haunted by the misdeeds of creatures she had never before imagined to exist? She looked harmless in her sleep, untroubled and innocent. But in her head swam secrets no human should possess. Soon, if she finished the book, the most horrible secret of all would be hers.

He was frustrated by her silence, by the absence of her, though he knew it was absurd he should feel so. He should be grateful she had closed the book, for the longer she slept, the less she would know of what was not hers to know, not ever. Yet *he* wanted to know. He wanted to hear more of the story of Matise, his brother . . . and Brianna, the female who had forever changed everything he once had thought was true.

Brianna, he thought. *Had you never been born, none of us would be where we are today. There would have been no bloody massacre in New York, no bomb aboard my private helicopter, no accident contrived to murder my father. I should hate you for this and more . . . yet, strangely, I cannot*. Was this, then, why his father had insisted he read the story of Brianna that was bound between the covers of that red book? There could be no other reason. What possible secrets could that book contain that were more horrible than the ones he knew already? Alexander Devoncroix had been far too pragmatic a man and shrewd a leader to imagine Nicholas would be swayed by sentiment for the adopted sister he had never known. There must be something more. Why didn't the human wake up and read?

And that, of course, was a foolish wish. As innocent as she looked in her sleep, the human was far from harmless; Nicholas knew that. It was not what she might tell other humans that concerned him, for the pack had little to fear from humankind. What might she tell her brethren that would impress them in this day of satellite television and special effects and truths that grew more stranger than fiction every day? Hardly a week went by, after all, that some human tabloid or another did not feature tales of the inexplicable that could be traced back to the pack, often with photographs. No one cared. No one was interested. Human minds were focused on more immediate problems than the fate of their species.

Ah, but what humans knew, the pack would know. And it *would* make a difference to them. It would make a difference because they would know it for the truth. And the truth would shake them to the foundation of their souls.

What would become of the pack while he lay helpless in this place? How long had he been gone? How long had his people been without a leader of any sort? Panic would set in quickly once they knew, or began to suspect, that the heir of Alexander Devoncroix was missing or dead. Stock markets around the world would begin to plummet, factories would close, commerce would stumble, trade would halt. And what if some ambitious young werewolf—a member of the Dark Brotherhood, for example—seized this opportunity to step into his place and take over the pack? Was anything preventing Michel from doing so?

The bars upon the cage confounded him. If only he could escape this place, lives might yet be saved. But he was too weak to break the locks with his teeth, and too confined to Change so that he might use his hands. If she unfastened the doors again to bring him food or water, he could overpower her effortlessly. But he knew with a sinking despair that she would not unfasten the locks again. She might be stupid, but she was no fool, this human. She was accustomed to wolves in the wild, and she had a healthy respect for claws and teeth. She had proved as much the last time she had passed the water dish into the cage without opening the door.

The wind thundered against the side of the building and the human stirred on the couch where she slept, drawing the quilt more tightly around her shoulders. Nicholas could smell the storm and hear the snow. He could hear something else, not far in the distance yet almost lost in the wind: a call, wordless and long and instantly recognizable. It caused a chill to seize Nicholas's spine.

I am here, it said.

His heart began to beat very hard. He summoned all of the will at his control not to answer back: *I am here!*

The human awoke with a start, almost as though she had heard the cry as well. She sat up groggily and rubbed her face, then she threw back the quilt and came over to him. Nicholas watched her carefully. He remembered how she had picked up the SCU when he had willed it before. Coincidence? She had awakened to a sound she simply could not have heard. Was it possible—was it at all possible—that she possessed sentience beyond which any werewolf had suspected before?

"How are you, fellow?" she said softly. She smelled of warm sleep and cotton, woodsmoke and wool. She rested her hand atop the cage and bent close.

Without her, he would be dead. He knew that. But so much more was at stake here than the life of one human.

Again his mother's face rose up to haunt him, her angry, urgent voice: *In all these centuries the one discipline we have had is that we have no power over human life. Give the pack that power and we become omnipotent. Do you realize the danger in that?*

And his reply: *You talk like a human.*

Those were his last words to his mother. *You talk like a human.*

He could see the human woman was about to turn away. He caught her with his gaze. She seemed confused; she glanced at him. He held her tight with the power of his eyes.

Human, he thought distinctly. *Go to the briefcase. Remove the* (here he formed a clear picture of the SCU). *Slide the switch on the back of the device upward. Leave it there. Do it.*

Hannah took a groggy step backward, shaking her head a little.

He shouted, *Do it!*

She gasped and pressed her fingers to her temples, pressing hard against a sudden stabbing pain. She blinked, and turned away. The headache began to dissipate almost immediately.

Hannah went toward the kitchen for a glass of water. Her attention was caught by the briefcase lying open on the table. She hesitated, then picked up the electronic organizer again. She felt another stab of pain in her head, and pinched the bridge of her nose, frowning, until it eased.

She started to put the organizer down; then, curiously, she turned it over. There was a black switch on the back she had not noticed before. She made a soft sound of surprise—"Hmm"—and pushed the switch upward. Nothing happened.

She returned the organizer to the briefcase and poured a glass of water from the bottle on the kitchen counter. By the time the glass was filled, however, her headache was gone.

She checked on the wolf on her way back to the chair, but his head was on his paws, and his slitted eyes were not interested in her. She resumed her place in the chair, and once again began to read out loud.

The transmitter on the table sent its steady silent signal, and Nicholas closed his eyes, and listened to the words.

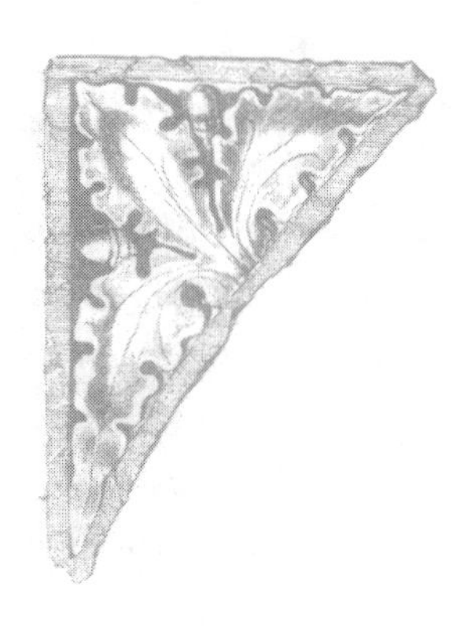

From the Writings of Matise Devoncroix

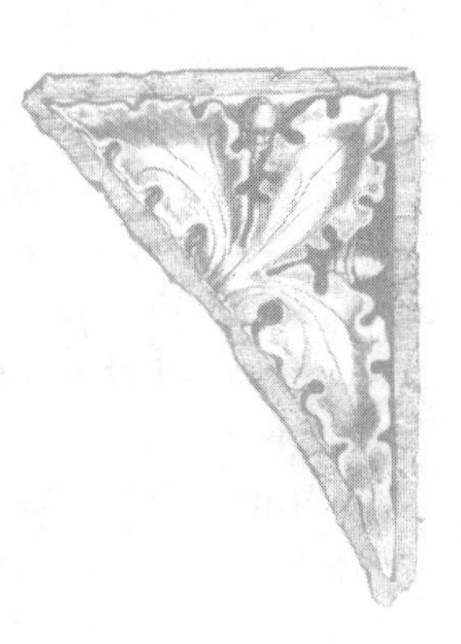

XXX

AND HERE IS THE STORY OF THE GREAT QUEEN EUDORA, THE REASON that all my other stories have been told; the story without which none of the others would matter.

You recall how it was when we abandoned Rome: our great experiment reduced to shambles, civilization lay in smoking ruins. Pillars tumbled, papyrus scrolls gave up the greatness of their thoughts to greedy flames, statues sank to the bottom of the cold dark sea. When we failed, we failed magnificently.

A new wave of barbarism and superstition overtook the humans, and we had not the spirit to fight it. For the first time in untold ages, we were feared, hunted, set up in legend and campfire tale to terrify human children. It was quite disgusting, really. And perhaps the worst of it was that in the face of such rejection we retreated—to our stone fortresses and castles deep, to the rich dark forests of myth and lore, to the wilderness of Siberia, where, under the rough but practical rule of the Antonovs, we learned new lessons in survival—without humans.

Without us, human civilization took a great backward plunge, of course. But history barely bothers to record that without them, ours did not fare much better.

Oh, we survived, it is true. We survived by avoiding humans, by hiding from them, by killing them when we could. Does that shock you? That such savagery should have afflicted our line in such relatively recent history? This is how it was then:

In a little village in Germany, it happened that a cow was brought down, a man was bitten, a child disappeared. The humans believed that a werewolf was at large, and a bounty was put upon the creature's head. In a single day a human brought back a sled piled high with the carcasses of thirty-seven wolves.

How many of their kind did we bring back upon our sleds, I wonder, when we heard this tale?

There was no peace between us. And for it, both our races were plunged into a long Dark Age of the Soul.

What happened? you will wonder. How did this terrible black age come to an end, how did any of us survive it to tell the tale? There is no simple answer, of course, for the factors are many and complex. Some say the process was greatly aided by the decimation of the human population during the fourteenth century. And that occurrence, as we know, was brought about by a mysterious plague to which our species was fortunately immune . . . a plague, it is said, that had its origins in the Crimea, an Antonov stronghold. It is not my purpose here to speculate further, but I might suggest that history should be kind when looking back upon the fierce, strong rule of the Antonovs. We may owe them more than we think.

But the world was changing. We grew tired of wildness, of hiding in forests and castle keeps. Our souls thirsted for the grandness we had once known, for art and music and pleasant indolence. The cities were clearer now, the countryside free of ravaging humans.

Many of our population drifted out of the north, toward sunnier climes, and there they found, in the lush wine country of France, the kernel of a new beginning.

In A.D. 1250, Silos Devoncroix of Gaul overthrew, by chance and cunning, Leo Antonov of Siberia, and claimed the pack for the Devoncroix. This was the beginning of a new, expansive age for our people, but very little had changed regarding humans. We built magnificent châteaus and villas on the water, we claimed a hundred thousand acres for vineyards, we gradually began to recall our great treasures of art and song and philosophy and to enjoy them again. Around us, humans continued to die of filth and disease and ignorance, and we ignored them as long as they didn't lie too long in the streets.

For almost two centuries we persevered in this manner, increasing our own greatness while avoiding humans when we could, despising them when we could not and disposing of them when they became too troublesome. And then a young queen called Eudora inherited the pack.

It is said that while returning to the Palais one stormy night the queen's carriage left the road and cracked a wheel in a ditch. The queen was persuaded to take shelter in a nearby human church while her attendants made repairs. As it happened, the priest of that church struck up a conversation with her, and she was quite astonished by his articulation, as he was, no doubt, by her charm.

Now, it was the custom of those times that no werewolf should perform a physically demeaning task when a human was available to perform it for him, and as humans were quite accustomed to serving those wealthier and more powerful than they themselves, there was rarely any argument on that score. When the queen's guards found the human conducting conversation with her, they were outraged, and immediately commanded that he come and remove the carriage from the ditch. He went willingly to do as he was bidden.

But his human strength was not up to the task. He slipped in the mud, became trapped under the weight of the vehicle and was gravely injured. The queen was overwhelmed with remorse, and insisted upon taking the broken human back to the Palais, where he could benefit from the healing skills of her own court.

What developed between them over those next months is a speculation too complex to relate in this time and space, and opinions vary widely as to the details. It seems certain, however, that for the first time in more than a millennium, humans and werewolves began to discover in each other the remarkable miracle of reciprocity. Humans were not animals. Werewolves were not monsters. What amazement this must have caused both parties; what astonishment.

But cultures do not change overnight, prejudices do not evaporate simply for saying they must, and whoever claims otherwise tells you a fiction. The human priest and the werewolf queen struggled in their souls with their newfound knowledge of each other, exploring it cautiously and with suspicion, not knowing how to act upon it or whether to act at all. The queen dared not let it be known among her court that she regarded this human as anything more than a beast of burden she had nursed back to health; certainly she was in no position to declare her growing belief that *all* humans might possess sentience. And the young priest, in whom was he to confide his secrets? Only his journals, and his God.

For years they met in secret, the human and the queen, learning of each other, growing with each other, dispelling the myths and superstitions in which time had immersed the separate species. Very subtle changes began to occur around the Palais. Instead of burning out the peasants' huts when they became infested with disease, as would have been the practical method of dealing with them in times past, the queen sent down elixirs to cure them. Instead of working the human laborers to near death for scraps of food and water, as was customary, she began to pay them in coin. As a result, both her vineyards and the village thrived.

But the one thing she would not do, could not do, was to declare her friendship with this human openly.

What happened was inevitable. After years of conversing together, learning together, coming to understand each other and to depend on each other and to love each other at last as only the deepest and truest of friends can know love—the human was discovered unexpectedly in the one place no human should ever have been: the queen's bedchamber. The guards reacted appropriately and instinctively. Before the queen could stop them, they fell upon the human and tore him asunder.

Perhaps you have seen the magnificent DeFranco painting of our good Queen Eudora, kneeling amidst the remains of her slaughtered human, her hands dripping with blood and her face uplifted in a cry of agony and despair, of wretched guilt and bitter, bitter sorrow. So much more than a human died that day. So much more than a life was lost.

Yet from the rubble of this tragedy was built an empire that endures to this day, and the blood of this poor human is the mortar that holds the foundation together. The great Queen Eudora arose from his body, with bloodied fists raised to the sky and shaking with power, to make the vow that would change our world, and his, forever.

It is a promise that has endured to this day.

XXXI

ASK YOUR PARENTS, FREDA HAD SAID. PAPA WAS IN PARIS. I COULD have made the crossing in the morning and been back in London in two days if I used my wolf form for the land portions of the trip. But two days seemed an eternity when the truth was burning a hole in my heart, when hope was pounding in my chest and quaking in my soul. Hope and remorse and desperation and need and great, tremulous joy—how could I wait two days when Brianna was less than twenty minutes away?

And besides, I'm not sure that destiny would have been changed by waiting, anyway. I don't think that anything could have made a difference then.

I pulled on my human clothes, trousers and a shirt, and I made my way to Brianna's home, wild-haired, barefoot, needful. Please understand. It was for her sake I did this thing. It was for the love of her.

The street was empty and quiet, the windows of her house dark. I leapt the garden wall and went to a side door so as not to disturb the servants. The lock confounded me for a moment, for I had never known a werewolf to lock her doors and had not expected it, but I snapped the flimsy thing between my fingers and stepped inside.

The darkened room where I found myself was a small library in which no fire had been lit that night; my breath frosted as I got my bearings. It was good to be among the things that smelled of Brianna, even if they also smelled of humans. This was her world. I basked in it.

But with my first inhalation of breath I knew she was here, and I knew she was not alone. A surge of anger and disgust propelled me down the corridor. I mounted the stairs, I sought out her bedchamber, I flung open the door.

Brianna's bed—a graceful sleigh style with many feather mattresses and coverings trimmed in Venetian lace—was situated adjacent to the window whose draperies had not been closed, and although the room was completely dark by ordinary standards, there was enough ambient light through that window to allow me to see perfectly. The naked human man was upon the bed, with Brianna astride him, his hands holding her hips and her back arched to better pleasure him, and herself. He was too intent on the sensation that consumed him to notice me as I paused in the doorway, arms crossed upon my chest, scowling at them. But Brianna had known, of course, the moment I entered her house, and now I think she put on a little show, mocking me.

Her pretty breasts were upturned, her torso long and smooth, her red curls tangled around her shoulders and caught in places with the moisture of his kisses. She lifted her hair with both hands, showing her figure to its best advantage and allowing her curls to spill from her fingers like autumn leaves caught in a gentle breeze, and the human's hands caressed her breasts; then she followed their sliding pattern down her torso with her own fingers, a shadow dance of motion. Her hair swung forward as she leaned over him, her tongue flicking and circling over his face and his neck while her pelvis rocked rhythmically against his, and through the veil of tumbled curls she cut her eyes to me in triumph, and in daring.

And so it was. I fed my savage nature by running in the snow and feeding on fresh kill; she satisfied the wildness in her by defiling herself with a human. This I understood. But understanding did not make it any the more acceptable.

I let the door swing closed behind me as I strode over to the bed and snatched her to her feet by her arm. The smell of human sex and Brianna's own compelling musk assaulted my nostrils; too much human, too little of Brianna.

I was tormented, I was enraged, I was repulsed. And yet the combination of all these emotions barely mitigated the joy I felt for simply being in her presence, the great exultation of the discovery I had come to share with her. And it was only because of this that I was able to deal with the situation with such very great restraint.

"Get dressed," I told the startled, gasping man she had earlier introduced to me as Walter. My tone was short, but otherwise polite. "And then kindly leave this house. I need to speak with Brianna alone, if you please." I glanced at Brianna and wrinkled my nose. "But not," I added, "until you've had a bath."

Brianna jerked her arm away from my grip impatiently, and the human Walter scrambled among the bedclothes for his trousers—concerned first and foremost, as humans invariably are at such moments, with protecting his modesty. Brianna tossed her head, glaring at me. "What are you doing here, Matise?"

"Saving you from further humiliating yourself, at the very least," I returned, and I made an angry gesture toward the human and the bed. "Is this the best you were born for? Have you no pride at all?"

"I'll choose my companions without any help from you, Matise Devoncroix, as I have been doing for quite a few years now! How dare you talk to me like that! How dare you break into my house—"

I gave a short, loud bark of laughter. "I wouldn't have to 'break in' as you so eloquently put it, if you didn't put locks on your doors. What has become of you, Brianna? Hiding behind locks, having sex with"—I waved a dismissive hand toward the bed—"creatures like this—have you no pride at all?"

Her eyes glittered dangerously in the dark, and she drew close to my mouth. "You," she said softly, "have blood on your breath."

The smell and the noise of the fumbling human were making it hard for me to concentrate, and I had no more patience for Brianna's theatrics. She swept a filmy pink peignoir from the tangle of clothing on the floor, and as she slipped her arms into its sleeves I strode forward and picked her up bodily. She screeched and twisted, but I withstood her efforts. "Be still," I told her, and with a single mighty kick of my foot I knocked the closed door off its hinges, flat on the floor, and carried her through. I didn't think how this must have looked to the human. I didn't think about him at all.

I took her to the cold dark library from which I had entered this house, because it was familiar to me and because it was far from the human. I set her on her feet and she pushed away from me with dark and glittering eyes. "You," she told me distinctly, "are a brute."

I put my hands on her face, her hair curling around my fingers again, her breath brushing against my skin again, her warmth seeping into my blood again—my breath quickened, my heart ached, for a moment I was unable to speak. I simply gazed at her, so full of possibility that all I could feel was awe.

And she must have sensed it, she must have known something monumental was about to happen, or perhaps she was as affected by me as I was by her. She did not reprimand me again, and I felt her heart go heavy and slow. She drew in a soft breath, but did not release it at once. Waiting.

I said, "Ah, Brianna, we have made a terrible mistake."

I covered her mouth with mine and kissed her deeply, and she thrust her fingers into my hair and drank of me, and we were like drowning creatures gasping for air, filling each other with life-giving force, taking it desperately, taking it greedily, this kiss, this touch, this blending of scents and tastes and thundering heartbeats. Then she twisted away from me with a wrenching force and she said in a hoarse, ragged bubbling of words, one spilling atop the other with breathless intensity, "No, don't do this, Matise, it wasn't a mistake, you know it wasn't, oh please don't come back here and break my heart again, Matise, please don't!"

"Ah, my love, my sweet girl." I kissed her throat and her breasts, and she was trembling so; it made me weak to feel her tremble. I sank to my knees, my head pressed into her belly, my nostrils filled with the rich dark scent of her sex, and even though it was mixed with human, even though human permeated every cell of her skin and hair, I didn't mind it so much now, because the scent of Brianna was that much sweeter. "I've come back for you, yes," I whispered. "I've come back."

I knew what I did to her. I could feel it in the heat of her skin, its sudden suppleness and glow; I could hear it in the rush of her blood and the stutter of her breath and the fine high singing of her quaking muscles, I could smell it and I could taste it. And when she said, low and shaking, "I shall hate you forever for this," I did not believe her, for every part of her except her lips told a story of adoration and need, and it filled me with soaring triumph.

I lifted my face, I tilted back my head to look up at her. I said, "Imagine it, just think about it for a moment, just pretend—if I weren't your brother, would you hate me then? Or would you adore me with every beat of your heart, would you melt to my touch, would you weep for my kisses, would you want me for your lover? Would you, Brianna?"

"You are a wretched creature!" She tore away from me, her face anguished. "Is this why you came here tonight? To mock me? To punish me for my enjoyment of humans, to make sure I never know a moment's peace from you? Why are you doing this to me?"

I got to my feet. I blocked her exit from the room. I didn't touch her. I didn't have to. The fever in my eyes held her captive, the quickness of my breath, the roar of my pulses. "I am not your brother, Brianna," I said, pinning her in my gaze. "You are not my sister."

The pain in her eyes slowly became mitigated with confusion, uncertainty.

I said, quick and soft, "I've come to believe—something I've learned—Brianna, I'm sure of it, you were a foundling. Not of my parents' blood. When they went to Alaska, there was no pregnancy. Yet you appeared, without witness in the wilderness, and six months later I was born . . . Think of it, Brianna, think of it. It's the only thing that makes sense."

But even before I finished speaking I saw the recoiling in her eyes, the draining away of blood from her lips. "And so," she said, with a forced steadiness that was denied by the roar of her pulses, "now I am denied not only the pack and my only love, but my parents as well. As you wish, Matise."

She started to move past me, but I caught her arm.

"No!" she shouted, and flung me away with such violence that I crashed into the desk and overturned a lamp. "No, I won't have it, do you hear? You will not come here and tell me your miracles and expect all to be well simply because you say it must! I have made my choice, Matise, don't you see that?"

I was incredulous. "That weak-livered human with his bony limbs and dangling penis—*that* is your choice?"

"He loves me!"

"What can a human know of love? He cannot even *comprehend* you! Brianna . . ." I approached her again, careful now because her heartbeat was skittering and her fists were clenched and I could smell the salt of her tears deep in her throat. I ached to hold her, to draw her against my chest and make all her pain go away and leave her for all time. But when I lifted my hand, the only thing I felt free to do was to touch her hair, very lightly, merely adoring it.

My throat was thick and my voice husky as I spoke. "Brianna. Long ago I promised you we would be together always. I know I've done my best to break that promise, but . . . I can't leave you. We've known it since we were children, this magic between us, this need to be together—and now, don't you see it's possible at last? Torment me if you will, chastise me and make me suffer, I deserve all of it and more—but, Brianna, don't deny us both what we were meant to be! If we are not truly brother and sister, then there is no shame in what we feel for one another. We're free to be together! How can you not celebrate that?"

She lifted her hands and put them lightly over both of mine, bringing them down from her hair. But she did not let go. She held my hands, stilled and obedient to her touch, and she looked at me solemnly. "There was never any shame in it for me, Matise," she said. "So don't you see? For you, everything has changed; for me, nothing has. You are still werewolf, and I am still an anthropomorph. We can never mate. We have no life together."

But oh, no, I would not accept this. To be so close and to have her snatched away from me again . . . no. There was no room for this in my imagination.

I said, "We'll leave for Dover now—we can be in Paris by the afternoon. We'll tell Papa everything. When you hear it from his own lips, Bri, you'll know the truth and he can help us. But if you continue with this human, if you go through with this mockery of a mating and make it public, the pack will turn its back on you well and true and there will be no one to help us, not ever!"

She pulled her hands away, and the look in her eyes was despairing. Wordlessly, she tried to push past me.

I caught her against me. "I won't let you do this."

"Let me go!" She wrenched away, eyes blazing, blood hot. "I didn't ask you here, Matise—I didn't ask for any of this! I didn't leave because I wanted to, and you know that! I was driven out! I can't go back because there's nothing to go back to! This is all that is left to me, don't you understand that? Why must you torment me so?"

A sound behind me caught my ear. It was such an unfamiliar sound that at first I didn't recognize it, didn't even turn around. Then the man Walter said, "Let her go."

It was the very coldness of his voice that made me glance in his direction. He stood in the doorway, his stance relaxed yet oddly poised. His eyes were steady upon me, and in his hand he held a small revolver trained upon me.

I looked from him to Brianna, incredulity and annoyance sharpening my tone. "This is what you would choose over me? A human with a *gun*?"

She stared at me for one terrible moment, and then she broke away. Ah, it was so quick. And that is the way it always is with humans and their guns: so quick, so senseless, so impossible to predict or to recall. Brianna went to Walter, I think to wrench the gun from him. I lunged for Brianna in anger and impulse, just to stop her from going near the creature; just to stop her.

The gunshot clapped in my ears and the impact of the bullet caused me to stagger, but it was not until a moment later, not until I smelled the hot scent of my own blood and looked down, in some surprise, to see the blossom of red upon the white linen that covered my shoulder, that I realized I had been struck. Brianna gave a cry and tore the gun from the human's hand and tossed it aside, and she made to rush for me and he caught her back and that is all I recall as the fireball of agony spread from my shoulder down my arm and into my fingers, seizing my spinal cord, inflaming my brain. I tore at my clothes, I threw back my head, I let the Passion take me.

And when I regained myself I was deep into instinct, for although the wound was not serious, the pain was great and my senses were confused by it. The room, the night, the smells, none were familiar to me. The hot traces of cordite lingered in the air and reminded me of terror and hatred. Only Brianna, only the scent of Brianna, made sense to me. And when I staggered around to look for her, I heard the sounds of struggle and I heard her shout, "Walter, no!" and I smelled the smell of human terror and deadly intent and I saw Brianna holding his arms, trying to keep him from reaching the gun she had discarded.

I sprang for him. I couldn't stop myself. I was inflamed with pain and the room stank of guns and danger, I saw Brianna struggling and I smelled fear and anger, and an instinct stronger than reason rose to protect her. How could I know, considering the state I was in then, that the human wanted only to protect her from *me?*

But I tell you this, and it is a truth I have held close in a tight secret knot of shame, locked deep inside an unbreachable part of myself, for all of my life. I leapt upon the human, I flung him to the ground, I dug my claws into his flesh and my teeth into his throat and I tasted his blood, I tasted it hot and thick as it spurted into my mouth, and I liked it, I tell you, I loved it. I felt his struggles, the ineffectual clawings and kickings, and I was filled with satisfaction, oh, yes, a satisfaction that resonated deep within the core of me with an almost orgasmic thrill, to feel those struggles weaken, and then cease.

For this is the truth of it, my friend, the heavy and unshakable truth: the taste of human blood is good. The fever of the kill is ecstasy.

But then I felt something else. Through a fog, distant and vague, I heard a voice that was familiar to me, I felt fingers digging into my fur; words began to form, wild and ragged, in my ears: "Matise, don't; stop, please, you're killing him, *you are killing him!*"

It was Brianna. Brianna, flung full-body atop me, pulling at me, trying to save the life of her human . . . trying to save me.

I unclenched the muscles of my jaw, withdrew my teeth from succulent flesh. Trembling convulsively, quaking to the very root of my being, I backed away.

And when my vision cleared, what I saw was Brianna covered in blood, kneeling on the floor beside her human, sobbing in great gasping breaths, trying to wad the flimsy fabric of her peignoir against one of the many wounds upon that poor frail body, trying to stop the flow of blood. "Alive," I heard her whisper. "Yes, alive, Walter, hold on, you're alive . . ."

I was dazed, reeling, still drunk from the combat and weak from the stress of my own injury. It seemed like a dream to me. No, a nightmare. The kind from which you never wake up.

And then she looked at me, her face twisted with anguish; she held out her wet red hands. Kneeling there over the torn and broken body of her human lover, she pleaded, "Help me. Matise, please help me . . ."

I heard the human's beating heart, his weak ragged breath; I heard my beloved's plea and smelled the desperation on her, and oh, how noble I would be to say that in that instant, reason returned and I was filled with horror for what I had done. I was quaking, yes, but it was with a great and powerful need, for every muscle in my body, every cell and fiber and neuron within me wanted nothing more than to leap for the human again, to take his neck between my jaws and feel it snap.

There was no noble creature of reason within me then. I was a killer, and I loved myself for it.

I crouched low. I felt the growl rumble through my throat. My muscles tensed to spring and nothing could have stopped me, nothing *would* have stopped me. But Brianna smelled my intent. I saw it flash in her eyes in that moment, that split second before I leapt to finish off my prey—horror, and fear. My Brianna was afraid of me.

She flung herself over her lover to protect him from me, but there was no need. I backed away, heart pounding, dry-mouthed, so awash with shock that the Change back into human form was almost involuntary.

I sank to my knees, gasping and weak, but as soon as my voice returned I managed to say, "Freda—call her on the telephone. She knows about human physiology. She can help him. Hurry!"

Brianna got to her feet and ran to the telephone. I went over to the human and did what I could to stop the bleeding, then I lifted him in my arms and carried him upstairs.

XXXII

LOOKING BACK OVER THOSE LAST WORDS, I WONDER EVEN NOW WHY I bothered to write them down. Do I try to portray myself in a heroic light, or to convince you—or myself—of a lack of culpability? I hope not. Because if I can do such a thing now, it makes all that I suffered before meaningless.

I therefore report the remainder of this episode in as factual a manner as I am able. It does me no credit to relate that, near fainting with the great expenditure of energy demanded by my wound and two Changes in quick succession, I left the human where I dropped him on the bed and staggered to the kitchen, where I gorged myself on whatever I could find there. I tore at the larder doors, sank my teeth into a side of bacon without bothering to remove the cotton bag it was hung in; I dug into a wheel of cheese with my fingers and consumed two loaves of bread and a pie without tasting them. I made my way to the icebox and drank a bottle of milk in a single swallow, licked the butter dish clean, consumed the remains of the previous night's dinner and a half-dozen eggs, raw. By the time my head had cleared enough for me to recognize my surroundings, Freda was in the house.

I dressed, although my shirt was shredded beyond repair. I put on the human's shirt, and hardly noticed the smell for the taste of anxiety that was swelling in my throat and dampening even the edge of my hunger. I went to Brianna.

Brianna had washed and changed into a clean garment, and had tied back her hair. But she had blood under her fingernails. I recall the smell of it, mixed with the clean silk smell of her clothes and the cold fearful smell of her skin. She looked at me when I came up the carpeted stairs and into the small corridor where she sat outside the bedroom. There is a special communication we are supposed to know only in wolf form, but our eyes met, and everything that must be said was said. Words, after that, would have seemed irrelevant.

I sat beside her on the small silk-covered couch outside the bedroom where the human lay bleeding from wounds I had inflicted. We listened, the two of us, to the sounds Freda made behind the closed door of the bedroom, but neither of us suggested going in. We listened to the sound of the human's heartbeat, to the uncertain rhythm of his breathing, to the click of broken bones being snapped into place.

And then, without any warning at all, we heard the human's heart stop beating.

Ah, that I had words to describe that moment. And if I could but give my own life that you may never know it.

It was as though all life—not just the human's—stopped at the moment when he ceased to be, as though each solitary molecule, each atom and thought of an atom, was flash-frozen for an instant of intense, superattenuated existence, poised on the threshold of eternal magnificence, yet . . . stopped. Inert. Lifeless after all.

A clock chimed downstairs: a single loud, reverberating note, frozen. Brianna took a breath, and was still. The pattern of the wall-paper was suddenly brilliantly clear in every etched detail and satin furbelow; the wood grain of the floor revealed a hundred thousand footfalls that had gone before and had left their marks; the tapestry upon which we sat was exposed in every intricate detail as though the lifeblood of those who had sewn it suddenly infused their labor with a preternatural light—brilliant, but frozen.

The smell of Brianna, sweet and clean, and the blood under her fingernails. The smell of death and drugs and human blood. The cold stale smell of my own sweat. Each fragment of perfume throbbed like a living thing—but it too was frozen in time. And in the midst of this miasma of lifeless intensity I swam, disoriented, icy, helpless. This is death. This is what I had done.

The door opened and closed again softly. Freda had blood on her hands and death on her skin. Her eyes were quiet, her tone composed. She looked at Brianna.

"His spine was crushed, Bri," she said gently. "He was really quite beyond repair. We'll have to call the human authorities now, for the death certificate."

She glanced at me. "You'd better leave, Matise. There will be an inquiry. A gun discharged and the police will come. We can tell them some tale of an intruder, I suppose. But it would be more credible if you were not here."

How calm she was, and reasonable. How perfectly in control.

Brianna stood. She started toward the door beyond which lay the dead man, and then she looked back at me. "You asked me if he knew what I was," she said. In her eyes was the great blank sky of eternity, of sorrow beyond comprehension. In her eyes was the life she might have known, now gone forever. "He knew. In his own way, he knew." Then she smiled, very faintly, sadly. That smile I shall remember all the rest of my life. "And he loved me anyway."

Brianna went into the room with the dead human, and closed the door.

I do not remember how I left that house. I walked out into the cold and the fog, too weak to Change, but changed forever. I walked and walked, and I walked to the edge of the earth.

PART THREE

I do solemnly vow,
by all that I hold most sacred,
by the blood of my father and the
bones of my mother,
that from this day forward
I will act with honor and respect
toward all living creatures;
I will discipline my power to
the defense of the weak and the moderation
of the strong;
I will hunt for the nourishment of my spirit
and kill only for the nourishment of my body;
that above all things no human
ever shall know harm from my hand
except as required to defend myself from harm;
that I shall not cause or know to be caused
the spilling of one drop of human blood,
for the human is my brother,
and his life is my own.
This I swear freely and gladly upon my most glorious nature,
and upon penalty of death and the shame of all my kind.

—EUDORA'S VOW, CIRCA 1400

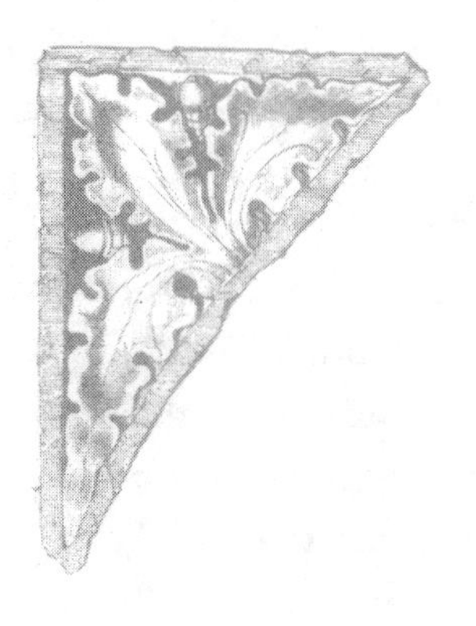

Thirteen

THE WILDERNESS
16:16
ALASKA STANDARD TIME
NOVEMBER 25

IT WAS FOR HER SAKE THAT I DID THIS THING, MATISE DEVONCROIX HAD said. *It was for the love of her . . .*

It is for the pack I do this thing! Nicholas had cried to his father. *For the sake of the pack . . .*

And now he couldn't get the images out of his head. The good Queen Eudora, her face raised in anguish toward the heavens, her hands covered with human blood. Brianna, kneeling in a pool of the blood of her human lover. *Ah, Father,* he thought in despair, *is this what you wanted me to know? Is this why you wanted me to read the book?* If even a werewolf as strong as Matise Devoncroix could be brought low by his own passions, seduced into savagery by the taste of human flesh, what chance did the ordinary werewolf have to resist the call of his own wild nature? That was what his mother had tried to tell him, but he would not listen; he could not listen. A vow had been broken; lives had been ruined. How many more lives would be destroyed now?

Yet what choice had he had? What choice did he have even now?

He looked at the human and then at the transmitter, which was lying on the table, channel open, sending its steady silent signal for help. Perhaps the signal would reach Garret in time; perhaps it would reach his enemies. Perhaps, in the end, it would not matter; perhaps nothing he could do would save the pack now. The irony was this: if the pack survived, it would owe its future to this human woman. If it did not, Nicholas could blame no one but himself.

I, Nicholas Devoncroix, do as my first act as leader of the pact reinstate the ancient Law of Separation and the attendant penalties thereof, which have been flagrantly ignored these five centuries or more . . .

Hannah turned away from the window, hugging the book to her chest. Her brow was faintly furrowed, her expression thoughtful. She could not have described, had she been questioned, what it was she had observed through the window during these past few minutes, or if she had seen anything at all. In truth, she had not been looking.

Brianna Cross. Why did she suspect that if she looked that name up in an encyclopedia of theatrical personalities, she would find an entry, complete with a photograph of a striking young woman with riotous red curls? And the name Pennington was not unknown in British peerage. If she made inquiries, would she discover that he had died of injuries sustained while fighting off an intruder at his paramour's home?

Ah, but fiction was regularly built on less fact than that. And fiction it was . . . until she chose to believe otherwise.

She put the volume aside, wrapped the quilt around her shoulders and went over to the cage. The wolf was quiet, and in the dimness it was hard to tell whether he was awake. She knelt beside him. Blue eyes looked back at her. Eyes so blue they made her throat dry.

"Hi," she murmured. Her throat ached from hours of reading, and her voice cracked a little when she spoke. "The storm seems to have died down. How're you feeling?"

Impossible to tell in the poor light, but the savagely burned flesh on his back and flank seemed already to be covered with a downy coat of fur. The gash on his hip was nothing more than a faint white line. She swallowed hard.

"Who are you?" she whispered.

I will lead my people into the coming century with a new rule and a new morality. We will no longer suffer the human parasites to feed upon our good graces. We will not be corrupted by their base morality and low-formed nature. They exist to increase our coffers and serve our interests, that is all.

She said raspily, "If it's true . . . if you are one of them, why don't you Change? Why don't you prove it to me?"

She watched as the wolf got to his feet: all four feet, standing solidly on legs which had only a few hours ago been nothing but fragments of shattered bone. Her heart was pounding hard. He seemed unsteady still, but growing visibly stronger. Soon he would be completely recovered. A little more rest, and he would be strong enough to take care of himself. To do whatever it was he had to do.

He looked at her. Hannah swallowed again, breath suddenly shallow, pulse racing. She moved back a few inches from the cage, moistening her dry lips. It was difficult for her to master enough breath even for a shaky whisper. "You have to promise me," she managed. "I've done my best for you, but I'm all alone here and I'm not strong enough to take you back where I found you. You have to promise me that when I let you go, when I open the cage door, you won't hurt me. I know you think you have to fight your way out of here, but you don't. You just have to leave. Okay?"

The intelligence in the eyes of the beast was sharp and unsettling, yet she saw no promise there. In a moment, however, he turned in the cage, releasing her gaze, and lay down again. Only then did Hannah expel a long-pent-up breath.

"Okay," she whispered.

She left the cage, stoked the fire and crossed the room. She made herself a cup of tea and laced it liberally with honey, then returned and picked up the book again.

From this day no werewolf shall be found to engage in social intercourse with a human. No human shall ever again break bread with a werewolf or enter into his home, nor shall a werewolf cross the threshold of a human house except in the company of another werewolf, and with the express permission of his immediate superior. No werewolf shall engage in sex play or other intimate behavior with a human. Failure to observe this edict, given this day and time by my own hand, shall be punishable by death . . . for both the werewolf and the human.

As it was so written in ancient times, it is written this day in my own hand, Nicholas Devoncroix.

Watching the human in the rocking chair with her eyes upon the book, Nicholas felt a profound and painful stirring of regret . . . for her, and for himself.

Garret, he thought, *hurry. Please hurry.*

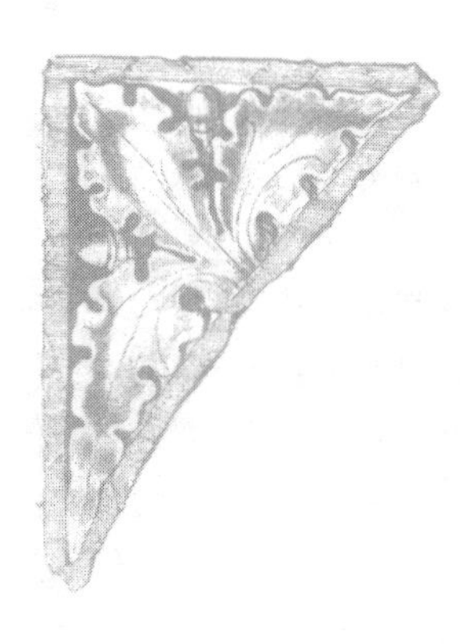

From the Writings of Matise Devoncroix

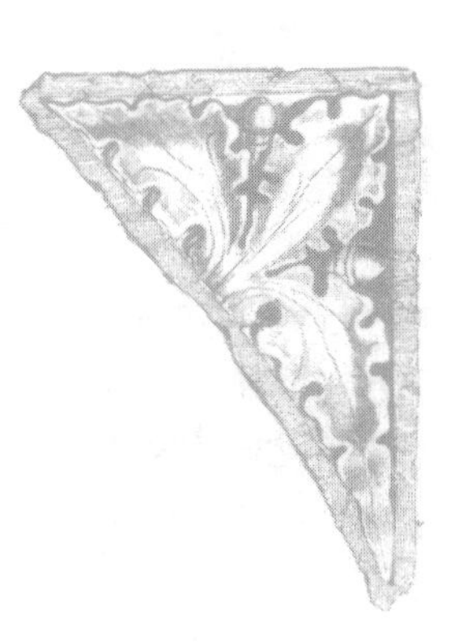

XXXIII

I SHOULD TELL YOU NOW OF THE DAYS AND NIGHTS OF MY DESPAIR, of the great dark bleakness that sucked up my soul like dust in a whirlwind. To this day I cannot fully recall that time, nor do I wish to.

The madness of grief and shock drove me to my natural form for an unknown time. I skulked through the city streets, I fed myself on small rodents and the refuse from human garbage bins. In this state I couldn't think, I couldn't feel, and I would have been pleased to remain so. But I could not prevent the resurfacing of consciousness, the horror, the self-loathing. I tried to outrun it, and eventually I ran to Dover, where I stole aboard one of our cargo ships bound for Calais. In this state I cannot say I had a plan. But I had a need, and I knew what I had to do.

I must have presented a terrifying sight as I strode into the Credit Devoncroix, which housed my father's Paris office. The building was a stately columned structure with polished marble floors and wide staircases that tossed back footsteps and murmuring voices into a gentle cacophony of dignified sound. There were tellers' windows and glass doors with gold stencilling on them. There were shocked expressions and swivelling heads as I swept by. There was the almost overwhelming smell of humans, and it clenched in my stomach and almost robbed my breath.

I plunged up the staircase, down a corridor, through a set of double doors, past a stunned clerk and into my father's private office. My hair was tangled, my eyes wild, and I had lost almost twenty percent of my human body weight. I was dressed in clothing I had snatched off a line behind a butcher's shop: trousers that were too short for me and a shirt that was too large. I had no shoes at all.

But I was convinced that none of this was the reason humans stared at me and werewolves recoiled when I passed. They could smell the murder on me and were horrified by it. I had broken the only vow a werewolf is ever required to uphold and they knew it. I had taken the life of a human. I was no longer one of them. I was a creature beyond understanding, beneath contempt. I must pass quickly before they became contaminated by me. They could barely bear to look at me, my scent was a mortal offense to their nostrils.

Perhaps all of this was true, perhaps none of it was. Truth, at this point, existed only in my perception of it. I knew only that every indrawn breath, every turned head, every shocked stare fuelled my anger and my shame until, by the time I flung open my father's door, I was quivering with these emotions.

There was a human with him, I recall, a man of some importance in political circles, and now that I look back on it, I realize they were discussing the state of the American stock market. From a historical perspective this is, of course, significant, but such was the state I was in that I now do not recall what they were saying when I burst in or, in fact, who the human dignitary was.

I do remember that both men got to their feet when I entered; the human with some alarm, and my father more slowly. I think

Papa said something about continuing the conversation later, or perhaps offered the human some refreshment in another room; at any rate, he got rid of him. The door closed and there we were, the two of us, alone.

The year was 1928. My father, Alexander Devoncroix, had been leader of the pack for over a quarter of a century. He had already taken what was essentially a family fortune and turned it into the beginnings of a global empire; he had rounded up a scattered, lackadaisical pack and united it into a splendidly efficient powerbrokering machine. He had not yet, perhaps, acquired the stature he would in later years, but already he was a towering figure in the world of both humans and werewolves. He stood quietly behind the desk, smelling of silk and strength, a handsome man of youngish features and slicked-back hair, expression unrevealing, blue eyes blazing cold fire. Another time, such a look would have brought me to my knees.

I stood perhaps a dozen feet from the leader of the pack in all his power, and I held his gaze even though it caused me to sway a little on my feet. I demanded, in a voice that was ragged with emotion and hoarse from disuse, "The truth, *mon père*. Tell me the truth about Brianna!"

He allowed me to see a flicker of distaste cross his features, for it must be said that a werewolf as powerful as Alexander Devoncroix can disguise his scent, his appearance, even his heartbeat to such an extent that one knows of him at any given time only what he wishes to be known. The fire in his eyes faded to mere impatience and he said, "I thought you were ill, but you are only impertinent. Go away and compose yourself, and return to me when you are fit for conversation."

He dismissed me with a wave of his hand and started to turn away, but I lunged at him. Of course he would not be taken by surprise and had but to lift his arms to foil my attack, and the force of his countermove sent me reeling across the room. I barely noticed. I held up my hands to him and I cried, "Look at me, Papa! I have killed for you! Can you see it, can you smell it? It's human blood that has been spilled for the sake of your lie! Now do I have your attention?"

He went very still. There was no disguising his scent now, nor the coldness of his skin, nor the shock in his eyes. He held my gaze in a painful lock and he said, very deliberately, "What have you done?"

And I replied, "I have fallen in love with my sister, Papa, and I have killed her human lover. But she is not my sister after all, is she, and this human, this poor human who thought only to protect the woman he loved from a monstrous beast, has died for nothing."

He held me with his gaze for another moment, drawing in the nuances of truth from my scent, my eyes, the words I had not spoken. Then he walked away from me and stood before the tall, ornately draped window that looked out upon the Rue St. Honoré, and he was silent for a long time.

When at last he spoke, he did so quietly, without turning, and his words filled up the big room one by one, swelling and growing, inhaling the silence and pressing against the walls and drinking up light and sound and life itself, until nothing existed in all the universe except his words, and the truth he had hidden for so long.

"I had a brother. He was a betrayer and a criminal, who plotted to assassinate the queen. For his crimes this creature was exiled to Alaska, which at that time was a great and empty wilderness where—it was believed—none of our kind had ever trodden. But during his exile . . ." This next seemed hard for him to say, and he hesitated for a fraction of a moment over the words. "He found a mate, and sired a daughter. Your mother and I tracked him down and arrived mere months after the child's birth. I make no secret of the fact that my brother fell beneath my own jaws, though I take no pride in it either. His—mate, the mother of his child, was dying already." The words were stiff now, painful, as though each of them was released at great cost. "Your mother, my queen, took the child to her own breast, for we had lost a son of our own at birth and our lives were filled with darkness for it. Brianna was a miracle.

How could we not love her? In every way but one she was our child. She has always been our child."

I don't know how long I stood there, letting those words swell up inside my head, eat away at my soul, leech the very air from my lungs. Like a very, very old man, I turned and groped for the door.

I heard Papa say, "There were reasons we couldn't tell you, Matise."

But I found the door and I went through it, and I didn't look back.

I returned to London. I had to. I did not expect Brianna to welcome me, but I could not stay away. The passion was gone out of me, for anger, for blame, for guilt, for shame. I was frozen in astonished emotion, and I wanted only to be near her.

I arrived in Mayfair still haggard but clean and fully dressed, and approached her house late on a rainy afternoon. The moment the shape of it came into view I was overwhelmed with memories. I had to stop the taxi a block away and send the driver along, for the sudden closeness of the interior and the pressing weight of sights and smells threatened to smother me. I stood in the rain in front of her house, smelling blood and smelling terror, and was as cold and as empty as I have ever been in my life.

I don't know how long I had been standing there before I came to understand that the emptiness I felt originated within the house itself. The windows were dark, the chimneys cold. Whatever trace of Brianna that lingered there was scrubbed almost clean by the smell of strong soap and floor polish.

"She is not here."

I thought at first the words were only in my thoughts, for the rain and my own shocked despair had hidden Freda's approach from me. But I turned and she was close, dressed in black with a frill of white lace at her throat and holding a big black umbrella which, as she drew near, she raised to shield me as well as herself from the rain.

"We shouldn't stand here," she said. "I believe the police are still looking for you, and it could be awkward."

I walked when she walked because I had no reason not to, I had no thought, I had no will. I walked and water dripped down my face and made squishing sounds inside my shoes, and Freda's umbrella bobbed over my head. When I left this place there had been snow on the streets. The snow was gone now, but the rain was frigid and the day was dark. Bony-spined trees hoarded their spring blossoms the way the Grim Reaper might guard his captured prey. Some of the windows we passed shone yellow with lamplight, but those windows seemed a world apart from us.

Freda said, "It was in all the papers, a tremendous scandal. He was a human of some influence, and Brianna was—well, she was Brianna. It's an odd thing about these humans, you know. As much as they adore their idols, they are always waiting for them to fall."

It occurred to me, in some vague and detached way, that if the news had been in all the British papers, my father would have known about the killing long before I had informed him of it. I said, without much energy at all, "He knew. And he did nothing."

It took Freda a moment to understand my meaning. "Your father? Don't be absurd. He sent someone around immediately to inquire after Brianna, and whether anything needed to be done to protect her. No one knew about your involvement, of course, and I didn't volunteer the information."

We walked for a few moments in silence. The rain splattering on the umbrella sounded like tiny cannons mimicking the beat of my heart. Then Freda said quietly, "It was self-defense, Matise. The human attacked you with a gun. You had every right—"

I interrupted her without emotion. "In a human court, perhaps. In the judgement of the pack, I interfered in the matters of humans, as did Brianna. You have said it yourself. The human authorities are involved, and this scandal could endanger the whole pack, and there is no forgiveness for that."

I did not say aloud the final judgement, the only one that mattered. I had killed a human. I had felt his lifeblood run out between my jaws and I had enjoyed it. I had at that moment turned my back upon the pack, upon civilization, upon all I had ever thought I knew about myself. I could never go back.

We walked without speaking for a time, the sounds of echoing footsteps and exploding raindrops upon the fabric of her umbrella our only companions. At length I said, "You were right. Brianna is not the child of my parents after all."

Briefly, and with very little emotion at all, I repeated the story my father had told me. Freda listened in thoughtful silence and, when I was finished, murmured only, "How very odd."

But I could delay no longer. Steeling myself for the answer, I stopped and turned to Freda, stepping out of the shelter of the umbrella so that I might read her face before her words. "Where is Brianna? Will she see me?"

Freda answered, "Brianna is in seclusion."

Ah, it was a knife in my heart. I was not surprised, but the pain was crippling. "That is what you told the newspapers," I responded evenly, because I had to try. "Where is my—where is Brianna?"

The pity that crossed her face was almost more than I could bear. She reached inside her black coat and pulled out a sheaf of papers. "She left these for you," she said. "Some letters, and a journal that she never finished."

I took them from her, and as I did I saw that her hand was trembling. She withdrew her hand quickly, and when I raised my eyes to her face she turned quickly in profile, half shielded by the umbrella. "I never meant for it to be this way," she said, her voice low and strained. "I only wanted—what was best. Never this."

And such was the vortex of loss and grief in which I spun that it did not even occur to me to question what she meant. I did not care for anyone's pain but my own. What a fool I was. We both were.

I tucked the papers inside my wet coat as though they were jewels of the most precious kind, which indeed they were. I lifted my face to the rain and walked away.

"Matise."

Only the sharp note of urgency in her tone caused me to stop. She stood with curtains of rain pouring off the small roof of the umbrella, stately and still in her aloneness, yet looking vulnerable for the first time since I had known her. She said, "Did your father say—who was Brianna's mother? There were no werewolves in Alaska before the turn of the century, at least none that we knew of. So who was her mother?"

It seemed to me a pointless question, and, in the enormity of my pain, absurdly irrelevant. I walked away without replying, or caring what the answer might be.

Again, what a fool was I.

XXXIV

I RETURNED TO MY TOWN HOUSE AND BEGAN, QUIETLY AND METHODICALLY, to put my affairs in order. I left a long letter of instruction for my housekeeper, and another for my attorney, which included instructions for my banker and my publisher. It was far after midnight before I sat down to read Brianna's papers. By dawn I was a broken man.

I have included most of her relevant writings already. Here is the last one:

Beloved,

I don't think I've ever told you how I envy your gift for language. Give me a song to sing and I will fill your heart to bursting, give me a role to play and I will transport you beyond imagination; let me dance and you will see angels. But give me a thing to say that is as hard as this and I am tangled in a mesh of good intentions, clumsy and tripping, not knowing where to begin. I cannot even imagine a thing so permanent as goodbye between us; how can I say it?

You will think I'm going away because of what we have done, because of the blood that lies spilled between us, because of the shame and guilt we share. Perhaps you think I blame you, but I beg you believe me: there is no blame. The humans have a phrase for what we have done: mortal sin. Sin unto the death of the soul. You and I, I think, are bound by destiny to be thrust, over and over again, into sin unto the death of the soul.

There, I've said it badly. But it's the best I can do.

Let me tell you what happened after you left that night, and we gave poor Walter over to the ghoulish humans who deal in such things. So many humans filling up my house, so many impudent questions, so many voices clattering, clattering, wailing and babbling. I thought my ears would burst with the voices and there was no peace from it, for everywhere I went they followed me. The policemen, the detectives from Scotland Yard, the boys from Fleet Street. What manner of madman, they demanded, could have torn Walter asunder in such a way? How could I not have seen it? Had he died in my arms? Why was there blood here and there and the other place, and why did my neighbors report seeing a man leave my house in the dark? And Freda, oh, my darling girl, what a rock she was. Even though she too was under attack for nothing more than being a female with medical skills, she stood stalwart, allowing me to say nothing, speaking in my place, keeping them away from me, all of them. For days, I tell you, I was a prisoner in my own bedchamber, and she would come to me at intervals and tell me that this human had come or that one had demanded, but that she had dealt with it all and I was not to worry. Oh, Matise, I am so glad you were away from the madness! Above all else during those dreadful days I never forgot to be thankful that you were safe, and that yours was not added to the blood I already had on my hands. I could bear anything as long as you were safe.

Did you see what they wrote about me? Did you hear what they said? "Lady Macbeth," they called me, who "kissed the noble prince with bloodied lips" . . . Horrible metaphor, of course, but that was the least of it. They used Walter's death as an example of the catastrophic consequences of mixing between the classes.

Classes! I almost laughed at that one. Walter's family called me a tart. Those lovely humans who had clamored to have me in their drawing rooms suddenly could not be bothered to pay a condolence call, and within days the theater had cancelled my booking. How fickle is the adulation of humans, how shallow their devotions. Was I surprised? I cannot say so. But I was very, very disappointed.

Freda says that in another month all will be forgotten, that I should tour the Americas and when I return I will be a bigger star than ever. No doubt she is right. But that's not something that interests me.

I came to the world of humans because I did not belong to the world of werewolves. Oh, yes, I adored them; yes, I wallowed in their adoration of me, I drank it in like mother's milk, I needed it like I needed air to breathe. But I needed more than to be loved by them, you see. I needed to be one *of them, and it was for this reason that I took a human lover, that I even agreed to marry him. Because by being part of a human, even in that shallow physical way, even in the ritualistic, symbolic way they celebrate in their silly ceremonies—don't you see that by being part of him, I sought, in my own way, to* become *human?*

But I am not human. And I am not werewolf. I belong in neither world.

I do not mean to diminish Walter, or what he meant to me. He was an extraordinary human, and I will love him forever for the gift he gave me—of total acceptance, of passion without question, of the illusion, however fleeting it might have been, of being completely normal. He is dead, and I am melancholy. But the greatness of my sorrow, you see, comes not from the loss of my lover, but from what his death has done to you.

We are mortal sinners, you and I. We have the blood of a human on our hands.

In the midst of the chaos, Gault came to me. You remember Gault, the servant of our father, the secretary of our mother? I went downstairs when I heard his voice, even though Freda didn't want me to, and there he stood in my front parlor, and in that stiff and formal way of his, he said, "I have been sent, Miss Brianna, to inquire whether you are in need of anything your family can provide."

And do you know what I did then, Matise? I burst into tears. Oh, yes, they were magnificent, those tears. Maman *had not forgotten me. Papa loved me. In all my travail, for all my failings, they had not failed me. I flung myself upon Gault and quite ruined the poor creature's coat with my weeping, but I will say this for him: though he never spared a smile for us when we were children, though he used to frighten us with his grim expressions and stern manner, I saw him soften then, and he patted my hair in a rather awkward way, and he mumbled, "There, there," and seemed, as best he could be, altogether un-Gault-like.*

At any rate, when my flood tide was past and I made some kind of feeble apology, he was feeling more kindly disposed toward me than I had any right to expect, and he said, "I have known you since your mother first held you in her arms."

I will never know why I said it. "She held me in her arms—but she did not give birth to me."

His expression grew very guarded, and I heard his muscles go stiff. "Who told you this?"

I asked, "Gault, will you tell me who gave birth to me?"

And then the most extraordinary thing happened. He lowered his eyes, and his heartbeat became strong and heavy. "Someone," he said, very softly, "who gave her life for you and who was loved by both your parents, beyond all that is reasonable."

So you see, my dear, you were right. You and I bear no blood relation, and this is one shame we may safely dismiss from our consciences. But it doesn't matter in the greater scheme of things, don't you see? It doesn't matter.

I knew Gault would tell me no more, and I didn't press. I had enough answers for one lifetime. And none of them made a difference now.

So when he asked again if there was anything I needed, I knew quite suddenly and surely that there was. I said, "A place to be safe, Gault. A quiet place, where I can belong."

He was thoughtful for a time, and very grave. And then he said that he knew of such a place.

Should you speak to our parents, tell them that it was I who pressed the promise from Gault, and that he should not be held accountable for the betrayal, if that's what they choose to think it is. I know in my heart that he never would have given his vow to me had he not first made a vow to them—to take the secret of my real parents' identity to his grave.

It was, I think, an equitable trade. The secret of my birth for the secret of my life.

The place to which he is taking me is known to only a few living creatures outside its perimeter. He himself has known it only in rumor, but assures me he can get me there. There is music there, he says. It sounds peaceful. I think I may be happy for the first time in my life.

The promise I ask from him is this: that he keep my destination private from all who ask, even my parents, even Freda, whom I love. All, that is, save one. I know you will not ask, my beloved, nor will you seek me there, unless it is necessary.

Be happy. Be at peace. I will hold you always in my heart, and in my song.

Brianna

I put her papers in a vault at Barclays Bank, which was one of the few in Europe my father did not own. In the morning I set sail for the Americas, leaving Europe, and civilization, behind.

It would be forty years before I saw either again.

XXXV

THEY CALL IT GOING WILD, TURNING SAVAGE, BECOMING FERAL, AS though it were a state so remarkable as to require its own designation and cautionary description. This has always struck me as odd. We are by nature savages, we are born wild, so how can we *become* what we in fact are?

In 1928 I surrendered to my nature, which has always been wild. I roamed the jungles and I ran the plains, I hunted the forests and even, occasionally, the city streets. I had adventures too numerous to be chronicled here, and I made discoveries both magnificent and mundane about myself and my world. But the things I needed to know eluded me; the only answers that mattered, I did not even know enough to ask.

The years slipped by. The American economy crashed, and the pack made a great deal of money restoring it. Another human war came to Europe, providing our scientists with unparalleled opportunities for invention and advancement. Slowly and invisibly, the pack took over industry, commerce, research, finance and technology around the world. All of this I knew after the fact and in the vaguest, most disinterested way, usually upon reading a name in a newspaper that would make me smile or, later, when that most astonishing of devices, television, came into vogue, by seeing a familiar face.

Of course, I did not spend all my life in the wilderness, or live it in savagery. Occasionally the need would rise within me like a great hunger, the need for words to read and a voice to speak languages and hands to hold objects and soft cotton against my skin and the taste of a good wine; for the smells of the city, the sound of machinery, the clutter of humans. These are as much a part of Nature as are the hunt, the run, the sex.

And so from time to time over the years I would return to the world of the humans, seeking among them the peace that had outrun me in the wilderness. I never found it, of course. Now and then I would write down an outrageously fictionalized version of my adventures, and invent some pseudonym for myself, and sell the book for the entertainment of humans. By this time all of the European presses and most of the American ones were owned by the pack, and it amused me briefly to speculate upon whether the distributors of my work guessed at my true identity. I never lingered long enough to find out.

I felt no desire to return to the pack. What it had become, I could never be. Like Brianna, I was between two worlds, belonging to neither. Yet, unlike her, I was compelled to keep searching for what I could never find.

Each time I returned to civilization it was with more desperation, less care. I was the wild man in Buenos Aires, running naked through the streets, laughing crazily at the sparkling glass towers that had sprung up to block the mountains. Why? Because I could. I was the mad poet of the New York coffeehouses, preaching nihilism and hatred to eager-eyed humans, sleeping in the streets and eating their pets for breakfast. I did worse things, yes, but I also did better. Most of the time, in truth, I did nothing at all except nurse the great aching emptiness inside me, and hunger and hunger for what I could not have.

XXXVI

IN 1968 I CAME TO CALIFORNIA, WHICH SMELLED OF ROTTEN FRUIT AND machine exhaust and far too many humans. It was also a place of many werewolves, and in this way reminded me of the lovely decadence and decay of Venice before the first European wars. These werewolves made films and rock music and bushels of money; they dressed in tight trousers and white boots and dark glasses to shield their sensitive eyes; they sunned themselves by concrete pools and sipped imported cocktails and gave outrageous parties. I could not help but wonder, as I wandered barefoot through the streets of Los Angeles, observing it all, whether my parents had anticipated *this* when they devised their grand scheme for bringing the pack to live and work in harmony with humans. The thought amused me.

And shall I tell you why I came to California? You will have guessed it already. It was the same reason I came to any city; the only reason, I think, I ever left my savage state. Without asking it,

Brianna had exacted a promise from me, and I would defend her wishes with my last breath. But always there was a part of me that waited for her to change her mind; to come again, as I had done, to the world of humans.

I had seen a photograph in a magazine of a young actress with milky skin and riotous red curls and piercing blue eyes. It was not Brianna. But it might have been. So I came to California.

And that is where the oddest kind of destiny took over. I have lived a full and varied life and have experienced very little that could actually be said to make sense in terms of cause and effect. By its very exception, if for no other reason, this incident deserves to be related here.

It was 1968. It was California, the land of motorcars and movie stars and machine guns. Still, I marvel at the serendipity.

I was hungry. I had just taken from a hotel room on La Cienega two hundred American dollars—it was simpler than accessing my own funds, and what moral obligation had I to foolish humans who leave their possessions lying about unguarded?—and though what I really craved was a thick beefsteak very rare, the smell of frying food lured me into an establishment where food is wrapped in paper and served from behind a plastic counter.

I had been away for a long time and some things still fascinated me: traffic lights, ballpoint pens, credit cards, fast food. The restaurant was filled with humans and their children—noisy, smelly, ill-mannered creatures—but they fascinated me too, so much that I was willing to take my place in line with them and wait to be served. In fact, I found it all rather amusing, and an interesting way to become acclimated to this place and time.

My hair was down to my waist and I wore the minimum acceptable clothing—soft denim half trousers and a cotton shirt and sandals—but it was 1968 and California and no one gave me a second glance. Well, perhaps a few did, but no more than is common for any werewolf in a public place. The truth is, I might have been in and out of that restaurant unnoticed; I might have disappeared into the wild for another ten or fifteen or twenty years and all of history might have been changed, except for serendipity. And it came in the form of a human with a gun.

Lest you ever become reliant upon your supernatural powers of perception, let me confess now I did not know he was there until I heard the gasps of humans and smelled their sudden dark, thick wave of fear. My senses were involved elsewhere—with the smell of frying meat, the sound of bubbling oil, the cackle of voices, the roar of automobiles, the soft brown breasts and thighs of a human girl in a very small dress. I was attuned for wilderness hunting and had not adjusted to the dangers of the city. I look back and wonder how much of a role impatience with my own failings played in what happened next.

This is the scene as I recall it. There were small orange chairs and tables lining the windows of this establishment. At the one nearest to me sat a young female with short, curly brown hair and two of her offspring: one was strapped into a mobile chair and made off-key vocalizations at the top of his lungs while tossing scraps of food on the floor; another tried diligently to avoid the ministrations of his mother with a paper napkin. The female looked tired and unkempt, and then she looked startled and terrified, and then there was the sound of a great explosion, and bits of her face splattered the floor and the high-backed orange booth and my sandals.

There was a human male in line behind me; he wore glasses and had little hair on his head. He fell to the floor and started screaming. The young male dispensing food behind the counter stood transfixed, round-eyed, immobile. Another shot was fired and a window imploded. The sound of screams was wild and cacophonous, sudden, discordant; like a herd startled while feeding, no one knew where to run.

And all of this happened in seconds, you understand. It takes a long time to tell, but it was less than the space between heartbeats.

In the human community it was a tragedy of monumental proportions, a crime to shock even news-jaded veterans; a female, two children and an old man were killed within the first fifteen seconds. This was during a time, you see, when such occurrences were not common in the human community and much was made of it. But for me it was not shocking, it was not catastrophic; I had witnessed so much worse in my lifetime, and these poor humans, though I was sorry to see them die so violently, had nothing to do with me. They are, after all, a violent, disorderly species who live and die by rules much different from our own. What I did, it must be understood, was not out of some misguided sense of heroism, or of love of the human species. Far, far from that.

Though the human Walter had held a pistol and this human held a shotgun, though this one smelled of madness and the other had smelled of fear, these were small distinctions to me. Blood and gun oil and cordite; I felt the outrage from forty years ago, the instinct to defend and protect, and this time—yes, I honestly think that some part of me was trying to rewrite the past—this time I would get it right.

So with the echo of gunfire thundering in my ears and the sound of human screams like little whimpers on the face of it, with the gleam of mad ecstasy shining from the gunman's eyes and the barrel of the loathsome machine already targeting its next victim, I strode forward. I'm not sure he saw me, certainly he never expected me, and even if he had he could not have stopped me. I was very fast. With a roar I twisted the weapon from his hands, and I remember the shock in his eyes, the angry cry he gave, like a child deprived of his toy, and then how very still he was as I tore the wooden stock from the metal with my hands and cast the two pieces of the gun onto the floor. I looked him in the eye, and there was a moment—just a moment—when I saw another human, from another time entirely. For a moment he was alive, and Brianna was happy, and I was free. But it was only a moment.

Then I seized him by the shoulders, this poor broken human with madness in his eyes, and I lifted him off his feet and threw him through the window.

I might have killed him, but I was careful not to. There was a certain satisfaction in that, and perhaps in my own way, a small bit of the past had been put right. Not because of the twenty-two people inside the restaurant whose lives—so claimed the evening newscasts—I had saved. But because of the one.

The essence of what happened after that is fairly predictable. This was the age of telephones, security alarms, hand-held cameras. My preference would have been to stroll out of that place, wash the smell off my skin and go on with my business. But the human policemen were there almost before I reached the door, with hundreds of guns and megaphones and flashing lights, and the photographs and the cameramen and the little humans with microphones were everywhere. My likeness must have been displayed in a hundred different broadcast and print venues that day. This is what I mean by serendipity.

There was one microphone-gripping broadcast journalist who was not human, but a low-status werewolf, and when he caught my scent his eyes went still and his skin went dry and little droplets of fear congealed in the folds between his legs and beneath his eyes. It is not so common a thing to catch the scent of a werewolf who is not of the pack; rather like, I would think, a human who sees a ghost. But this werewolf—for all that he lacked in status he made up for in courage—and he slowly, with great effort of will, pushed his way to the forefront of the crowd, even past the policemen to whom I was trying to be polite without much success; and he stood close to me and drew in my scent and caught my eye and, dropping his microphone to his side, whispered, "Who are you?"

It was really quite chaotic. The smell of dead and terrified humans, the filth of human blood and brains on my shoes, the policemen who smelled of more violence and madness than had the gunman, flashing lights, strobing lights, shouting, weeping and wailing; the perpetual cacophony of the human condition and all of it desperately trying to ensnare me in its web. Already I was plotting my way through the crowd, how I would crush a few limbs, bash some heads together, sprint for a private spot, resume my natural form and be rid of this filthy place. But then I looked at the young werewolf, I smelled his awe, and I remembered why I had come.

I held his gaze until a cold dew bathed his face. I said softly, "No one you want to know."

And I turned back to the policeman who, only a moment ago, had been so anxious to ask me impudent questions. But even he now seemed to have difficulty regaining his train of thought, and the werewolf with the microphone, when he walked away, was trembling.

In another age I *might* have walked away, bashed heads together, sprinted for safety. But this was the age of cameras and questions, and anonymity, if that was what I sought, would not be easy to regain. It was a peculiar thing, this celebrity, and I confess I was intrigued by it, amused even, though perhaps "amused" is not an appropriate term to use with so many dead and broken humans lying about.

But what foolish questions they asked me. What was my name and where did I live and what did I do to make money; how absurd. This would bring to life again their fallen members? And how fascinated they were by the damage I had done to the human killer's weapon; I believe I had twisted the metal. How was this done, they wanted to know, or was the weapon damaged when it was fired, for surely no man could have done such a thing.

I told them the fictions they wanted to hear for a while and finally I grew impatient and told them the truth. Indeed, no man could do such a thing and no man had. I had twisted the stock off the barrel in the same way I might twist the neck off a squirrel or the arm off a human's shoulder; would anyone care for a demonstration? As for the injured gunman, perhaps they would have preferred I destroy him, and if so, I would be glad to accommodate them now, for it was all growing very, very tiresome.

Human policemen, I quickly discovered, have little sense of humor in times of crisis. I discovered that, and I pushed it. It takes no imagination to understand why. A part of me, you see, was still in London in 1928, trying to make right what had gone wrong. A human was dead. A killer had escaped.

But in 1968 I was a hero. And the best humans could do for

their heroes, even those who frightened them, was to place them in a quiet environment for observation.

That is how I ended up in the human psychiatric ward of St. Mary's Hospital in Los Angeles California, America. Of all my adventures thus far, it was perhaps the most notable. And it is notable only because I chose to be there.

And, of course, because that is how Freda finally found me.

In this atmosphere, this hospital, there was the smell of chemicals and pain and death, and the constant sound of weeping. Ah, the conversations I heard. The torture I witnessed. It was in many ways the most perfect example of human savagery I have ever observed, in other ways a teaching model of stubborn, if misguided, hope. I spent a great deal of time pondering the human condition in that desperate place, and I learned more than I expected to. But the expiation I sought was denied me.

I was standing at the window, with it tiny flat bars and heavy mesh screen and thick, plastic-coated glass, absently watching the humans come and go in the parking lot below, when I caught the scent of werewolf. I'm ashamed to admit it had been so long that I almost didn't identify her; when I did, my heartbeat gave a jolt of surprise and joy that I knew she could hear. Nonetheless, I spent the last few seconds before she opened the door by composing myself, and pretending to be blasé.

She stood behind me without a greeting for a few moments, observing me, analyzing my scent, and I did not turn from the window, allowing her the time to do it.

"Brianna used to be so afraid of being captured in a place like this," I said eventually. "Did you know that? It was foolish of her. They're really very agreeable here, and she could have escaped anytime she wanted to."

Freda said, "You are the foolish one, Matise, to play such a game. What are you trying to prove?"

I turned to her and smiled. "It's good to see you, Freda. You are still beautiful."

The fashions of the day flattered her. She wore a deep green suit with the skirt cut above the knee and a white blouse with a high collar. Her hair had been cast with an artificial pale tint close to her face, and she wore it swept up high and softly coiled. There was a gentle maturity about her features and an authority in her bearing that came with age, but otherwise she was the same strikingly beautiful girl I remembered.

She scrutinized my appearance, and did not have to voice her opinion. There are certain inevitable physiological changes that come from spending too much time in one's natural form, and I did not try to hide them.

I made a gesture, my smile growing sardonic. "Will you come in? Shall I ring for tea? There is a young human nurse who is quite fond of me. I'm sure she could be persuaded—"

"Forty years," Freda interrupted abruptly. "You always were a master at running away, but this, I think, is a record even for you."

I replied, holding her gaze, "It is my nature."

In a moment she relented, and it was her gaze that wavered first. "So it is."

She came further into the narrow room, glancing around absently, pretending interest in the meager accouterments of such a place: the television bolted to the wall, the plastic pitcher of ice, the deck of playing cards, the paperback books I had borrowed from the small library down the hall. I smelled uneasiness on her and it made me sad that Freda should ever be uneasy around me.

I said, "If the pack has sent you, and I can't think why it would, you may rest assured. Humans are exceedingly stupid, and believe only what they want to hear. Their drugs have no effect on me, even when I take them, and I haven't allowed them to test my blood."

That made her smile. "I know. And the pack hasn't sent me. You have been dead to them, you know, for all of these years."

Now it was my turn to answer, with as little emotion as I could muster, "I know."

She faced me directly and said, "You are free to go. I have taken over your case and signed your dismissal papers."

I lifted an eyebrow. "I have always been free to go, with or without dismissal papers. However, it was kind of you to take an interest."

The tension in her muscles smelled like smokey incense, thick but sweet. It was contagious, and I felt my own chest tighten in anticipation, my senses quicken.

Freda said, "You may not think so when you hear what I have come to say."

With a quick, desperate stab of fear, I muttered, "Brianna?"

She shook her head. "She communicates with no one. Not even your parents can get news of her unless she wishes it. So far, she has not wished it."

There was more. I waited.

But all Freda said was, casting a disdainful glance around the room, "Let's get out of here, shall we? I can hardly form a coherent thought in this place. What you need is a bath and a civilized meal."

"You may not wish to go with me in public," I cautioned her. "The human photographers are really quite persistent."

She just smiled. "Darling, that was a week ago. They have quite forgotten you by now."

XXXVII

As it happened, she was right. We went to the hotel where Freda had a room, and I washed the smell of sickness off me and changed into a white linen suit and tucked my hair up under my hat and donned dark glasses to protect my eyes from the brutal sun. When we went down into the courtyard where all the humans had gathered to dine on large plates of fruit, no one even looked up.

Freda told me she had heard a rumor among the pack that there was a strange werewolf in California, and that she had found me through the American papers.

"You really must start leaving a forwarding address," she remarked with a faint, unconvincing smile over the edge of her menu. "I have been looking for you for five years."

I put down the heavy tasseled menu, which listed no meat of any sort. "Why?"

The waiter stopped to pour two glasses of chilled domestic white and I was surprised to note a bouquet not unlike the Devoncroix Sauternes. Freda answered the question I had not asked. "Oh, yes, Devoncroix grapes have done quite well on this coast, although the quality will never be quite what it is in France." She ordered two plates of chicken fruit salad without the fruit, and then lifted her glass to me.

"To your happy return," she said, "unconventional as it may have been."

I sipped my wine, watching her.

She said, "I want you to come back to Europe with me. I want you to take me to Brianna."

Ah, speak softly when you say those words. Utter them with reverence and with awe, a prayer half formed, a spell to bind the angels. *Take me to Brianna*. There is magic in those words. Tremble when you say them.

Yet we sat there under an obscenely bright Western sun in this courtyard cluttered with humans drinking imitation Devoncroix wine, and she said, "Bring the chicken and more chilled wine and, by the way, take me to Brianna," as though it were a thing that could be done as easily as said. As though forty years of my life had not been spent using every resource of will trying *not* to go to Brianna, as though every night of those forty years had not been filled with scenarios in which I imagined someone would come to me and say, "Take me to Brianna," and I would have no choice but to comply.

I looked at the contents of my glass for several moments, not trusting myself to speak. The fury that filled me was cold and bitter; it crept into every pore and seeped out of my skin. It was so thick I could almost see it in the air. Very carefully, I put the glass down, and got to my feet. "My wine has gone sour," I said, "and I do not care for chicken at all."

I turned to leave.

She touched my hand, a quick, birdlike touch, barely there and gone. The smell of her fear was sharp and she was right to be afraid. I was only half tame. Even the humans had had sense enough to put me in a room with bars on the windows.

She said, in as soft and urgent as a dying creature's last breath, "Please."

I did not want to. Every muscle in my body was stiff unto breaking, fighting any desire I might have had to yield. And yet there was her scent, pained and desperate, and her eyes, filled with years of sorrow, and I remembered how, when I had turned to run with the pack, Freda had risked her life for Brianna.

I sat down.

The place where we sat in the concrete courtyard was shielded by a stone arch with climbing greenery all around it, and the greenery was dotted with saucer-sized fuchsia blossoms whose perfume, when the breeze shifted, was like mango syrup, cloying and exotic. It gave the illusion of privacy, although, of course, the chatter of two dozen human conversations, the beats of twice as many human hearts, assured us of nothing of the kind. And yet for a moment the intensity of Freda's distress was so palpable that it blocked out all other impressions, and we were alone.

I was unwillingly intrigued.

She lowered her own dark glasses and let me see her eyes for a moment, then replaced them. She fixed her attention on her wineglass. She said in a low, still voice, "You did not kill the human Walter, Matise. He was quite alive when you carried him to Brianna's bedchamber. He was broken, it is true. But—he was alive."

The persistent blaze of the sun was muted suddenly by a passing cloud, throwing pale shadows over the table. Freda looked up, as though surprised by the phenomenon, toward the sky. She had no need to look at me. Everything she needed to know about me could be gained from her other senses.

I waited.

"He was a dangerous human, Matise," she said. "I don't think

Brianna ever understood exactly how dangerous. When I walked into that room and saw that you had not killed him, I was astonished—and angry. If he lived, he would have been crippled forever, barely a human at all. Brianna would have been more tightly bound to him than ever, and what torment would he have put her through because of you? Being bedridden would not have stripped such a man of his power, and to what lengths would he have gone to track you down, to ruin us all? It was an impossible situation, really. His life was ruined, Brianna's life would have been ruined, there was danger to the whole pack. And he suffered so. It was a kindness, really, to put him out of his agony."

She looked at me now, as was only proper. "He died quietly from an overdose of morphine, administered by my hand. And I would do it again."

As though orchestrated by a unseen hand, the cloud moved aside and bright sun spilled down again, luminescing off the white tablecloth, radiating from Freda's hair, turning her porcelain-white skin almost translucent. My eyes hurt from the brilliance of it, despite the dark glasses.

I sipped my wine, which was warm and tasteless. I waited for anger, even a killing rage, but it did not come. Forty years of running from guilt that was not my own. Self-exile for a crime I had not committed. The blinding white blaze of the California sun burned all passion out of me.

She said, steadying her voice with an admirable effort, "I wanted to save Brianna's life, not destroy it. I wanted to free her, not condemn her to exile. If I had known how deeply she felt the responsibility for the death of this human—if I had known . . ." Her voice betrayed her then, and would speak no more. She turned her attention quickly to her glass of wine.

I said, moved at last by a faint and rather detached sense of amazement, "You were never in love with me. It was Brianna, all along."

Freda put down the glass, steady again. "I would have given my life for her. I never dreamed that, in trying to protect her, I would drive her so far away that I could never have her. If I had known what she planned, how deeply she felt, I would have told her the truth about the human. But she was gone without a good-bye."

"You might have told me," I observed, but there was no reprimand there. Freda had behaved just as I would have done had the circumstances been reversed; there was no dishonor in the lie she had told.

"If I had told you, would you have stayed?"

I did not have to consider that question very long. "No. And neither would Brianna, I think. Whether it was your hand that cut off his breath or mine, the fact remains he would not have died had it not been for me—and Brianna."

"There is a proverb," murmured Freda, "that cautions against humans who love werewolves, for it never turns out well for the human."

"Or the werewolf," I added softly, and let my thoughts drift to Brianna.

Then I said abruptly, "And so you would have me break Brianna's only request of me and intrude into her peace just so that you may unburden yourself to her for this imagined wrong? Not if you were on your deathbed, Freda, and this was your last request."

"Thankfully, neither of those conditions applies." But she did not sound thankful. "I have written my confession to Brianna long ago, and begged Gault to deliver it to her. He may have done so. She may have read it."

I was impatient. My head hurt and my eyes were beginning to sting with so much brightness, and the smells of humans and overcooked food worked badly on my stomach. I wanted to run. I wanted to be alone. "Then why—"

"As deeply as I loved Brianna, that is how deeply she has always loved you. I thought I could make her happy, but I never came close. The only thing that could make her happy—the only thing she ever wanted from her life—was to be a full werewolf, your mate."

A bustling human waiter came at last with two plates of chicken and fruit, which we ignored. He refilled our glasses. We sat in stone-still silence until he was gone.

Freda said, "I have spent the past forty years researching the cause of anthropomorphism. It has to do with a recessive gene and the position it occupies in the chromosomal strain. I suspect it was Brianna's mother—whose identity is unknown to us—who passed on the gene. If I can find the exact location of the gene in Brianna's DNA, there is a possibility I can correct the defect. But in order to do that, I have to have a sample of Brianna's blood."

Now she met my gaze, and held it steady. "I think I have found a cure for Brianna's condition," she said. "Take me to her."

XXXVIII

THEY CALL SUCH PLACES SANCTUARIES, AND THEY ARE KNOWN TO most of us only through rumor and myth, for the mighty werewolf, most perfect of all creatures, so lacking in weakness or failure, rarely has need for the protection such places offer. How many Sanctuaries are there? What is the specific function of each, and where are they located? Gault told me not even the pack leader knows the answers to these questions.

They are established and maintained by werewolves who have sworn an oath of discretion and who have devoted their lives to the contemplation of intellect, philosophy and the arts. It is commonly held that the greatest of the pack treasures are held in the galleries, vaults and libraries of Castle Devoncroix. Not so. The sum of all our greatness for a thousand ages—our secrets, our history, our most magnificent creations—is kept safe from discovery by both humans and werewolves, deep in the hearts of Sanctuaries around the world.

Or so the rumor goes.

It was to such a place that Brianna had retreated, and I think, in my deepest heart, I had always known this. Even Gault could not direct me to her, but sent me instead to a location where I might leave a message for her. Over a week passed without a reply. At last the note was delivered, not in her handwriting and bearing no scent of her at all, containing directions to where she would meet us.

It was in Switzerland, deep in the Alps, and this pleased me. She would be at home in the Alps. She had always loved them so.

The journey took some days because we had to carry Freda's medical equipment and, perforce, travel in human form. We dressed in short trousers and hiking boots and divided the equipment Freda would need between two packs, which we carried on our backs. It was summer and the climb was pleasant, even though we were, upon occasion, required to use ropes. At night we hunted in wolf form and slept beneath the stars, and it would have been, under any other circumstances, exactly the kind of journey I would enjoy. But my skin was tight with anticipation and my chest full of anxiety. Would Brianna forgive me for bringing Freda here? Would Brianna even meet us? She had made no promises, and we had nothing but a set of instructions to a place that might not even exist. But if she was there, if she did forgive me, if Freda was right and there was a cure . . . oh, how my dreams spun at night. How my thoughts plodded during the day.

During the long dark ages of human ignorance and our despair, human travellers were so in dread of attack by canids and their kin that they came to build alongside their travelling paths small stone fortresses in which to hide. Such little buildings became known as "loup holes." I was amused to discover that the shelter to which we had been directed greatly resembled a loup hole, though I was certain no human hands had constructed it.

It was small, windowless, built completely of stone—and empty. The interior smelled of cold night and winter snows and long disuse, and contained nothing but a row of sleeping shelves around the walls. It was twilight when we arrived, and we waited expectantly for a while. But as darkness fell and our hunger grew, we Changed and hunted, and returned to the little cottage to sleep. The moan and whistle of the high winds sounded as melancholy as I felt.

At dawn I went outside, still in wolf form, and relieved myself and drank from the stream, and buried my nose in a froth of snow that had fallen during the night to glisten upon the grass. I luxuriated in the clean, cold smell, the night creatures who had passed that way, the freshness of a rising morning, the cold green, the black earth, the crisp, cutting mineral smell of ancient rock . . . oh, how I pity the creatures who cannot know such a moment, to drink in the essence of life captured in a breath, to absorb it into their bones, to feel it in their souls, to become one, for an instant, with all that is pure and essential about a blade of grass tipped with snow, the spoor of mole, the crispness of pale tuber deep beneath the ground.

What a poor imitation of living it must be for all those not werewolf, for we can know in a single moment such simple intensity as I have described and in the next a sudden recognition, a jolt of remembrance, that floods the thinking mind with joyful anticipation and words, yes, words that burst to be spoken. That is what happened to me as I caught Brianna's scent and snapped to attention. I caught the shape of her in the mist, and unrestrained welcome, shattering relief, the wrenching need of forty empty years, robbed me of control. I leapt for her and burst into the Passion. Trembling with it, on fire with it, I ran to her and heard the music of her laughter as she ran to me and we flung ourselves upon each other, fiercely, hungrily. I buried myself in her scent, her touch, the soft trilling gasps of laughter and the salt of happy tears. Strong slender arms tight around me, soft skin warm and rich, hair like sunshine. She was wearing a thin gauze dress, I recall, of a fabric so fine it might have been woven by woodland fairies, a pale thing with pink flowers blended in whisper-strokes into the background, and it clung to her body and flowed from it like frosting on a cake. Brianna, Brianna, Brianna. My soul throbbed with her.

We both sensed Freda standing at the threshold of the little building and perhaps it was that which brought us back to the present, even though, when we separated, we could not bear to take our eyes from each other. The words I had so longed to say now crowded up my throat and made it impossible for me to speak. I could only look at her in helpless, adoring silence, and let her sense from every pore of my body the things I needed to say.

She was sixty-eight years old, and she had the appearance of a thirty-year-old human female. Her figure was slim and firm; her riotous copper curls had lost none of their luster. But there was a lovely maturity about her face, a softening of the mouth and a quietness of the eyes, a gentleness of bearing that quite took my breath away. I wish Leonardo da Vinci could have painted her. I wish Brahms could have written a symphony for her.

She caught a strand of my hair in her hand and looked at me questioningly. The years of carelessly remaining too long in one form had turned my hair silvery white.

I found my voice at last. "I thought you might not recognize me."

Her eyes brimmed with laughter, although tears still stained her cheeks, and she kissed the strand of my hair and said softly, "How life has changed us both."

And then she turned to face Freda, who had quietly taken her human form and robed herself, and there was a second of hesitance, no more, while they acknowledged each other, and she flew into Freda's arms just as she had into mine, and the two of them embraced with the same singular, all-encompassing intensity that she and I had shared. I saw Freda's face and I caught the scent of ecstasy that wafted from her, and though it shames me to admit it, I was jealous.

The embrace ended with a moment of awkwardness for them both when Freda said, "I tried to write you—"

And Brianna said gently, "I know what you did. It was all so long ago. It doesn't matter now."

This was good. And still somehow it hurt me to hear her say it.

I went into the shelter and found a robe to cover my nudity, and we sat outside, the three of us, as the slow-rising sun melted the snow on the grass and painted the landscape in shades of yellow and pink. It was enough to simply look at her. I think I could have spent my life simply looking at her.

Brianna said, "How odd. Until this moment, I thought I was content. But now I ache for your company, for news of the outside, for everything you can bring me."

She had not asked me to validate the reason I had broken her request for privacy. That she respected the fact that there was a reason made me feel small, and humble.

I said, "This place . . . you've been happy there?"

She considered this. "I must have been. There is nothing to constrain us to stay—only against bringing outsiders in." And she smiled. "I asked for a place to belong, and I found one. Everyone there is like me, you see. They are all anthropomorphs."

I heard Freda's soft intake of breath, but I felt little surprise. Brianna's reply seemed perfectly logical.

Brianna looked from one to the other of us, and she said, with only a slight hesitance, "I smell no mate on either of you. So many years to live alone."

Freda said, "No more years than you have."

I could not meet Brianna's gaze, though I felt hers upon me. She answered softly, "Yes."

And then she said quickly, brightly, "Tell me of the pack, of our parents and siblings and of the lives you two have led. We hear nothing here that isn't at least a hundred years old!"

"I came to bring you news," I replied, "but not of the pack." My tone was abrupt from the rising anxiety within me. "Freda has pursued her studies of physiology and she thinks she may have found a cure for your condition."

Freda explained. "It would require I draw a small amount of your blood, Brianna. Since we don't know who your mother was, this is the only way I can continue my research. If I find what I expect to find, it would be only a matter of weeks before I could begin to reverse your condition."

Brianna was very still when Freda finished, almost as though she had not heard. I could discern no change in her heartbeat or her scent; simply stillness.

She said at last, "This . . . cure. You have tested it on others?"

"Your condition is very rare, Brianna. I have tested my theory on two others and had one hundred percent success—but they were both under the age of twenty. You would be the first adult."

"So there's no guarantee."

"I would not have come here if I didn't believe I could replicate the results for you."

"And I wouldn't have brought her," I added.

Brianna nodded thoughtfully and got to her feet. She walked away from us, hands clasped loosely behind her back, and Freda and I shared confused looks. This was not the reaction we had expected.

I went over to Brianna and we walked a few steps in silence. Brianna said softly, without looking at me, "You smell like a thousand Passions."

"And you smell of a hundred thousand days apart from me."

"I have never been apart from you. I have carried you here . . ." She touched her breast. "Every moment of every day for all of my life."

"Did I do wrong in coming?"

She didn't answer immediately, and when she did, her voice was small and puzzled. "I thought I was content. I have work I love and the company of others like me. I'm not afraid or ashamed, and I have nothing to hide. I have missed you, desperately, and Freda, and sometimes I wonder about *Maman* and Papa and the brothers and sisters I never knew, but I have never been tempted to leave this place. I thought I was content."

Her eyes were clouded now, like a tropical sky before a long rain. "Now you are here and I realize I was never content at all. Now all the old emptiness and yearning come tumbling back, all the desperate dreams and wild, mad need. I could have stayed forever, believing I was happy, before you came. Now I can never go back."

"Why would you want to go back? Don't you see—if Freda is right, you can be whole at last, you can be healthy, you can be free! And if she is wrong, what have you lost but a few drops of blood? Brianna, why would you hesitate? It may only be a chance, but it is a *chance*!"

She looked so sad. I had wanted her to be jubilant, joyful, excited. But she looked so sad. "Hope is a greedy lover," she said. "It steals my peace and eats out my heart, and leaves nothing of me to share with other loves."

But then she smiled at me, or attempted to, and lifted her hand to my hair. She tightened her fingers and brought my hair to her nostrils, closing her eyes, inhaling deeply. "A thousand Passions," she whispered.

She was still for a moment, her eyes closed, the strand of my hair pressed to her face. But then, slowly, the tension unwound from her body, her breath exhaled, her eyes opened. We looked at each other, and the decision was made. I understood then what she had been trying to tell me—that the decision had been made the moment I first contacted Gault, and there was no going back. Without another word passing between us, we returned to Freda.

XXXIX

FREDA SET OUT HER MICROSCOPE AND SLIDES AND TEST TUBES AND heparin-treated syringes, and Brianna offered up her arm like a grand sacrifice. "There was no record of your blood analysis anywhere I looked," Freda said. "You never had a sample taken before?"

"I should say not. *Maman* was so protective of me, I don't think I ever even spilled a drop of blood, much less gave it up voluntarily."

What mundane talk for the last few moments of our three lives which would never be the same again. A pale milk sun, streaking color across the sky. The drip of melting snow from the roof of the shelter, a stirring of leaves high in a tree, the smell of a warm-blooded rodent nearby. Ordinary. Mundane.

Freda tapped a vein on the inside of Brianna's arm and when it swelled, she slipped the needle inside. Simple, painless. I could smell Brianna's tension, the anxiety she tried hard to hide, as the small clear cylinder began to fill with blood. And then I smelled something else.

Brianna's blood, sweet and hot, raw and pure, bubbling into the glass tube. Iron and salt and hemoglobin and plasma, the sweet-sharp cinnamon scent that was Brianna, the bitter wild scent of werewolf . . . and more.

We all three caught it at once. Human. The scent of human was clear on the air and my first instinct was to whirl and defend against an intruder. I actually half turned before my confusion stopped me. The scent was not in the air. The scent was in her blood.

There was a moment when time stopped, thought and reason faded, even shock was suspended, all controlled by the slow, steady flow of Brianna's blood into the tube. No bird rustled its wings, no ground creature dug, no breeze blew. Understanding hovered, half born, in the ether of our unconscious.

And then, with a rush as swift and sharp as the first breath ever drawn, comprehension burst through us. I whispered, "Human," and Brianna said, "No," and at the same time Freda raised her eyes from the syringe to Brianna and she said, "Brianna, your mother—"

"No," Brianna said.

"—must have been—she had to have been—"

"No!"

"—human."

"No!"

Brianna jerked her arm away from Freda and I heard the small *snick* as the needle broke off in her arm; smelled the flood of hot human-smelling blood as the vial broke and spilled its contents on the ground. Brianna's eyes were wild, her skin was tight; even her hair seemed to bristle with electric light and mad denial. Blood trickled from the open vein in her arm and she plunged her fingers into it, bringing them to her nostrils, breathing deeply, exhaling a choked, "No!"

"Brianna, your blood has the smell of human—a human-werewolf mix! There were no werewolves in Alaska before you were born, so your father must have mated with a human—"

"No."

"How else can you explain it? I know it should be impossible, but somehow a human and a werewolf mated and you—*you* are the result. An incredible, impossible result, but—you are here. You are living!"

Freda's voice was trembling with excitement, her face alight and her gaze focused on possibilities beyond this moment, but I was watching Brianna. Her face was streaked with blood as she tried to wipe the offending scent from her nostrils, her arm dripped red liquid and stained her dress, her eyes were dark and her expression twisted with repulsion, terror and self-loathing.

"Half human," Brianna said, choking on the word. Half pig. Half monkey. Half dog. All of our life you are one thing, and suddenly you discover you were never that at all. A freak. An impossibility. A monster.

She took a step back, as though to escape the truth, but it was a truth she took with her. Quick, hot breaths. Thundering heartbeat. She looked wildly at me, questioning, daring, begging, but what she read in my eyes, what she smelled on my skin, was shock and horror, was truth. I reached for her, but too late. She slapped my hand away and took another stumbling step backward.

She brought her bloodied hands before her face and looked at them with loathing and dread. "Human," she said. And then she screamed at Freda, "Why did you come here, why did you do this? I can smell it, I can! It's in my blood and I can't get it out!"

An awful pain twisted her face and she dragged her fingers through her hair and lifted her face to the sky and screamed a scream that should have rent the heavens. It echoed off the forested mountains and shuddered through the trees and stilled the burrowing rabbits in their holes; it brought ice to my blood and stopped the beat of my heart.

She sank to her knees, her arms wrapped around her middle, and I saw a shudder rack her body; a sudden fierce cramp of pain contorted her face and choked a cry from her and it terrified her. I lunged for her, but Freda was there before me, understanding before me, dropping down on her knees beside Brianna, pushing back her hair, wiping the blood and tears from her face, murmuring, "It's all right, all right, don't fight it, Bri, don't be afraid . . ."

Brianna screamed and doubled over as another wave of pain struck her, and I could smell the fever on her skin, the terror in her blood. I caught Freda by the shoulders and flung her away, taking her place beside Brianna, trying to embrace her. "Do something!" I cried. "Help her! Can't you see she's ill? What have you done to her?"

Freda struggled with me. "Matise, leave her be, you don't understand! Stand away from her—"

Freda pulled me away just as Brianna, with a great and powerful cry, rose to her feet. There was madness in her eyes, a white-hot glaze, and agony on her face. Purple veins throbbed in her throat and her hair crackled and sparked with little snaps of flame. She clawed at her skin, she screamed aloud.

Freda moved toward her with a softened voice and gentle manner. "Brianna, listen, focus on my voice, I can help you, I can—"

Brianna roared with agony and turned on Freda and knocked her aside with all her force. Freda crashed into the side of the stone building and fell at its foot, where she lay, crumpled and still.

I shouted Freda's name and ran to her, falling onto my knees beside her. There were broken bones, and her pain smelled thick and dark, but she was not mortally injured. The effort to retain her human form against all instinct drained her skin of color and heat and painted it with thick, oily perspiration. Her lips trembled as she tried to form words, and I knew it was only for what she wanted to say to me that she held on. I gathered her in my arms, close to my ear. She clutched at my shoulder.

"Help her!" she gasped hoarsely. "Only you can!"

"Freda, let go, you'll die if you don't! Don't try to keep this form!"

Behind us, Brianna screamed, and doubled over on the ground with pain. Her dress was in tatters where her fingers had clawed it.

Freda's fingers tightened on my shoulder. "It was—the shock," she whispered. "The smell of her blood, knowing the truth . . ."

Passion. A powerful, intense emotion.

I looked quickly over my shoulder again at Brianna. She was sobbing, gasping, and the smell from her was hot and bitter. The fever from her body had turned the grass around her yellow and limp.

"She can't Change without you!" Freda said urgently. "Her body doesn't know how!"

I stared at Freda in horror. "I can't! I'll kill her!"

But Freda, who had loved Brianna enough to give her to me, loved her too much to abandon her now. "She'll die if you don't! Go! For the love of all that is holy, go to her!"

I got to my feet, backing away respectfully as Freda gave way to the pain, released her hold on human form and sank into a healing Passion. I started toward Brianna.

Ah, but Freda was wrong. Brianna did not need me. Whether it was the pheromones released by Freda's Change or her own sudden assumption of will, Brianna was on her feet. Her clothing was discarded, her head thrown back in a portrait of exquisite anguish, slender throat arched, quaking.

I felt the heat, I smelled the combustion, and the power of it, the terror and the wonder, robbed my legs of strength. I threw up my hand against the brightness of her glow as her hair seemed to catch fire, swirling about her body in a thousand orange red-ribbons. Her face became incandescent, emitting heat and light and joy; her skin was a thousand candlepower, a hundred thousand; the air around her took on a life of its own, inspired by her energy; the treetops were singed, the damp grass crackled. It was terrible, it was rapturous; it shook the foundation of my soul.

Brianna slowly raised her arms to the sky; she closed her fists to embrace the sorcery. I shook with need for her, with joy for her, with the greatness and magnificence that was her. She opened her arms to me.

I threw off my robe and went to her, drawn as if polarized, swept by her ecstasy. I caught her fists in mine, I breathed the essence of her, I basked in her glory. I felt the glow of her on my skin, in my eyes, burning in my soul. I *was* her. Even before we were one, this was the greatness of her power.

She gave a mighty cry that reverberated to the heavens of rapture, of victory, of grandeur, and the heavens answered back as she took me into her Passion.

XXXX

WE NAME OUR CHILDREN FOR THE MEANING THE HUMAN-LANGUAGE sounds have to our ears, and for their translation into our own wolf song. Sometimes our names sound exotic in human language, like Icharus; sometimes they are prosaic, like Michael. But they always mean more than the humans would interpret. My name, in wolf song, means Warrior. Brianna's means Miracle.

We named our son David, which in both our languages means Peace.

This, then, is your story, my son, which I have written for you, of how you came to be; of the parents from whose deep failings and great love you are sprung; of the sacrifices we have made and the wrongs we have done. Here too is the greatest secret of all, of two species come together at last, of a birth that should not have been yet miraculously thrived to mother a new race of creatures upon this earth.

You are the first of your kind. You know already the extent of your power, and now you know from whence it is sprung. How you use your gift must be your choice, and yours alone.

This is our legacy to you. Treasure it.

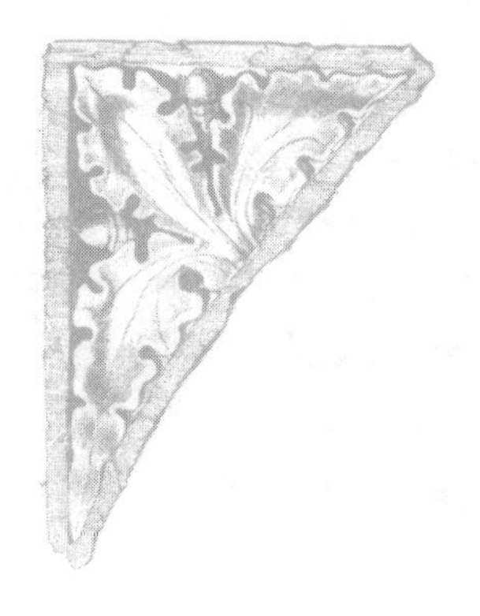

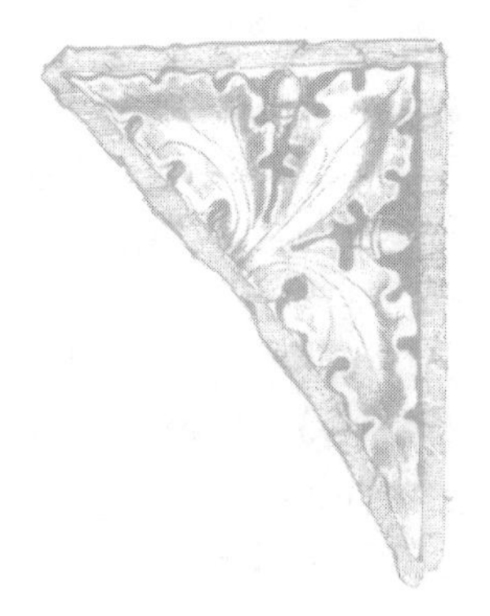

Fourteen

THE WILDERNESS
6:12
ALASKA STANDARD TIME
NOVEMBER 26

HANNAH DID NOT KNOW WHEN THE STORM HAD DIED DOWN, OR when the distant drone of the engine of the first search plane had whispered into the edge of her consciousness. The room was cold, and her breath frosted on the air. Still she sat there for a long moment after she had closed the book, watching the wolf.

He was on his feet, head low, spine touching the top of the cage. And he was watching her.

She got up and went over to the cage. She stood over it for a moment, hesitating. "We have a deal, don't we?"

She knelt down in front of the cage door, and unfastened the top latch. "My name is Hannah Braselton North," she said softly. "Remember me."

She unfastened the bottom latch, and opened the door.

It all happened at once, in an explosion of fury and sound that took her completely by surprise. The unshuttered front window of the lodge burst inward beneath the force of the two enormous gray wolves who jumped through it. Safety-coated glass rained like hail from the sky, along with a flurry of snow and Arctic wind. Hannah screamed and ducked her head, protecting her face from the glass, and before the scream had died out, the Great White was through the window and, in a single leap, upon her.

The force of his impact knocked Hannah to the floor so hard that the breath went out of her lungs in a single vacuumed gasp and she lay helpless and choking, drowning in the airless void of her own lungs, for a small eternity—long enough for one of the dark wolves to lunge at her with teeth bared. She rolled away, throwing up her arms to protect her face, and felt the stab of razor incisors in the flesh of her upper arm. She tore away with the sound of ripping cloth, a great gash in her sweater and sweatshirt and thermal top but no flesh torn, and breath, at last breath.

She got to her knees and flung herself toward the gun rack opposite the door, but the Great White brought her down with a bone-jarring force, the sound of snarling and snapping, teeth tangled in her hair, bruising paws on her back and her ribs, and now the pressure of teeth on her shoulder—and now nothing, now freedom, as the blond wolf, her own wolf, leapt into the fray with a furious barking growl.

The Great White turned to meet him and the two mighty wolves clashed in midair, fell to the ground, snapping and twisting, knocking over furniture, spraying saliva and blood. The two darker wolves circled excitedly; one darted for an attack and yelped in pain. Sobbing, Hannah stumbled to the gun rack, jerked down her rifle.

The Great White suddenly broke loose, almost as though warned by the sound of a round being chambered, and leapt through the open window, followed closely by his two lieutenants and, without a backward look, the blond wolf.

The silence left in their wake was penetrating. Hannah sank to the floor, steadying herself against the wall with one hand. She was shaking convulsively, and every indrawn breath sounded like a rasping sob. Her shoulder throbbed and so did the wound on her arm. A dozen bruises ached and pulled muscles were stiff, but she was alive. Alive.

She spent another few minutes filling her lungs with air, steadying her shaking muscles, regaining her strength. Then she donned her outdoor gear and went after them.

Fifteen

THE TWO LIEUTENANTS DISAPPEARED, FANNING OFF INTO THE MURKY gray morning until they simply were no more. The white wolf stopped, and awaited Nicholas's approach.

They had come to a hilly stretch dotted with towering firs. The recent snow had snapped limbs and littered the drifts with their remnants, but the driving wind had cleared a path down to hard crust through the valley, so the running was easier than it might have been. Still, Nicholas was limping and weak. The wound on his hip had been deep and still ached, and his lungs were not yet strong enough for such sudden and intense exercise. He had begun to fall far behind. It was almost as though the white wolf sensed this, and that was why he stopped.

The snowfall had ceased, but the wind slanted its force through the white wolf's fur and stirred up little drifts at his feet. Otherwise he was perfectly still, waiting. Nicholas approached cautiously, his heart pounding with exertion and expectation. When he was within a few feet and smelled no aggression, he moved closer.

The two wolves circled each other, taking each other's scent, confirming what they had known the moment they clashed in battle. Still, Nicholas could not disguise his astonishment. He took a step back and sat down, regarding the other with narrowed eyes.

The white wolf moved a polite distance away, leapt and transformed. Because it would have been a challenge not to do so, Nicholas called up the last of his energy and Changed into his human form as well.

Arctic wind bit into Nicholas's newly healed human skin, and blew a veil of long white hair across his brother's face. Pushing it back with an impatient hand, his brother gestured to the east and shouted, "Shelter! Come!"

Nicholas bent his head to the wind and followed the other's lead.

The shelter was a shallow indentation of a cave piled with several furs. His brother pulled a fur around his own shoulders and tossed another to Nicholas. He gave him a single appraising look, and rubbed the back of his neck where the impressions of Nicholas's teeth were just now fading. "You fight well," he said, "for someone we thought to be near death."

Nicholas drew the fur tightly around his nakedness, drinking in its warmth. He looked at the other werewolf long and hard, and he said at last, in words that were slow and soft, "You are Matise. My father told me you were dead."

Matise inclined his head. "You will find our parent was a master of lies. That is one characteristic that made him such a powerful pack leader."

Nicholas said, "They have left this life, our parents."

"I know."

The two shared a moment of respectful silence.

Matise moved to the front of the cave. There was enough space for the two of them in human form to sit in the threshold and have an unimpeded view of all approaches, and that was what they did, side by side, away from the bite of the wind.

Matise said, "We haven't much time. Those who search for you have already left their airplanes. They will pick up your trail easily now that you're in the open."

"And you? How did you pick it up?"

A smile softened Matise's weathered brown features, though he kept his eyes straight ahead, narrowed on the distance. "It wasn't you I was interested in. It was the book. It was stolen from me some time ago."

"By our father?"

"Yes. We did all we could to keep David's existence secret from the pack. We couldn't risk the pack's reaction to him. If Brianna was cast out for being an anthropomorph, what might they do to the whelp of a half human? And more—he was of Devoncroix blood, a blight upon our name, a threat to almost a thousand years of Devoncroix rule. It was quite a burden for one small boy to bear. So we kept him secret."

"Here? In Alaska?"

Matise shook his head. "In my years of travels I came upon a small island in Micronesia little explored by humans and of no interest to werewolves. There we built our home, and lived in peace until three years ago. That was when Father found us. We barely escaped with our family intact. We were forced to leave our possessions—including the book—behind."

"And you came to Alaska." Nicholas could not keep the note of incredulity out of his voice.

Matise smiled. "It sounds foolish, I know. But it's sometimes easier to hide in the last place an enemy expects. And we were successful—until a few weeks ago. David was captured by Alexander Devoncroix's minions and taken to a laboratory in New York where he was caged, drugged and studied—"

"And from which he escaped last week, leaving three dead scientists behind."

Matise shot him a sharp, penetrating look, and then made his expression bland again. "There was a rescue operation, yes. One of my operatives died in the attempt."

Nicholas drew a long, slow breath. This, then, was the reason for it all. Brianna, the hybrid who never should have lived at all, had mated with a werewolf and produced a living offspring. A new race had been born. Not an accident, not a freak of nature, but a mutation in the genetic code that created an entirely new species.

That was the secret of the book. That was what his father had wanted him to know but had not had the courage to tell him. A rush of anger filled Nicholas, anger and resentment and hot, furious regret for the lives that had been lost—for his mother, his father, the innocent victims on the helicopter—all for the sake of a handful of words unspoken. But the anger faded almost before it had registered as he understood a new truth. Nothing Alexander Devoncroix could have said would have changed Nicholas's mind, and most probably would have made him only more determined. Until he knew the story for himself in the words of his brother, until he knew the tragedy and power that lay behind the tale, Nicholas would have understood nothing.

He focused again on Matise, and spoke with difficulty. "And this—David. What became of him?"

"You will not find him," replied Matise, "unless he wishes you to do so."

"My father found him."

Matise gave a small sorrowful shake of his head. "He was his grandfather, after all. David trusted where he should not have done. I doubt it is a mistake he will make again."

"You attribute to him a great deal of power."

The very nature of his silence gave Nicholas a chill. "Where is he?" he repeated.

"He is no threat to you, Nicholas Devoncroix," Matise said quietly, firmly. "Nor to any werewolf or human living. Mind your own house. Leave him be. I can assure you, David is the least of your troubles."

They were silent for a time. Nicholas said uneasily, "Your pack . . ."

Matise saw his meaning and smiled. "They are no relation. Feral werewolves, looking for a home, as we were. Brianna was at the end of her reproductive years when we mated, and we had but one child."

"And Brianna? What became of her? My father told me she had died."

Matise was thoughtful for a moment. "That was kind of him. He did it to protect her. As hard as it is to believe now, my parents always loved her, in their way. But she did not die."

Matise directed his gaze to the south, and Nicholas, catching the faint snatch of scent upon the wind, followed with his eyes. There upon the crest of a hill some quarter mile distant stood a female in wolf form, watching them. Her fur was pale and sprinkled with faded red, her bearing composed, her eyes Devoncroix blue.

Nicholas said softly, "Brianna."

"After that first time," Matise said, "she was never able to Change back. She has lived the last half of her life confined to this form, just as she spent the first half of her life in the other."

Nicholas did not know what to say. The stark tragedy of it left him numb.

After a time he said heavily, "You are too late to save your book. The human woman has read it already."

"What is to be done with her?"

A longer silence this time. Brianna, child of miracle, mother of a new breed, turned and walked away unhurriedly, blending into the snow and the pale gray day.

Nicholas said, "I have met many humans. As a species I do not think them trustworthy. But there have, occasionally, been individuals who have proved themselves exceptional . . ."

Nicholas let the words trail off, gazing at the place where Brianna had been. He had issued the Edict of Separation to ensure that no such mismating as had conceived Brianna should ever happen again. But even then it was too late. He had given his people license to kill humans for nothing. And it was wrong. Useless . . . and wrong.

He got to his feet abruptly. "I must get to a radio immediately."

But Matise's hand closed around his arm, and at the same time Nicholas picked up the scent. Their eyes met in wordless acknowledgement, and as one, they moved outside.

Sixteen

THE TRACKS IN THE SNOW WERE EASY TO FOLLOW. JUST OUTSIDE THE cabin, the pack had seemed to scatter, going in three different directions. But one path was distinct and straight: two wolves running together. The blond wolf and the white, one chasing the other. That was the trail Hannah followed.

Her heart was pounding from more than the exertion, and her breath wheezed in and out, and she knew she was a fool to follow. But she would have been a fool not to.

"Did you see that, Tom, did you fucking *see* that?" She paused atop a steep ridge to get her breath, blotting her damp forehead. "He attacked me. He came through the window—through a safety-coated, double-insulated window—and he attacked me. He could have killed me." And then, because the marvel of the incident was not only in the very unwolflike attack through the window, but in the aftermath, she had to add softly, "But he didn't."

She glanced around the ridge. There was no sign of Tom.

A half mile farther, the tracks became farther apart; one wolf outdistancing the other. She followed through the shadows of evergreen forest, of deep drifts and smooth trail. And then, abruptly, the tracks ended.

Here the snow was melted away into a muddy slush of about six feet in diameter. On the other side of the slush, the tracks in the snow resumed. But they were not wolf tracks. They were human.

Throat dry, heart threatening to crack the ribs in her chest, Hannah eased the rifle off her shoulder and proceeded cautiously ahead.

Two men came out of the woods on either side of her; as stealthily as ghosts, they did not so much walk as *appear*. They stood no more than five feet ahead of her, blocking her escape to the left and right. Both were wrapped in full fur cloaks with slits for the arms, but the garments had no fastenings and where they gaped open or were caught by the wind, Hannah could tell that the men were naked beneath. Both were barefoot in the snow, yet appeared to be oblivious to the fact. They were both tall and slim, with a vague resemblance in facial features. One was middle-aged, though younger than his waist-length, silver-white hair would imply. The other looked to be in his twenties or early thirties, with silky blond hair, now faintly tangled by the wind, that fell to his shoulders. Both had sky-blue eyes.

Neither man flinched as Hannah swung the rifle into position. Her heart was slamming against her ribs, sending shaking staccato puffs of breath through her lips that frosted on the air.

The blond man dropped his gaze to the rifle, then looked at her. He said mildly, "So, Hannah North, is this what it has come to between us?"

His eyes. She didn't want to look too long into his eyes. She was afraid of what she might see there, of what she had already seen. She fought to keep the rifle from shaking, her voice from shaking. "I—I don't know you."

Oh, yes, you do, said Tom, but she did not look around. She knew he wasn't there.

A faint hint of a smile softened the man's features. "That much is true. You don't know me at all."

The white-haired one stepped forward. Hannah jerked the rifle toward him, but he did not acknowledge the gesture with so much as a raised eyebrow. "You know me," he said quietly. "You have something that I wrote."

Her throat convulsed. She looked quickly from one of them to the other. Oh, yes, she knew. *She knew.*

She lowered the rifle slowly. With every muscle quivering, she reached into the deep pocket of her coat, fumbling for a moment with the Velcro fastening, and pulled out the red book. His eyes. They burned like a fever in her brain.

She held the book out to him. His fingers closed upon it. But with more courage than she had ever known she possessed, Hannah held on to the book. "Just tell me." Her voice was steadier than she had hoped, but it hurt her throat to keep it that way. "Your son. Was he more like us—or like you?"

"Like neither," replied the werewolf, oddly gentle. "And more than both. Far, far more."

Hannah released the book.

He tucked the volume inside his cloak and walked away. As he came abreast of the other one, there was a ululation from the woods behind them, far too close, a quick, sharp howl of warning. Hannah jerked the rifle back into position and swung around, heart slamming again, but the two males merely exchanged looks.

Feeling foolish yet unable to make her adrenal glands believe the danger was past, Hannah turned back. Only the blond remained.

He said, "I am not accustomed to being under obligation to a human." The word "human" seemed to echo on the air, odd and unfamiliar, startling her as much as it did him. He frowned a little, as though with annoyance at the awkwardness, before proceeding. And then it was with a simple statement, an acknowledgement and no more. "You saved my life."

A simple acknowledgement, but it was enough.

Hannah felt her muscles slowly begin to unknot, her breathing, though still heavy, was less ragged. The gun barrel jerked with every beat of her heart, but it did so less often and with less force.

She said, "What will happen with us now?"

He smiled. It was a heavy thing, weighted with sorrow and with care, but it was a smile. "Hopefully," he said, "peace."

He extended his hand and took a step forward. Hannah smiled uncertainly. She started to lower the rifle.

And then Nicholas caught a scent that had been disguised from him before; hidden among the familiar werewolf scents of guards and members of the rescue team, or perhaps well hidden because it *was* so familiar. For a moment he was frozen with shock, with absolute astonishment that the enemy could have gotten so close without his being aware of it. He spun toward the tree line, but too late. Michel in wolf form burst out of the snow and launched himself at Nicholas with teeth and claws bared.

Nicholas was too weak to Change again so soon, and had no time to do so even if he had been able. He threw up his arms to block the assault with his body and even then knew he had no chance of surviving the attack in human form. By the time the rescue team crested the hill and saw what was happening, Nicholas would be dead, and Michel would be gone.

The future played out in an instant in his head: the last of the Devoncroix dead and burned to ashes, the pack vulnerable and unguided, civilization in chaos, and from the ruins arises a great leader from the Dark Brotherhood, his rule harsh and his justice swift, and all the world beneath his command. For this the bonds of friendship were easily cut; for this a month, a year or a decade in exile was small sacrifice. For this Nicholas would die.

He looked into the cold bright eyes of one he once had called friend; he felt the hot bitter rush of his breath and smelled the scent of his ambition, and thunder roared and blood sprayed like rain from the sky. Michel fell to the ground, dead from the gaping wound Hannah's shotgun had inflicted in his side.

Nicholas turned to her, and she was gasping, wide-eyed and shaking, staring at the dead wolf not six feet away. The air was thick with the smells of human terror and black gunsmoke and singed fur and hot blood and death, cold and final. Nicholas took a step toward her.

The guards came at her from the back and the left, huge black wolves with sharp green eyes and flashing teeth. It was the classic assassin's posture, perfectly executed. Nicholas shouted, *"No!"* and flung himself forward, but too late. She whirled around and tried to get the gun into position, but she failed, and the only sound of her defeat was a small, choked cry. One guard knocked her to the ground; the rifle went flying. The other sank his teeth into the vital femoral artery and tore; blood spurted.

Nicholas roared, *"NOOOO!"* and he lunged for the first wolf, who had dug his teeth into the jugular vein of the human's throat. With his bare hands Nicholas seized the wolf by the neck and threw him aside; the wolf yelped and tumbled, the blood that dripped from his jowls turning the churned-up snow pink.

The second wolf backed off, head lowered, tail between his legs, as Nicholas turned on him. Nicholas sank to his knees beside the human woman, in a drift of red snow. Quickly, frantically, he searched for the source of the spurting blood in her leg. He pressed his hands tightly over the wound, but blood dribbled through his fingers, warm and slippery, and blood seeped like a wellspring from the gash in her throat; he could do nothing to stop it.

"Hannah North," he commanded, low and harsh, "hold on. I'll get help for you . . ."

But her fragile human body had not the healing resources to survive such an onslaught, and her eyes, when they fluttered open, were glazed and unfocused. The spurt of blood between his fingers was growing less vigorous. He said urgently, "I swear to you, this was not my will." His voice was hoarse with emotion, almost a whisper. "I swear it."

And he thought she heard him. Her eyes focused, though not on him, and she seemed to be listening intently—but not to him. Her lips moved, and the words she formed would have been inaudible to any but werewolf ears; they lit up her eyes. "Tom," she said. "I knew you'd come back."

She smiled, and closed her eyes. Her heart stopped beating, her blood stopped flowing, and she died.

Nicholas straightened up slowly. His hands were wet with blood. He got to his feet. His eyes searched the landscape until they found what he sought. He strode over to the rifle on the ground and snatched it up, examining it closely. He smelled no ammunition in the chamber. Having used her weapon to save his life, she had rendered it helpless to save her own.

With a roar that brought him to the edge of Passion, he broke the weapon in two over his knee, and then he turned upon the two guards who were cowering in his shadow.

Strong hands upon his shoulders restrained him. "Nicholas, don't! They were doing their jobs! She killed Michel, didn't you see? They were protecting you!"

Nicholas jerked away, spun around, and recognized the face of his closest friend and second in command, Garret Landseer. As unit leader, he was in human form and dressed for the climate in heavy clothing and boots. His eyes were dark with concern, his features tight. "She had a gun, Nicholas! Why are you angry?"

"*She* was protecting me!" Nicholas shouted. "Michel attacked me and would have finished me if she hadn't used her weapon! He put the bomb on the helicopter. He meant me dead! How could *you* not know that?"

Color drained from Garret's face. "He was the infiltrator?" He looked at Nicholas for another shocked moment, and then lowered his eyes. "I'm sorry. I have no excuse. My attention has been occupied with finding you; instead, I should have looked to the reason for your disappearance."

Nicholas stared at him wildly, and then at the two guards. He walked a few steps away, staggering a little in the snow, and stood with his fists clenched upon his chest and his jaw locked against the rage, face uplifted to the sky.

Gradually, his breathing slowed, his tremors ceased. The tension left his muscles, and he stood strong and still, but no longer a threat.

He said, without turning, "You're not to be held accountable. You did what was right."

Garret approached to him. "We thought you were dead," he said. "The storm came up so suddenly, we couldn't track any survivors . . . we thought you were dead. Then, from out of nowhere, we got the open transmitter signal, and it led us close enough to pick up your scent. Without it, we wouldn't have found the wreckage before spring."

Nicholas glanced at him, but he felt no urge to tell his friend how the transmitter signal had been sent. Another time, perhaps. But not now.

Beyond Garret's shoulder a movement caught Nicholas's eye, and Garret turned in time to see the two wolves, the large white male and the more delicate red female, disappearing over the ridge. Garret's nostrils flared.

"We caught their scent earlier," he said. "Who are they?"

Nicholas took a moment before replying. Then he said simply, "Wild ones. They helped me . . . when I was ill. Leave them be."

Garret said, "As you wish."

Nicholas walked away from him, and was out of sight for a moment. He returned carrying the fur cloak in which Matise had wrapped himself. He knelt beside the body of Hannah Braselton North and, very gently, he covered her with the cloak. The members of the rescue team, in human and wolf form, gathered some yards away in heavy silence, watching their leader.

Nicholas touched the hair of the human where a lock of it lay upon the snow uncovered by the cloak, and then he stood up. He turned to Garret, his voice sharp. "The edict I sent the Council before I left New York. I must retract it before it is read. Do you have a telephone?"

Garret's face went very still. A gust of wind caught a strand of his dark hair and whipped it over his throat, ruffled the fur at the edge of his parka hood.

"Do you?" Nicholas demanded. "Give it to me!"

Garret said carefully, "I do. But . . . Nicholas, we thought you were dead. The edict you sent was read to the pack, and honored by the Council as your last command. It went into effect twelve hours ago."

Nicholas felt the blood drain from his face, his fingertips, his toes. He stared at Garret without seeing him. *Five hundred years of peace ends this day.* Five hundred years . . .

He looked down at his hands, which were wet with the human's blood. Almost absently, he wiped them on his cloak.

Garret said, "The plane is waiting to take you back. We should get word to the pack as soon as possible that you're all right."

"Yes," Nicholas said. His lips felt numb, his voice sounded far away.

"The important thing is to keep the pack together, and safe."

The pack. *What I do, I do for the pack . . .*

The muscles of his throat worked almost against his will, forming words that were automatic and mechanical, yet no less true for that. "Yes," he said. "The pack."

He rested his gaze upon the form on the ground, now covered by the fur cloak, but his thoughts were already beyond it. The pack. That was all that mattered now.

"It may not be too late to contain the damage," he said abruptly, glancing at Garret. "I'll need a satellite relay and a clear channel. I'll address the pack as soon as we can get a hookup. Was there a panic in the financial market? Have you been able to stabilize Wall Street?"

"Matters have been unsettled on all fronts," admitted Garret guardedly, "but I think we can bring things back under control. Your appearance, alive and well, will go a long way toward reassuring the pack. I left a team to establish a camp less than three kilometers away, and you can do a satellite broadcast there. But we should hurry."

One last time, Nicholas glanced back at the human. "I want her moved to a safe place," he said quietly. "I will not have her left here for predators. Her people should be notified so that they can come for her."

"Of course."

Garret looked at his friend, and smiled gently. "It's good to have you back." He touched Nicholas's shoulder, briefly, and gestured the way.

In a moment Nicholas followed, still trying to wipe the blood from his hands.

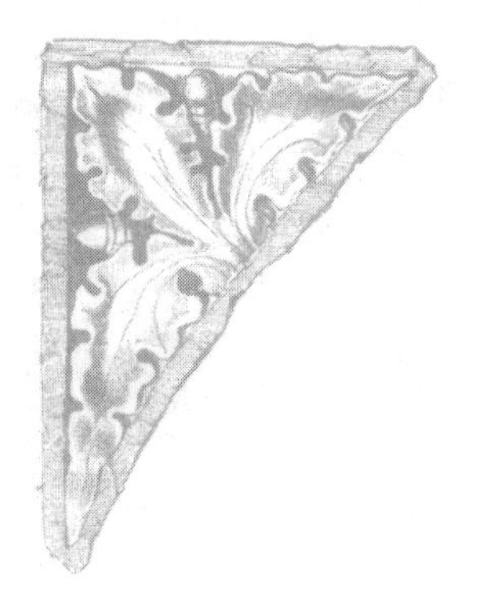

Epilogue

AND SO MY TALE IS DONE. I HAVE PROMISED YOU THAT HISTORY WOULD be changed by what was in these pages, and so it has been done. As with all great changes, there will be upheaval, there will be rebirth. But only time will tell whether the transformation will be for good or ill.

In a Sanctuary deep in the heart of Switzerland is a young werewolf whose destiny it is to inherit the earth. He will appear among you when he is ready, this new breed of Man, this first of his kind. He will walk beside you, but you won't know him. You will read his writings, but you won't believe them. You will hear his voice address the nations, but will you listen? Will it by then be too late?

I have done my part to prepare you for his coming. I have written my story as best I know how, I have told all the truth I am able to tell. For this I have paid the price already, and may yet know consequences even more terrible. But I will hide no longer.

Let the future bring what it may. I put my hand to this confession this twenty-ninth day of December, 1998.

I am Matise Devoncroix,

werewolf.